The Color of Justice

Kentapoos shook his head. "Your *justice* is only for Whites. If Whites had been murdered at the river, they would hunt us down like dogs and hang us."

Steele got up, shoved his hands in his pockets, then joined Kentapoos at the window. "Some things never change, Jack. So much hatred and distrust. If it is not the Indians, it is the Chinese. If it is not the Chinese, it is the Negroes. For you, it is the other tribes—now the Whites. Everyone has to have someone to look down on." Steele rubbed his temples. "Perhaps to hate."

Kentapoos turned to face Steele. "You are right, my friend. There is much hatred. And now I will not be able to hold back my men."

LOST RIVER

Paxton Riddle

BERKLEY BOOKS, NEW YORK

LOST RIVER

A Berkley Book / published by arrangement with
the author

PRINTING HISTORY
Berkley edition / June 1999

The Penguin Putnam Inc. World Wide Web site address is
http://www.penguinputnam.com

ISBN: 0-425-16940-5

BERKLEY®
Berkley Books are published by The Berkley Publishing Group,
a division of Penguin Putnam Inc.,
375 Hudson Street, New York, New York 10014.
BERKLEY and the "B" logo
are trademarks belonging to Penguin Putnam Inc.

PRINTED IN THE UNITED STATES OF AMERICA

10 9 8 7 6 5 4 3 2 1

DEDICATION

Virtually all the characters in this story lived, fought, cried, loved. For many of them, we will never know their innermost thoughts and desires. We can only surmise.

I dedicate this book to my distant Modoc cousins, Roxanne Williams and Debra Herrera, who still live in Modoc country. Both of these strong women exhibit the salient characteristics of what I imagine were those of their great-great grandmother, Toby (*Kai*tchkona Winema): love of family, intrepidity, leadership, personal warmth, and of course, pride in, and dedication to, their Modoc heritage.

Two other Modocs to whom I would like to dedicate this book are: the late and sadly missed Ed Lawver, great-great grandson of Hakargarush—Ben Lawver, one of Kentapoos's warriors. It was Ed who helped immeasurably with the Modoc language, who so magnanimously presented me with a beautiful honor gift, and who said in a recent television documentary, "I will always be a Modoc." And special thanks to the late Wilma Walker, great-granddaughter of Akekis, also one of Kentapoos's warriors, who I met so briefly yet who gave me so much, and to her husband, Cal, who loved her so deeply, who offered additional help with the Modoc language. Finally, I thank Lynn Schonchin, great-grandson of Chief Skonches, for his valuable input.

In some small way, I hope I have shed more light on the complexities and tragedies regarding the nexus of White and

Modoc cultures. That there were good and bad people on both sides is obvious, but that there existed a tragic lack of sensitivity on behalf of the white majority cannot be denied.

People like Winema were statespersons. I feel they were unsung American heroes—human bridges that could have been used to cross cultural barriers. Influential Whites unfortunately, chose to take a different road, as did, in the end, Kentapoos. But no one tried harder than he to build the red road to peaceful coexistence. In fairness, however, I remain aware that some will always view Native persons like Winema as "sell-outs," turncoats, because they chose to work with Whites rather than fight them during armed conflict. Perhaps we are pretentious in trying to portray people who lived in a time none of us experienced.

I should also say a word about Albert Meacham. Even after he was seriously wounded at the doomed peace commission meeting that fateful April day of 1873, he continued to be an outspoken defender of Indian rights in a time and place socially dangerous to do so.

This book must also be dedicated to Frank Riddle and all the men like him who were strong enough to love, and legally marry, Native women at a time when they would face contempt—and to their children, like Jeff Riddle, who most likely bore the scars of racist slurs and discrimination during his life.

Some mention should also be made of General Edward S. Canby. From what we know, he was a decent man, who was yet another victim of settlers' greed and the government's inept "Indian Policy."

To all these people I say *humast*.

NOTE TO THE READER

Every effort has been made to make this story historically accurate. Many of the conversations between the characters, telegrams, and articles and advertisements from the *Yreka Journal* are as originally translated. Good fiction, however, requires the author to fill in the blank spaces, to flesh out the characters, and to make certain changes that enhance the readability of the book. I have worked to keep these changes to a minimum, or at least, within the confines of realism. The reader will find a glossary of Modoc and Chinook words at the end of the book.

In Memory of:
Toby "Winema" Riddle

ACKNOWLEDGMENTS

Special thanks to my hardworking and patient friends at the Cincinnati Writer's Project Fiction Critique Group. Chapter by chapter, month after month, they hung in there with me. Without their advice and counsel I could never have completed such a personally-imposing project. I must also thank my wife, Sally, who encouraged me to write full time while she took on the role of sole breadwinner.

Also, thank you to the wonderful reference staff at Union Township Library in West Chester, Ohio. Their cheerful assistance and their enthusiasm about the book made my research task a pleasure. I am also in the debt of Chief Bill Follis and the Modoc Tribe of Oklahoma for allowing me to peruse their records and photographs.

A special thanks must also go to my good friends and fellow writers, Mary O'Dell and Ryck Neube, for their patient editing and words of encouragement.

PROLOGUE

*Near the gentle confluence of Lost River and Tule Lake,
less than half a day's pony ride from the Oregon-
California border, tall shade trees and swampy wetlands
embraced the village of Kalelk. Game, medicine herbs,
clear placid lakes, and the tule reeds needed for basket-
making were abundant. It was* Mowatoc, *the land of the*
Modokni, *the people the Whites called Modocs.*

K'chilwifam, 1853, village of Yuwa'Ina

STONEY BOY STIRRED from his warm bed and
stretched. He was half-asleep, but could ignore his bladder no
longer. Stepping outside, he yawned and peered at the horizon.
Dawn's crimson light fanned out across the sky like spilled
blood. He could see that only a handful of the women moved
about the small summer village. Elders and children slept
peacefully in their summer bread loaf–shaped latches. The men
were off on a hunt.

A dog barked and Grandmother Seelush hushed him with a
well-aimed pebble. She returned to her camas root preparation
as she chanted the sun-greeting prayer.

Stoney Boy shuffled into the bushes. A bluejay landed on a
branch above his head and chided him. "*Getak tika!* It is too
early."

A flock of sparrows flared, piping thinly, startled by a
rumbling sound to the west. Stoney Boy listened. The rumbling

grew louder. He recognized the sound of running horses, which puzzled him. The men were not due to return for another two sleeps. He cocked his head. The horse sounds became more distinct. In that stark instant he knew what was wrong.

It was the sound of shod hooves.

He felt a prickling up the back of his neck as he heard the light clank of arms, the chink of bit-rings. Before he could react the *boshtin* riders broke through the manzanita, yelling and shooting—a wild frieze of headlong horses with eyes walled and teeth cropped, the riders with jaws clenched. Pale with dust, they appeared like an army of ghosts. Stoney Boy stood frozen to the ground, his breachclout warming with urine. In a flash they were upon him. Something burned his face, then a *boshtin* rode by him, clubbed him with his gun. Stunned, he felt himself whirling, falling.

The horsemen galloped past him, toward the village. Feigning death, he waited until the hoofbeats faded.

Move now!

Crouching, he darted into the manzanita bushes. With trembling hands he parted the leaves and watched in horror. The air thickened with dust and the acrid smell of gunpowder. Wild-eyed, the riders' lathered horses whinnied and bunched up at the sound of screaming and gunfire. Faces twisted with hostility, the men shot at latches, dogs and people—anything that moved.

The first to die were Grandmothers Likes Sugar and Looking East, washing at the creek. They looked up at the men, but did not run, their faces defiant as the bullets cut them down. They lay there, half submerged in the icy water.

She-likes-it, Mink, and Shouts-at-squirrels fell near their cookfires. Mink toppled onto the boiling pot, spraying steaming stew over her, and onto her baby, still strapped into its cradle board. She cried out, then lay still in the embers, her smoldering hair exuding tiny wisps of dark smoke. The baby lay next to her and screamed and screamed.

Two of the *boshtin*, a man in a red shirt and one wearing a white hat, dismounted and ran from latch to latch. Shots and cries erupted from inside. Two of Stoney Boys friends, Little Hand and the nearsighted Slow Eyes, managed to launch their training arrows, but the small shafts swished harmlessly past the attackers. Red Shirt shot Slow Eyes in the face. White Hat cut down Little Hand with a cavalry sword, the shoulder to hip gash spilling blood and entrails. Stoney Boy cried out, his scream lost in the bedlam of the village.

Little Hand's mother, Makes Bread, emerged from the latch, saw it happen. Crazed with grief she screamed curses at the invader and rushed him, knife raised. He shot her with his pistol, and she fell. She crawled toward him, still cursing, her eyes flashing with hate. Jumping off his horse, White Hat stepped on her knife hand, grasped her hair, and scalped her. Makes Bread cursed, "*WOCHAGALAM WEASH!*" and flailed at him. He laughed, waving her own bloody scalp in her face, then shot her again. She moved no more.

Finally the shots became sporadic. The attackers strode around camp, finishing off the wounded. Each shot made Stoney Boy twitch as if the bullet slammed into his own body. In silent rage, he clenched his fists until his fingernails pierced his flesh. Rivulets of burning tears rushed down his cheeks.

The militiamen had gathered in the center of the village. Two men he recognized. They used to be nearby miners known as Harley and Piney. They emerged from latches, herding small children. Harley carried an infant by its leg, dangling the child upside down. Stoney Boy recognized the babe as Bent Leg's daughter. She was to be named upon her father's return. He heard the men shout to one another.

"Hey, Ben."

"Whad'ya got, Harley?"

"Look what we found hidin' under some robes like a nesta' bear cubs."

"You know what to do."

A sick feeling burned in Stoney Boy's throat. NOOOOO! he screamed in his mind. It happened so fast he did not remember hearing the shot, only seeing the pistol buck. The impact of the heavy bullet all but disintegrated the girl's tiny head, splattering blood and brains on the other children, and on her killer.

Terrified, the remaining children bolted toward the creek. The men cut them down. His breath coming in rapid spurts, Stoney Boy squeezed his eyes shut in anguish, felt his knees give out from under him as he collapsed behind the bushes. The world spun like a vision gone mad.

A preternatural silence enveloped the village and surrounding forest. Nothing moved or made a sound—not a bird, not a chipmunk, not a cricket chirp. A pungent cloud of gray gunsmoke hung in the still air. Uneasy, the men looked at one another and around the dead village. No one spoke.

At last the *boshtin* they called Ben cleared his throat. "Piney, collect any usable firearms." He smirked and raised his voice for all to hear. "And hop to it. There's more villages south!"

The men cheered.

Soon another man waved his arm. "First Yreka Volunteers, form up!"

Stoney Boy watched the *boshtin* leave. Though he willed it, his body would not stop trembling. He touched his hand to his cheek to wipe away his tears and found his fingers wet with blood.

When it was safe to move, Stoney Boy stumbled into the village. Ashen-faced, he roamed among the dead. He found his friends Little Top and Shy Boy, faces caked with blood, eyes staring into space. He found his mother, his brother, and his sister—Carries Water, Small Thumb and Laughs-at-stars—their mutilated faces like grotesque masks, noses and ears cut from them. With small pudgy fingers, his sister still grasped her tule reed doll. Their dead eyes asked him unanswerable questions.

He fell to his knees, crying, choking on his own vomit. His mouth rancid with the aftertaste, he stumbled to the creek, bent down to drink, and saw his reflection. A deep red bullet track sliced a gash across his right cheek. Staring at the reflection, he knelt there, numbed.

Why was he spared while so many younger ones died?

Something hard—something base—began to grow inside him, like a fungus sprouting from decaying vegetation on the forest floor. He felt it filling his body with a strange heat. Hate. Bitter, teeth-grating hate. And with the all-consuming enmity came the reason why he was spared. The dark crusted wound on his face matched the fury in his heart. Lifting his head, he raged at the sky, "*Kemush!* Hear me! You have deserted us! You cannot be trusted! I am no longer Stoney Boy. I am Black Wound, Tetetekus, the warrior who does not need *Kemush*! I live to kill *boshtin*!" His words echoed through the forest. He screamed the words until his voice became hoarse.

Unable to desert his family, he stayed with them for two days as their bodies began to bloat and reek. Soon the men would return to the village and see what had befallen their loved ones. For now, all he could do was chase off the buzzards now wheeling above the high lacework of branches. A soft rain began to fall. Looking skyward, he had a bitter thought. *Now Kemush* cries for the People.

The bird sounds did not return to the forest those two days. Only the plaintive strains of Tetetekus's song for the dead, and the pattering of raindrops on bloodstained leaves.

PART ONE

Winds of Change

"God gave me this country; he put my people here first. I was born here, my father was born here. I want to live here. I have told the White man to come and share my country. I have tried to live peaceably and never ask any man for anything. Once my people numbered like the sands, now when I speak to them, only the wind answers."

—Kentapoos (Modoc), 1873

"If we would welcome the exiled patriot from other lands, let us give the hand of fellowship to those whose birthright to this land cannot be disputed.

"If our civilization is the most exalted on the face of the earth, then let us be the most magnanimous in our treatment of the remnants of a people who gave our fathers the welcome hand."

—A. B. Meacham, *Wigwam and Warpath;
or the Royal Chief in Chains*, 1875

"The witness clearly establishes the fact that unarmed and unresisting Indians were attacked and shot down like wild beasts, and that 'extermination' was the war cry of the White men."

—Joel Palmer,
Supt. of Oregon Indian Affairs, 1853

ONE

Fol'dum, 1860

FINGERING THE THREE dripping scalps, Tete-tekus's mouth formed a cold smile as he surveyed the scene of death. It was warm in the tree-skinned house, plus he liked the sweet smell of blood. The *boshtin* woman had been surprisingly feisty—a fighter. The man he had spit on—a coward. The boy he had killed quickly, in the fashion of his cousin Little Top's death.

He had kept count. Twenty-five *boshtin wachagum* had fallen under his weapons of vengeance. He had been careful, killing only four or five a winter since age fifteen. He had planned well, and had not been caught.

If only Kentapoos's father still lived. *He* would have appreciated his work. But not Kentapoos or Secot—they were soft. *Boshtin* lovers.

The settlers' homesteads had become the compass points of Black Wound's life, and the killings must be done in a sacred way. And as it did each time he killed, the memory of Yuwa'Ina flashed into his mind like chain lightning. He couldn't prevent it, did not *want* to prevent it. To forget even the smallest detail would be blasphemous to his family's memory. Each time he killed, he had the memory to serve as his guide. In his mind, the massacre didn't happen seven summers ago, it happened yesterday.

Black Wound stood, took a lantern from the dining table, removed the hurricane glass, and heaved it against the far wall. The smell of coal oil wafted through the room, but the flame went out. Cursing, he ripped the red and white cloth from the dining table. Overturned dishes with half-eaten cake, utensils, cups full of coffee, and a pitcher of milk crashed to the floor. Unable to resist sugary cake, Wound scooped up a hunk, picked out the strange white twig, and shoved the cake into his mouth. Revenge was sweet in many ways. He went to the cook fire in the fireplace, used the table cloth to grab a burning log, and touched it to the coal oil–soaked wall and curtains. The flames climbed the curtains greedily as he walked out the door.

Positioning the bodies, Black Wound stepped back and checked the details. They mimicked those of his loved ones in Yuwa'Ina exactly. Now the medicine would be right. Who were these white savages who took everything without asking? They had no right to be here. If enough were killed, they would disappear like smoke, and he, Tetetekus, would be honored for it.

Pleased with his work, he rode into the night. At the top of the ridge he stopped and watched as flames licked up the sides of the small cabin. Wisps of dark smoke shot up like gray lances in the windless air. A flake of floating ash burned his cheek, but he didn't notice. There was another *boshtin* to be killed. But he must be careful. She had protectors. He rode toward home, his plan becoming as clear as his image in a looking glass.

At Kalelk he dismounted and stretched, invigorated from the killing, anxious to share his plan with his wife. As he entered his lodge Woman Watching put down the herbs she studied and eyed him suspiciously. "And what tale do you have this time, cheating husband?"

He had told no one, not even his wife, about his killings. As usual, her first suspicion about his absences related to his strong sexual appetite.

"*Getak*, woman! We have better things to talk about."

"*Hunamasht?*"

"You should show more respect for a husband that would tell you how to rid us of White Hair . . . without suspicion," he tantalized.

"*You*, who watch her like a dog in heat?" She went back to her herbs. "I'm not in the mood for joking."

His smile faded. "Never have I touched that *boshtin kash* and you know it, faithless wife."

She snorted. "Only because you fear her husband's anger."

He looked at her with a boyish, hurt expression. He knew how to handle his wife.

Her eyes softened somewhat. She sighed. "Very well, what is in your mind, husband?"

He smiled, satisfied she had changed her tone. "How goes your learning of the medicine ways?" he asked, spearing a piece of boiled sucker from the cook pot.

She looked up, unsure of his direction. "Cho-ocks says I learn quickly. What has this to do with White Hair?"

"Did you not tell me of the *ihash* root that kills slowly?" he asked, eyebrows arched. "That could it not be put into food or water and go untasted?"

He had her attention now. "So I did, husband." Her face lit up like a summer moon. "So I did."

Two

Kalelk, Jkwo', 1860

Still early in the season-of-budding-trees, the slight chill in the air made Winema snuggle deeper into the warm robes as dawn's wan light eased into the crevices of the woven reed door, bringing the blessing of the morning sun. She dozed in the twilight of half-sleep, trying to recall a pleasant dream from the night. It wouldn't return. Once awakened, her mind always sprinted into motion, listing the innumerable chores for the day.

She arose and stretched. Swinging aside the mat door of her lodge, she chanted the sun-greeting prayer as her mother had taught her so long ago, then she turned southward and smiled. The sacred mountain loomed before her, its virgin snowcap reflecting the remnant pinks and golds of sunrise. Looking around her empty home, she stared at Big Arm's bow hanging on a lonely peg. In some ways she missed having a husband, someone to share her dreams and warm her body. Strange, she thought, how time dulls the edges of bad memories. Now she thought only of Big Arm's better qualities. But then freedom again at sixteen winters, with only her father to care for, tasted very sweet.

It didn't seem possible that only two winters had passed

since the white scab disease decimated the villages and took her husband's life. So many had died. At first there was time for mourning and proper cremation, but then the disease had spread like prairie fire. Some terrorized parents had deserted sons and daughters to escape the *gutkaks*, the rotting-face sickness the Whites called smallpox. Worse had been the village children. Their little bodies burned to the touch. They jerked and shook. Small shrunken stomachs spewed forth sickness with the force of flung lances. It was enough to break a heart of stone.

Now some of the People had returned to work for the White diggers and ranchers, wore the White's clothes, traded in the towns of Yreka and Frog Town, and drank the White's whiskey. Perhaps the *Modokni* would be able to live side by side with the *boshtin* in peace.

Perhaps.

Winema strolled to her father's latch and rekindled the still-warm cookfire. From the adjacent storage hut, she gathered epos roots and squashes for the stew. She smiled as she saw her father, Secot, approaching with cousin Kentapoos, One-who-has-the-Waterbrash. Like Winema, both men wore bowl-like, woven, reed-basket hats decorated with porcupine quills dyed red, yellow, and green.

"I see my prayers were answered this morning, Father," Winema said, taking two hares from him.

Secot smiled as he held out the rabbits. "*Kemush* granted us an easy hunt."

Kentapoos nodded. "And I am hungry as *kowitois* in winter."

A veteran of many war parties and successful horse-taking missions, Kentapoos had a strong, woman-pleasing masculine face framed by a handsome square jaw. The wolf was appropriate for describing his perpetual appetite, she thought.

Winema said, "The vegetables are already cooking. I will make the meat."

Her father grinned. "*Nent.* And make it quick."

Winema shot him a look and the two men chuckled.

As promised, Winema had the rabbits skinned, cleaned, and

on the spit with her usual alacrity. Kentapoos watched her work. His large dark eyes twinkled above a playful smile—the look of boyish innocence that made him so popular with the women. Seven years her senior, he seemed more an elder brother than a cousin. When they were younger, he brought her little gifts: a fallen bird, an orphaned baby mink, a swallow-tailed butterfly. And he served as her protector from some of the rougher boys and girls.

But by the time she was eight winters, she no longer needed protection. After Chases Squirrels, now called Woman Watching, had tripped her and viciously pulled her hair, Winema threw her off as Kentapoos had instructed, then wrenched the bully's arm behind her back until she shrieked her surrender.

When the meat had boiled enough, Winema dipped a gourd bowl into the stew for each man and handed it to them.

"Unless you have other needs, I will eat with White Hair."

"More gossip?" Kentapoos quipped. He grinned at his uncle, then at Winema.

His easy smile creased pleasant laugh lines on either side of a generous mouth, giving him an open and gentle expression. He saved his dour, warriorlike frown for his friends, or for the elder men.

"We gossip less than you men, Waterbrash," she quipped with a sarcastic twist.

The two men laughed. Secot waved his hand. "Go, Daughter. Enjoy yourself," and Winema headed toward White Hair's lodge.

~

SECOT and Kentapoos ate without speaking. When finished, each produced his personal *paksh*, held it over his head toward *Kemush*, in thanks, and lit it with a smoldering stick from the cookfire.

Kentapoos arched his eyebrows and belched. "Winema is a fine cook."

Drawing a deep puff from his pipe, Secot nodded, then exhaled the first puff with his head back, coaxing the smoke toward the Creator.

"And wise beyond her years," Secot added.

With a wry smile Kentapoos said, "Now that her mourning time is over, she will soon have young men singing her *kamis'no stinti* outside her lodge. Perhaps soon you will have grandchildren playing on your lap, Uncle."

The *laki*'s eyes closed, his mouth upturned slightly as he mulled over the idea. "Perhaps, but I hope the love songs will come later." His expression turned pensive. "Since my *dekes* was killed in the fight with the *Siastai*, she has been a great comfort to me." To use Secot's wife's name would bring misfortune now that she was dead.

Secot thought well of his deceased brother's son, but placed his trust in Skonches—a seasoned and highly respected warrior—as the better choice to be next in line for Chief. Kentapoos had the right mixture of compassion and mental toughness, Secot thought, but was too easily swayed by the more hot-tempered young men. Though Kentapoos descended from the original line of *Modokni* chiefs, he was too young to assume the mantle at the time. Secot knew his nephew expected to achieve his rightful position and he had strived to prove himself. The People however, felt he needed seasoning.

A commotion at the north end of the camp cut short the conversation, bringing both men to their feet. In a heartbeat they heard the all too familiar sounds—rifle shots and shouts.

"*Alamimakt!*"

Secot turned to Kentapoos. "Help Skonches gather the men and meet the attack. I will collect the women and children."

Kentapoos wheeled and darted off. Winema stopped mid-stride at hearing the familiar gut-twisting sounds. She ran back and saw her father shouting orders to the stirring camp.

There had been no warning. The Pit River warriors overwhelmed the Modoc pickets before the alarm could be raised. Thirty men strong and painted for war, they rushed the northern perimeter. Handing Secot his rifle, Winema's face creased with worry and anger.

"Help me move the women and children into the reeds," Secot ordered.

They sped from lodge to lodge, gathering what women and children they could. The battle sounds grew louder. Wailing and keening permeated the air.

⌐

As Kentapoos and forty warriors reached the northern perimeter, Kentapoos saw two of his men fall, the first cut down by a hissing arrow that punctured his neck, the second thrown back from a rifle ball that smashed into his forehead.

Two *Alamimakts* rushed him. He raised his aged, blackpowder rifle and shot the first man through the mouth. His head snapped back, spraying blood and teeth in an arc. Kentapoos dropped the single-shot weapon, unsheathed his knife, and braced himself for the second man, now only five feet away. The *Alamimakt* hefted a tomahawk in his right hand, a knife in his left. He let out a piercing yell, swung the tomahawk in a vicious downward arc at Kentapoos's skull.

Deftly Kentapoos feinted left, then right. The *Alamimakt*'s tomahawk chinked against Kentapoos's knife, cartwheeling it through the air. Kentapoos shot out his leg, tripping his attacker. The *Alamimakt* fell forward, landed on his hands and knees. Kentapoos pounced on him like a *sloa*. The two men grappled and rolled, Kentapoos gripping viselike onto his adversary's wrists. But the warrior still held both tomahawk and knife. Kentapoos thrust his knee into the man's groin, heard him suck air, his eyes growing big as gourd bowls, and the strength in the *Alamimakt*'s arms weakened.

Kentapoos grabbed the warrior's knife hand, jerked it downward, plunged the man's own knife into his straining throat. The man gagged as blood spurted, hot and thick, into Kentapoos's face and hands. The sweet smell of it, coupled with his anger, brought a pulsing wave of excitement. Kentapoos tilted his head back and shouted a war cry. Above him he saw *witkat'kis*, circling. He knew now he would be victorious.

⌐

FOURTEEN-year-old Mehenulush wailed over the crumpled, lifeless body of her father. Two *Alamimakts* rushed toward her and her mother, Tall Woman. Crazed with grief, Tall Woman lunged at the warrior with her knife, but not quickly enough. His war club thudded into her skull, stunning her. The man picked her up, threw her over his shoulder. A second warrior struck Mehenulush a numbing blow to the temple. Her legs buckled like broken twigs, and the two warriors disappeared into the brush, each with his prize for the day.

A high yipping sound signaled a retreat from the *Alamimakt* leader, and they turned and raced for their horses, waiting a bowshot away. A screening force of ten men covered their retreat with a fusillade of rifle fire, the balls thwacking and ripping through branches and leaves. Modoc warriors ran for cover and returned the fire, but the *Alamimakts* were already on their horses and at a hard gallop.

Kentapoos shouted, "To the hors—!"

"Getak!" Skonches interrupted. "We have wounded here. There will be time for revenge after the hunts."

"Wait? I say we pursue them, *atui*. They have taken two of our women!"

Skonches's face hardened. "You have done well, Kentapoos, but if you pursue them and they think you will overtake them, they will kill the women to lighten their load. The summer hunt must begin tomorrow. First we feed the people, *then* we avenge them."

Kentapoos's brow furrowed, his jaw tightened. The two men faced off for several heartbeats. But he knew the war chief was right. *"Nent.* We will take our revenge after the hunts. Then we will take back our women and take *Alamimakt* slaves in the bargain!"

The *laki* nodded. *"Oka ilagen."*

❧

LATER, when Secot entered their latch, tears were in Winema's eyes—tears of bitterness, not fear. This was hardly her first raid, but it was hard knowing Mehenulush and her mother were taken. Winema had often watched over Mehenulush and the other young girls of the village.

Secot stroked her face. "Hush, *ketchkani tchili-lika*. The *Alamimakt kash* are gone."

The childhood endearment did not soften her heart. "Father, what of Mehenulush . . . and her mother? You know how the *Alamimakt* treat their slaves."

His face hardened. "Skonches will lead a war party and steal them back. Then we will make *their* women cry. Mehenulush and Tall Woman will soon be with us again."

Outside, Jakalunus, the holy man, chanted plaintively. There would be much to do in preparing for the cremations of the dead. Both grief and bitterness stewed in her belly. "I grow sick of these raids, Father. They bring only misery and death. They solve nothing!"

Secot looked at her first in surprise, then in disdain.

Winema ignored the frown. "I know it is the way of our fathers, but there must be a better way."

The chief's face clouded. "Enough, Daughter. You forget your place."

The wails outside broke into their conversation. Winema knew she must join the other women in the grieving way—a ceremony she knew all too well. Now was not the time to push her point. At least the mourning period would be shortened somewhat, for the pond lily gathering season began in three days. This, and the coming hunts, would help take everyone's mind off the recent attack. Still, she was *Modokni*. And in spite of her distaste for war, seething thoughts of revenge rolled across her mind like gathering storm clouds.

Even after three suns had passed, Winema's mood did not improve. The attack, followed by the death ceremonies, contaminated her spirit. Her father had taught her to care for her spirit before all else. The sweat lodge helped some, but only the sacred springs could provide the total cleansing she needed now. Winema visited the springs often, earning her childhood name of *Nanooktowah*, Strange Child, as few felt as comfortable near the-place-where-*Kemush*-left-his-footprints, a sacred and mysterious place.

Skoks nickered knowingly at her approach. She patted the pony's neck and spoke softly to him. After mounting the scrubby piebald, she rode out of the sleeping village of Kalelk.

The short ride was calming, and nearing the springs, Winema inhaled deeply. She loved the aromas and sounds of forest and water. Misted ferns, fresh mint, and wild lavender skirted the spring. Small puffs of steam rose lazily from the fissure, and she wondered if this was where clouds were made. Smooth flat rocks shaped like footprints snaked across the meandering stream, and small patches of hairlike moss waved, beckoning her to step across them as did *Isees*, the son of *Kemush*.

She peeled her buckskin shirt and grass skirt, then stepped into drifting billows of steam, letting them mist over her. Her eyes closed as she felt the soothing warmth envelop her body, protecting her from the crisp morning air, cleansing body and mind. She felt even closer to the Creator here than in the sweat lodge.

There was no doubt as to the sacredness of this place. She could feel it. But spirits were everywhere. Her uncle had taught her that since the Creator had given man a spirit, then would he not give the tree or the fox a spirit as well? "*Kemush* has created the earth for the benefit of all creatures. All things are connected in the great circle of life. Honor His creations as you do yourself."

She prayed for long life, for successful hunts. She gave thanks for all the Creator had provided: for mother earth, for the four-leggeds, for the two-leggeds, for the things that swim and crawl.

Kneeling by the small adjoining stream, she scooped up the tepid water and splashed it on her face. She stood, looked at the lightening sky and made her closing prayers for peace.

THREE

It was not until eight sleeps after the *Alamimakt* attack that Winema was able to share a morning meal with White Hair. The mourning and cremation ceremonies, followed by pond lily gathering and the hunts, kept everyone, especially the women, busy.

In her before-life, White Hair was Amanda Slocum, a survivor of the great cloth-wagon battle at Bloody Point. Amanda was only thirteen, her sister twelve, when rescued by Squinter and his hunting party six winters ago. Now she shared Squinter's lodge as his wife.

When Winema arrived at White Hair's latch, Squinter was leaving for a hunt. White Hair was speaking to him in Modoc. "Why do you not wear the mittens I made? It is cold this morning." She looked at Winema and smiled, switching to English. "I swear, this man would freeze to death if I didn't dress him in the mornin'."

Squinter frowned. Winema knew he had little interest in learning the *boshtin*-talk and disliked them speaking it, leaving him to guess what mischief they were up to. She felt sorry for Squinter. Modoc men did not wear mittens, and she knew the other men would tease him unmercifully.

White Hair rose on tiptoes, gave him a quick peck on the lips. He frowned again, eyed Winema. Then, nodding curtly, he left at a trot.

"He's such a prude," White Hair complained good-humoredly. She had a flair for the dramatic and took her normal stance: left hand on hip, right hand free to swirl in the air. "Once I got him on to kissin', he liked it, long as nobody sees. He keeps tryin' to make a proper Modoc girl out of me, but he's wastin' his time."

"You are a stubborn one, White Hair." Other than Lodge Woman, Winema had no dearer friend. They had learned a fair amount of each other's languages. In time, they had shared their secrets.

"What is kissing like?" Winema asked, curious and repulsed at the same time.

"I know what you are thinking." White Hair grinned, "I have been teased by the other women about it. They think it is dirty." She leaned closer. "But I will tell you—it is delicious. And it adds a lot in the blankets."

They chuckled.

White Hair switched back to Modoc. "Did you eat? I got some fine stew brewing."

"It smells good. I could eat tree bark this morning."

They sat in front of the latch as White Hair prepared two bowls of stew. Winema sighed. "I was thinking of Big Arm this morning."

White Hair squinted and curled her lip in scornful surprise. "You miss him?"

"In some ways."

"Your father picked him, not you."

"It is our way," Winema said resignedly.

White Hair waved her stew spoon in the air. "I must be honest with you, Winema. I never cared for the man. He was hard on you."

Winema made a rueful smile. "I did not bear him children. He had a right to be angry."

White Hair frowned and cocked her head. "You ever think it might have been *his* fault? Remember Rough Foot? She had no children with her first husband, and then had three with her second."

Winema smiled and nodded. She had considered this but worried nonetheless.

White Hair went on, "Maybe we expect too much. Men are men, I figure. Of course I don't know if White husbands are different." Her brow furrowed in concentration, White Hair stirred her stew a moment. Winema knew White Hair no longer thought of returning to the White world. They had discussed it before. She had no family left from her before-life, and she was content at Kalelk. After the *gutkaks* struck the villages, and so many died, Woman Watching and her friends attacked Nellie and Amanda, blaming them for the deaths, accusing them of witchery. Winema remembered helping Nellie's and Amanda's husbands break up the fight. But things quieted when Nellie caught the sickness and died.

Still, Winema worried for White Hair's safety. The attack by the three women reflected jealousy as much as vengeance. Nellie's death provided only a short reprieve from their bad-talk.

"Do you not think you have mourned enough?" White Hair continued.

"*Ih*. Father said my mourning period is over, but I've told no one. For now, it keeps unwanted men away."

"I know there are few interesting men here in Kalelk. Why do you not look for a man in E'Uslis, or one of the other villages?"

"Perhaps. I will think on it."

This was the best way to get White Hair off the marriage topic. White Hair liked men, and some of her White manner-isms appeared flirtatious. She still hadn't learned the proper way for a married Indian girl to act. Winema had cautioned her about this. Some of the village women's husbands watched White Hair move about the village, her long blond hair cascading down to her hips. They hungered for her, and their wives knew it. Black Wound's wife, Woman Watching, made trouble for White Hair at every opportunity. She had an evil tongue.

"I had another dream last night," Winema said, changing the subject.

"You did? I never dream." White Hair grinned, cocked her eyebrows. "Was it juicy?"

"Is that all you think about, White Hair? Does Squinter not scratch your itch?"

They laughed.

"It was about the lake spirit."

"Oh, I love fairy tale dreams."

"Fairy tale?"

"It means—ah—a silly story."

Winema frowned. "My dream was *true*." Her sincerity brooked no argument.

White Hair said, "Let's not argue religion again. I can't help it if my poor dead pa beat it into me." She thought a moment. "Maybe that's why I don't dream anymore. It took two years before I stopped dreaming of that day at the canyon. I saw my mother's body, you know. Right after that *kash Alamimakt* pulled us out of the wagon. Jesus help me, I want to forget it." She became misty-eyed. "I was lucky. If it were not for Squinter and you, I would be a half-starved slave, or dead. I guess my Bible is all I have left of my before-life."

Winema took White Hair's hand. Her friend had a right to her religion. Spirituality was a very personal thing, never forced on others. Winema decided, however, not to chide White Hair again about "luck." There was no such thing, Winema had told her. The Creator guides the world and all within it. Nothing happens by chance.

Winema had taught White Hair about *Kemush*, the sky spirits, and other complexities of the *Modokni* way. And White Hair taught her about the Christian way, sometimes reading from her holy book. Winema enjoyed the Christian-way stories, noticing there were many similarities, especially about the son of God, whom the *Modokni* knew as Isees.

White Hair looked pensively at the sky. "Now Nellie's gone. I miss her. But she is better off, I suppose."

A chill crept up Winema's back. She fingered the small

medicine pouch on her belt. "You should not speak her name," she hissed, her eyes scanning the area worriedly.

White Hair rolled her eyes. "Oh, Winema. I'll say the proper prayer later."

Winema relaxed but held on to her medicine pouch. "Your sister was not happy here. It was difficult for her, I know."

"She just couldn't get used to it. I *do* hold that against the men. She was too young to marry, and she never got over the massacre."

"There are good and bad among all people. People sometimes forget this."

White Hair looked into Winema's eyes, then covered Winema's hand with her own. "I'm just glad I got such a good friend as you."

Winema smiled wryly, "And you have Squinter."

They laughed.

"Yes. I have Squinter."

After the meal Winema started back to her lodge in good spirits. She never left White hair's lodge without a warm glow. The night was cool and the stars shone like brilliant bits of creek mica. A scuffing sound, followed by running feet, broke Winema's reverie. She strode quickly in that direction and saw a woman's form dissolve into the darkness. She couldn't be sure, but something about the gait reminded Winema of Woman Watching.

FOUR

SPRING BLOSSOMED INTO hot summer and after several days of gambling, drinking, and fandango wrecking, Frank Riddle and his mining partners, Four Eyes and Whitey, rode the fifteen miles to Hawkinsville in a light drizzle. They had prospected together since 1850, when they met on the wagon train west. Years of back-breaking work and disappointment brought the twenty-five-year-old prospector to Siskiyou County, California, and the once-booming town of Hawkinsville. Behind him lay Hangtown, Rich Gulch, Rough and Ready, Cut Eye, and a hundred other flash-in-the-pan mining camps up and down the Sierra Nevadas.

He always arrived too late. Creeks and rivers like the American, the Tuolumne, and the South Fork had numbed his hands and frozen his legs while he waded and panned. The payoff for his effort was a bout with scurvy, a mild case of rheumatism, and enough money to live from day-to-day. But he struggled to put aside a little money—the one lesson his mother taught him that stuck.

The bespectacled Four Eyes, otherwise known as Nathan Hopkins, had been a schoolteacher out East before he was struck with the gold bug. Whitey on the other hand was at least twenty years older than his two partners, a grizzled veteran of the fur-trapping days.

"You certainly picked fine weather to leave in, Frank," Eyes grumbled. "Left a nice dry room and a good card game for this. And on a Sunday."

Frank's gray mood matched the belly of the clouds. "We laid around Yreka long enough. It's time to get to work."

The men noticed Frank had been in a funk the past two days, so they didn't push it. He got that way sometimes. It proved best to ignore his sulk until he pulled out of it.

Entering Hawkinsville, they rode past the only hotel in town. A crowd of scruffy miners and several fancy-dressed gamblers milled around under a balcony. Frank reined up and they watched from horseback. A tall man dressed in black stood erect and self-assured on the balcony. Frank caught the eye of a gambler sporting a red vest and asked what was going on.

"It's that damned preacher, Hill. He waltzed in here yesterday like he owned the damned town. Said he was gonna hold services this morning from that balcony."

"What's wrong with that?" Frank asked.

The man looked at Frank as though he were dumb. "Don't you know what an outbreak of religion will do to us? He'll start rantin' and ravin' about the sins of card playin' and most of us will go broke. By God, I won't have it."

Whitey chuckled. "Well, bud. Looks like yer outta luck. Seems to me he's gonna start preachin' any minute."

"The hell he will!" the gambler huffed as he started to push through the crowd.

The crowd grew noisier. A number of the gamblers yelled curses or waved their fists at the preacher. But most of them watched, waiting to see what would happen. The preacher raised his hands to quiet the crowd.

"Good morning, gentlemen. I am the Reverend Mr. Hill. Let us start our service this morning with the beloved hymn, 'What a Friend We Have in Jesus.'"

His rich bass voice carried out over the crowd and a few of the miners joined in. The man with the red vest pushed his way to the foot of the balcony stairs. "Hey, you. Quit that singin' and get out of town!"

Reverend Hill eyed the man but continued singing. The gambler yelled louder, "I said get a move on or I'll toss you over that balcony."

Reverend Hill stopped singing and smiled. "Just help yourself anytime, sir."

The red-vested troublemaker scowled. He sprinted up the stairs, two at a time. Frank saw the Reverend pull a heavy Colt revolver from under his frock coat and hold it patiently by the barrel. When Red Vest reached him, the preacher whacked the man squarely in the middle of his forehead with the butt. Red Vest fell backward down the stairs where he lay in a heap, unconscious. Calmly the Reverend replaced the weapon inside his coat. The stunned crowd gaped.

Turning back to his flock, the Reverend smiled and announced, "Now, boys. If any more of you object to hearing the word of the Almighty, come on up here before the service proceeds. I do not like to be interrupted."

A loud cheer erupted from the miners. Men threw their hats into the air and whistled. Several miners fired their guns in the air.

Whitey stood in his stirrups, hands cupped to his mouth. "Go ahead, Parson. The show's all yers!" He looked at Frank and Eyes, grinning. "Any preacher with that much sand is worth listenin' to, I reckon."

Even Frank had to chuckle. He had soured on religion years ago. His father, a fire-and-brimstone Baptist, had tried to beat it into him. How could you love a God who was cruel and vengeful? It never made sense to him. He felt his mood lifting as the drizzle stopped and the sun peeked through broken clouds. Reverend Hill was certainly a different sort from the dour, self-righteous preachers he'd met in Kentucky. Here was a man's man.

Only when he was alone in the woods did Frank feel close to something greater than himself. On the Oregon Trail, Jacques Dubois, the train's mixed-blood scout of French, Sioux, and Cheyenne parentage, had introduced him to Lakota and Cheyenne spirituality. Jacques had said that although *mitakaye oyasin*—we are all related—"Whites are not spiritual people like Indians. They do not understand the meaning of earthly life. They do not understand the earth is their mother who lives beneath their feet, that she provides sustenance and must be respected. They do not understand that every living thing has a *matasooma*, a spirit. The rock, the tree, the river—they all have a purpose, and were put here to make life better, sometimes to test us. All of Grandfather's creations deserve *na-éà-touo*, respect."

Frank respected Jacques too much to scoff at this concept, and they had many more discussions over the four-month trip. The more Jacques explained, the closer Indian philosophy and spirituality matched his own.

Frank had always heard Indians were godless savages, but he had discovered the opposite. He had been impressed with their deep reverence for an understanding God, and for the importance of all things natural. And people had misunderstood prayers to spirits as prayers to false idols.

"What is the difference between praying to a saint or to the Thunder Beings, for rain?" Jacques asked in his lilting French accent. "Like saints, the spirits answer to Grandfather."

Frank soon found himself out on the prairie, joining Jacques in his dawn prayers and experiencing the intense spirituality and blissful afterglow of the sweat lodge. He found himself talking less and listening more—not only to others and to the sounds around him, but to his own spirit. His love for God and all His creations buoyed suddenly clear and meaningful. But after parting with Jacques, who returned to his scouting duties, and after ten years in the mean and godless mining camps up and down the Sierra Nevadas, he had hardened, had regressed into the realities of the White world.

MAKING a claim near Long Branch, the three partners worked it for three months, graduating from panning, to a rocker, and finally to Long Toms.

"Well," Frank said, mopping the back of his neck with a red

bandanna, "we've got our investment back out of this claim, but it sure as hell ain't going to make us rich."

He and Whitey had run the Long Tom all day. September proved hotter than August, sweat soaking their clothes and running off their noses like drain spouts.

"Maybe we oughta sell out and go over to Humbug," Whitey suggested.

"Maybe." Frank was tepid on the idea. Years of mediocre-to-poor success had made prospecting seem more and more like gambling as a profession. But it had become habit.

Whitey studied Frank's face. "You been mopey as a sick calf. What's ailin' you, boy?"

"I don't know, Whitey. Nothin', I guess," Frank said, his thoughts distant.

"We'll hit it big soon. Then you'll perk up, I gawrentee it," Whitey said, hoping to rejuvenate Frank's worrisome loss of interest.

Frank smirked. "My daddy told me not to count your coon dogs till they get back to camp."

Frank's eyes darted over Whitey's shoulders. He nodded toward the far creek bank. "Looks like we got a visitor."

Whitey watched a young Indian man step across protruding rocks in the creek and approach them. He wore a red wool shirt, jeans, and moccasins. His long black hair extended from under his high-crowned hat to his shoulders. A friendly smile lit his face.

"Hey, I think that's Cap'n Jack. Some of the miners mentioned him. They say he comes 'round pretty often," Whitey pointed out.

Frank was glad to see an Indian. He hadn't seen *any* Indians for quite a while. There had been trouble during the past months between Whites and the Modoc, Shasta, and Pit River tribes. He knew the killings had something to do with revenge for "Bloody Point" on the White side, and revenge for raids on Indian villages on the Indian side—all over a wagon-train massacre several years ago.

"How do?" Jack said, stretching out his smile and hand at the same time.

Frank and Whitey shook his hand.

"Coffee?" Jack asked.

"Sure," Frank said. The men walked to the campfire and poured coffee for the three of them.

"Sugar?" Jack asked, smiling. It came out sounding like "shoo-gar."

Frank picked up a tin container and handed it to Jack. Jack poured in half the container.

The Indian smiled widely. "I like sugar."

"Have a seat. Take a load off," Whitey offered, watching the man carefully.

As they sat and drank their coffee, Jack scrutinized Frank. "I am Jack. You new here, yes?"

Frank noticed Jack spoke broken English. He decided to try his rusty Chinook, gleaned from his years in the mining camps. "*Ni'ka mem* Frank, and this is Whitey. We came north *taghum* moons ago."

Jack looked pleased and eyed Frank more seriously. "You been with *mak'laks* before, I see. Who taught you *Tchinuk*?"

Frank remembered Jacques's Cheyenne name. "A good friend taught me some. His name is *T'kòpe chak'chak*. White Eagle. The rest I learned in the camps."

Jack nodded. "A strong name, White Eagle, but not from here."

"*Wak'e*. He is Cheyenne."

Jack thought a moment. "I have not heard of these people."

"They live far to the east. Over the big mountains."

Jack nodded.

Whitey frowned. "Hey, why don't you boys speak English so's a man can join the conversation?"

"Sorry, Whitey," Frank said.

Frank and Jack decided to speak English, using Chinook for any words Jack had trouble with. Frank was interested in Jack's tribal affiliation. "What is your *til'ikum*, Jack?"

"*Modokni.*"

"We've heard about the Modocs," Whitey said.

The young Modoc's eyes narrowed. "What have you heard?"

"Well . . ." Whitey started to respond, but couldn't think how to put it in a positive light.

Jack frowned slightly, studied his coffee mug.

"Frank and I been around Injuns and White folk long enough to know you cain't believe ever'thing ya hear," Whitey said, looking happy he'd found a better reply.

Jack looked up. "You are wiser than most."

"How did you get a name like Cap'n Jack?" Frank asked, remembering Jacques had said: "Always wait for an Indian to *tell* you his name. He will do so when ready."

"The Whites think Indian names too hard to say, so they give us White names. My name is Kentapoos."

Frank nodded. "We understand there's been *mam'ook sol'leks* between your people and the Whites."

"Yes. There has been fighting. I have not visited the miners for a while."

"Is it about the wagon killings?" Whitey asked.

Jack's smile faded, his face reflecting guarded impassivity. Frank had learned Indians were masters at masking their feelings, especially to strangers.

"Perhaps we will talk of it some time," Jack said, standing. "I must go. *Klow howyah*."

The men shook hands. Jack crossed the creek and disappeared into the trees.

"I must'a asked somethin' he didn't like," Whitey said.

Frank watched Jack walk into the woods. "I hope he comes back. I'd like to hear his side."

THE Howlin' Wilderness was the only saloon in Hawkinsville, and it ran a poor second to even the seediest saloon in Yreka. But it saved a fifteen-mile ride, and the liquor tasted just as wet. The walls were low, painted plank. Paintings and pictures of race horses, prizefighters, and bulldogs festooned the walls. A bloodstained Monte table stood in the center of the room.

Whitey, Frank, and Four Eyes stood at the bar. Whitey was good-humored as always, but Four Eyes wore a pinched expression. He nursed a sore finger mashed in the rocker that afternoon.

"You gotta pay closer attention on that rocker, Eyes. It'll bite ya if ya don't," Whitey lectured.

"If we'd found another partner after Pickpan left, it wouldn't have happened. I'm trying to do two jobs at once," Eyes retorted, trying to clean his spectacles while favoring the aching forefinger.

"Maybe you oughta have the doc look at that," Frank suggested.

Eyes snorted, "I haven't seen a qualified doctor since I left the East. These country quacks are nothing more than butchers in frock coats."

Farther down the bar a young man with beady eyes raised his voice. His black hair hung in long curly locks over his shoulders. Several men gathered around him, apparently enjoying the discussion. Frank, Eyes, and Whitey couldn't help overhearing.

"Notice you ain't heard a peep from them Shastas or Pits since," the boy-faced man said. He grinned, then tossed down another shot. "Yessir. Five hundred of them red bastards we killed."

"You're right, Ben. What's left of 'em are about starved out. I doubt if they make it through the winter," one of his audience remarked.

Frank whispered to the bartender, "Who's that?"

"Him? That's Ben Wright. Famous Indian fighter."

"And the two miners next to him?" Frank asked.

"Piney Hobbs and Harley Sievers. Some of the trouble we've had 'round here is their doin'," the man remarked out of the corner of his mouth.

"What's he talking about—five hundred killed?" Frank asked.

The man looked at Frank, surprise in his face. "You new here?"

"Only been here a few months."

"Well, back in fifty-three a bunch of Injuns massacred a wagon train near here. Cut up and killed everyone—men, women, and children. Two hundred souls was the last count I heard. Anyway, Ben formed a militia and they cleaned the countryside of the scoundrels. He's been a big man 'round here ever since. I hear he's killed Injuns all over Oregon and northern California. Sort of a one-man army."

Frank was shocked. If what this man said proved true, some seven hundred people were slaughtered on both sides, and that was seven years ago. How many more since then he could only guess. Frank had seen small scuffles with Indians while in the Sierras, but nothing like this. Usually somebody just ended up with a bruised head or a missing horse. This was all-out war. The wanton killing of women and children, on both sides, fired his sense-of-fairness fuse. He wondered what caused the Indians to attack the train in the first place. Ben Wright and his cronies broke into another fit of laughter.

Frank had met too many of their kind in California—killers who found a way to make a legal living at rape and murder. Kentapoos had avoided the wagon train subject. Knowing how stories about Indian massacres were often blown out of proportion, Frank wondered if the wagon train incident really happened. Or, if it did, what the true number killed was. There were always two sides to these stories and, thanks to his friend and mentor, Jacques, Frank felt he understood Indians. Cap'n Jack would most likely discuss the subject only when he trusted Frank, and then, only when he thought it the right time.

FIVE

THE SUMMER HAD been long, hot, and financially disappointing for the three miners. September brought no relief from the heat. Nathan gave up prospecting and took a job as schoolteacher for the Yreka Community School. Frank envied him. Nathan had an education and a profession to fall back on.

The states were at war, but that was far away. Most agreed it would be over in less than six months. Frank's sympathies lay with the Confederacy. The South had taken too much guff from the hypocritical northerners. And Frank had enjoyed a close relationship with Daisy and Tom, the two slaves his parents owned. In fact, they had been better parents to him than his own. The system had worked well for the Riddles.

Frank and Whitey sat at their favorite corner table at the Howlin' Wilderness, discussing their prospects.

"All the ice we had this winter a-scrapin' up the riverbeds oughta free up some gold," Whitey said optimistically.

"Maybe," Frank replied, unenthused.

Whitey looked frustrated. "Maybe what? Maybe we oughta stay here, or maybe we oughta move on?"

Frank figured this as good a time as any. "I need some time to think, Whitey. I guess, well, I sort of need to be by myself for a while."

Whitey looked dejected but not surprised. "I seen it a-comin'. You're tired of bein' partners? Is that it?"

"No, that ain't it . . . exactly."

"Well, what then?"

Frank sensed Whitey's frustration. He knew Whitey worried about his recent moodiness. They had always been honest with each other, but Frank was not sure how to voice his jumbled feelings. If they seemed vague to him, how could he explain them to Whitey? Also, Captain Jack had visited their camp several times, and Frank wanted to learn more about the Modocs. He liked Jack and wanted to visit with him on his own turf.

"I'm thinking about heading over to Modoc country. Do a little panning. Maybe some trapping, too."

Whitey leaned back in his chair, his eyes widening. "Modoc country. That could be dang'rous."

Frank shrugged. "Jack'll be there."

"Jack's only one man. Ya know he said there's some in them villages what ain't so friendly."

Frank shrugged. "I never had trouble with Injuns. Mostly, if you treat them with respect, they'll return the favor. You just gotta know their ways and mind yer manners, like Jacques taught me."

"Well, Jacques ain't here. 'Sides, Jacques never met any Modocs. I expect they're diff'ernt."

"Course they're different. But, like Jacques says, 'yet they are the same,'" Frank mimed, doing a Kentucky imitation of Jacques's French accent.

Whitey slumped, peered down at his glass of whiskey. "Awright. There's no augerin' with a moon-eyed *Kai*ntuckian. I guess ya gotta get *somethin'* outta yer system."

Whitey's good-natured response buoyed his spirits for the first time in months. "You're a true friend, Whitey."

"I guess I could keep workin' our claim down here whilst you palaver with your Injun friends. Assumin', that is, ya keep your har." Pleased to see Frank smile, he said, "By Gawd, its good to see ya cheered, though. Looks like yer spirits shot up like a Sunday mornin' pecker."

Whitey slapped his leg and made his wheezey laugh. Frank

found himself laughing along. It was as if a great load had been lifted from his shoulders. Tomorrow he would head east—to Modoc country.

~

AT daybreak Frank rode across a sage-covered plain, cutting through the budding forest on the northern base of Willow Creek Mountain, then south toward Lower *Klamath* Lake. Setting up camp on Willow Creek, near the base of Dome Mountain, Frank picked a site near a grove of high-reaching alders and sugar pines. There, were the rich smells of burning juniper and manzanita bushes. A day later white-tailed does with their spotted fawns approached guardedly to drink, as did foxes and badgers. Frank often heard the mournful call of an unusual white-headed owl from the arches above. It made ideal thinking country, and Frank relished the natural surroundings and solitude. Here, he felt in his element. And the panning went reasonably well—about three ounces the first five days. It gave time for Frank to think about the past several years since he left Kentucky. Other than the harsh disappointment of mining, his trip on the Oregon Trail and his travels through the Sierras were everything he'd hoped for. When he was a youngster he read everything he could get his hands on about the West. Hat brim-high prairie grass, buffalo hides, tipi smoke, tumble-weeds, wild horse sweat, wagon trains, gun smoke, and sagebrush. Every greenhorn guidebook and thumb-worn trappers' chronicles were dog-eared and safely secreted away behind a loosened board in the barn.

His thoughts returned to the Modocs. He figured Kentapoos would find him soon, and in Modoc home territory he could learn more about them without the interruptions of "civilization." He wondered if the Modoc villages looked anything like the Indian villages he'd seen on the plains.

On the sixth day two Indians came. The man looked to be in his forties. There was something proud and sagacious about him. The young woman accompanying him interested Frank even more. She had smooth dusky skin and long braided hair.

A funny little multicolored reed basket sat on her head. She had eyelashes as thick as sable brushes. Delicate shell disks decorated her earlobes.

"*Klow howyah*," Frank greeted them in Chinook.

"*Klow howyah*," the man answered, moving closer.

"You Modocs?" Frank asked.

The man nodded. "This is our country, yes."

Frank figured he'd better drop Jack's name right off. "Do you know Kentapoos?"

Only a slight rise of one eyebrow revealed the man's surprise. The woman looked on but remained silent.

"How do you know him?" the man asked.

"We talked many times. Near Frog Town," Frank answered, using the Indian name for Hawkinsville.

"Ah!" the man exclaimed, his face relaxing somewhat.

"He invited me to visit sometime, but I did not know the place of his village."

"He is from our village, Kalelk. Not far from here."

As much as he tried Frank found it hard not to stare at the woman. Although built differently from Sweet Grass, the Arapaho girl he'd known at Fort Laramie, and not as finely featured, she had the same proud air and special allure about her.

She canted her head slightly and a stray ray of sunshine broke through the branches and splashed her hair, revealing an intriguing hint of auburn. She was handsome rather than pretty, he thought. High, wide cheekbones underscored almond eyes that shimmered like pools of liquid onyx. They glistened with intelligence and curiosity. The color of her skin reminded him of cinnamon. Her jet-black hair was tied with the strong tule reeds the Modocs used to weave their fine baskets with. He had seen Indian women selling them in town. Frank guessed her age at seventeen or eighteen.

Remembering his manners, Frank said, "I have *kau'py* and *itl'willie*," gesturing to the cooking coffee and meat on his campfire.

The man looked at the young woman. They dismounted and the threesome sat.

Frank poured coffee and cut off a piece of venison for each. "*Shu'kwa?*" he asked.

The man nodded. Frank poured a healthy amount of sugar into their cups. At the first swallow the young woman smiled briefly, revealing attractive white teeth. Frank heard this was attributed to the camas and epos roots in their diets.

"*Ni'ka mem* Frank Riddle."

"I am Secot. This is my daughter, Winema. We go to the digging camps to trade. How long will you stay in our country?"

Secot seemed to exude authority. He got to the point faster than Frank expected. Frank was careful to avoid the rudeness of direct eye contact. "As long as the Modocs will allow, Secot."

Again, Secot's eyebrows revealed mild surprise. "You may stay as long as you use only the pan. The wooden digging tools muddy the water, drive away the fish."

Frank nodded. "I will do as you ask, *Pusuep*."

As Jacques had taught him, Frank used the title of *uncle* in respect for a man of about his father's age.

There was a hint of a smile on Secot's lips. He nodded. "Then you are welcome. I will tell my people."

Frank drank his coffee and nibbled at the venison jerky, allowing a respectful amount of silence to pass before he probed further. "Do you think Kentapoos might pass this way?"

"I will tell him you are here."

Frank caught Secot watching him as he stared at Winema. Embarrassed, Frank cleared his throat. "Forgive me, Uncle. I do not wish to be impolite. It's just that your daughter is a very handsome girl."

Secot smiled, raised one eyebrow, but said nothing. After some additional small talk he glanced at Winema and they stood.

Frank rose. "More coffee?" He hoped to extend the visit.

Secot smiled easily now. "*Humast*, but we must go if we wish to be back to Kalelk before the sun sets."

The two men shook hands and Frank's eyes met Winema's. She smiled politely, then cast her eyes downward. Her grace and modesty—in fact, everything about her—captivated him. The Modocs mounted their ponies and rode west, and for the first time in years Frank felt he had something to look forward to.

That night, under a purple vault of shimmering stars, he slept fitfully. His mind wandered back to the wagon train that brought him from Independence to South Pass eleven years ago. A vision of Sweet Grass, his first lover, floated into his mind like a minnow breaking the surface of a pond, and he let himself drift into the past. After three glorious days with her, it was his last night in the Indian camp outside Fort Laramie. . . .

❦

AFTER waking him with her hand over his mouth, they had snaked under the tipi's side, careful not to wake Jacques. Outside in the moonlight he saw her cheeks were freshly rouged with vermilion. Her dark eyes danced mischievously as she held her finger to her lips, then loped toward the Platte with him in tow.

At the riverbank they arrived at a glade in a copse of oak trees, well concealed from probing eyes. She had spread a buffalo robe on the ground. The night was July-warm. A faint breeze flowed from the river. Choruses of crickets chirped in a minor key.

Frank wasn't sure what to say. "Sweet Grass, I—" She placed her finger on his lips. Untying the small leather strings on her shoulders, her buckskin dress fell around her ankles. She looked at Frank and smiled.

Frank's mouth hung open. It was all he could do not to flee. She giggled at his expression. Her form was lithe, her breasts firm and round, her nipples the color of pipe clay. He had never seen a naked woman, never thought it would happen this way—so abrupt, so open. Yet here, with Sweet Grass, it seemed natural, not sinful as his mother would have deemed it.

She unbuttoned his shirt while, dry-mouthed, he groped with his trouser buttons. Both naked, she pulled him down to the robe. Skin to skin, the sensations caused his fear to fall away like a discarded robe. Frank kissed her eyes, then her neck. She smelled of musk and sage, smells that caused his mind to swim with desire. She let him explore her body, which he did haltingly, with awe. Some places he touched made her giggle, then he found places that made her sigh, or inhale sharply.

She guided him into that mysterious place he had so often wondered about. It was more pleasurable than he ever imagined—too pleasurable, and it ended prematurely. After, they lay together staring at the stars, not even trying to struggle with language. Somehow it seemed inappropriate to diminish this special time with clumsy words. Frank just liked looking at her, touching her, feeling her warmth against him. She was laughter, a cool breeze, the dip of a bird's wing.

When they made love again it was unhurried. A cloud drifted across the moon. An owl hooted softly. His moans and her muted cries mingled with the night sounds of the river. There was no tomorrow, no wagon train, no California. There were only the two of them, the shadowed moon, and the endless prairie.

Six

JAKALUNUS KNELT BESIDE White Hair and took her hand. She was sweating and clutching her belly. Her voice was strained and weak.

"It hurts, *kiuks*."

Squinter took his wife's hand.

"How long has she been sick?" the holy man asked.

"Since the rise of the sun. The pain comes and goes," Squinter said, his speech rushed, worried.

Jakalunus's face grew dark. "Gather some helpers."

"*Ih*." Squinter ran to Winema's lodge, and she helped him spread the word. White Hair was well-liked. Soon a concerned crowd gathered in front of, and inside, Squinter's lodge.

Jakalunus looked up at the lodge supports and spotted a tied leather thong hanging from a beam. Squinter was offering a horse as payment for the cure. The holy man packed and lit his *paksh*. He drew two puffs, then offered the pipe to *Kemush*, to the four directions and to *Kaela Ena*. He drew another lungful and blew measured streams of the sweet smoke along White Hair's body. Laying the pipe aside, he placed his hands gently on her belly, closed his eyes, and prayed softly. White Hair's pain seemed to subside for the moment. Her face relaxed, but her breathing remained shallow and rapid. She looked at Jakalunus with beseeching eyes.

Jakalunus placed his medicine bundle carefully on a reed mat he had blessed earlier, and prepared a mixture of sage, cedar chips, and some of his own personal ingredients, mixing them in a large mussel shell. From the fire he took a burning stick and touched it to the mixture. Blowing on it softly, it smoldered to life, and the air in the lodge became heavy with the blended aromas.

The *kiuks* chanted the opening prayer. "*Plaitalántnish nu shuína*. I am singing to the heavens above."

The bundle had to be opened in a sacred way, the prayers said precisely in order for his healing powers to remain at peak level. The chant finished, he unrolled his bundle, checked the sacred items spread upon it. He kept in mind the bad spirits, the *skoksi*, who watched for every opportunity to make mischief, to take advantage of any error. Shaking the rattle, then turning it in leftward circles, *tusa'sas skoks*, would frighten away the joker skunk spirit.

The doctor waved a wand decorated with woodpecker, mallard, and bluebird feathers, purifying the sacred items by wafting the sweet vapor onto them. The preparation-way completed, he began the interpretation-way. The correct spirits must be called from *skoksum kalo*, the land of the spirits.

First, he called *kowe skoks*, the frog spirit, a keen examiner of food. "*Kowe welä'kash nû tchalekíya, welwáshtat nú tchalíka*. I the decrepit she-frog, sit down here by the water spring." Then the lightning spirit, *lolukum skoks*, was called to make light, to help him *see* the sickness. Five songs were sung, the crowd of helpers joining in.

The rattles had been laid aside, but now they shook by something unseen—a sudden draft that chilled the lodge and all within it.

The spirits had arrived.

Jakalunus convulsed as if struck by something sharp, then cried out. The crowd hushed. White Hair moaned. Winema mopped her friend's brow with a damp cool cloth.

Strange voices came from deep within the *kiuks*. The rasp-like utterances spoke in unknown tongues. They seemed to argue for some time as his head jerked back and forth. At times a hissing, quavering voice, like mice moving through dry grass, emanated from his throat.

Jakalunus's eyes snapped open. He looked worriedly at White Hair. "The spirits cannot agree on the *nebaks*. I must call the ghost spirit."

There came a communal gasp and Winema squeezed White Hair's hand. Calling the ghost spirit was dangerous, for he manifested death.

Jakalunus rested a moment, drank from the gourd bowl. He needed all his strength, all his wile, to confront the cunning spirit of darkness. The holy man's assistant, Cho-ocks, rubbed sage on the *kiuks*'s forehead, back, and arms. Picking up the shell, he smudged the senior doctor and all within the lodge with the protective smoke. After doing the same for White Hair, he went outside and smudged the helpers and onlookers. Three children were discovered in the crowd. Lodge Woman gasped and chased them off, no doubt fearing the ghost spirit could make off with them.

Jakalunus stood and began the ghost chant. "*Nulidshá nulidshá nulidshá ko-idsnántala kälátala Kailpákshtala—tchiá.* I am sliding, slipping, sliding. Toward that wretched land, toward that burning place—to remain there."

The air in the warm lodge became as cold as ice. The flames shrank as if in fear. A violent spasm shook the *kiuks*. His eyes widened and rolled back in his head. He groaned, a sound so terrifying, the helpers shrank from him. The once starving fire now whooshed to life, singeing the hairs on the backs of his hands as he covered his face. Then he spoke to the spirit using unfamiliar words, spirit words. Winema was sure she heard the sounds of the wolf, the bear, the cougar.

Suddenly the lodge filled with voices, ancient voices—whispering, shouting, groaning. Men and women yelped as invisible icy fingers pulled at their bodies. Macabre shadows writhed and danced along the inner walls of the latch.

The lodge shuddered, raining down bits of thatch and dirt. People shrank back and hid their eyes, covered their ears. The *kiuks*'s body trembled, his arms straight out. He screamed as if his own spirit had been wrenched from him.

Time seemed suspended. The lodge grew death-still. The fire relaxed and the room warmed again. Ghost spirit had returned to the dark land.

The *kiuks*'s eyes closed before he collapsed to the dirt floor. It looked as though his breathing had stopped. Cho-ocks ran to him and the holy man slowly opened his eyes, his entire body glistening with sweat. His voice was a hoarse whisper. "Ghost spirit has"—he gasped for breath—"confirmed my suspicion. White Hair has been"—The old man took a drink to soothe bone-dry lips—"poisoned."

. Winema felt White Hair's hand flex within hers. Anger supplanted her fear.

With considerable effort Jakalunus began the curing-way. "*At gé-u steínash wakídsha!* Now my heart has returned."

Two baskets sat next to him. He dipped his fingers into the water basket and moistened his mouth in preparation. Moving to White Hair's side he made loud sucking sounds on her belly, then on her temples and forehead. Next, the fish hawk, eagle, and coyote spirits were called, each possessing increasingly greater curing power. "*Kapkablandaks! O'kst ah tkaléga ndéwa!* Be silent! Her body arises from the dead to scream!"

The healer's breathing became labored, then he coughed and gasped. The pelican spirit was called—he who scoops things into his baggy mouth. Choking and gagging as if something caught in his throat, Jakalunus turned and spat blackened blood into the second basket.

Winema felt relief. The poison had been removed.

As the doctor slowly raised his head from White Hair's body, something jerked him back violently. Cho-ocks caught him, eased him onto the ground. In a moment Jakalunus struggled back to a sitting position. He looked years older, wizened. Weakly he shook his rattle and sang, "*Gé-u hû gépkash käíla shuáktcha.* After I had arrived in the spirit land, the Earth wept and cried." He turned to Squinter. "I am not sure I got all of the poison. We must wait and see."

The ceremony had ended and the helpers dispersed. White Hair lay in deep sleep, her breathing ragged. Winema saw there was nothing more she could do for her friend. She left the sick house with Secot, anger flickering in her eyes. They walked toward Secot's latch. Woman Watching must pay for her witchery, Winema promised herself. There was no doubt as to the medicine woman's guilt. "Father, you and I both know who did this to White Hair. She must be punished."

Secot frowned. "Watch what you say, Daughter. Talk like that could bring about the wrath of the village on Woman Watching. It would mean her death. You have proof?"

Winema stiffened. "It is well known who White Hair's enemies are."

"And if she has more than one enemy, who do we blame?"

"It is Woman Watching. I know it."

"And how do you know this?"

"She is jealous of White Hair, and she soon completes the herb medicine training. She has the knowledge."

He stopped and considered this for a moment. "Even if I agree with you, Winema, you need proof before she can be punished. You must not speak of this to anyone but me."

Winema knew her father's mind. After all, it was from him she inherited her stubbornness. She could think of no way to prove Woman Watching's guilt. Until she could, justice would not come for White Hair. For now, all they could do was wait.

SEVEN

A WEEK HAD passed and a pallid, gaunt White Hair still slept the deep sleep. But it was the acorn-gathering time and Winema appreciated the diversion from the sadness of Squinter's lodge. She joined the other women gatherers and they laughed and joked while they batted the tiny nuts off tall oaks with long poles and gathered them into their *wekkis*.

It was one of Winema's favorite times. Her mother once told her acorns were made especially for the *Modokni*, their shells the color of the People's skin, their heads fitted with rounded basket hats like their own. And there was nothing better than the smell of fresh baked acorn bread. She loved the season of falling leaves. It often filled her with warm melancholy, the bittersweet memories of times gone by. *Kemush* painted the forest in magic colors: pumpkin golds, fire reds, and maize yellows mixed with the eternal green of firs and pines. The manzanita berries turned as yellow as the *boshtin*'s gold.

Winema's mind jumped unbiddenly to Frank. Over the past two moons Secot had asked frequently about Frank. She knew what her father was thinking. He grew impatient with her reticence to remarry and provide him with grandchildren. He obviously viewed Frank as a valuable husband. He had lately become convinced Winema would, in this changing world, benefit from a White husband. This surprised her since Secot

had never been an open advocate of intermarriage. Perhaps—
frustrated by her lack of interest in the village men—this was
his latest plan to get her interested in a man. Then again, times
were changing and mixed-race couples were hardly novel.
White Hair thought it enticing if only to find out how white
men were in the blankets.

Secot was impressed with Frank's skill in *Tchinuk* and his
understanding of Indian ways. She had to admit the man
seemed better behaved than most *boshtin*, but that didn't mean
she wanted to marry him. Besides, like most White men, he
wore a beard. Not only were they ugly, but she imagined they
would be scratchy as well.

Their baskets filled, the women returned to Kalelk only to
hear mourning cries. A twinge of dread crept up Winema's
spine. Instinctively she ran to Squinter's lodge. Her worse fears
realized, Squinter and several women mourners stood outside
the latch. They sang a death song.

The basket dropped from her hand as an all-too-familiar
feeling of dread filled her heart. Once again she would mourn.
Once again she would sing a death song for someone she loved.

~

EVERY day Winema saw Woman Watching about the village.
The evil-tongued woman strutted around with a smirk on her
face until she saw Winema, then she avoided Winema's eyes
and hurried away. Winema stopped and watched her. Dark
feelings churned and swirled inside her. She did not share her
suspicions with anyone, especially Squinter. She knew Squinter
would take revenge on Woman Watching, starting a blood
feud. Then Tetetekus would try to kill Squinter. If successful,
Squinter's family would take revenge on Tetetekus, and so on.
No, this would be between her and Woman Watching.

Deep in thought, she hadn't noticed Kentapoos approach.
He touched her shoulder. "I grieve with you for White Hair."

"*Humast*, Cousin."

"If I knew who was responsible for her death, he would pay
a heavy price."

His offer pleased her. It reminded her of when they were youths, when Kentapoos had been protective of her.

"Do you have any suspicions, Cousin?" he asked.

"None," she answered.

She knew Kentapoos and Tetetekus were friends, so she changed subjects. "I forgot to tell you I met a *boshtin* digger several suns ago who says he knows you."

Kentapoos reacted with mild surprise. "Who?"

"His name is Frank Riddle. Father gave him permission to use his pan in The-little-white-water, and to trap."

Kentapoos smiled expectantly. "So he finally comes to *Mowatoc*. What do you think of him?"

Winema ignored the inference. "He seemed better than most *boshtin*, that is all."

"*Ih*. He *is* different from most Whites. He likes *mak'laks* and knows about our ways. I have been thinking of inviting him to my lodge."

"And what would Tetetekus say about that?" she asked.

He stiffened. "Tetetekus does not decide who will be my guest."

She looked at him, a pinprick of doubt in her eyes. "I am glad to hear you say that, my cousin," and headed toward her latch.

~

THREE days later Frank and Kentapoos stood at the edge of the gaming fields. Over the past two months Frank had hunted and gambled with Kentapoos and several other Modocs. A friendship was growing and Frank had finally been invited to the village. The fall hunts had been fat with meat, and Secot called for a day of celebration and games. The sweat houses were busy the night before as men and women prepared physically and spiritually.

The playing fields teemed with shouts and laughs. Children played tule ball, agilely dodging the *dasi*, thrown by the child struck by it last. Some of the boys held slingshot contests. There were one-legged races, wrestling matches, lance-throwing, and archery contests. But the two contests no one would miss were the women's and men's ball games. Here, the most serious *kakla* took place. People bet everything from horses to latches, the gambling sometimes more important than the games themselves.

The Kalelk women had challenged the E'Uslis women, and Winema had offered to play on the E'Uslis team. They were surprised but happy to have her. A highly skilled player, she did not hesitate to get rough when necessary, and it looked good for the *laki*'s daughter to show a lack of favoritism.

Frank had heard of the game but had never seen one. Jack explained the concept. "Each woman uses two sticks to carry and pass the *dasi* to a teammate, or throw it at the other team's goal."

Frank examined one of the rackets—a hard wooden pole with a small net made of sinew lashed to one end. A bent willow stick formed the frame for the net. Examining the thick Kalelk posts in front of him, Frank then squinted to see the E'Uslis posts several hundred yards down field.

Jack continued, "The team *tyees* decide how many points they will play today. Each time the *dasi* passes between the goalposts is one point. The first team to reach that number for the day wins."

"Look. There's Winema," Frank said. Bouncing up and down on his toes like a player waiting to get into the game, Frank nodded toward her, careful not to show rudeness by pointing.

"Yes. You would do well to bet on her team today. She is the fastest and strongest woman player in Kalelk, perhaps in all of *Mowatoc*."

Frank turned to Jack and the group of Modoc men around them. "All right, I'll bet an ounce of gold on Winema's team." This created a flurry of cross-betting and shouting. Gold bought valuable things in the *boshtin* camps and towns.

On the field the team *tyees* met and decided the game would go to fifteen points. Secot threw in the ball and bedlam broke out. A tremendous shout erupted from players and spectators alike, followed by the sharp cracks of a hundred wooden poles whacking and thudding against wood and flesh.

～

WINEMA rushed toward the ball, shoving and elbowing opponents aside. Woman Watching beat her by a heartbeat and the group raced toward the E'Uslis goal. Winema smiled to herself as she thrust her pole between Woman Watching's pumping legs. The pole angled in at shin level, tripping her. Woman Watching yelped in pain and went down hard with a grunt.

The ball sailed upward. Winema caught it with her left stick. Confronted by a bevy of opposing players, she passed the ball backward to a teammate.

The E'Uslis team spread out smartly as they ran full-out toward the Kalelk goal. They feinted and passed efficiently, outmaneuvering their opponents. Although she sustained a painful blow from behind, Winema's teammate managed to swing her stick accurately, hurling the ball between the goalposts for the first point before another woman collided into her. At a run the shove knocked her off balance and into the goalpost, her head whacking the left post, stunning her for several breaths. The spectators exploded into cheers and resumed betting furiously. Two players were helped off the field, one with a broken nose, the other with a badly sprained ankle.

The ball was again put into play. Woman Watching and her team had apparently planned ahead. Two Kalelk players had sprinted toward the opponent's goal the moment the first point was scored. Woman Watching stole the ball from Wind Walker, took two giant strides, and threw the ball with all her strength. It arced high and far ahead of the body of players. An accurate pass, one of the two forwards caught it.

Groans and yells from the audience accompanied the whoosh of the ball through the Kalelk goal—a perfect play, tying the game.

⁓

FRANK watched in amazement. "These women play rough!" he yelled over the crowd noise to Jack. He tried to picture the White women he knew playing such a game—the vision wouldn't take shape. He felt proud of these tough, hardworking women. They managed to be incredibly rugged and spirited on the ball field, yet soft and feminine—even shy—in private.

As the game continued into late morning, the women's stamina impressed Frank. They kept at a constant run, in addition to the hitting, shoving, and falling. Winema, however, seemed to concentrate more on outwitting one particular player than on scoring goals. Frank saw Jack watching his cousin with an uneasy eye, the score now 13–12, Kalelk.

"I do not understand Winema," Jack said. "She should have three or four goals by now. She wastes her time, staying so close to Woman Watching."

Frank nodded. "*Ih*. I noticed that. Like they was hobbled together."

⁓

BY midmorning the E'Uslis team had lost eleven players to injuries, Kalelk, nine. Her face closed and wary like *wus*, the fox, Woman Watching eyed Winema. It was unusually warm for October and both women breathed heavily. Rills of sweat painted muddy streaks through the grime on their foreheads. Their sweat-soaked hair clung in strands around their faces and necks.

Recovering a missed E'Uslis goal throw, the ball passed to Winema, and she jogged down field toward the E'Uslis goal. Woman Watching attacked from Winema's left rear. Using her stick like a lance, she gave Winema a vicious kidney jab. Winema gasped in pain but kept running. Woman Watching attacked again, whipping her pole down hard on Winema's shoulder, causing Winema to lose her grip, and the ball jiggled out of her net.

A wild scramble for the loose *dasi* ensued, but Woman

Watching deftly scooped it up and sprinted for the goal. She swung hard and the ball nicked the post and bounced through the goal, tying the game once again.

The E'Uslis supporters cheered. A scuffle broke out among the spectators. Designated crowd-calmers interceded, preventing an all-out fight.

Winema's shoulder and back ached, but she ignored them. She crouched and looked at Woman Watching like a wolf stalking its prey. An E'Uslis team member won control of the ball, and the players dashed after her toward the Kalelk goal. Winema charged from Woman Watching's left side. She swung her stick, hitting the back of Woman Watching's running legs with a loud smack. Woman Watching stumbled. Slowing, Winema swung her stick in the opposite direction and whacked Woman Watching on the chest. The medicine woman grunted, tumbled forward to the ground.

Winema sprinted to catch her teammates. Before she reached them, she saw the ball arc high into the air and pass through the goal. She shouted happily—they had pulled into the lead, 14–13.

Winema squinted skyward. The piercing-bright sun was almost directly above her. Bone-weary, thirsty, and hungry, she nevertheless hoped the game would not end too soon. She was not finished with Woman Watching.

Lodge Woman trotted up, her face pinched in concern. "Winema, what are you doing? You know the rule."

Winema shot her a look that brooked no argument. Her friend sighed and ran off to join her teammates. Standing at midfield, Winema waited for the play to move toward her. She heard running feet behind her and turned just as Woman Watching's stick smashed into her chest. The wind knocked from her, she fell backward.

Woman Watching bared her teeth and raised her stick for a head blow, but Winema jammed her stick into Woman Watching's right knee, bringing her down with a yelp. Woman Watching cursed, reached for her dropped pole, but Winema got to her knees first and rammed the butt of her racket into

Woman Watching's nose. Woman Watching reeled backward, blood spraying in an arc.

The players raced by them, intent on the goal. On the sidelines Tetetekus started to go to his wife's aid, but Kentapoos and two other men held him back.

Exhausted, Winema slumped on her knees. Woman Watching rolled over and grasped her stick. Struggling to her knees, she swung clumsily at Winema. The stick whooshed a finger's width from her head and Winema felt the rush of air. Looking up, she raised her stick, swung wildly at her opponent, who parried, their sticks clacking ferociously. Lacking the strength to stand, they remained on their knees, thrusting and parrying like drunken fighters. Woman Watching's nose oozed blood and mucus down her lips and chin.

At the far end of the field, most of the players had reached the E'Uslis goal, but several had stopped to watch the fight at midfield. The distraction allowed the E'Uslis team to score the winning point.

Winema and Woman Watching continued flailing at each other like cornered animals. They grunted, cursed, and snarled as they traded blows to the arms and thighs. Woman Watching's reactions became slow and careless, and Winema saw an opening. Woman Watching's stick swung downward. Winema parried it, jabbed her stick into her opponent's belly, then followed up with a powerful upward flick of her wrist. The butt of Winema's stick caught her adversary under the chin, snapping the woman's head back with tremendous force, blood spurting from her mouth.

Sitting back on her legs, Woman Watching put her hands out behind her to prevent herself from falling over. Only half-conscious, she tried to regain her balance, raising her upper body up to her original position. Winema saw this and with her last measure of strength, swung her stick downward. It cracked heavily on Woman Watching's head. The woman's eyes rolled back in her head as she fell over like a heartshot deer.

"That was for White Hair," Winema panted, her eyes cold, her voice harsh as a rasp.

➤

FRANK watched the fight with astonishment. He'd never seen two women fight with such brutal determination. What was it about? It was supposed to be a game. Yet his respect—and desire—for Winema took on a new dimension.

Jack, Secot, and Tetetekus loped toward the two women. As they closed on them, Frank saw Winema hold up her arm and wave them back. With great effort she used her ball pole to leverage herself to a standing position and walked erect, head up, toward the spectators. She faltered several times, yet waved her father and cousin away at every offer of assistance.

Frank desperately wanted to go to her but sensed she would disapprove. He watched her disappear into the village. Tetetekus picked up his wife and carried her to their latch. As he passed, Frank could see her chest heaving, her face a bloody and bruised mess.

Both Jack and Secot were frowning. Frank assumed they were concerned about Woman Watching.

"I must go to Winema," Secot said. "Stay and watch the games." In after thought, he said, "Will you come to the feast tomorrow?"

"I would be honored," Frank answered. "Please tell Winema of my concern for her." But his words did not reach Secot, who was loping toward Winema's lodge.

➤

WINEMA entered her latch followed closely by Secot. She collapsed in her robes, completely drained.

Secot's face was tight with anger. "You have shamed us."

She was barely able to speak. Her face ached as did every muscle in her body. She did not answer.

"You, above all people. The *laki*'s daughter. What am I to say to the People when I hear them talking, saying Secot's daughter dishonors the game?"

Winema raised up partially, her eyes flashing. "Tell them your daughter is a woman who honors her friends above all.

Tell them she lets off White Hair's killer with only a beating, that Woman Watching should have been publicly *killed* for taking the life of a fellow *Gumbatwas*."

Secot's face reddened. "*GETAK*! Tomorrow I will gather the People. You will give gifts of apology to Woman Watching and Black Wound. Then you will tell the People that you shamed yourself by bringing personal feelings onto the playing field."

They stared at each other, a test of wills. Finally Winema sagged. She knew she had broken a time-honored rule.

The following morning, the People gathered in a large semicircle. Winema walked up to a smirking Woman Watching and her husband. Her face was one massive, purple bruise, her eyes virtually swollen shut. Handing them her best trade blanket, Winema bowed her head in apology and tasted bile.

THE following evening Frank returned to Kalelk. He found Jack, Winema, and Secot in front of Winema's lodge. Several other Modocs sat around their fire, eating and talking.

"Ah, Frank. Sit here," Jack invited, indicating a space between Jack and Winema.

Winema stood and smiled a welcome. There were several purple bruises on her face and arms. Her lower lip was puffy, but, overall, she seemed recovered.

"We are glad you came, Frank," she said.

She served him a bowl of sucker fish soup and two freshly cooked epos roots, then sliced an ample hunk of venison for him from the spit. The rich aromas reminded Frank of how hungry he was. The seared *mow'itsh itl'willie* was rare inside, increasing the meat's gamy taste. Juice dripped from his fingers and chin.

Jack introduced the other guests. Nodding politely to each, Frank found it difficult to take his eyes from Winema. Only yesterday she had fought like a cougar, and now she was the modest, soft-spoken daughter of Secot. He caught himself wondering which she would be in the blankets—the lion or the mouse—then felt a little ashamed of his thoughts. This woman was no Hawkinsville whore.

It had been a long time since he felt interest in a *proper* woman. But he felt a bit intimidated by Winema. Looking at Laulauwush—Wild Girl—sitting across from him with her round face and mischievous grin, he wondered if she and Winema should trade names.

"What did you think of our games?" Jack asked. "I know you won your bet on the women's contest."

"Yes, I won three horses on Winema's game, but lost one on the men's game. I have never seen a game where the ball is kicked, not thrown. Next time, I will understand the men's game better." Frank smiled wryly. "And I will know not to bet on *your* team, Jack."

The group laughed.

Kentapoos returned the sally. "You had a good day indeed. Horses are valuable and you can always get more gold from the stream. Perhaps next time you will play *with* us and improve the odds."

"I might just do that."

"*Kloshe*'." Kentapoos looked pleased.

After the meal Frank conjured enough courage and asked Winema to walk with him. She assented and they walked to the river. They ambled by tall oaks and elms, their leaves splashed with golds and yellows, and past leaning poles of river cane. They picked and ate sweet blue elderberries. Passing by deep-scarlet serviceberries, she explained how their crotches were used to anchor the swamp grass mats of their latches, and how beautiful their snowy white flowers were in early summer.

Fascinated, they watched a large flock of sparrows which seemed to suspend in midair, then form an hourglass shape. The strange formation undulated in and out as if it breathed a life of its own. A portion of the birds broke out of the configuration, formed spirals that curved out, around, then melted back into the hourglass. It seemed the birds had designed this performance for *them*, and they watched spellbound until the strange formation burst into a random-shaped flock and flew off toward the east.

"I think it an omen," Winema said.

"An omen?" Frank asked.

"A good omen," she said, smiling at him. Her eyebrows pinched together in a question. "Why do White men not remove their face hair?"

He looked at her, bewildered by the sudden change of subject. "Well—I don't know. It's just the custom. Some men *do* cut them."

"And which do White women like best?"

Frank frowned in thought and scratched his head. "I . . . never thought much about it. I guess some women like beards and some do not."

He realized Winema had taken over the conversation. He mentally fished for a way to get back to yesterday's game. "Are your ball games always that rough?" he said, hoping to draw her out about the fight.

Her expression remained impassive. "The game is always rough."

"Are there usually fights like that?"

Her answer was almost imperceptible. "No."

They walked in silence, Frank having no luck in getting her to reveal anything about the fight. Their thoughts were interrupted by a squirrel which ran across their path, then skittered up a nearby birch. It scurried out onto a limb, looked down, and scolded them. Winema made clicking noises back at the squirrel.

"Feisty little *skwis'kwis*, isn't he?" Frank said.

"*She* is a *moi*," Winema answered, smiling. "No doubt she is angry with me for taking her acorns today."

Eyebrows knitted, she said, "I think it is time you learn more Modoc and less *Tchinuk*."

"Would you teach me?" Frank asked, one eyebrow raised.

"*Nawit'ka*. Anything to rid you of that poor language."

They laughed together.

"I could teach you more English in return," Frank offered.

"That would be nice."

She smiled and looked into his eyes, her directness causing his heart to jump. Those eyes. Depthless black pools.

"Now I will have someone to speak it with since my good friend has gone to the land of the dead."

He grasped her hand and they walked. The sun felt warm on their faces. The air was alive with honeybees and the aroma of loamy earth. Frank hadn't felt this good since his days with Sweet Grass. He knew what he would do first thing in the morning. He would shave off his beard.

EIGHT

Fol'dum, Winter, 1861

WINEMA RETRIEVED AN armload of swamp grass from the winter-stocked storehouse adjacent to her latch. Reentering her lodge, she sat near the warm fire and began tying new floor mats. She thought about Frank. He had visited often since their first walk together four moons ago. On his second visit he arrived carrying a bundle of wildflowers, his face clean-shaven. She had been impressed. That Frank thought so well of her to cut his face hair enhanced her warm feelings about him.

The bird omen proved true and their relationship deepened. Beardless, he turned out to be more handsome than she had guessed: a gentle face, a strong jaw, an easy smile. She liked his laugh and his good Indian manners. Even better, he was learning Modoc quickly, his understanding of *Tchinuk* proving helpful.

Sometimes she had arousing dreams of Frank. She wondered how White men made love. It had a been a long time since she had been in the blankets with a man, and she burned. Many nights she waited for him, expecting him to make his heart known, but he did not come. Unless White men were different, he must not have the right feelings for her. Yet if he did, how would she respond?

Secot stuck his head in on his way to the sweat lodge. "I saw Woman Watching this afternoon."

"*Ih?*"

One corner of his mouth upturned. "She is healing well."

Without a flicker of emotion Winema returned to her task. "That is a shame."

Frowning, Secot stretched, then shuffled his feet, a nervous habit when he had something on his mind. Winema knew he liked Frank. He brought the White miner up often, but did not wish to be too obvious, she knew. Not only was it unmanly, but talking too much about him might turn her away from Frank. Secot called him Tchmu'tcham, One Who Shoots Straight. He had given Frank the name one moon ago after Frank impressed him with his marksmanship.

"How does it go with Tchmu'tcham?"

Winema's lips formed a half-smile, but she kept her eyes on her lap work. "He has almost finished his skinned-tree house, a ca-bin he calls it."

"It must be lonely for him in that house . . . all alone."

She wouldn't give in. "I do not think so, Father. He hunts with Kentapoos, Bostin-ahgar, Cho-ocks, and the others. He visits me sometimes, and he has no wife to nag him. *Kai*, I do not think he is lonely."

She looked at him out of the corner of her eye, seeing the frustration in his face as he sighed and turned to look out the door. It became harder not to laugh. She enjoyed teasing, and her father was an easy mark.

Secot turned back toward her. "Perhaps he needs your help, your advice, on the house."

"He has not asked," she said evenly.

Secot threw up an arm in exasperation. "Then *you* should *ask* him. I go now to the sweat lodge."

Winema stretched a too-wide smile, "Have a good sweat, Father."

BEFORE Secot got five steps, Frank rode into the village at a gallop. He pulled rein and spoke to the chief from horseback.

"There is trouble. Another White family has been killed, near Dry Lake."

Secot frowned. "Who has done this?"

"I do not know, *laki*, but the townspeople are angry. The men in Yreka have asked Ben Wright to find and punish the killers."

"Why involve us? It is the *Alamimakts* who usually make this trouble. Who is this man—Ben 'White'?"

"He is the one who led the raid on the *mak'laks* the winter of the five hundred killed."

Secot stiffened. Kentapoos and Tetetekus had joined them now, and many others, curious about Frank's hurried entry into the village.

Tetetekus scowled at Frank. "The *boshtin* will attack. They send this one as a spy."

Kentapoos gave him a sharp look, "*Kai*, Tetetekus. Tchmu'tcham comes as a friend."

Tetetekus, his face filled with contempt, elbowed his way closer to Frank. "How do you know of this trouble?"

Frank didn't like his accusatory tone, but answered his question. "My friend rode out to tell me. He fears for our safety."

"*Our* safety? *You* are in no danger. You are White."

Kentapoos stepped forward. "*Getak*. Tchmu'tcham has come to warn us."

Tetetekus glowered at the Waterbrash, but did not reply. Winema looked on without betraying her feelings.

A shout interrupted the discussion. Wieum, a runner from one of the western villages ran up breathlessly. "Secot, a *boshtin* called Ben Wright came to our village with a white flag. He wants to talk about the killing of the Whites. He says there will be no trouble, only talk. I am to take your answer to his camp in two suns."

Tetetekus snorted, "It is a trick. I say we attack them before they attack us."

"No!" Frank took a step forward. "The man came under a white flag. If you attack them, there will be much trouble. Many more Whites will come—*shuldshash* maybe—and they will make war on you." He turned to Secot. "Let me go with you, *laki*. I will tell him the *Modokni* are innocent."

Secot considered this a moment. "This is not to be decided here. I will call a council tomorrow after the other men return from their hunts." He looked around him. "Kentapoos, Skonches, advise the elders."

Secot hesitated, then turned back to Frank, his expression softening. "*Geo' sut'walinai.* I do not know what the council will decide. If there is trouble, I will need your help here. Will you stay?"

Frank felt a mix of pride and disappointment. Secot honored him by asking him to help protect the people remaining at the village. On the other hand, he rejected Frank's offer of help. In any case, Frank had no choice. He looked at Winema. "I would be honored, Secot."

Secot nodded and headed for his latch. After the men had gone, Frank complained to Winema, "I do not understand why your father will not let me go. I know I could help."

The corners of her eyes crinkled in appreciation. "My father is a proud man and a chief. It will take time before you will be allowed to speak for him. But I think he is pleased you offered."

Though her answer was designed to soothe, it nonetheless grated. Over the past few months Frank felt he had earned the Modocs' trust, that he had been thought of as one of them. But once again he experienced an enigmatic line he could not cross as a White man. There were certain ceremonies and meetings closed to him. Lively conversations sometimes trailed off as he approached. As much as he enjoyed being with Indians, they maintained a frustrating barrier that kept him from knowing their innermost selves. It made him feel . . . unworthy, even unmanly.

Looking into Winema's eyes, Frank realized that only recently had she replaced Jack as his binding connection to the

Modocs. Over the past three months he found himself thinking about her constantly, their visits becoming the most important part of his day. Sometimes they looked at each other, knowing what the other thought or felt. Many nights he lay awake listening to the burbling creek beside his cabin, imagining them making love. But beyond the sexual, new feelings churned within him as if he were a child discovering the wonders of a butterfly emerging from its cocoon. There were times he ached to tell Winema of his feelings, but at each opportunity he lost his nerve.

Winema studied his face. "I feel like riding. Will you go with me?"

Dusk shadowed the forest as they mounted their horses and rode toward the creek.

WINEMA seemed to read his thoughts. "You feel you are not trusted."

She caught him by surprise. Perhaps he had become lax in controlling his facial expressions lately: "Be careful. Your face is the *miroir* of your soul," his French-Cheyenne friend, Jacques, had taught. "Indian people can read it like trail sign."

"It seems that way sometimes," Frank said, looking ahead.

"Do not let it bother you, Tchmu'tcham. It is only natural. Do *your* people not trust Indians?"

He hadn't thought about it in the reverse, but she was right.

She continued, "I think it takes longer to trust those who are different, *ih*?"

Her voice had a way of soothing, rather like his mother's Rose salve. "I suppose you are right. Do you remember I told you of my friend, Jacques—White Eagle?"

"*Ih.*"

"He said Indians are the same, yet they are different."

Winema chuckled.

A puzzled smile on his face, Frank asked, "Why do you laugh?"

"Kentapoos once told me that, only he spoke of Whites."

They both chuckled.

She turned to be sure they were out of sight of the village gossipers, then reached over and took his hand. "It has been a while since I have seen your ca-bin."

Their eyes met, probing each other.

Frank cleared his throat. "Well, it . . . it is not finished."

She smiled. "Perhaps I can help."

They arrived at the half-completed cabin, the roof finished only over the back sleeping area, sheltered by a piece of hanging canvas. Pushing the canvas aside, Winema inspected the dwelling while Frank built a fire in the stone fireplace. He felt self-conscious about the tiny incomplete house now that Winema stood in it. He slipped into English. "It ain't much, I know."

She turned and looked at him. "How do you say *cul'tus wau'wau* again?"

Frank smiled at the familiar Chinook word. "Nonsense."

She nodded her head. "Nonsense. It will make a very strong latch."

She stared at the half-finished front wall unhappily.

"What's wrong, Winema?"

"You could become sick if you live in a lodge where the door does not face east to receive the blessing of the morning sun."

Frank pinked in chagrin. "I can fix that."

He looked into her eyes—dark, lustrous pools that pulled him in. Putting his hands on her shoulders, he pulled her to him, kissed her gently, then drew back, fearing she would be repulsed. But anger didn't come. Instead, she blinked—a funny look on her face, as if deciding how she felt.

She ran her tongue over her lips and grinned. "I have wondered about this—" She searched for the word.

"Kissin'?" Frank prompted.

"Kiss-in, *ih*. My friend told me about it."

"Can we try it again?" Frank asked, one eyebrow arched.

"That would be good, I think."

More confident, he took her face in his hands and softly

kissed her forehead, each eyelid, then her mouth. As they kissed, he tenderly caressed her neck, then brought his hand to the small of her back and pulled her tightly to him. The kiss became more passionate. Frank felt the heat of her body against him. She kissed him back now, no longer a curious student, but a woman responding.

They broke for a moment, their breathing rapid.

"Winema, I never felt this way before."

For a moment her brow furrowed in thought. Frank knew of the tribal disdain of sex outside of marriage, but Winema was no longer a girl. She was a mature woman and a widow.

Her face relaxed. "It is time then, as I feel the same."

She removed her rabbit and wildcat fur jacket, untied the thong around her waist and pulled off her buckskin dress. Through the small window moonlight played over her body, revealing full breasts, a firm belly and rounded hips. The chilly air coaxed tiny goose bumps to the surface of her soft cocoa skin.

Frank stared, frozen for the moment. She unbuttoned his shirt and slipped it off, then gently pushed him onto the small bunk and removed his boots and socks. He stood, quickly peeled off his pants and long johns, then pulled her to him. She sighed and they kissed again.

Falling onto the bunk, he held her tightly, as if he could not get her close enough, wanting her to melt into him. She seemed to throb with life and vitality. He felt the warmth of her hand, her fingers, a soft caressing touch that made the hair on his neck stand. A shudder sprinted up his back. She seemed to know just how to touch him, how to excite him. He kissed her neck and inhaled the familiar smells of musk and sage and wildflowers.

Her breathing quickened and she mumbled Modoc words he did not understand. God, he hungered for her, wanted to devour her. But he held the rushing feeling back. He wanted this moment to last a lifetime. Caressing her breasts, he moved his mouth to them, taking his time to fully explore each with his lips and tongue. A faint taste of wood smoke teased his palate. She arched her back, then inhaled sharply as his fingers moved lower.

He never dreamed it could be this good with a woman. "I need you, Winema." He had never said anything like it before, but there it was. It just tumbled out. Then, like a hummingbird delving for nectar in the heart of a flower, he gently probed her mouth with his tongue.

When he entered her she moaned, then moved with him, responding in kind to his every motion as if they had always been lovers—fast, slow, then fast again. They fell into a rhythm, bringing waves of soaring pleasure unknown before to either of them until their bodies arched in the flight of climax.

Later, lying there holding each other, catching their breath, the sounds of the forest enveloped them. Lissome reeds rustled in a light breeze. A coyote questioned the night. Hidden in the branches above, a poor-will called.

Winema snuggled closer into his shoulder, their legs intertwining. He caressed the side of her face, tracing the inner ridges of her ear with his finger, and felt her warm breath against his neck. Now he realized love was far more than a vague word. Exhilarated, he felt commitment, complete happiness—a oneness he had never imagined.

Winema began to sing softly:

> *Ka-ila nu shu-le-moke'dsha,*
> *kenta ka-i-latat*
> *tgi'ke-lan shu-ina . . .*

"I didn't understand all the words," Frank said.

"It is a happiness song. It says, I take the earth up in my arms and with it, whirl around in a dance. On this spot I am standing and singing."

He hugged her, kissed her forehead.

"Did you hear the poor-will?" she asked. "She brings good omens."

He pulled away slightly so he could see her eyes in the

firelight. His finger moved wisps of hair from her face. "You bring me all the luck I need. Will you be my wife, Winema?"

The question came easily, which surprised him, yet he never felt so sure of anything in his life. She searched his eyes a moment, then seemed satisfied. A teasing gleamed in her eyes, and she smiled. "That is a question you must ask my father."

"I would ask *Kemush* himself if I had to." He held her face in his hands and gazed into her eyes. "I will honor the *Modokni* way. But I want to be sure it is what *you* want. That's *my* way."

Moonlight glistened in her onyx eyes. "*Ih*, Tchmu'tcham, *ih*."

They kissed deeply, the fire renewing in them. This time their lovemaking was more languorous, more committed. The clear night air brought the lonely call of a loon from Tule Lake and the poor-will once again beckoned its mate. But the lovers didn't notice.

NINE

THE FOLLOWING DAY was cold and clear, a turquoise sky dusted with lacy clouds. The council of elders and senior warriors were sitting hip to hip in Secot's lodge. Secot opened the council with a prayer: "Hear us, Grandfather. We ask you to grant us clear thinking. Our minds must be calm, for we have important matters before us. Give us wisdom, Grandfather, so that we may decide wisely."

"*Heya*," muttered the men.

Jakalunus blessed, packed, and lit the pipe, then passed it to his left after drawing several puffs. After the pipe had made its rounds, Secot said, "Brothers. Tchmu'tcham and Wieum have advised us of the *boshtin* killings at Dry Lake, and that the White townsmen wish to talk about it. We must give our answer at tomorrow's sun. I ask now if any man here knows *anything* about these killings."

Each man looked at the faces around the circle. No one spoke. Tetetekus wore his best impassive expression.

Krelatko shrugged. "It is of no concern to us. We led no war party on the Whites. Let them go to the *Alamimakts* and talk their talk."

Heads nodded and voices murmured agreement.

Kentapoos waited for the muttering to die down, then spoke. "We cannot avoid the council with Wright. We may not like it, but it is *we* whom the *boshtin* accuse."

Secot nodded. "I have tried to live in peace with the Whites. I want no more trouble with them. They are too many."

"*Ih*." Skonches agreed.

Tetetekus's face reddened. "Peace? What peace? We have had no peace since they arrived in our country. I say if the Whites want trouble, we should give it to them, *atui*! Skonches and I will lead the attack!"

Skonches's face pinched in annoyance. "Do not include me so quickly in your plans, Tetetekus. My thoughts are much closer to Secot's."

More heads nodded.

"*You* were not at Yuwa'Ina," Tetetekus growled.

"Perhaps not, but I lost a sister there, and I have lost other relatives to the *boshtin*," Skonches countered.

"*Tchawai na*! Again *Modokni catkum* was spilled for something the *Alamimakt* had done!" Tetetekus retorted.

The murmuring and nodding became more pronounced. All of the men had lost loved ones in one of these incidents.

"This is up-in-the-air talk," Kentapoos said. "Let us meet Wright and tell him we did not do this thing, that we are at peace, and let that be the end of it. Besides, we have White friends now like Tchmu'tcham, the ranchers Fairchild and Applegate—the Yreka *tyees*, Steele and Roseborough."

"Ha! Any one of which would betray us for their own if there was trouble," Hakar snapped, anxious to support Tetetekus.

Secot waited. Satisfied all had their say, he decided, "We have all suffered from the Whites, but their numbers are greater than the stars. We know they will not stop coming. My decision is to talk to this Wright and convince him we know nothing of the killings. Wieum shall tell 'White' we will meet him in three suns. *Otwe-katuxsè*. I am finished."

Tetetekus jumped to his feet and kicked ashes from the fire onto Secot's feet. "Coward! You are all cowards! You crawl to these Whites like whipped Paiutes even when they shoot down your own relations!"

Skonches leaped to his feet, pulled his knife, the blade flashing in the firelight. Secot grabbed his wrist as he scrambled to his feet. "*Kai!* We will not turn our knives on each other."

The chief frowned at Tetetekus. "You have a right to your say here, Tetetekus, but I forbid you to attend the council with White."

Tetetekus spit on the ground, whipped the mat door aside, and stalked out of the latch, followed closely by his growing entourage—Hakar, Skiet-teteko, and Bostin'ahgar.

FRANK and Winema awaited the outcome of the council at Winema's latch. Pacing the entire time, Frank stared at Secot's lodge as if he could *will* Secot to let him attend the Wright meeting. The fact that it was poor timing to discuss the marriage proposal added to his frustration. Now it would have to wait. He saw the reed door fly back on Secot's lodge and Tetetekus and three others stalk out. Kentapoos soon followed, walked over, and related the meeting results. Frank felt relief mixed with apprehension. While he wanted the Modocs to peacefully convince Wright of their innocence in the killings, he distrusted Wright's motivations.

"Use caution, my friend," Frank said.

Kentapoos smiled. "*Oka ilagen.*"

That afternoon preparations began for the Wright meeting. In Frank's opinion too many people decided to go. Several families would accompany their men, which wasn't unusual for peace councils. But still only a guest, there was nothing Frank could say or do about it.

"Something tells me I should make my marriage proposal to your father tonight."

She studied him with both curiosity and concern. "You've had a dream, a vision?"

Frank shook his head. "No dream. I can't really explain it."

"You must follow your spirit."

Frank smiled and held her face in his hands. "I love you, Little Swallow," he said, using Secot's pet name for her.

Frank found Secot in front of his latch, finishing a conversation with Skonches. He waited patiently at a polite distance for the two men to finish, then saw Skonches leave.

"Uncle. May I speak with you."

Secot turned toward him. "*Oka ilagen*, Tchmu'tcham. Come inside where an old man can warm his bones by the fire."

Frank waited for Secot to light his *paksh* and pass it. They smoked for a while in silence, not rushing into serious talk. Finally Secot looked at Frank expectantly. "Secot—Winema and I—well—"

Damn. He had this well thought out before he entered the lodge. The chief withdrew his pipe, raised an eyebrow.

Frank tried again. "We, ah—"

Secot smiled slightly now, firelight dancing in his eyes.

Frank's mouth felt dry as ashes. This was crazy. He felt like a tongue-tied schoolboy. He licked his lips. The words finally came, rushing out in a stream. "I-wish-to-marry-your-daughter-I-offer-six-horses."

Secot nodded gravely as he took another puff. Removing the pipe from his mouth, he asked, "Only six? Winema is a chief's daughter."

Frank blinked. Fear and humiliation washed over him. His heart hammered in his ears.

Secot's face broke into a wide grin that erupted into a belly laugh. "I wish Kentapoos could see your face." The laughs continued to shake his entire upper body, and he patted Frank's knee reassuringly.

Frank realized he was being teased—again. The relief brought a nervous chuckle.

The two men stood. "My heart is glad." Secot beamed. "I shall be proud to have you as a son, Tchmu'tcham. We shall have a great feast."

Frank pumped Secot's hand. "And I could not have a better father."

Frank rushed out of the latch to tell Winema, waiting for him at her lodge. Her glowing face showed she knew well beforehand her father's answer.

"I have to go to Yreka to buy three more horses," he said after their embrace. He had already collected three of the six over the past three weeks.

"And we will need gifts for the People," Winema added.

Frank was surprised. "Gifts? I figured *we'd* be the ones gettin' the gifts."

"We will, but it is the custom for us to have a giveaway at our wedding. We must have something for everyone."

"For everyone?" We'll go broke! he thought.

Winema formed a playful smile. "There you are, being White again. Wealth should be shared, then it will always return to you twice fold."

Frank felt a bit ashamed. He had prided himself on understanding Indian customs, then something like this would remind him of how much more there was to learn. "I guess we should wait until the Wright council is over."

"It is only a peace council, and it is three suns away. I want to go with you to Yreka. It has been a long time since I have been there."

Frank grinned. He felt giddy as a kid. "You're right. I want to show you off to Whitey and Four Eyes, and buy you a fancy weddin' dress. We will leave at first light. It will be Saturday. Eyes will be off."

Winema's eyes glittered in anticipation.

━◣

THE following morning Winema and Frank stopped by Long Branch. They found Whitey operating a rocker.

"Well, stranger. Looks like you found a purty lady." Whitey grinned.

Frank swelled. "Whitey, this is my betrothed, Winema."

Winema smiled shyly as Whitey doffed his hat and made a clumsy bow. "Pleased to meet ya." He regarded them a moment. "Excuse me for starin'." He held his hat against his heart. "She reminds me so much of my dear departed Rabbit."

Frank turned to Winema. "Whitey was married to a Bannock woman. She died of the *gutkaks.*"

Winema nodded. "My mother and my husband were taken by the *gutkaks*. You must miss her. Has it been long since she passed to the other side?"

Frank translated. Whitey smiled thinly. "Ten years ago." He replaced his hat and grinned. "By Gawd. I guessed this was comin'. Frank's been over here sloppy-eyed about you for months. Gonna have a big fandango, are ya?"

"You bet," Frank said, "and you're invited. Day after tomorrow, in Kalelk."

"Whoa, that quick?"

"Well, let's just say we got our reasons."

Whitey nodded knowingly. "Mmm. Ben Wright, eh? All right, I'll be there. I wanna be the first to kiss the bride." Whitey winked.

Whitey looked around, then pulled Frank closer. "You keep a look out for Wright. I don't like what I been hearin'."

Frank's smile faded. "Yeah, I hear ya."

In time, Frank and Winema said their good-byes and rode toward Yreka. Winema looked lost in thought. Frank recognized the look, her brows knitted in puzzlement. He visualized her nosing over the problem in her mind like a mouse seeking cheese. He waited for the impending question.

"I have never seen a *boshtin that* White. Is he of the first of the *t'kope* clans?" she asked.

Frank chuckled. "No, he's just Whitey."

She looked at him with puckish annoyance.

"All right." He chuckled. "Some call him an albino. He was born that way. Nobody knows why."

She mulled it over for a while. "There must be a reason Grandfather has marked him that way. He must have strong medicine."

Frank laughed. The idea of Whitey having magical powers struck Frank as hilarious.

Winema's expression told him she did not appreciate being laughed at.

"I'm sorry, darlin'. I didn't mean to make fun."

He reached over, took her hand. Her face relaxed somewhat.

"I'll make it up to you tonight," he said piquantly.

She squinted one eye. "You had better."

TEN

➤ ARRIVING IN YREKA, Frank and Winema tied their horses in front of Engler's Boarding House. Both animals dragged travois packed high with pelts and baskets. Horses, wagons, and people crowded the streets on Saturday errands.

"That's the last time we drag those fool travois, Winema. I'm gettin' us a buckboard."

Winema wasn't paying attention. She took in the large house in front of them. Freshly painted green flower boxes underscored the windows of the recently whitewashed frame building. A small brass bell tinkled as they entered. The warm foyer felt good after the cold ride, and the aromas of bacon, skillet grease, and fresh-baked muffins curled around them.

A portly woman with rosy cheeks bustled out of the kitchen, removing her apron. "Coming," she sang.

She stopped short and regarded Winema with surprise, her smile fading rapidly. Her tone became businesslike. "Can I help you?"

"Mornin', ma'am. I'm here to see your guest, Four Ey—ah, Mr. Hopkins," Frank corrected. "Is he in?"

"He just went upstairs. Who's callin'?"

Frank took off his hat. "Frank Riddle."

"Very well." She scrutinized Winema. "Wait here." Frowning, she disappeared upstairs.

Wide-eyed, Winema looked around the room. "How many people live in such a house?"

"Don't know, exactly. Maybe ten, twelve."

Two men stared over their newspapers at them from the parlor. They sat on either end of a black, medallion-backed serpentine sofa.

Winema moved over to a long shelf and studied the small knickknacks arranged carefully upon it. She breathed a Modoc word as she gently fingered a small ceramic bird. The figurine captivated her, and Frank enjoyed her expressions.

Mrs. Engler's voice slapped at them from the stairs. "Don't touch that!"

Winema jumped, accidentally brushing the small statue off the shelf. It tumbled to the floor, chipping off a wing.

"Now see what you've done," the woman barked as she rushed toward Winema.

Winema backed up a step, eyeing the woman warily.

Mrs. Engler's face pinched and reddened. "We don't allow Indians in here for just this reason."

Annoyed at the woman, Frank said, "It wouldn't have happened if you hadn't yelled at her like that."

The woman stiffened. "You can wait on the porch for Mr. Hopkins."

"That suits me, lady. C'mon, Winema. Seems we ain't wanted here," and they walked out onto the porch. Winema was about to say something when Four Eyes emerged, grasping a copy of *Silas Marner.*

"Frank, what in Sam Hill—" He stopped short when he saw Winema, his mouth still open.

Frank laughed, grabbed his friend's hand and shook it enthusiastically. "Good to see you, Eyes. It's been too long. I want to introduce you to my betrothed, Winema."

Eyes shook Frank's hand. "Ah, yes . . . it's been too long." He cleared his throat, leaned closer. "Best to call me Nathan here in town, me being the schoolteacher." He smiled sheepishly, but with a degree of self-importance.

An uncomfortable pause followed as Frank considered the

strange request. Deciding it was unimportant, Frank perked, "Well, Nathan, get your coat. It's cold out here. We can go over to Delmonico's for some coffee."

They walked to the restaurant and settled around a table toward the back. A waiter appeared. He eyed Winema but said nothing. Frank ordered coffee all around.

Nathan rambled on about current events: the latest states to secede, the coming income tax, the transcontinental telegraph. Frank sensed his old friend was avoiding any personal conversation or direct eye contact. Also, it soon became too difficult to keep up, having to explain all the new words and concepts to Winema. Frank invited him to the wedding, but he made excuses.

"I'd like to, Frank, but I have school." Nervously he seemed to search for something else. "And there's lesson preparation. You know how it is."

The table talk seemed to lose energy and drift. They walked back to the boardinghouse and onto the narrow porch. Frustrated, Frank grabbed his friend's sleeve. "Eyes. This is Frank you're talking to. What's wrong?"

Nathan's face hardened. He looked at Winema, then cocked his head toward the far end of the porch. "Over here—in private."

Frank looked at Winema. She squeezed his hand and nodded. Frank and Nathan walked a few paces away, then Nathan turned and regarded Frank. His eyes lacked warmth, as if he were a stranger.

"Have you thought this thing through, Frank?"

"What do you mean?"

"Well—she's—" He peered over Frank's shoulder at Winema—"she's an Indian."

Although Frank guessed what was coming, the words cut him like a razor. He set his jaw. "Yeah?"

Nathan blinked. He spoke in an urgent whisper. "Frank, you have to think about your future here. Not only is she an Indian, but she's a Modoc. You know how people feel about them right now."

Frank felt the sting of betrayal. "I never expected this from you, Eyes. You're supposed to be an educated man."

Nathan's left eye twitched. He grabbed Frank by the shoulder. "And a practical one. Damnit, it's *because* I'm your friend that I'm saying this. What about children? Do you want them to suffer all their lives, being called half-breeds? Think about it Frank. It—"

Frank's face flushed in anger. "Get your hands off me Eyes, before I knock you on your ass."

Nathan dropped his hands to his sides. He looked more sad and frustrated than frightened. "I'm sorry, Frank. I *am* your friend. I didn't want it to come out this way." He shoved his hands into his pockets. "Damn!"

Frank glared at him a moment, then wheeled, took Winema by the arm, and walked away.

Winema watched Frank's expression. "Something is wrong, Tchmu'tcham?"

"No. Nothin'." He patted her hand. "C'mon. Let's buy that weddin' dress."

A AT the dress shop Winema fingered every dress, every bolt of cloth with the wide-eyed excitement of a cat on a birdhouse. She finally settled on a blue satin dress with matching shawl and bonnet. Frank picked out an everyday calico dress for her as well.

Over the course of the day the pelts on the travois and the gold dust in Frank's purse were replaced with bags of sugar, tobacco, blankets, beads, needles, thread, bolts of colorful cloth, and one superbly carved ivory-handled knife. They laughed and talked, Frank taking pleasure in her pleasure. Stopping by the U. S. Bread and Cracker Factory, they bought twelve loaves of bread for a dollar. The bread would make excellent and inexpensive giveaway gifts.

As they walked arm in arm down the street, they approached couples on the sidewalk. With some, the usual amenities were exchanged. Others, their smiles melting into frowns, stepped into the street and skirted around them. In the shops matrons with furrowed brows and scorning eyes whispered to each other behind their hands.

Just then there was a commotion in the street and a horse's frantic whinnying. They turned to see a dappled mare rear after she was struck by a rock thrown by a young boy on the sidewalk. The rider barely managed to stay in the saddle as the frightened horse bolted down the street. A man came out of a shop, jogged over to the boy, grabbed the back of the youngster's collar, and proceeded to whale at his backside.

Winema's eyes widened in shock. She frowned and squeezed Frank's arm. "We go now. I want to show Lodge Woman and Wild Girl my new dresses."

Frank knew she wasn't really ready to leave. There were more shops to explore. He assumed the negative public reaction to their presence had taken its toll on Winema. He hadn't considered the Yrekan's reactions. In the mining camps, Indian wives were hardly uncommon.

They snugged the tie ropes on the travois and headed back to Kalelk. A few miles outside of town Winema said, "Many do not like Indians in Yreka Town."

Frank frowned. "The hell with them."

The troubling conversation with Eyes and the cold stares of the citizenry threw a wet blanket on what had started out as a perfect day. More troubling were Frank's nagging reservations about his impending marriage. Did Eyes have a point? Was Frank letting his feelings for Winema cloud his judgment? Were he and Winema only setting themselves up for heartache?

Winema interrupted his thoughts. "I have decided why so many Whites are rude."

Frank's eyebrows arched. "Rude?"

"*Ih*. Like when they point or stare or laugh at the wrong time."

Frank chuckled. "Jacques hated it when Whites interrupted him all the time. So you think Cho-ocks is right?"

"*Kai*. I do not think it is because they are not human beings." She attempted a wink, a mannerism Frank had taught her that she liked. "I would not have married you if I thought that. I think it is because of the way they raise their children."

Frank nodded. "Ah, the boy getting the whuppin' back there." He hadn't thought about it at the time, but now realized the negative impact it would have on his future wife. It was very rare for Modocs to strike their children. Now that he thought of it, this applied as well to the Cheyenne and Sioux he'd met. In his mind they spoiled their kids. Yet, somehow, it worked. He never saw a disrespectful Indian child.

"*Ih*. It is why their children do not have respect. Like how Whites treat Indian people. We could teach them how to raise their children if they would let us."

Frank said, "Ah, you mean by shaming or teasing them when they misbehave."

"*Ih*. That way it does not break the spirit. When you break a child's spirit, he will not respect others or himself."

Frank was glad Winema created the opportunity to explore this topic. "You got a point, Winema, but then how do you explain rascals like Black Wound or Woman Watching?"

Her brow creased in thought. "Some people's spirits are poisoned when too many bad things happen to them. Black Wound's heart is black like charred meat because he saw his people murdered. His wife's heart is heavy with, ah, how do you say . . ."

"Bitterness?"

She shook her head.

"Suspicion?"

She shot him a confused look.

"Jealousy?"

"*Ih*, jell-a-see. Something happened to her in her before-life, before she came to Kalelk. I do not know what."

They rode in silence for a while, staring ahead at the dusty ribbon of road. Winema pursed her lips. Frank could almost hear her mental gears grinding.

"There is something else."

"What's that?"

"I think many Whites have lost their spirits. In his heart the White man does not honor himself."

➤

AFTER leaving Winema with Lodge Woman, Frank rode back to his cabin. Building a fire in his fireplace, he thought about the conversation he'd had concerning mixed marriages with Joel Palmer, his wagonmaster on the Oregon Trail. Palmer used their scout, Jacques, as an example. It had been the end of another dusty, seventeen-mile day on the trail. The two of them sat in front of a campfire near Chimney Rock. . . .

"Jacques is a *Métis*," Joel informed. "His mother is Cheyenne and Sioux, his father a French Canadian—a fur trapper. Quite common out here. It is a hard life for them, though, caught in between two races."

Frank pondered this, stirring the campfire slowly with a stick. "I reckon so." He stopped stirring and sat back on his haunches. "Don't seem right, though. A man can't pick his folks."

"True. But that is the way of it out here."

They sat quietly, the campfire bathing their faces in hues of orange and red.

Palmer continued, "For some people, these mixed marriages are acceptable. For others, Indian and White alike, it is a travesty."

"What do *you* think, Cap'n?" Frank asked.

Palmer stroked his chin. "I think it is wise to keep with one's own kind. It makes life, well, easier." Palmer freshened his coffee. "On my first trip out here I met an old Indian medicine man at Fort Laramie. I overheard him talking with his niece. She was in love with one of the soldiers. The old man said, 'The hawk does not marry the crow.'"

Frank pushed his hat brim up a notch on his head and scratched the side of his neck. "I guess I need to think some on that." He took a thoughtful sip of coffee. "But it's powerful hard to make rules about ro-mance."

The cabin was dark and cold. Firelight stretched Frank's

shadow behind him. Pale moonlight shone through the one finished window. Frank shivered and warmed his hands by the struggling fire. It was too late to back out now. Besides, he was never much on rules. He loved this woman. She was everything he wanted. True, it would be safer not to marry Winema. But sometimes the safe thing to do left a bad taste in his mouth.

ELEVEN

➤ WINEMA'S EYES GLEAMED with pleasure as she watched Frank, in his "biled" shirt, hand the tethers of six horses to her waiting father. The sky was a cloudless azure blue, the sun so bright people shaded their eyes. Only scattered patches of melting snow cobwebbed the ground—a January thaw, Frank called it.

Winema looked up and thanked Sky Chief for the mild, clear weather. It had warmed enough for her to discard her fur jacket, allowing her to show off her new dress, shawl, and bonnet. A fifty-strand necklace of dentalium shells draped across her shoulders and chest, reflecting her wealth and position as a *laki*'s daughter. The gifts they purchased in Yreka lay to their right in neat stacks.

Frank, looking nervous but happy, joined her in front of Secot. Secot nodded to Lodge Woman, who draped a white, yellow, and green trade blanket over the couple's shoulders, then Secot made a short prayer and speech.

"*Heya, Kemush*! Grandfather! We thank you for this beautiful day and for causing this man and woman to be in love. They are good people, Grandfather. Help them bring many grandchildren to play in their grandfather's lodge. *Heya*!"

The crowd echoed, "*Heya*!" As Secot continued speaking, Jakalunus moved around the couple, holding his clamshell of burning sage, wafting the sweet smoke over them.

"To all here today, let it be known that my daughter takes this man as her husband. We all know him. He is a good man and a good provider. He is not of our kind, but he came to us as a friend. Now he is my son. And as my son, and husband of my daughter, he is *Modokni*. Let us hope they live in peace and prosper. And let them always remember *Kemush* and the old ways."

"*Heya!*" shouted the crowd and they enveloped the couple with yips and whoops, shaking their hands.

Frank said, "That's it? We're married?"

Winema chuckled and hugged his arm. "*Ih*, Tchmu'tcham. Now you have a wife to feed."

Frank looked both relieved and buoyant. He pulled her to him for a kiss. The crowd laughed, yipped, and yelled suggestively. Winema looked embarrassed. Some of the women made faces or turned away. Winema used to agree with them that kissing seemed an unsanitary thing to do. One eats with one's mouth, not makes love with it. But she had learned to appreciate its interesting effects on her.

The newlyweds distributed the gifts and shook at least two hundred hands. Winema could tell from Frank's face he enjoyed the giveaway, and she was pleased. Kentapoos was the last in line to receive his gift, but saw the ground was bare. Frank grinned, reached inside his shirt, and produced the handsome, ivory-handled knife. The new silver blade flashed like a mirror in the bright sunshine. There were "ahh's" from the onlookers.

"This is for you, my friend."

Kentapoos smiled and admired the knife, moving his hand over the cool blade, the intricate carved handle. "Not friend," he said, looking up at Frank, "*Wakatahtekeh*—brother."

They grasped each other's arms, and Winema saw the bond between them strengthen. It couldn't have been a more perfect day; surrounded by the three men she loved most, by her friends, and by her people. Her smile faded slightly as she glimpsed Woman Watching and Black Wound scowling from the rear of the crowd. Glimpsing Whitey, her smile returned. She was pleased at least one of Frank's friends came to the wedding. Besides, today she could have no bad feelings even if she wanted to.

Four men took seats around a rectangular drum and began beating out a strong rhythm, their high voices singing an honor song.

Winema took Frank's arm. "Come, husband. This song honors *us*."

The crowd shuffled into a large circle. Winema and Frank danced around the drum by themselves, Frank unsure of his feet; Winema, erect and proud, making small graceful steps. The fringe of her shawl swayed back and forth in time with the beat like tule fronds waving in the currents of the lake. After they had completed the circle, people danced into the arena from the east, shook the honoree's hands, and then fell in behind them. Soon they headed a long procession of dancers.

Winema couldn't remember when she had felt so proud, so happy. Behind them danced relatives and friends. Even Whitey danced. Toddlers held their parents' hands and bounced along to the beat on bowed, stubby legs. Young children hopped and jumped, the beat stirring their blood. Other children squealed, teased, and chased each other only to be shooed out of the dance arena by elders with mock stern faces.

People placed gifts on a large bear skin spread on the ground for the bride and groom. Older women bent over cookfires and tended spits of roasting meat. Others stirred pots of steaming stew in preparation for the feast, using small willow switches to chase off hungry dogs and giggling children. Dancing, eating, storytelling, and joking went on the rest of the day and into the night.

After dark, Winema gathered the children. Seeing Frank's curious expression, she explained, "It is a tradition for the bride to gather the little ones and tell a story. This shows she loves children and will have many of her own."

Several children chorused, "*Nanihlas*! Nanihlas!"

Winema signaled for quiet. "*Nent*, I will tell you about Brother Bat."

The children shouted their approval, then settled down to hear the story.

"A long time ago, when the animals could talk, there was a war between the beasts and the birds. Bat was on Bird's side. In the first battle, the birds were badly beaten. As soon as Bat saw the battle was going badly, he crept away, hid under a log and stayed there 'til the fight was over.

"When the animals were going home Bat slipped in among them. After they had gone some distance they saw him and asked one another: 'How is this? Bat fought against us.' Bat heard them and said, 'Oh, no! I am one of you; I don't belong to the bird people. Did you ever see one of them with double teeth? Go and look in their mouths and see. If you find one bird with double teeth, you can say I belong to the bird people. I am one of your own.' They said nothing more and let Bat stay with them.

"Soon, there was another battle. In that battle, Birds won. As Bat's side was getting beaten, he slipped away and hid under a log. When the battle was over, and Birds were going home, Bat went in among them. When they noticed him, they said: 'You are our enemy, we saw you fighting against us.'

"'Oh, no,' said Bat, 'I am one of you. I don't belong to those beasts. Did you ever see one of those people who had wings?'

"They didn't say anything more and let him stay with them. So, Bat went back and forth as long as the war lasted.

"At the end of the war, Birds and Beasts held a council to see what to do with him. At last they said to Bat, 'Hereafter, you will fly around alone at night and will never have any friends, either among those that fly or those that walk.'

"And to this day, brother bat flies only at night."

Frank, arching his eyebrows, jerked his head, signaling Winema that he wished to speak with her. The flock of children suddenly scattered and ran laughing into the night, making batwings with their arms.

"When's a husband get some time with his wife, *alone*?" Frank finally asked.

"Is now a good time?"

He grinned, took her hand, and they headed toward their horses.

At the now finished cabin Frank picked her up and carried her across the threshold.

She laughed, taken by surprise. "What are you doing?"

"A little tradition White people have. I'm s'posed to carry you in the first time after we're married."

"A strange custom. What does it mean?"

Frank looked stumped. "Damned if I know. You're just s'posed to do it."

He carried her into the warm bedroom.

"When did you build the fire?" she asked.

"I asked Jack to come down here an hour ago and start it."

"My husband thinks of everything. He is very smart." She kissed him and pushed him down onto the bed. "Now for a *Modokni* wedding night trad-shn."

Frank's eyebrows arched expectantly. Winema began to sing, her hands moving sensuously up his arms, across his shoulders, and onto his face.

> *Ah yeh ah yeh yeha yeha*
> *ah yeh ah yeh yeha yeha*
> *ka-a mish nu ka-a ni*
> *ka-a mish nu ka-a ni*
> *m-bush e-al-u-ap-ka*
> *hu-masht tuma tu-a git-ku-apa*
> *ah yeh ah yeh yeha yeha ha*

Frank wasn't sure how to react. The words were hardly complimentary. "I think I got most of it: Very much I want you for a husband, for in times to come you will"—he made a face—"drink like a fat man?"

She covered her mouth and laughed. "Your Modoc improves every day, husband. But it is *live* as a *rich* man."

Her laughter felt like warm sunlight. He grabbed her waist and pulled her to him. "I doubt we'll ever be rich, but I love hearing you call me husband."

"Ah, but we are already rich," she said, and pushed him back, lowering herself onto him. She whispered in his ear, "And tonight, *I* will make love to *you*."

TWELVE

THE MORNING OF the Wright meeting brought an overcast sky and a chilling wind. Secot mounted his horse and pulled his bearskin coat tighter around him. "How many go with us?" he asked Skonches.

"Forty. Kentapoos sent four scouts in advance. Each will approach the campsite from a different direction. We will know if there is treachery long before we arrive."

Secot nodded and gave the starting signal. "*Waquset*. We go."

Skonches and three others provided the rear guard. The women and children hustled about, packing travois. Such meetings often meant feasting and gifts, and spirits were high.

"HEY, you!"

The two men grappling with an iron spit snapped their attention to Ben Wright.

"I want that cookfire and spit set closer to the river." Under his beaver coat Wright wore his favorite Indian hunting outfit: buckskin trousers with a matching fringed jacket, and a yellow scarf. His fringed buckskin gloves—finely beaded with a colorful floral design—were no doubt traded or stolen from a Nez Perce or Yakama. One side of the brim of his Stetson hat was pinned up against the crown. The pin secured an ostrich plume he had traded for in St. Louis.

Seeing the two men placed the spit correctly, Wright squatted down by the fire to finish his coffee. Harley Sievers and Piney Hobbs sat across from him, waiting expectantly for him to finish his story.

Wright grimaced as he tasted the liquid again. "Piney, this coffee would float a hammer." Leering at the little man, he continued, "As I was sayin'. I left Indiana and arrived at the Willamette Valley just in time for the Cayuse war. You remember that. When those red bastards killed Mr. and Mrs. Whitman after they'd been so good to 'em?"

Harley and Piney frowned and nodded.

"I learned how to fight like an Injun and how to kill like an Injun." Wright grinned and cocked an eyebrow.

"I hear you got a bag full a' fingers and noses," Piney said.

Wright's eyes sparkled. "My collection."

Harley grimaced. "Must get pretty ripe."

"That's why I gotta keep refreshing 'em." Wright looked at Hobbs and Sievers seriously. "When I finish with an Injun, their people know who done it. Course, the scalp money from ranchers and farmers ain't bad, neither."

"How many ya killed, Ben?"

Wright squinted an eye in thought. "Don't rightly know. A hundred, two hundred? Some of 'em were still kickin' when I cut 'em. I knew they'd go home and spread the word. That's why I keep workin' south. Injuns up there know when I'm within ten miles, make themselves scarce."

Piney giggled. "Well, them Shastas and Pits weren't no match for ya. We all but wiped them sonsabitches out."

Wright snorted a short laugh. "You got that right."

There was a shout and a man loped up to Wright. "They're here, Ben."

~

SECOT rode slowly into the camp, dismounted, and shook Ben Wright's hand. Wright grinned, effusing geniality. He spoke in

Chinook. "*Klow howyah*, Secot. I have heard heap good things about you."

Secot's face remained impassive. The compliment rang insincere. Although his scouts reported no traps, he remained alert.

Wright continued, "I thought we'd have a friendly feast tonight, then talk in the morning. We got plenty of meat, coffee, sugar, and whiskey." Wright emphasized *whiskey*. "Your people can camp over there by the river."

Secot nodded. "*Kloshe'*." The *laki* relaxed a bit. Wright seemed to understand Indian ways. He even looked Indian in his dress and manner. Also, Wright did not seem angry nor did he rush to make serious talk. The whiskey worried Secot, however. It would be more difficult to manage the young men when under its influence.

The feast was a success and the whiskey flowed. By late evening most of the men and some of the women were drunk. The Modocs put on a war dance for the *boshtin*'s entertainment, but most of the dancers were to too drunk to stay on their feet. Some did not collapse in their lean-tos until the twilight of impending dawn.

Secot was pleased. Other than two drunken brawls he broke up, the evening left everyone in good spirits. Apparently, Wieum and Tchmu'tcham overreacted about Wright. Still, apprehension tugged at him. But he, too, had succumbed to the wiles of the *boshtin* whiskey. Fuzzy-minded from the strong drink, he couldn't keep his eyes open and sleep came quickly.

~

CLICK.

The sound awoke Kentapoos and he jerked upright. He listened, cocking his head one way, then the other. The stillness of the winter dawn was unsettling. Something in his mind urged wariness. Holding his Navy Colt at his side, Kentapoos nervously set the hammer at half-cock. He emerged stealthily from his lean-to and stepped outside into a gray, dripping twilight. A thin red line slashed across the horizon like a fresh cut.

Click, click.

He recognized it now. It was the sound of a pistol cylinder as it moved from chamber to chamber. A man paced back and forth five body-lengths from Secot's lean-to, his breath puffing small clouds in the chilly mist. Kentapoos recognized him by the silhouette of his plumed hat. Strange, he thought. The council was to take place this morning, but why the rush? Wright's hands were busy with something.

Click, click.

There was movement in Secot's lean-to now. Kentapoos heard the chief cough. Wrapped in a blanket, Secot emerged, shivering in the morning cold. Secot spotted Wright, who moved closer, muttering something in Chinook.

Then, before Kentapoos could blink, Wright raised his pistol and fired twice into Secot's chest. The sound ripped through the still air. Kentapoos jumped. Secot groaned and stumbled back into the entrance of his lean-to, collapsing it as he fell.

Wright yelled, "NOW!" and the world exploded.

Rifle fire opened up on the sides and front of the camp. Kentapoos crouched, cursed at Wright, "*Kailash stani!*" and fired at him.

Wright crouched, snapped off two wild shots, then ran for the tree line. Kentapoos's pistol bucked as he emptied it at Wright but with no effect.

The noise of the fusillade was deafening. Bullets whopped and whacked into the lean-tos. Two of them whirred menacingly by Kentapoos's ear. Screams and piteous cries from the shelters stabbed at his ears.

"STAY LOW!" Kentapoos ordered.

Still groggy from liquor and sleep, Skonches and several warriors stumbled out of their shelters. They returned fire at the invisible targets. Skonches looked confused, his mouth agape, as he tried to take in the situation.

"Secot is *luelótan!*" Kentapoos yelled.

The death of Secot seemed to stun Skonches for a moment,

then he recovered, started to bark orders. "Kentapoos! Get the women and children to the river. Bostin-ahgar, Cho-ocks, Krelatko, return fire!"

Hearing Skonches's commanding voice, the warriors rallied, started firing in the three directions of the enemy muzzle flashes. One warrior was shot as he stumbled out of his shelter, another, while trying to get to the horses. Two others lay wounded.

Kentapoos heard Wright yell, "Give 'em hell, boys! Don't spare the nits or squaws!"

In the confusion, She-takes-it and Morning Sun ran toward the Wright camp. Kentapoos's gut twisted. "NO! TOWARD THE RIV—"

Several bullets tore into the women, cutting their screams short as they fell. The warriors' covering fire slammed into the tree line, dissipating the gunfire from the ambushers. Confused yells and shouts came from every direction.

Crouched down, Kentapoos scuttled from shelter to shelter, yelling at the women and children to stay low, to cross the thinly iced river—the only escape route. At least it was narrow and shallow this time of year. In two of the shelters he was too late. Left-Handed Woman and She Gets Water, the warrior Skiet-teteko's wife, lay lifeless over the bullet-ridden bodies of their children. Kentapoos's eyes pinched shut in pain. Skiet-teteko had asked him to name the little girl last winter.

Wait—a small cry.

Lifting the woman's shoulder he saw the child was bleeding but alive. He pulled her out and thrust her into the arms of the first woman he passed running for the river. Twice, Kentapoos felt sharp grazing stings. He kept going. All the shelters were empty now, the warriors retreating to the river behind the women and children. Kentapoos glimpsed several bodies floating in the river. He gulped down the sick feeling in his throat. Hate throbbed in his temples.

Half-dressed men, women, and children ran onto the ice only to break through, slowing their escape, further exposing them to the murderous rifle fire. Kentapoos and the warriors began their withdrawal, covering each other as best as possible. Sloshing through the water, it felt like a cold blade cutting into him. Floating pieces of sharp ice impeded their movement, pinched and cut their legs.

Two of the Modoc women reached the far bank; one holding Skiet-teteko's child close to her chest. They slipped and struggled on the now muddy bank only to be shot down. Screaming, they slid back into the freezing water, their long hair spreading in the water in spidery tendrils.

Kentapoos's eyes caught fire as he watched helplessly. "NOOO!" He screamed curses at the invisible attackers. Firing furiously in the three directions, he ran out of ammunition. He saw the child then, swaddled in a blanket, floating in the river. She was screaming. He swept her up and made it to the top of the far bank.

"Kentapoos!" Green Basket waited for him there, lying prone under a fallen tree trunk. He gave a prayer of thanks that they had left Laughs Loud with his aunt in Kalelk. "Here. Take the child and run. Have everyone meet at the deer lick." He grabbed her shoulder. Wide-eyed, she looked like a frightened doe, frozen to the spot. "Do you remember where it is?"

"*Ih*," she said.

He felt her trembling. "Go now."

Heartsink spread across Green Basket's face. "*You* lead us."

"I will be along shortly. Now, go!" and he gave her a shove.

Kentapoos watched her disappear into the forest. He heard sporadic shooting. Shoving his rifle under the log, he unsheathed the ivory-handled knife, felt the heft of it in his hand. He ignored his freezing legs and arms, feeling only cold fury. Crouching, he ran toward the shooters, toward Ben Wright.

As Kentapoos stalked through the tree line along the opposite bank, he periodically stopped and listened for Wright's voice. The *boshtin* were not pursuing his people. *Waquset*, he could complete his plan. Reaching down, he dabbed his fingers on his muddy jeans and painted two dark lines from his forehead, over each eyelid, down to his jaw line.

Totally focused now, his mind was as clear as the air high on the sacred mountain. He thought of the hawk. His father had told him, "Grandfather has seen to it *witkat'kis*'s mind is not cluttered with the concerns of man. He thinks only of survival, only of the kill."

The sun now appeared as a bloodred thumbnail on the horizon. Murky light filtered through the trees. Kentapoos heard men's voices across the river. Foxlike, he loped an arrow's arc upriver and recrossed, his teeth clenched to his mission.

~

DRUNK with victory, Wright's twenty volunteers poured into Secot's camp. Flasks and bottles were passed as they scrambled in and out of the temporary shelters and probed bodies for life, then mutilated them.

After discovering not one of his men was hit, Wright ordered, "Take your scalps, boys. There'll be scalp money in Yreka." Spotting the bodies floating in the river, Wright waded in and scalped them. He was undeterred by their staring eyes, their frozen grimaces, their lips set close, and blue and cold like steel.

As he walked back toward the camp, he saw Harley and Piney. "Harley, Piney! How 'bout stoking that fire up. We'll have breakfast before going back to town."

Harley looked at Piney. "You heard the man. Go get some more wood."

Confusion painted Piney's face. "I thought he said for both of us to get some."

"Well, you heard wrong." Pointing to another man, Harley continued, "There's Dick. Have him to help you." Nodding toward Wright, he said, "You'd best hurry. Ben ain't a patient man."

Piney's eyes shifted from Harley to Ben Wright and back to Harley. He squared his shoulders. "I ain't afraid of that little shit."

Wright heard the argument and started toward them. Piney watched Wright coming, carrying several dripping scalps in one hand, his twelve-inch skinning knife in the other. Piney turned toward Dick Miller. "Hey Dick! Ben wants us to get some more wood," and hustled toward him.

Wright walked past Harley, his gaze fixed on Billy Foley, the fifteen-year-old son of Ed Foley. The boy and his father stood over the bodies of a Modoc woman and child. Billy sobbed. Vomit stained the front of his coat. "Jesus, Pa. I . . . I didn't know it would be like this. Jesus. They're just women and kids."

Sorrow lined Ed Foley's face, and he squeezed his son's shoulder. Wright stomped up to them.

"You boys gonna take them scalps or am I?"

Ed Foley wheeled to face Wright. "Christ, Ben. This has got out of hand."

Wright sneered at him. "If you ain't got the belly for it, Ed, you can take your sniveling kid and head back to Yreka. *Men* will finish your work."

Foley's face flushed. "You sonofabitch." Foley swung at Wright, but Wright ducked, maneuvered, and kicked the man in the groin. Foley sucked air, groaned, and doubled over in agony. Wright slammed the butt of his knife straight down on the crown of Foley's head. He yelped and fell to his knees.

Billy screamed, "You fucking bastard!" and rushed at Wright. Wright jeered and slapped the boy hard across the face with the wet, bloody scalps—once, twice. They whipped against his face with a loud wet smack. The boy staggered back with a look of horror. Billy touched his cheek with his hand, then looked at the watery bloodstains on his palm. He gagged and retched.

A crowd had formed now and Wright turned to them, scorn-faced. "Anybody else here with no grit?"

The crowd remained silent. Finally three men brushed past Wright and helped Ed and Billy to their horses. Several others followed.

Trembling with anger, Wright watched them walk off. "You dumb bastards!" he yelled after them. "You think these red niggers had second thoughts after they killed your kin and neighbors? You think they cried and puked over it?"

The defectors didn't respond. They helped the Foleys onto their mounts, mounted their own horses, and rode away. The crowd dispersed, leaving Ben Wright to fume as he watched the defectors trot down the road.

❧

KENTAPOOS took a position inside the treeline and watched the camp. He saw the strange confrontation with the other man and boy. It appeared not everyone respected Wright. The remaining men moved to the campfire and started cooking. At last Wright turned and walked toward the tree line.

Kentapoos stalked his prey in a diagonal toward a point that would intersect with Wright. With the tenacity of a black widow, the Waterbrash moved when his prey moved, but quicker. He glided across the snow-covered forest floor, using all his senses. His hand sensed every groove and burl of the ivory-handled knife. He could almost taste the sweetness of revenge.

Wright tromped arrogantly through the brush. A yell from the camp below interrupted him. Surprised, Kentapoos flopped into the snow.

"HEY BEN!"

"WHAT!"

"THERE'S ONE STILL ALIVE DOWN HERE. WHAD'YA WANT US TO DO WITH HIM?"

"I TOLD YA. NO PRISONERS."

Wright listened a moment, then moved next to a large alder and unbuttoned his jeans. The cold of the wet snow burned against Kentapoos's skin as he began to snake up to the other side of the tree. He heard Wright sigh, then the pattering stream into the shrubbery.

Looking around the trunk he could see Wright looming above him. Rising to his knees, Kentapoos crawled around the trunk until his face was level with Wright's rump.

Hearing something, Wright snapped his head around, half-twisted his body. "Huh?"

With all his strength, Kentapoos thrust the cold gleaming blade straight up into Wright's groin. Wright grunted at the impact, then let out a scream so loud and animal-like it startled Kentapoos. Wright's hands flew to his crotch. As he tried to turn to see his attacker, Kentapoos took advantage of the position. He pulled out the knife and rammed his shoulder into the back of Wright's knees. Wright's knees buckled and he collapsed as Kentapoos rolled out of the way. Wright continued to hold on to his crotch, moaning and howling like a wounded cougar.

Kentapoos turned him over and straddled his chest. Wright was wild-eyed. Kentapoos spit into his face. "You will kill no more of our women and children. You will die slow."

"Nooo!" Wright groaned as he shook his head from side to side.

Time was running out. Kentapoos could hear Wright's men shouting, searching through the forest. Kentapoos grabbed a handful of Wright's long, dark hair and started his cut just above the forehead. Wright bucked and screamed as Kentapoos sliced and tore the scalp piece off his head. Moving off Wright's chest, Kentapoos showed him the bloody hair. "You like scalps?" and threw the bloody mass in Wright's face. There was no honor in this scalp.

Wright sobbed, his eyes squeezed shut in pain. To assure death, Kentapoos thrust his knife into his enemy's belly. A sickening gag cut short Wright's moans. Kentapoos wiped the blade clean on Wright's coat and melted into the forest, leaving his enemy in agony, his genitals exposed.

As he sprinted through the forest, Kentapoos felt that somehow the vengeance was not as sweet as he had imagined. The Whites, unlike the *Alamimakt* or Siastai, would not retire to their own lands to await good weather or full bellies. They would keep coming. And coming.

THIRTEEN

HALF A DAY'S ride from the ambush site Winema sat cross-legged in front of Secot's latch, preparing a simmering pot of venison stew. The rich aroma mingled with those of other stew pots bubbling throughout the village. She knew everyone would be hungry after the Wright meeting. Frank sat on a tree stump chair and whittled as he watched her prepare the meal.

She washed and peeled several camas roots and cut them into small pieces. After tossing a handful into her gourd bowl, she used a *dunwa* to mash them, then added a small amount of water and produced a paste. Satisfied with the consistency, she added various herbs and a pinch of ash from the fire.

Her fingers wiped the paste into a large, thick green leaf. Rolling the leaf, she folded the two ends under, making a neat packet. She laid the packet in a depression made in the smoldering coals and used a small wooden hand hoe to push hot ashes over them. She looked admiringly at her work. In an hour they would have some fine camas cakes to compliment the stew.

A shout drifted from the south end of the village, and several people hurried in that direction. Winema looked at Frank, who was already on his feet. He helped her up, and they hustled to meet the returning party, anxious to hear about the meeting.

Then, the wailing.

Winema felt the familiar knot in her gut as they raced toward the cries.

"It is Skonches!"

"They were attacked!"

"Many killed!"

In the rush to learn the status of loved ones, people mobbed the survivors, and more cries rose into the chilly air. Winema spotted Green Basket carrying an infant. They were all on foot.

"Where are the horses?"

"What happened?"

"Where is Secot?"

Questions flew like arrows at the survivors. After trudging twenty cold miles in light clothing they looked like frozen ghosts. Winema removed her blanket, put it around Green Basket, and took the infant from her. The infant felt unnatural. Winema removed the ice-covered wool from it's face and gasped. She had frozen blood on her face. Her body was stiff and lifeless. Winema recognized her as Skiet-teteko's daughter, and hot tears burned her cold cheeks.

"Secot is dead," someone wailed. "Our chief is dead!"

The words hit her like a cold rain. Winema whirled around. "Who said that?" Her voice was harsh. She felt a hand on her arm, and she turned, looking into Green Basket's face.

"It is true." Tears filled Green Basket's eyes. "Ben Wright murdered your father. My husband . . . he went after him. Then we heard more shots. We couldn't wait." She broke down and wept.

"Jesus," Frank croaked. He put his arms around Winema, hugged her tightly.

For a moment Winema's mind went blank. She felt numb. But there were people to be cared for, maybe wounded to be treated. The part of her that was the *laki*'s daughter took command. In emergencies, her mind managed to focus on the immediate needs of the moment. She would grieve later.

❧

THAT night Kentapoos returned. He went immediately to Winema, expecting to find her in Secot's lodge, grieving. Instead, he found her caring for frostbitten children. Winema saw her cousin shivering from the cold. Dark, crusted blood stained his clothes.

Frank jumped to his feet, grasped his friend. "Jack. You're hurt."

"No. It is Wright's blood."

Winema stood. Kentapoos went to her, took her hands. Kentapoos's safe return, the blood on his clothes, thoughts of her father, all came together like a crashing wave. The grief came in great, undulating shudders as she sobbed in Kentapoos's arms.

Frank's face twisted in anger, the cords of his throat distended and rigid. "Those bastards—those filthy sonsabitches. They'll all pay for this. By God, I'll kill them myself."

Kentapoos turned slowly to look at Tchmu'tcham. "No, my brother. You will do nothing because you believe in the *boshtin* law."

"You watch me, Jack. I'll get the sheriff and we'll find out who those men were and—"

Kentapoos shook his head. "There is no use, Tchmu'tcham. The law is for Whites."

"Horseshit!" Frank growled. "We got laws against murder."

Winema moved closer to her husband. Her voice shook with rage and sorrow. "*Kai*! There are no laws against killing Indians."

Green Basket approached Kentapoos, whispered in his ear. He nodded, left the lodge, and moved around camp, gathering several men. A heavy snow had begun to fall. He spoke quietly. "Let us go now to the river and collect our dead relatives."

It took several trips back to the river before the last three bodies floated to the surface.

✦

THROUGH the frigid night and all the following day, Kalelk mourned. Winema and Frank stood at the head of the mourners

as they prepared her father's body, their faces drawn with grief.
In her grief Winema thought of her father's countenance, his
voice, his quiet words. Until Frank, he had been the most
important man in her life. It was as if the wind spirit had come
and sucked everything out of her, as if it had taken part of her
own spirit to join that of her father's. She was not sure if she
could function with half a spirit and wondered if it grew back,
like *kekina*'s tail.

Most of the men were at Yainax, a high butte revered by the
Modokni, preparing the *chi-pi-no*, the burning place. Relatives
from Winema's band, the *Gumbatwases*, joined hundreds of
other mourners from the *Kokiwas* and *Puskamas* bands as well.
Jakalunus would oversee the ceremonies.

Winema had selected Secot's finest ceremonial clothes. The
women had bathed his body and dressed him. Many of the
women cried or moaned, but Winema kept her composure. She
would grieve later, privately, in the sweat lodge. For now, she
was a *laki*'s daughter, and she would conduct herself accord-
ingly.

An honor guard placed Secot's body on a woven reed
stretcher. The four men lifted the litter, and the mourners began
the trip to Yainax. At the cremation site a brisk wind moved
across the high lonely butte. Jakalunus donned his medicine
skullcap fashioned from buckskin dyed red and decorated with
woodpecker feathers. He stood and faced north. "Spirit of the
north. You who bring the winds from the ice mountains, grant
this man cool breezes against his back on his journey to the
Above World. See that his path contains no stones, that it is
smooth and free of worry." He turned about. "Spirit of the
south. She who brings peace and happiness. Grant your favors
and your warm winds upon this man."

Facing east, he prayed, "Spirit of the east. He who provides
the warrior and hunter success. Provide much game and good
hunting for this man." Turning to the west, he said, "Spirit of
the dead. Accept the spirit of this great chief with honor; that he
may take his honored place among the Old Ones."

The holy man held the shell above his head and asked

Kemush to bless the ceremony. Last he held the shell toward the earth, asking *Kaela Ena* to accept Secot's ashes back into her womb from where all things come. Many special prayer-songs were sung, some by Jakalunus's assistant, Cho-ocks, others by the elder medicine man himself.

The deep timbre of the drum beat slowly, representing the perpetual heartbeat of the earth. Each slow, measured drumbeat thudded within her chest like a fist of sorrow. It was hard to keep her composure when they sang the slow pensive death song: *Nä'nu wíka-shítko mú'kash hä'ma.* I hear the owl's cry and very near it seems to be."

An honor song composed for Secot by his nephew, Slolux, followed. The men placed the stretcher on the large funeral pyre prepared earlier. Kentapoos and Bostin-ahgar led Secot's favorite horse onto the pyre and shot it. The horse would help Secot hunt, assure his speedy journey west to the land of the dead.

Winema lit the fire. Staring into the flames, she muttered her final farewell, "*Chowotkan, akroh.*" Stepping back, she joined the other women in a high plaintive death song as the flames consumed her father's body.

＝

UPON their return to Kalelk, the elders of the three clans gathered to select a new *laki*. A people without a headman was vulnerable, an opportune time for an attack on the village. The council met only briefly before selecting Skonches as principal chief. A wise politician, Skonches immediately announced Kentapoos as his war chief. Kentapoos had to accept. A leader does not refuse such an honor. The new war *tyee* stalked out of the village, where he happened upon Winema outside her sweat lodge.

"The *laki* will be missed," he said.

"*Humast,* cousin."

Frowning, he pretended to adjust the lodge coverings. "They have chosen Skonches."

Winema knew Skonches would probably be selected, and

she knew Kentapoos would be upset about it. Her mind awash with her own grief, she hardly felt like consoling anyone.

"It is not that the people think you unworthy, Waterbrash. Skonches is older, and respected for his great bravery." As soon as the words tumbled out, she wished she had put it differently.

"I have also shown my bravery in battle. My father was a chief and his father before him."

"In your heart you know it is the right decision. Your time will come."

"I will be an old man before then."

"Then you will be all the wiser."

He glowered at her. "You side with *them*, against your own blood?"

Winema's eyes sparked. "You know better. It is just that—"

"I get more support from my friends than from my relatives!"

"You listen too much to those hotheads. You are not like Hakar and Tetetekus."

"Psha! I am a warrior. You speak of the *tsakiag*, the little boy of long ago."

"Not that long ago. And you have not changed as much as you think." She grew impatient, in no mood to deal with Kentapoos's whining.

The war chief scowled.

That finished it. Her emotions were strained to the limit from the ceremony. "My father is dead and you come to me with this? Is this how you show respect for him on the day of his death ceremony?" Her voice rose with her emotions. "The earth is still fresh over his ashes, and already you have forgotten him!"

Kentapoos stood abruptly and glared at her. "I can see I am wasting my time speaking to a woman." He turned and tramped off.

She watched him stomp away. It hurt that her favorite cousin did not comfort her in her time of need; that he only thought of himself. They never argued when they were younger. Kentapoos was changing somehow. But then, so was she; so weren't they all. Still, she didn't like what she was seeing. Was it the influence of his friends? Perhaps. She was too consumed with grief to worry about it.

≈

FOR the next several days Kentapoos considered his conversation with Winema. While it hurt that she took Skonches's side, he was embarrassed he had picked such a poor time to seek her sympathy. Like many times before, he struggled within himself, a tug-of-war between two hearts—that of Kentapoos the warrior, and that of Captain Jack, the affable diplomat. Yet he could not be one or the other for any lengthy period, which added to his frustration. Things used to be so clear. He had known who he was, had been filled with self-assuredness. But lately . . .

In any case, the people had spoken, the issue of Skonches's selection now immutable. But Green Basket would listen. Most of all, she would soothe, he thought as he walked toward his lodge. Their lovemaking was as passionate as always. And as they talked quietly afterward, someone scratched at the door. "Kentapoos. It is Tetetekus, Cho-ocks, and Whusum."

Kentapoos invited them in, prepared his pipe, and they smoked. Green Basket left to fetch water at the creek.

Tetetekus spoke first. "We share your anger. You are the rightful chief. I have spoken with many and they agree."

Cho-ocks sneered. "Skonches shames us. He is a Paiute and plans no revenge on the *boshtin*. He prefers us to hide in our villages and tremble like rabbits."

"Heya!" Whusum noised.

Kentapoos arched an eyebrow. "You, Whusum? Skonches's own brother?"

"I am ashamed of him."

Tetetekus continued, "You showed the courage of a chief when you killed Wright and escaped. It is Kentapoos we want to lead us."

Kentapoos felt a wave of pride wash over him. His friends

had not deserted him. "I hear you, my brothers. Who else supports me?"

Cho-ocks called off the names. "Kankush, Krelatko, Slatus-locks, Skiet-teteko, Akekis, many others."

"Especially Skiet-teteko," Whusum jumped in. "He remembers how you tried to save his daughter at the river."

Tetetekus's voice rose in anger. "How many of our women and children must we lose to the lying *boshtin*? I told you they cannot be trusted. The cowards use whiskey and words to trick us!"

Kentapoos closed his eyes and nodded slowly. The old feelings of self-confidence and pride washed through him. "My heart is glad you have come to me. I will fast and pray on this. Do not act yet. In the meantime we should press these matters vigorously in our council meetings. Let us see what Skonches will do."

THE following day Kentapoos climbed the sacred mountain. He crossed foaming streams that meandered down among the boulders, between leaning walls of yew and great cedars, past clumps of White thorns and maldroño. Other than a partridge calling her flock together, the mountain maintained a spiritual stillness.

Kentapoos built a makeshift sweat lodge among some chaparral on an outcropping of rock. He fasted and prayed for three days while he hefted heavy stones up and down the mountain side. The body must be totally exhausted before his prayers to Sky Chief.

As he struggled he reflected on yesterday's meeting in his latch. He knew he had to handle this situation carefully. He needed these men's support, but as the son of a chief, he also respected tradition and rank. The undertones of Tetetekus's remarks troubled him. Did he expect Kentapoos to participate in the killing of Chief Skonches? Unthinkable. Kentapoos wished for uncluttered thoughts, like the hawk's. But he could not ignore the logical side of himself. It poked and buzzed at him like a mosquito in the night. Unlike Tetetekus and Cho-ocks, he knew several of the Yreka Whites. He even called them friends.

For two days he battled with the phantoms of self-doubt and apprehension. If he thought himself ready to be principal chief, why then could he not come to a simple solution? Surely a chief's mind would not be so muddy, so irritatingly indecisive. Frustrated, he heaved bigger and heavier rocks up the hill until he collapsed, totally fatigued. As he lay there the sun eased itself down, leaving broad crimson banners that hugged the mountaintop, then streamed away to the south in hues of gold. And he slept.

In the afternoon of the third day *witkat'kis* circled above him. Had it come with its unsullied mind to mock him? Fatigue and dizziness from lack of food overtook the war chief, and he lay down in his lean-to. His mind swam in a river of muddied thoughts. Through bleary eyes he could still see the hawk now low in the sky. Its fingered wing tips caught a flash of reflected sunlight off the mountain's snowy peak, then spun golden spirals as the raptor wheeled lower.

Suddenly, like a splinter of light in his mind, he sensed a familiar presence. The voice in his head was unmistakable. *Father? Is that you*? Kentapoos squinted at the proud bird. *Father, help me.*

Strange, he did not hear his father's words; rather, he felt impressions. The fog in his mind dissolved as it does before the warming sun. There was a way out—a way he could attain prestige, achieve revenge, even prevent more bloodshed. Why hadn't he thought of it before? It was time to make use of his friendships in Yreka, to find out if the friendships were only one-sided. *He* would go to Yreka and talk with the *tyees*, Elisha Steele and Roseborough. Captain Jack could convince the Yrekans to rub out Wright's men—the *boshtin* law way.

FOURTEEN

THE DAYS AFTER the cremations brought a brutal winter storm. Gray clumps of clouds like bundles of dirty socks hovered low over glistening white snow that covered the ground. Frank couldn't remember when he had felt so depressed. He blamed himself for Secot's death. The *laki* had treated him like a son, and Frank had felt closer to the chief than to his own father.

It was hard to face Winema, let alone the *su a suuks*, the relatives of the slain. He had offered to help Jack recover the bodies, but Black Wound and some others protested so bitterly, Jack and Skonches recommended he stay at the village. For a while Frank helped Winema care for survivors and relatives, but their faces haunted him. So he stayed at the cabin.

Winema tried to assure him no one blamed him, but he remained unconvinced. He knew some maintained their suspicions about him, especially Black Wound, and anyone he could influence. Frank also knew that Winema was beginning to suffer from Woman Watching's vicious gossip. After all, wasn't it he who argued with Black Wound, saying, "No. The man, Wright, came under a white flag. If you attack them, there will be much trouble"? That phrase festered in his mind like an old wound that would never completely heal. If Jack hadn't killed Wright, Frank would've done it himself—in the middle of

Miner Street if he had to. Then he could have proved his loyalty.

The cabin door opened, admitting a sudden cold breeze, and Winema's shadow eclipsed the weak sunlight on his legs. She frowned. "The mourning is over, Tchmu'tcham. We are in the land of the living, not of the dead."

He looked at her but could say nothing. Everything had been discussed already, hashed and rehashed. She toed the cabin door shut and carried an armful of wood to the fireplace. Residual bits of ice glimmered on the wood, then melted into dark stains as she laid two pieces on the fire.

"I do not know how to live with a dead husband," she said, squatting by the blaze. She stared into the flames. "Do you wish me to prepare your cremation fire?"

He flared. "What do you want me to do, Winema? Christ. I was the one who told them to trust the white flag. Me. The fool of Kalelk."

Winema sighed in frustration. "I have told you—"

"Yeah, I know," Frank interrupted, "but I see those women's and kids' faces in my mind, bobbing in the river, their eyes staring up." He closed his eyes against the gruesome vision. "They're looking at me, Winema. Asking me why."

Her eyes widened in fear as if she had seen a *skoksi*. "You never told me of any dreams."

Frank slumped farther in his chair. *Damn*, he thought. "I didn't mean to, either." He knew Winema believed spirits often revealed truth in dreams. As a Modoc, she did not believe in coincidence, there was a reason for everything.

Confusion clouded Winema's eyes. She mumbled, half to herself, "I do not understand. I know the truth, yet your dreams . . ." Her voice trailed off and she stood suddenly. "Will you go to Jakalunus with me? I want you to tell him about this *peshak moosum nanitch*, your bad-seeing-sleep."

Frank was jolted. "Are you joking?"

"You know I do not joke about these things."

Frank stared at her for several moments as apprehension filled his mind. "He'll think I'm guilty of treachery for sure.

Hell, I might as well stand in the middle of Kalelk and confess I'm a traitor!"

Her face reflected disappointment. "I thought you respected Jakalunus more than that. I ask you to do this, husband, because I know you are not to blame, and because I know Jakalunus sees truth. He will tell the People and your mind will be cleared . . . and my husband returned to me."

Moving to him, she knelt by his chair, rested her arms on his knees. "The People do not doubt you. Remember that you are my husband, and that my father took you as his son."

Secot's words floated back into Frank's memory: "And as my son, and husband of my daughter, he is Modoc."

"But Black Wound and Skiet—"

"Do not worry about them," she interrupted, squeezing his hand. "*I* will handle them if need be."

Frank gazed into her eyes. Besides feeling ashamed of his own self-pity, he was shaken with the realization that Winema was emotionally braver than he. He studied her face, as if for the first time, and recognized an enduring strength there. Perhaps this was part of what had drawn him to her. She always seemed so confident, never questioning who she was or what she stood for. While the realization made him feel diminished as a man, it also uplifted him, and he couldn't help feeling a sense of pride that she was his wife. It hadn't occurred to him before, but now it struck him like some profound truth from the Gospel on Sunday morning. He trusted her above all. "All right. Let's go see Jakalunus."

❧

KENTAPOOS rode up to the back door of the law offices of Steele & Roseborough. He was glad for the cover of winter's early dusk. He didn't feel like running into any familiar faces in town, friend *or* foe. Not until he spoke with Steele and Roseborough.

The war chief peered through the wavy glass in the top half of the door. He could see Steele bent over his desk. The outer waiting room was empty. Entering, a host of interesting aromas greeted him: rich woods, leather books, pipe smoke, and Steele's New England Rum hair tonic—smells Kentapoos associated with his friend's fairness and prudence.

Elisha Steele sat at a large, gothic Victorian desk made of black walnut. At fifty-seven his neatly barbered gray hair was beginning to recede. His long thin face, sad eyes, and trim beard made him look like the man in the picture hanging behind him—the one the Whites called Lincoln. Steele looked up. Surprise and concern creased his face. "Jack! Thank God you're all right."

He jumped up and pumped Kentapoos's hand. As usual, they spoke in a familiar mix of English and Modoc.

Kentapoos shook his friend's hand. "You heard, then?"

"Yes." The law-talker motioned to a chair. "Sit down, Jack. Tell me what happened." He returned to his desk chair, propped his elbows on the chair arms, and entwined his fingers.

Kentapoos related the facts of the massacre, leaving out the nature of Wright's death. Steele listened. From time to time the lawyer's eyes closed and his mouth tightened as he shared Kentapoos's pain. "Secot's death is a great loss, Jack. He was a fine man and a respected chief. Ben Wright was an animal. He got what he deserved."

Kentapoos cringed at hearing aloud the names of the dead but went on. "*Tyee*, the People burn for revenge. But you and I know we are too few to root out the murdering men and kill them. And it will be hard to hold the young men back from taking revenge on nearby White settlers. Our relatives cannot rest until avenged, this you know. Innocent people may die. I did not know what to do and went to the sacred mountain to pray. On the third day my father's spirit spoke to me. And so I am here to ask you for help."

Steele folded his arms on the desk and leaned forward. "Just as I thought. Sievers and Hobbs told everyone it was the other way around, that Secot attacked them during the feast."

Kentapoos sat straight up in the chair. "Lying *kash*!"

Steele raised his hand in a gesture of supplication and shook his head. "Not to worry, Jack. I didn't believe it."

"What about others in town?" Kentapoos asked apprehensively.

"Well—you know how it is. Some do, some don't. In any case I want to help—anything to prevent the spilling of more blood." Steele leaned back in his chair, frowned, and sighed. Already he looked defeated. "But I'm not sure what I can do."

Kentapoos's eyebrows arched in surprise. "But you are a *tyee*. You talk the White man's law."

Steele stroked his beard nervously. "That's true, Jack. I could bring charges—that is, accuse Wright's men, but there would have to be White witnesses who would testify against them." His face lit up as if he had a sudden idea. He leaned forward in his chair. "Was Frank Riddle there?"

Kentapoos shook his head.

Steele's face turned cloudy again. "Ah, well, even if I had a white witness I doubt a Yreka jury would convict them."

Kentapoos didn't understand all the legal terms, but understood the gist of Steele's words. He launched himself from the chair. "So again your *justice* is only for Whites. If Whites had died at the river, they would hunt us down like dogs and hang us with ropes. How can I hold my men back when they hear of this?"

"Jack. You forget why Wright's militia was formed. Innocent settlers—including women and children—have been killed by Indians."

"We know nothing of those killings! Now twenty Modocs have paid with their lives. Why don't they punish the *Alamimakt* or the Siastai or the *Yahooskin*—whoever is guilty of these deaths?"

Steele regarded Kentapoos over his spectacles, remembering him as the big-eyed young boy who walked quietly in his father's shadow when they visited Steele's old trading post at Fort Jones. "They've been punished plenty over the years, and you know it."

"Argh," Kentapoos noised in frustration. He turned away from Steele and looked out the window.

The Seth Thomas wall clock tocked away the seconds.

Steele got up, shoved his hands in his pockets, then joined Kentapoos at the window. "Some things never change, Jack. So much hatred and distrust. If it is not the Indians, it is the Chinese. If it is not the Chinese, it is the Negroes. For you, it is the Pits, or the *Klamaths*—now the Whites. Everyone has to have someone to look down on." Steele rubbed his temples. "Perhaps to hate."

Kentapoos turned to face Steele. "You are right, my friend. There is much hatred. Now I will not be able to hold back my men."

Steele's face paled. "Jack. Those settlers out there are innocent people. Maybe Skonches—"

Kentapoos flared again. "And what crime were Skietteko's wife and daughter guilty of? Or Harkar's baby son? Or Bad Leg's wife and sister?" Kentapoos stopped and collected himself. "Your settlers are not so innocent, *tyee*. They have taken Modoc land without asking or payment. We will wait five suns for you to bring the guilty men to us for punishment."

Kentapoos wheeled and rushed out the door. Before Steele could stop him, he was on his horse. Steele stood at the open back door. He knew there wasn't a chance in hell of turning over the killers to the Modocs. All he could do was send a warning to the settlers and hope Jack would cool off.

Kentapoos turned his horse. "It will be up to the men of Yreka, *tyee*. I hope *they* will act wisely," and he rode into the night.

FIFTEEN

FRANK HANDED JAKALUNUS the one-pound bag of tobacco. The craggy-faced holy man accepted it, then motioned for them to sit. Jakalunus lit his pipe and passed it. It seemed the medicine man had aged considerably over the past months. How old was he now—sixty? As Jakalunus smoked he studied Frank's face, then Winema's. Droplets of perspiration formed around Frank's hairline and forehead. He respected the old man a great deal and wanted to believe Winema's prediction. Still, he couldn't help but worry about the possible repercussions of a confession.

When he was a boy Frank had to tell his father why his horse had become lame. Frank had been jumping fences again when expressly forbidden to do so. A flicker of remembered pain returned to his backside. But here, the consequences could be far more ominous than a whipping.

After the usual small talk, Jakalunus set the pipe aside. "Something weighs heavy on your mind, Tchmu'tcham." He nodded toward Winema. "It worries your wife."

Frank addressed the *kiuks* as his respected elder. "Yes, Grandfather," he said haltingly, "It weighs very heavy. But I am not sure I should talk of it."

Jakalunus nodded. He glanced at Winema, then returned his gaze to Frank . . . and waited. The latch was as silent as death save for the occasional creaking and popping of green firewood. Frank felt Winema's prodding elbow. He cleared his throat. His mouth felt dry as the salt flats.

"I had a dream, Grandfather."

"*Ih?*"

Frank slowly related his nightmares of the bodies in the river, trying to underplay it as much as possible.

Jakalunus said, "You have told us you did not know of Wright's true plan."

"Yes, Grandfather. I never met him, only overheard him talking one day. I knew then I despised him. After the killing at the river, if Kentapoos had not killed him, I would have. I did not trust Wright. I asked Secot to let me go to the meeting, but he refused. Now I feel I should have followed my spirit and gone anyway. Maybe I could have done something—"

Winema broke in, "*Kiuks*. I know he is innocent. You know my heart."

Jakalunus looked at Winema. "*Ih*. I know your heart." He reached to his right and produced a painted deer skin bag. Untying the drawstring, he laid the skin flat on the ground. It contained five small pieces of multicolored quartz. Chanting an ancient prayer, he gently moved the stones around, touching each with his fingers. When he finished, Jakalunus studied the design, pursed his lips, and nodded. Lifting his clam shell of burning sage, he took a large painted condor feather, its quill wrapped with buckskin and gourd-stitched with beads, and walked around Frank, smudging him with the sweet smoke as he chanted.

The *Kiuks* returned to his place. Looking at Frank, he said, "As I have told your wife, everyone dreams, but few of them are prophesy. Yours is a dream of false guilt. You will dream it no more."

Frank peered into the deep, black eyes of the medicine man, feeling a renewal of admiration. Jakalunus could indeed see truth. "*Humast*, Grandfather. I—"

Jakalunus held up his hand. "But . . . the sacred stones say it is best if you move away from *Mowatoc*."

Frank's feelings of relief fizzled like a pinched flame. Winema gripped his arm.

Jakalunus continued, "For your own safety."

"But our place is here—near Winema's people," Frank reasoned.

"Winema's place is with her husband."

Frank gazed at Winema. Her eyes looked frightened and immensely sad. But she nodded and took his hand. "I go where you go, husband. It is our way."

Frank shot an anxious look at Jakalunus. "But, Grandfather. It is not right that Winema should leave her home, her people."

Jakalunus gave him a patient stare. "Winema married you. She has chosen a different path. But she will never be far from her people."

Frank shifted uncomfortably. "But—"

Winema's arm squeeze stilled his argument. She gave him a stern expression, signaled toward the door with her eyes.

Emerging from the dark lodge, they squinted into a pale yellow sun that offered no warmth. Frank felt he had only exchanged one heavy burden for another. Now he felt responsible for causing Winema to leave her home and family. Raised in a fundamentalist household bereft of affection, he had grown to love the closeness of his Modoc family. It had taken some getting used to. Cousins, uncles, nephews; a never-ending—sometimes exhausting—flow of visitors came to their cabin. Some nights he had to step over sleeping relatives to get outside to relieve himself. Now he was sorry he had groused about it to Winema. Sad, he thought, how you don't realize the value of some things until you have to give them up.

Winema's voice interrupted his thoughts. "I think Jakalunus does not mean for us to be away from the People forever. In time we can return."

A touch of bitterness crept into his voice. "Then why leave?"

She thought for a moment. "Because of men like Tetetekus and Cho-ocks. Their blood is up, and no one can protect us all the time. We just need to 'lay high' as you say."

Frank smiled in spite of his mood. "That's 'lay low,' darlin'. And we don't need protectors. Nobody's gonna harm you. It's me that's in danger and I can damn well take care of myself."

As they walked she hooked his arm with hers. "*Oka ilagen*, husband. But think of the result if you killed a Modoc who attacked you. In these times, it would be very bad for us. No, we must do as Jakalunus says." There was a catch in her voice. "It is for the best."

They mounted their horses and rode slowly toward the cabin. As they approached the tiny house, one thought lightened Frank's mood a bit. "You know. I seen a nice little ranch for sale between here and Yreka. I been thinkin' I'd like to try my hand at ranching. I could still hunt and trap."

Winema tilted her head. "True. Our relatives could visit us there just as well."

"And you could visit them whenever you want. Maybe it won't be so bad after all."

Winema formed a cheerless smile, "You see, husband. Jakalunus knows these things."

As they secured and fed the horses Winema sprouted that impish look he loved—a flick of the eyes that switched between mischieviousness and questioning.

"We may *need* a bigger house. I think this one is too small for three."

He stared at her for a moment as the unexpected riddle unraveled in his mind. He dropped the feed bag. His mouth moved, but nothing came out. All he could do was stand there slack-jawed and wide-eyed.

Her faced beamed. "Aunt Kweelush says it will be a boy child."

Frank bellowed his best Kentucky hog call, then hugged Winema and twirled her around. They laughed and talked and planned the rest of the evening.

Later, as the veil of sleep enveloped him, Frank relived the day's surprising turn of events. Just this morning he had felt like a man facing execution. Tonight he was the giddiest man in Siskiyou County. One thing his father had often said now rang true: life is mostly guesswork.

～

THAT night Winema tossed and turned from a troubling dream. The thought of leaving her childhood home, her people, frightened her more and more. She knew nothing of living in the White world, in a square, tree-skinned house, by herself. Frank would be gone often, trapping or hunting.

She awoke suddenly in the middle of the night. The dream flashed through her mind. Strangely, it had nothing to do with her fears. Instead, it was an incident from childhood she hadn't thought of in years. She was Strange Child again, fourteen winters old. It was a lazy summer afternoon, and she was in charge of the younger village girls. . . .

～

"STRANGE Child, can we go now?" an excited Laulauwush had pleaded.

"We wish to try the new canoe," Mehenulush added.

Strange Child had smiled down at the girls. "*Ih*. We go now. Meet me at the canoe."

Laulauwush darted off to get Saukadush. Strange Child was relieved there would only be three girls to watch over. The other girls were helping their mothers weave baskets.

When they had gathered at the riverbank, Strange Child turned serious. "Girls, we've had much rain lately and the river runs fast. No matter what, we are not to go any farther down river than The-swimming-place."

Little heads bobbed in agreement.

"Very well then, who would like to sit in front?" she asked with a wry grin. The simultaneous outcries of "Me, me," reminded Strange Child of three baby birds, stretch-necked and straining for a morsel from mother's beak.

At The-swimming-place Strange Child remembered wild raspberry bushes close by and suggested the favored treat. Everyone liking the idea, she picked up her *yaki* and headed into the dense brush, Mehenulush in tow. No sooner had she left than Laulauwush and Saukadush jumped into the dugout, cedar canoe, and Laulauwush paddled out toward the middle of the river. Excited at first, she gradually realized she had been overconfident. Looking toward shore, she saw she had drifted too far out. Their campsite was passing from view.

Both girls started to paddle, but the current proved too strong after the spring rains.

"Turn! Turn!" yelled Laulauwush. "Paddle harder!"

Saukadush attacked the water with her paddle, but the current strengthened as they moved faster down river. "Strange Child!" she cried out. "Strange Child, help us!"

Laulauwush felt the growing panic and joined Saukadush in the cries for help.

Strange Child and Mehenulush had filled their baskets with berries and were halfway back to the bank when they heard the faint cries. Strange Child dropped the basket, the berries quickly forgotten. Various scenes of disaster flashed through her mind as she rushed toward the fading voices. Were they being attacked by an animal? Captured by passing *Alamimakt*? Drowning?

She arrived at the bank, looked in every direction for the girls. Sound carries a long way on the river, she knew, and it fooled the ear as to direction and source. At last she spotted them, a diminishing speck moving downriver. Dread covered her like a trade-wool blanket. Turning quickly to the frightened Mehenulush, she ordered, "Stay here."

Strange Child knew the riverbank was too cluttered with hanging roots, brush, and driftwood. She would not be able to pace the girls that way. She sprinted back into the woods, then down a path through the forest that paralleled the river. The path dipped in and out in places, affording spotty views of the river as she ran. This way she kept the girls in sight.

When she got a little ahead of them she moved to the bank and called out, "Paddle toward the bank, toward me!" She knew the rapids were ahead, studded with menacing rocks just under the surface. Again, the canoe carrying the struggling girls passed her, only somewhat closer to the bank. She realized they did not have the strength to overcome the current. Her mind raced. She started to tremble, a feeling of helplessness flooding through her. She fought it off as she continued her run.

Soon her lungs began to burn, her shins ached, her head pounded. Small branches and vines whipped unmercifully at her face. *This is not happening. This cannot be happening.* She prayed silently, *Kemush, creator of all things, help me, give me strength. Protect them, Kemush.* Tears flowed from her eyes, blurring her vision. Approaching the last, small clearing by the bank she could see that she had passed the canoe and would have little time, precious little, to find a way to save the girls.

At the head of the rapids, head pounding, her strength all but gone, Strange Child desperately searched the area. Then, upstream, she saw the fast-approaching canoe.

No time . . . no time.

Then she saw it. A fallen tree limb lay half submerged in the water, it's broken end extending just into the foliage on the bank.

It might be . . . has to be long enough.

Under normal circumstances the limb would have been far too cumbersome for Strange Child to maneuver, but a special power suddenly surged through her. She screamed at the approaching girls, "Grab the branch, grab the branch!"

The girls' paddling had helped somewhat and they were closer to the bank, but still caught in the swift current. There was stark terror imprinted on their faces. But Saukadush seemed to understand, relayed the message to Laulauwush, who fervently nodded her head. At the head of the rapids water thundered and sprayed over man-killing rocks and drowned their voices. Laulauwush gave an arm signal, confirming she understood Strange Child's order.

As she waded into the river, Strange Child felt the undertow suck at her legs, pulling her out and down. She leaned into the torrent, stopped at the point where she felt she could still maintain her footing, and extended the branch as far as she could. Her arms ached from the strain. Bottom rocks jabbed painfully into her moccasins.

Saukadush reached for the branch too soon. In her panic she lunged for it, rocking the canoe to one side. Laulauwush felt the sickening roll, knowing she was going to be thrown into the roiling river.

Horrified, Strange Child witnessed the crisis in the canoe. Laulauwush screamed, tumbled into the water. Strange Child shouted, "LAULAUWUSH!" then felt the tremendous tug as Saukadush's sudden weight almost yanked the branch from her grip. But she held on by sheer will as she backed toward the bank, hauling in the branch and Saukadush with it.

Devastated, Strange Child watched the empty canoe careen by. Laulauwush had vanished.

"HOLD ON TIGHT, SAUKADUSH. KICK YOUR FEET!"

Saukadush kicked like a madwoman, and Strange Child pulled until she thought her arms would be pulled from their sockets. When at last the river bottom met her kicking feet, Saukadush managed to stand and be pulled-walked out of the river.

Strange Child let go the branch, rushed to the youngster, and embraced her. "Oh Saukadush, *Kemush* be thanked you are safe. Are you hurt?"

Trembling, Saukadush shook her head, holding on so tight Strange Child felt her ribs would break. Strange Child knew she must look downriver for Laulauwush. She could never leave here, returning home to face the girl's family with not even her remains.

Prying Saukadush from her terrified embrace, Strange Child looked into her eyes and with as much calmness as she could feign, explained, "Saukadush, you are unhurt. You are safe. You know I must go to find Laulauwush, don't you?"

The smaller girl looked into Strange Child's eyes and slowly nodded.

"Do not move from this place until I return, do you understand?"

Again, the girl nodded. With this assurance, Strange Child

stood and moved toward the roar of the rapids. She felt as if her
heart had turned to stone, her legs heavy as tree stumps, but she
moved anyway. As she sped down the path she heard a
high-pitched sound over the bellow of the rapids. Then, another
sound—very faint. At first she thought it an animal's cry, but
soon it clarified—the muted high-pitched cry like small
children playing in the distance.

Sprinting down the path, she fought vines, thickets, and
dead trees to reach the bank, then strained to look downstream.
An arrow's arc farther down, she saw an object pinned on
the rocks. Rushing water roared as it crashed against half-
submerged stones.

She yelled, "LAULAUWUSH?" but realized her voice was
washed out by the din of the rushing water. Hustling back to the
footpath, she ran half the length of a stickball field and again
fought her way to the bank. *There*, she could see it! A canoe
paddle suspended between two jutting rocks, Laulauwush
desperately holding on to it.

Laulauwush glimpsed Strange Child on the bank. "Strange
Child, help me, hel—" Torrents of water pounded her like
liquid sledgehammers, forcing water into her mouth, choking
off her words.

Strange Child could hardly believe her eyes. "HOLD ON,
LAULAUWUSH, I AM COMING, I AM COMING, HOLD
ON!" Strange Child's tired mind cleared. Her eyes scanned the
rock layout between the bank and Laulauwush. She saw a way
she might move from rock to rock to reach the girl.

Wading into the river, she grabbed the first rock, then, using
her legs, thrust herself forward to the next, encircling it with
her arms. The third rock was slick with wet moss, and she
almost lost her grip. She progressed this way until she reached
Laulauwush.

Terror and exhaustion lined Laulauwush's bruised and cut
face. Hanging on to the rock with her right hand, Strange Child
reached out. "TAKE MY HAND!"

Laulauwush grabbed Strange Child's wrist with her left
hand and, letting go of the paddle, did the same with her right.

The current almost sucked her away, but she maintained her grip.

Strange Child felt as if her arm would tear from her body, but she held on. Pulling with every ounce of her remaining strength, she struggled to get close enough to be heard. "All right, I've got you. Grab my belt!"

Laulauwush nodded, felt for the belt under the water, then moved one hand then the other to the belt. With Laulauwush secured, Strange Child retraced her movements, rock by rock, back to the shore.

Exhausted, the two girls lay on the bank unable to speak. When she had caught her breath, Strange Child sat up and looked at Laulauwush. "Your father named you properly, Wild Girl."

When they returned to the village, Strange Child reported to Laulauwush's parents that the girls had taken the canoe without her permission and had accidentally overturned the craft close to shore, spilling her against some large rocks. Hence the bruises and cuts on Laulauwush's face. To protect Laulauwush from further trouble, she did not mention the rapids. The girls had already learned a life-changing lesson. They would not soon forget the power of the river.

The next morning Secot came into the latch. Smiling broadly, he said, "Daughter, there is much talk about you in the village today. Mehenulush has told the whole story. The elders wish to honor you with the warrior ceremony tonight. You will be the first woman so honored for three generations." He rested his hands on her shoulders. "You have made your father proud, and I have prayed for a new name for you, one that is appropriate for the ceremony. From now forward, you will be called Winema, Brave-Hearted Woman."

WINEMA arose and put two more logs on the dwindling fire. What was so troubling about this dream? The incident had ended happily and she usually remembered it with pride. But tonight a shadow hovered over it, bringing an uncomfortable feeling of foreboding. Why?

Then she realized the dream mirrored the actual incident, yet it differed. Closing her eyes, she concentrated, reached deep into the recesses of her mind.

The dream, she now recalled, transfigured Laulauwush and Mehenulush into her and Frank paddling the canoe toward the rapids. On the far bank watched Jakalunus, Kentapoos, Wild Girl, and the others. Fear gripped her again as the true dream played across her mind with frightening vividness. Her heart jumped as she felt the helplessness and panic Laulauwush must have felt as the canoe entered the rapids. No matter how hard she and Frank paddled, they could not overcome the forces that sucked them toward the vortex. Frank shouted from the back of the canoe, but she couldn't hear him over the roar of rushing water. She felt the sickening roll as the canoe tipped. The shock of plunging into the cold speeding river jarred her into wide-eyed consciousness, and she sat up with a start. A quick glance at Frank assured her she had not awakened him.

She tried to coax back sleep but could not. Her thoughts merged and ran like a herd of wild ponies. She lay there quietly until dawn, and trembled.

SIXTEEN

March 1862

BILLY FOLEY NEVER heard the shot that killed him. The impact cut short his whistling just after he broke the surface ice in the galvanized stock trough. It felt like someone hit him in the back with a ball peen hammer, the last thing his conscious mind sensed as he flopped headfirst into the trough.

Ed Foley didn't hear the shot, either. He was a mile away in the barn, nailing a new shoe onto his Bay. But Ida Mae Foley heard it as she tossed feed to several clucking hens in the front yard. "Ed? ED!" she yelled toward the barn.

"YEAH?"

She peered out across the snow-covered plain, glimpsed riders, then walked quickly toward the barn. "Ed, I heard a shot. Sounded like it came from the east pasture. Is Billy hunting out there this morning?"

"Better not be. He's supposed to be mendin' that fence and clearin' ice out of the water troughs."

They heard riders then, coming at full gallop.

Ed looked at his wife. "You expecting vis'tors?"

She shook her head and they walked out into the barnyard. Recognition came too late.

"Jesus!" Ed croaked. "Run for the house!"

Ida bolted inside and in moments the Modoc riders, yelling and whooping, surrounded Ed Foley. He wouldn't run. He had had a premonition this would happen, that he would be called to task for his part in the river massacre. It was fate.

Foley recognized the two Modoc warriors leading the group. He'd seen them at the river. So he stood there, tears forming in his eyes as he looked up at Captain Jack and Black Wound.

"You killed my boy, didn't you?"

Black Wound spat, "He is dead. Now you."

Foley looked at the ground, sighed, and spoke resignedly, "I told Ida you'd find us. I knew it."

The loud rifle report in the barnyard brought a startled cry from inside the house. Ida Foley knew her husband was dead.

~

WITH Foley dead, the Modocs' attention turned toward the dwelling and the scream inside.

"Leave her," Kentapoos said.

Black Wound jerked his head around, his expression baleful. "Leave her?" He snorted and turned to one of the warriors, "Pakol. Bring her out!"

The young warrior grunted, slid off his pony, and ran into the house.

Kentapoos frowned at Black Wound. "It would be foolish to kill the woman. There is no need."

Black Wound's mouth formed a grin that looked more like a grimace. "Oh—we should spare them as the Whites have spared ours?"

"We have already talked of this. Their women and children did not kill our people."

Black Wound's grimace turned into a condescending smirk. "Ahh. You worry about what *tyee* Steele and your White friends will think." A scowl replaced the smirk. "There is another useless *boshtin kash*. We waited not five suns, but seven, for him to bring us the guilty Whites who slaughtered our people at the river."

Cho-ocks added with a leer, "*Ih*. So much for your White friends."

Kentapoos shot them a blistering gaze. *GETAK*! I am here, am I not? I lead this war party and have done my share of killing. Now—"

A scream followed by a muffled blast came from within the house. The men recognized the report of a shotgun.

"PAKOL!" Kentapoos shouted at the kitchen window.

The woman's hysterical voice came from within. "He's dead! You sonsabitches! I know you've killed my Ed. I got a shell for each of ya, you murdering red BASTARDS!"

"BURN IT!" Black Wound ordered.

Shouts of wild approbation came from the ten warriors. Two of them slid off their ponies and ran into the barn. They returned with a lighted lantern, threw it through the kitchen window. Kentapoos watched the flames shoot up the curtains, then snake quickly throughout the rooms. He could not fight the mood of the men. He could lead only as long as he held their respect.

Horrific screams came from inside, then the woman burst out the kitchen door, her hair and dress in flames. Black Wound, Cho-ocks, and several others laughed as she staggered around the barnyard, screaming, slapping desperately at the flames with her blistered hands. Appalled at her suffering, Kentapoos jumped down and grabbed his horse blanket, ready to throw it over the woman. Wound pulled out his pistol and shot her in the head. She collapsed like a straw doll.

Black Wound looked at him and smiled. His eyes were dark and cold like water under ice. "You see, Kentapoos? Vengeance tastes sweet."

FOR most of the Modocs, the first three months of 1862 were especially harsh. After the revenge raids, most fled to the mountains in fear of retribution. But White revenge was sporadic and ineffectual. The soldiers did not come. Most were fighting a great war in the East.

Frank and Winema lived quietly at their ranch on Bogus Creek, a day's ride from Kalelk. Winema missed her relatives and friends, but busied herself with housekeeping and thinking about the tiny life inside her. She sang Modoc lullabies to it as she moved about the house or sat in her rocker, a gift from Frank. Frank would come in for dinner and place his hand on her belly. He loved to feel the child kick and move.

Assuming it was important to her husband, Winema tried hard to become more like a White wife, finding it not too dissimilar from her life in Kalelk. Woman's work was woman's work. In one way it was easier since it was unnecessary to tan hides—back-wrenching and tedious work she did not miss. Clothes came from Yreka, along with some food items, making cooking easier and more interesting.

With the help of a neighbor lady she applied herself to learning how to cook dishes like fried eggs and grits, baked pies, cornbread, and gravy. And she had become quite good at it. Still, she couldn't give up many of her best liked recipes and continued to gather roots and herbs for her favorite Modoc dishes.

Frank had helped her build a sweat lodge behind the house. There she could pray and sing and cleanse her spirit as she did in Kalelk. Sometimes Frank joined her. They could never have done this in Kalelk of course—sweating together. Mixed sweats weren't done. But she enjoyed the experience. Sitting together thigh to thigh in the cramped, dark lodge, it felt like First Man and First Woman. Just the two of them and the Creator.

But Frank was often away and Winema became lonely. She wondered how White women got used to it. Sometimes the silence of the open fields felt as if it would crush her, and she would jump on Skoks and gallop to the village just to talk to someone, anyone.

At Kalelk work got done, but usually with company. She desperately missed laughing and talking with friends and relatives as she worked. She missed Wild Girl, who had gone to the mountains since her husband, Wieum, was one of Kentapoos's warriors. Lodge Woman and her husband, Krelatko, however, remained at Kalelk, and she hoped they might visit soon.

When *Jkwo'* finally arrived, wildflowers sprang up like promises of good things to come, and the People trickled back to the villages. It almost seemed as if the fighting never happened. Peace, albeit uneasy, had returned to the Lost River Valley.

On a bright, clear day Lodge Woman rode up with her daughter, Moonlight. Winema saw her coming and rushed to greet her. She yipped and called to them as she ran. When they dismounted Winema embraced them warmly. "Aiee. Look how big Moonlight has gotten," Winema fawned, hugging the three-year-old, "and how beautiful she is."

Lodge Woman beamed with pride, then patted Winema's belly. "Yours has grown as well. How much longer?"

Winema grinned with pride. "He kicks like a warrior. He comes in four moons."

"I remember now. Your aunt Kweelush said it is a boy child."

"*Nent*, she has never been wrong." Winema studied Lodge Woman closely, then touched her friend's belly. "I thought so! You, too, are with child!"

Lodge Woman beamed, patted her belly. "*Ih.* Finally I will have a son for Krelatko."

Winema's eyebrows arched, and she covered her mouth with her hand. "*Ai*, where are my manners. Come in and eat. You must be tired and hungry."

In the house Lodge Woman and Moonlight stared with big eyes at the interior and the strange furnishings. Winema worried they would find the house uncomfortable, which might shorten their stay. "You must stay with us a while. I want to hear about everything back home."

"We can stay only three suns." Lodge Woman suddenly looked excited. "Krelatko will come then. At last we will go with him to Yreka town."

Winema understood her excitement, remembering the thrill

she felt the first time she visited the stores. "I am glad for you. You will enjoy it. But be careful. There are still Whites there with bad hearts."

Lodge Woman waved her off. "Krelatko has been there many times and knows the *boshtin*. Never any trouble."

Winema dropped the subject and steered them toward the kitchen. "Come. We eat."

Lodge Woman looked around. "Where is Tchmu'tcham?"

"In Yreka, at the blacksmith's. He will be home later. He will be so surprised."

They settled in the kitchen with coffee, fresh baked bread, and honey.

"How can you sit in these things?" Lodge Woman asked, as she studied a kitchen chair, then looked at the floor. "It feels wrong to be so far from Grandmother."

Winema laughed. "You become used to it."

She did not and they ended up sitting on blankets spread on the floor while Moonlight raced about the house, her mouth and fingers sticky from honey. The two women watched her for a while, chuckling at her wide-eyed excitement at all the strange sights and smells. She fingered every object she could reach with her sticky fingers, but Winema didn't mind. She was thrilled to have company.

"She will not want to go home now," Lodge Woman said, shaking her head.

"Moonlight is welcome to stay with us. She has always been like my own. She would give me much pleasure. I am alone often while Frank does his work and hunts."

Lodge Woman sympathized. "Ah. You have no one to talk to. I think I would go crazy."

Winema nodded in sad agreement. "Sometimes I think I might. But tell me of everything at home."

Lodge Woman mirrored her friend's pensive expression. "It was hard on those who went to the mountains. Two children and three elders died from the cold. The snow was deep, and much of the game had moved to the lowlands. There were only fruits and berries to eat. There was much hunger."

Winema's face pinched. She knew hunger and she knew cold. Shaking her head, she said, "As I told my father, there must be a better way. Our people lessen in number every year, yet the Whites increase like *gailawa*. I have seen the White families around here. Would you believe some have eight or ten children?"

Lodge Woman stared at her in disbelief. "Aiee. How is it possible?"

"Their husbands are home every sleep."

Lodge Woman listened with rapt attention.

Winema continued, "And their religion allows mating at any time . . . except for one sleep in seven."

Lodge Woman palmed her right cheek. "Aiee, no wonder. Last moon I counted. We had only nine sleeps available for loving, and even those sleeps were interrupted with horse guard duty or hunts." Her brow furrowed in puzzlement. "What is special about this one day?"

"Their belief is that *Kemush*—they call him God—created *Kaela Ena* in six suns and then rested on the seventh. So they do not work or mate on that day."

Lodge Woman's eyebrows bobbed in understanding. "Ahh." Her expression turned to disbelief. "The White men must be stiff all the time."

This caused Winema to fall into a fit of laughter, which infected Lodge Woman, who was surprised that what she said was so funny. Laughing now herself, Lodge Woman said, "Perhaps we should send our men to them for teaching."

Both women laughed so hard tears streamed down their cheeks. Moonlight ran in to see what the clamor was about and found the laughter contagious. She had the hiccups, and when these mixed with her high-pitched giggle, she sounded like a tiny, braying mule. It made the two women laugh all the harder.

"No more!" Winema pleaded.

When they regained control, Lodge Woman said, "Winema. Tcmu'tcham is White. So if the Whites have eight or ten children, perhaps you will have at least four or five!"

Winema considered this with knitted brow. She hadn't

thought about it before. "Perhaps you are right, Lodge Woman. It would be a wondrous thing." A thought struck her. "One good thing about living here is that Frank does not send me away at my moon time. We have no moon lodge here."

Lodge Woman was aghast. "Winema. Surely you do not wish to bring bad *lam'etsin* upon your husband by being near him at that time?"

Winema shook her head. "He does not believe in such things."

Lodge Woman's eyes grew as big as saucers as she covered her mouth. She apparently had no answer for this sacrilege.

Winema felt herself blushing and decided to change the subject. Leaning forward, she looked at Lodge Woman conspiratorially. "Now, tell me the rest of the gossip from home, especially, the *good* gossip."

SEVENTEEN

⮞ THREE DAYS LATER White Loon and Lodge Woman stood with their families, staring at the hustle and bustle of downtown Yreka. They had successfully pestered their husbands into bringing them to see for themselves if their husbands' stories about the town were true. White Loon brought her two young boys, and Lodge Woman brought her daughter, Moonlight. The children clung to their mother's dresses and eyed the commotion along Miner Street with nervous anticipation.

"I would like one of those White women's headdresses," Lodge Woman advised Krelatko. "It would look nice with this dress you bought me."

"*Ih*. So many kinds," White Loon commented.

"They call them 'hats,'" corrected her husband, Smoke, pleased with himself.

Lodge Woman's husband paid only scant attention to her. His mind was on the clapboard building in front of them—the Yreka Saloon. The two men had developed a liking for whiskey over the past few moons and looked forward to trading for some. They led their wives to the back of the saloon, where two dirty bearded men lounged on whiskey crates by the back steps.

⮞

SITTING on an empty whiskey crate, Piney Hobbs grinned and winked at his partner as he watched the Modocs approach. "Looks like we got some customers, Harley."

"Appears so," Harley Sievers responded dryly, leaning against the shaded back wall of the saloon.

Prospecting had turned out far less profitable than Piney and Harley expected. Believing Indians became more easily addicted to popskull than Whites, they went into the whiskey-selling business. Harley put on his best sales smile, revealing a dark gap from a missing front tooth. He ogled the wives as he spoke to the men. "Howdy, boys. I see ya brought your kin this time."

Krelatko smiled back. His hands moved in symmetry with his few English words, making it known the women wanted to see the town.

"Well good, good. Glad to see you took us up on our suggestion. So, what do you boys have to trade today? Whiskey ain't cheap, ya know."

Krelatko produced a small bag and handed it to Harley. Many Modocs now worked for miners and had learned how to pan the yellow dust.

"Looks like you Injuns been busy. Doin' some of your own panning lately?"

The *Modokni* just smiled.

Harley opened the bag, inspected the contents, then passed the open bag to Piney. The two men looked at each other and grinned. About four ounces of dust filled the pouch, equaling $72. This would be a high-profit day.

"We got a good place to enjoy this fine whiskey. It's just over here a ways," Harley said, waving in a westerly direction as he walked. Piney packed a half case of whiskey on his mule, and the group walked to a small grove of trees a half-mile outside of town.

❧

WHITE Loon and Lodge Woman grew vexed. Now they were leaving the town when they had just gotten there. Lodge

Woman yanked on her husband's shirt and whispered, "Where are we going? We want to see the town and get hats like you promised."

"Be patient, woman, first we must do business with these men."

"I do not trust these two *boshtin*. Their eyes belie their smiles," White Loon warned.

Lodge Woman frowned. "Business, ha! You two want to drink whiskey."

Krelatko gave her an angry glare. "*Kapkablandaks*! You know nothing of these things."

Sulking, the two women trudged behind the men. The men retired to a large shade tree in the middle of the grove. Lodge Woman and White Loon remained fifty or sixty strides to their rear, settling under a shade tree of their own. Happy for the free time, the children began to play with a *dasi*.

The two wives watched the men for a while. White Loon sighed. "My man used to be good in the blankets. Now he is only interested in whiskey."

"*Ih*. The same with mine. His *wiga* seems only good for wetting himself at night," sympathized Lodge Woman.

White Loon noised an agreement. As she watched Lodge Woman's little girl playing, she grew wistful. "Sometimes I think I would like a girl child so I could make her clothes and braid her hair. The boys, I cannot share secrets with as I did with my mother."

Lodge woman stared at her friend in surprise. "You? With two sons? Every woman prays for such gifts." Smiling wryly, she quipped, "You can borrow my daughter any time you wish."

The children lost interest in the ball and began to chase a *kekina*.

"Did you hear about Salalush?" White Loon asked.

"Good Hands' daughter?"

"The same."

"What has she done now?"

"She dressed in her brother's clothes again, tried to join the men on a hunt."

White Loon clicked her tongue. "She is unmanageable. Poor Good Hands."

"Mm. The girl is twelve winters, yet she wants to be a boy. You see what troubles a daughter can bring?" Lodge Woman teased.

Boisterous laughter came from the men's camp followed by the clinking of discarded bottles.

"Do you think Slatuslaks will marry Tends Fire?"

"*Kai*. Slolux bargains with her father as we speak."

"She's a feisty one, that girl. I heard she was seen sneaking out of Slatuslaks's lodge two nights ago."

"She'd better be careful. If her mother catches her . . ."

The two women looked at each other knowingly. White Loon smiled mischievously. "Then again, I might think about sneaking into Slatuslaks's lodge myself."

Lodge Woman gasped in fake surprise, and the two friends laughed so loud the men stopped for a moment and looked their way. The women stopped laughing, glared at their husbands, then tossed their heads in defiance. Lodge Woman's husband frowned, waved them off, and returned to his merriment.

"I heard there was a raid on one of the Siastai villages by the White diggers," Lodge Woman said.

"*Hunamasht?* What happened?"

"They say the diggers were drunk. Many Siastai were killed—many children. Some of the women were violated. They are planning revenge against the Whites."

"I told my husband the *boshtin* bear watching. They have no respect. I am worried there will be war soon if this keeps up."

"Perhaps war would get the men away from whiskey," Lodge Woman quipped, "then they would rediscover what is between their legs."

Again, the women laughed heartily. White Loon's youngest son, Yawns-a-lot, toddled over, yawned, and rubbed his eye with his fist. He plopped down next to her, and she took him into her lap and stroked his long black hair. He snuggled against her, popped his thumb into his mouth contentedly. His older brother stopped by and kept worrying Yawns's toe. White Loon looked mildly annoyed. "*Iawne gan lawua.* Go yonder and play," she admonished. The older boy giggled and ran off.

The women grew silent and watched the men, knowing they could not wait much longer, for the children would have to be fed soon.

~

AT the men's camp Krelatko had passed out and now lay on his side, snoring. Piney and Harley drank from bottles containing three parts water and one part whiskey. They held out a full strength bottle to Smoke. He grabbed for it, but Harley pulled it away.

"You drank up all your money an hour ago. If ya want more, it's gonna cost ya," Harley teased.

Smoke looked at Harley, but Harley's head weaved and bobbed. He could not quite pull the man's face into focus. The one thing he *could* focus on was the desperate need for more whiskey. He craved the floating, unreal feeling the liquor brought on. He thought of it as the vision-bringer. Never having had a real vision, he felt jealous of men who experienced them. Potent medicine, the whiskey not only washed away his cares, but conjured powerful dreams.

Smoke stared blankly at Harley and reached for the bottle Harley held out.

"Ah, ah, ah. You gotta pay for it, Injun," Harley said, pulling the bottle just out of Smoke's reach and handing it to Piney.

Smoke groped his shirt and pants pockets, feeling for the pouch, but he had given it to Harley. He tried to stand but only rose half way before he lost his balance and fell backward, landing hard on his rump. Harley laughed.

"Tell you what, chief. You want this bottle?" Piney waved the bottle in front of Smoke's blurred eyes.

"I trade *tchilikum* for it," Smoke slurred.

"No, no. You done drunk up that gold. You need more now."

Smoke struggled with the damnable *boshtin* language. "No

more gold. Trade horse." He pointed toward the women. "Woman take."

He wanted to get up and tell his wife to take the White men to his horse, but the sky started spinning in preparation for the vision-bringer. He fell over sideways and dreamt his dream.

"Did you hear that, Harley?" Piney said with mock sarcasm. "Imagine, an Injun so in love with the bottle he would give you his squaw for more."

"I heard it, Piney. He said, 'Take my woman.'"

Piney made a loud sucking sound on his lip and winked. "I guess we'll just help ourselves."

❧

LODGE Woman noticed them first. The two White men swaggered toward them, but without her husband. A moment ago all of the men sat under the tree laughing and talking. Now she saw their husbands lying still on the ground. White Loon moved the sleeping child from her lap to a blanket she had spread for him. Then she, too, saw the approaching men.

Both women were immediately concerned and a little frightened. Neither had dealt much with White men and, without their husbands, could not understand the *boshtin* talk.

Harley and Piney strutted up to the women. The men's faces wore unsettling expressions. They had seen such expressions before on men—White and Indian.

"How do, ladies," Harley said. "Looks like we now own your red asses."

The two women grew seriously frightened. They did not understand the words, but they sensed trouble was afoot. White Loon looked at Lodge Woman. "I think we should gather up the children and leave, *atui*."

"Hey, none of that Injun talk now," Harley ordered, his expression and inflection sinister. "I'll take this one, you can have the other one," he directed to his partner.

Both men pulled out large skinning knives and hauled the women up roughly, holding the knives to their throats while confiscating the women's waist knives.

The children had moved their play into the forest, out of sight. Fearing for their safety, and their husbands', the two mothers offered no resistance. In addition to the knives, the *boshtin* had rifles scabbarded on their horses.

"These squaws got nerve wearin' dresses, Harley. I guess they wanna be White women," Piney said in a biting tone.

Harley leered at White Loon's chest. "Let's see what's underneath them dresses."

Piney cackled. "I'll bet whatever it is, it's red."

Moonlight had emerged from the tree line and ran to his mother to see what was wrong. She saw the knife and cried out. Piney cuffed her hard. She stumbled and fell.

Startled and enraged, Lodge Woman yelled at the man, "*Getak, watchaga auk lum weyus!*"

Piney jerked and twisted her arm behind her back, touching the knife to her throat.

"Get the other children and wait here," White Loon ordered.

Moonlight was no stranger to violence and stood frozen to the spot. The two men marched their women in separate directions, toward the nearby woods.

Lodge Woman couldn't stop shaking and found it difficult to walk. Panic jolted up her spine, then settled like a wet ball of rawhide in her stomach. When they stopped deep in the brush, she decided she would rather die fighting than allow this *boshtin* have his way with her. She would wait for the right time.

"All right squaw, strip!"

Lodge Woman got the meaning. She slowly unbuttoned her dress, letting it fall around her ankles together with her dignity. She tried to hide herself with her arms and hands, ashamed at her nakedness. Only Krelatko had seen her this way. For the first time in her life she felt totally helpless and humiliated.

Harley's eyes grew big as gourd bowls. "Wooee. You sure are cat-bodied." He yanked her arm away, ran his hand over her breast, down to her belly, and grinned. "What's this? A little Injun in the oven. That'll increase your price considerable."

He grabbed her shoulder, tried to push her down. She spit in

his face. His face flushed blood red. "Why, you squaw bitch."
He slapped her, hard, and she fell backward, hitting her head on
a low rotting stump.

＊

PINEY held on to White Loon's long single braid. He yanked
and twisted it so that she faced him. She blanched with terror.
He seemed energized by her fear. Slipping the point of the
knife under the lower buttons on her dress, he jerked the knife
upward, ripping the material and buttons, bearing her breasts
and stomach. He gaped at her body, saliva leaking out of the
corner of his mouth. The fetid odors of whiskey and rotting
teeth assailed her nose. Surely this could not be happening. Her
husband will be here any moment to kill this *kash*.

＊

THE blow to Lodge Woman's skull dazed her. When she could
again focus, Harley was laying on top of her, trying to force her
legs apart. Desperately she felt around. Her hand closed on a
small rock. She swung at his head, striking a glancing blow
against his upper cheek.

"Sonofabitch!" he roared. "You red whore!"

He switched the knife to his left hand and bludgeoned her
head with the butt of the knife—once, twice, three times. As
she slipped into unconsciousness, she felt him ram himself into
her.

＊

"GET down. Now," Piney ordered, pointing to the ground.

Terrified, White Loon laid down. Perhaps if she cooperated
he would spare her. She had to survive this ordeal for the sake
of her boys. Piney flopped on top of her, kissed her. She was
startled. Was the rape not bad enough? The act of kissing
disgusted her, his stale whiskey breath and probing tongue
added to the abhorrence. His chopped red hair stood straight
out at odd angles, adding to his ugliness. She jerked her head
from side to side, trying to escape his gaping mouth. He bit her

breasts painfully and she cried out. Still, she could not bring herself to open her legs to this stranger.

Tired of trying to force her legs open one-handed, Piney punched at them until she relaxed them. Then he forced himself into her, bucking and thrusting like a wild animal. Her humiliation was unbearable, far worse than the pain.

Approaching climax, Piney mewled like an animal. In his ecstasy he lost coordination, and the knife he held on her throat cut deeply. White Loon felt a sharp pain in her neck, then a warmth flowed over her upper body.

The world started to blur. She seemed to disconnect from herself, almost as if she were watching this happen to someone else. Then she saw her grandmother standing there, radiant and smiling. White Loon reached for her, but she seemed pinned to the earth. *Grandmother. Help me.* The old woman smiled and held out her hand. White Loon grasped it and felt their spirits meld, felt the brilliant warmth of her love.

❧

HARLEY struggled back into the glade, the unconscious Lodge Woman thrown over his shoulder, her wrists and ankles bound with rawhide thongs. He stumbled over to the mule and heaved her across the saddle, then secured her with a rope. In a few minutes, Piney tromped into the glade leading the three children by a tether. He had tied them in a daisy-chain and they stumbled along behind him, single file. The two older ones looked defiant yet frightened. Only the youngest cried.

"Whew. These little dust devils gave me a hard time. Had to box some ears." His face, flushed from the exertion, highlighted the long, white scar across his narrow, red forehead.

"Where's the squaw?" Harley asked.

Piney had practiced his response. "She had a knife, tried to cut my gullet out. I had to defend myself."

"In other words, idgit, she's dead, right?"

Piney hung his head.

"Damnit, Piney, its gonna have to come out of your end. She was worth ten double eagles to the slavers."

Piney's face reddened and he whined, "Aw hell, Harley. Weren't my fault. 'Sides, I got these nits here. They're in big demand down state. They'll make up for the squaw."

"Yeah, lucky for you—maybe. We'll see when we meet Axel."

"What about them two drunk bucks?" Piney asked.

"We'll have 'em picked up for vagrancy."

Piney slapped his knee and giggled. "That'll keep 'em locked up for thirty days. I almost forgot about that new Injun Vagrant Law. We'll be able to claim 'em in thirty days and sell *them*, too."

An hour later the men met Axel and his partner outside Hawkinsville. The slavers drove a wagon containing five Indian children who sat silent and motionless, their eyes staring blankly into space as though their spirits had been sucked out of them. Blow flies buzzed around their dirty, bruised faces. The deal struck, Piney loaded the three Modoc children into the dray. The five Shasta children did not react to the new children one way or another.

Headed for central California, the wagon trundled south. Tears now flowed down the cheeks of the Modoc children as they huddled close to the unconcious Lodge Woman. The Shasta children were long past tears. Hollow stares reflected their emptiness as they were swallowed by the lonely dusk.

EIGHTEEN

THE HEAT FROM the midmorning June sun felt like the blast from a smith's forge. Frank sweated profusely as he coaxed the obstinate mule into one last pull. The recalcitrant tree stump, now almost exposed, was the last obstacle standing in the new garden plot. The mule's tongue lolled and his ears wilted. Frank knew this was the sign he had lost his ambition.

"C'mon, Mule, we're almost there."

Frank had yet to think of a name for the animal. It's contrariness had frustrated him to the point where he could think of no endearing feature that might furnish a name other than "Mule." Frank was in no mood to deal with the animal. He had been testy ever since he received the news about the Union victory at Gettysburg last month.

Readjusting the harness, Frank readied her for the final pull. He gave a loud whistle and slapped the reins. Mule jolted forward, hawed, then danced backward and stepped on Frank's foot. The pain was sharp. "Goddamn it!" Frank leaned over to remove his boot so he could massage the injured toes. Mule whipped his head around, eyed his master, then bit Frank on the top of his shoulder. "Yowch. Sonofabitch!" Frank wheeled to face the mule, prepared to give her a solid punch, but she swung her head forward to look at an approaching rider. Rubbing his injured shoulder with his left hand, Frank shielded his eyes as he squinted into the distance. The form took shape—it was Kentapoos.

Frank waved and yelled, "*Wuk lucee?*"

Kentapoos waved back. "*Moan ditch hosoyuk! Domli ditchki?*"

Kentapoos slid from his horse and the two friends embraced. Frank was delighted. It had been three weeks since he'd seen his cousin by marriage.

Kentapoos surveyed the mule and the stump, then looked at Frank. "You and Mule not understand each other yet?"

Frank shook his head. "Nobody understands that mule except maybe Winema. He's more fractious than Black Wound."

Kentapoos smiled. "You have to know how to talk to animals."

The young war chief slowly approached Mule, speaking Modoc in low tones. He stood next to Mule's head, stroked her nose and throat, and whispered into her ear. He turned and grinned at Frank, then walked to Mule's rear, took up the lines and made a strange sound that seemed to come from deep within his throat. Mule's head snapped up and she started forward, the powerful muscles in her shoulders and back rippling against the pull of the dogged stump. In a moment the last of the stump's front root section pulled free.

Frank watched with hands on hips. "Well, I'll . . ."

Mule pulled the stump several feet, then stopped and turned to stare belligerently at Frank.

"Damned if I don't hate a smart-assed mule worse than a stubborn one."

Kentapoos laughed. "You will learn by and by."

Frank pursed his lips, shook his head. Kentapoos had picked up the phrase *by and by* from Whites and had become enamored with it. "I'd shoot him and buy another if mules weren't so damned scarce and high priced lately. C'mon up to the house. Seein' you will make Winema's whole week."

After warm greetings and a meal of bacon, hot biscuits, molasses, and coffee, Kentapoos said, "I look for cousins Smoke and Krelatko. I see they are not here."

Winema's brow furrowed. "*Kai*. They went to Yreka two suns ago. They have not returned to Kalelk?"

Kentapoos shook his head.

Winema said, "Perhaps they have gone to E'Uslis or one of the other villages to visit relations?"

Kentapoos shook his head. "Smoke and Krelatko were to return last night to assist Cho-ocks with the New Moon dance."

They looked at each other, each with their own thoughts of dread.

Kentapoos stood, a sense of urgency on his face. "I will leave for Yreka, *atui*."

Frank shared his anxiety. Winema's kin might be in trouble. He experienced a sudden feeling of protectiveness for the missing families. Besides, someone needed to watch Jack's back. While Jack had friends in Yreka, his enemies far outnumbered them. "I'll go with you, Jack. They're part of my family, too."

IN Yreka, Kentapoos let Frank do the talking. Frank asked around about the missing Modoc families. No one seemed to have seen them. With some trepidation, Frank suggested they check with the sheriff.

Sheriff Eben Cantwell sat with his feet propped on his desk, his face buried behind a copy of the *Yreka Journal*. As Frank and Kentapoos entered, Cantwell scrunched the paper down and peered over it. He eyed Kentapoos suspiciously, then measured Frank with a questioning look. "What can I do for you?"

Frank didn't look forward to seeing the lawman. He had seen him operate in town but had never met him personally. All he knew was Cantwell had kin who were killed by Indians at the Bloody Point wagon train fight.

Cantwell's mustache protruded over his lip and drooped to his chin on either side of his mouth. He wore tan brogans and a clean white shirt. Every item on his desk seemed to be in its place. The office, recently cleaned and swept, smelled of polish and pomade.

Frank cleared his throat. "We're looking for two Indian families that came to town about three days ago. The men are known around here as Smoke and Scarface Charley. Have you seen 'em?"

Cantwell eyed Frank and Kentapoos. "I seen 'em."

Frank waited for him to continue, but nothing more came. Frustration crept into Frank's voice. "Well, what became of 'em, Sheriff?"

Cantwell's eyes narrowed. "And what might be your interest, Mister . . ."

"Riddle. Frank Riddle." Frank angled a thumb toward Kentapoos. "They're kin of my friend here."

A glint of recognition shone in the Sheriff's eyes as he scrutinized Kentapoos. "Can he speak English?"

Kentapoos said, "I can speak."

Cantwell's eyes narrowed again. He squinted one eye. "You look familiar. Do I know you?"

Frank touched Kentapoos's arm and stepped slightly in front of him. "Look, Sheriff. If you've seen our people, we'd appreciate knowing where to find them. We just want to take 'em home. Quiet like—no trouble."

Cantwell's gaze returned to Frank. "Got'em right here. Locked up in back."

Frank exchanged anxious glances with Kentapoos. "Locked up? For what?" As if the constable needed a reason, thought Frank.

The sheriff smoothed his waxed mustache. "Drunkenness and vagrancy."

Frank knew about the Indian vagrancy law. "We'll take 'em off your hands. According to the law, they're free to go if kinfolk claim them within thirty—"

"Don't quote the law to me, squawman," interrupted the sheriff.

Frank felt a flash of anger. He glimpsed Kentapoos's hand move toward his knife. No one had ever called Frank that name

to his face. The word seared him like a hot poker. Frank stayed
Kentapoos's hand and willed his own racing pulse down.
Trouble here would put them all in jail.

Tight-lipped, Frank said, "Sheriff, we'd like to take these
people home."

Cantwell stood, looked down his knife-like nose at the two
men. "You can have 'em after you pay their fines. Ten dollars
each."

The whipcord-lean sheriff took them to the rear jail room.
Smoke and Krelatko were sullen and hollow-eyed behind the
bars. Frank paid the fine. It was painful. The twenty dollars was
every cent he had set aside for the month.

Frank eyed the sheriff. "If these two men was drunk, that
means somebody in town sold 'em whiskey. As I recollect,
that's against local ordinance. Seems to me the saloon owner
oughta be in here with them."

The sheriff bristled. "That's twice you tried to tell me my
job, Riddle. Those Injuns didn't buy their whiskey at a saloon.
They bought it from whiskey traders."

"Then, shouldn't *they* be in the hoosegow?" Frank bristled.

Cantwell shoved his thumbs under his waistband. "They
will once I catch 'em."

"You mean they ain't in town? Who were they? Where'd
they go?"

"Two scalawags by the names of Harley Sievers and Piney
Hobbs." The sheriff looked down his nose. "Unfortunately,
they didn't see fit to consult me on their travel plans."

Inside the cramped jailhouse it felt hot enough to bake
bread. Frank mopped his sweating brow with his handkerchief.
"Look, sheriff, could you help us out—maybe describe these
two. You know, in case I run into them I could let you know."

Frank's conciliatory tone seemed to disarm Cantwell for the
moment, and he gave Frank a description of Hobbs and
Sievers. "You can be sure they'll decorate one of my jail cells
the first time they set foot back in town," Cantwell intoned.

As they turned to leave, the sheriff added, "A word of
advice, Riddle. I'd take your Injun friends home and keep 'em

there. If I see 'em in town again, I'll figure they're still vagrants."

Frank glared at him but kept his mouth shut. Jack muttered a Modoc slur under his breath.

Out on the street, Smoke and Krelatko waited impatiently for news about their families. Their expressions became icy when they discovered Frank and Jack had not seen their wives and children.

Kentapoos shot Frank an apprehensive look. "Slavers."

Frank's lips tightened. He massaged the back of his neck while the thought sank in. He knew about slavers, but the idea of them taking someone he knew was almost inconceivable. "Christ. They've got three days on us, Jack."

Kentapoos shook his head. "They will go south by road. They do not know we follow and we know that country." He looked at Smoke and Krelatko. "Tchmu'tcham and I will start now. You return to Kalelk, get fresh horses, and join us where the south road crosses Miller's Creek."

Frank spoke up, "No reason to go that far. Go to my place and see Winema. She'll give you the horses. Smoke, tell her to give you my shotgun." Smoke and Krelatko sprinted away. Frank knew they were capable of running the entire fifteen miles.

Frank looked questioningly at Kentapoos. "How do you know they'll head south?"

"We have heard that is where they sell their slaves." Kentapoos stood a bit straighter, "We have run them out of *our* country."

~

WHEN Smoke and Krelatko arrived at the Riddle ranch and told Winema of the events in town, she decided to ride with them. They saddled three horses, packed food on Mule, and made up three bedrolls. Winema gave Smoke Frank's old Holland & Holland shotgun, and shoved her own Colt, Pocket Model pistol in her wide belt. Frank had given her the five-shot, small-caliber revolver on her birthday. She cherished it and admired its compact three-and-one-half inch barrel, which was just right to tuck in her belt comfortably. She smiled at the irony of the engraved picture on the cylinder. It depicted a man standing with a Colt in each hand, firing at Indians.

NINETEEN

"NO, DAMNIT. IT'S too dangerous."

Winema had predicted Frank's reaction at Miller's Creek when she arrived with Smoke and Krelatko. She set her jaw. "I will, and that is the end of it."

She enjoyed tossing Frank's more interesting phrases back at him. Frank grabbed his hat and slapped it against his leg, raising a small cloud of dust. He glared at her, started to say something, then turned and looked down the road, combing his fingers through his dark sweaty hair. He turned back to her. "Look at you. You're gonna have a baby soon. You need to be at home where you can rest."

She crossed her arms defiantly. "Rest? You mean finish plowing and tend the stock, I think. Modoc women do not rest. We work until the baby comes." She knew she'd get her way. Frank denied her little, especially when she set her jaw that way.

Frank turned to face the group, then focused on Kentapoos. "We're losin' daylight, but I figure we'll have moonlight tonight. Won't be hard going as long as we're on a road. What do you think?"

"*Ih*. They lead us by two suns, but they will camp at night. We must not stop if we wish to catch them."

They rode all night and part of the next day before Krelatko

yelled, "*Getak!*" They reined up while he squatted and retrieved something from the road.

Krelatko looked excited. "It is a sign from Lodge Woman."
He showed them the flat rock with three evenly spaced lines
gouged on both sides.

"Are you sure?" Frank asked.

"*Ih*! It is our sign." His finger traced each of the three lines
as he spoke. "Me, Lodge Woman, and Moonlight."

Five miles farther down the road they stopped in front of a
farmhouse. Frank knocked on the door. A tiny woman, her face
deeply tanned and wrinkled from sun and work, answered. She
wore a faded calico dress covered by an apron smudged with
flour and rhubarb juice. Moving out onto the porch, she eyed
the unlikely and dusty group, brushing aside a shock of damp,
dirty-blond hair.

"You lookin' for a wagon full of Injun kids?" she asked.

Her words caught Frank by surprise. "Why, yes ma'am, we
are."

"Thought as much," she said. "Passed by here a day and a
half ago. Told those two clabber-faced men what I thought of
'em, too." She dried her hands on her apron and shook her
head. "Never seen a sorrier bunch of kids in my life. Did what
I could for 'em. Washed their faces and gave 'em some water."
She went on without taking a breath. "Ain't right to take little
ones away from their mas and pas. Even Injun kids." She
shielded her eyes as she peered down the lonely road. "Poor
little waifs."

"That was mighty kind of you, ma'am. We appreciate all ya
done. Did the slavers say where they was heading?"

"Naw. Didn't give 'em a chance, I was so mad. I gave 'em
a piece of my mind, though."

"You say they was only two?"

"Just two," she said matter-of-factly.

"The two Indian women all right?" Frank asked.

The woman knitted her brow in confusion. "I only seen one
squaw. They had her tied up. She looked wore out and dirty, but
she didn't seem hurt or nothin'."

Frank thanked the woman and rejoined the search party where he informed them of the woman's information. It was good news, but they were alarmed only one woman accompanied the children. Smoke and Krelatko exchanged worried expressions.

Smoke said in Modoc, "Could they have sold one? Maybe one of us should backtrack?"

Frank shook his head. "I think we should stay together. So far, we're moving at twice the speed of the slavers. If we keep it up we oughta catch up with the bastards by noon tomorrow."

Kentapoos's eyes hardened as his hand closed around the ivory handle of his sheathed knife. "They will tell all when they feel my knife."

The setting sun stretched long shadows across the road. Winema mounted her piebald and smiled thinly. "Let's ride."

❧

VARYING between trot and canter the search party made excellent time. They hadn't seen any road traffic all day, and they were exhausted and hungry. Thanks to a wobbling left wheel, and the mark left in the dirt by an unusual weld mark, they had been able to follow the slavers' wagon tracks, and they continued to find more of Lodge Woman's stones along the road. Late the next morning a dust cloud appeared ahead, reinvigorating them.

"There, ahead," Kentapoos said as he pointed down the road.

Frank reined up and the group halted. "By damn, we got them." Frank grinned as he removed his hat and wiped off sweat and grit with his sleeve. "For sure those slavers are well armed. There's no need in any of us to get shot. I say we trail them until they stop for the night, then move in quiet and take them while they sleep."

"*Nent*," agreed Kentapoos, who turned to Smoke. "Take my horse. I will circle ahead through the trees, make sure it is them and see what guns they have. I will meet you up ahead." Kentapoos slipped off his horse and raced into the tree line.

The group slowed to a walk. Some three miles later Kentapoos emerged from the trees. His body gleamed with sweat. "It is them. I saw one rifle and a shotgun. Both men have pistols."

Smoke took up his reins and growled, "I will kill them now!"

Kentapoos grabbed Smoke's bridle. "*Kai*! We must follow the plan if you want your wife and children alive."

Smoke glared at Kentapoos, then relaxed his grip on the reins. He looked longingly down the road. Frank understood his reaction, but had little sympathy for the man. He couldn't help feeling this wouldn't have happened if Smoke took more interest in his family and less in whiskey.

Winema moved her horse closer to Smoke's. She spoke reassuringly, "Do as Kentapoos says, and we will get them back safely."

Frank watched his wife out of the corner of his eye and smiled to himself. *Everyone's mother.*

Pacing the wagon ahead, they ate another meal of stale biscuits and bacon while on horseback. From time to time towering oaks and maples formed a canopy over the dusty road, their shade a welcome respite from the sizzling, June sun. They took turns dozing in their saddles.

When Sun Chief retreated at last, he offered a sunset that splashed the horizon with vivid hues of orange, red, and purple. A cooling breeze from Bohemotash Mountain puffed faintly against their faces. Ahead, the dust clouds disappeared—the slaver wagon had probably stopped for the night.

"Let's stop here. We can take turns sleeping," Frank suggested. "After dark Kentapoos and me'll sneak ahead, make sure they're asleep, then come back to get y'all."

Everyone agreed. Frank had another thought, looked directly into the Modocs' eyes. "We need to take the slavers alive. I want to deliver them to Cantwell, personally."

Smoke, Krelatko, and Kentapoos looked at Frank as though he'd gone mad, then started talking simultaneously. Kentapoos held up his hand for silence and looked at Frank. "These *boshtin* must die. There will be no justice for us in Yreka Town."

Frank was unperturbed. "Not this time. They broke the law selling whiskey to Indians. People get cantankerous about that. It means a long jail term."

Regardless of how much he shared in the hatred of the two slavers, Frank respected the law. Also, the missing Modoc woman remained in the back of his mind. If the slavers had killed her, murder might be added to the charges. Frank knew it would be difficult to sway the Modocs, but he had convinced himself that if they saw these men jailed or hanged—that the law worked for everyone—the Modocs could begin to trust "the system." From harsh experience they had no confidence in the White man's justice. For now, if he could convince Kentapoos to take the slavers alive, the war chief would keep Smoke and Krelatko in check.

Kentapoos's face hardened. "Tchmu'tcham, you trust too much. If you were Indian, you would understand my words."

Again, Frank felt that invisible line being drawn. Sometimes they considered him Modoc and other times not. When would they accept him? "Y'all might be right, Jack. But I was raised to respect the law. It usually works."

Kentapoos snorted.

Frank tried a different approach. "Look, Jack. It's because we got laws that Whites can work together and keep the peace. It could help Indian people, too, stop the wars between the tribes and with the Whites. Without them, everybody just looks out for theirselves. This time give the law a chance to work."

Kentapoos gave him a doubting look. "How many chances should we give, Tchmu'tcham?"

Frank sighed. Before he could respond, Kentapoos continued. "Very well, my brother. Because it means so much to you, we will test this law. I hope we will not be disappointed—again."

Frank grasped Kentapoos's shoulder. "*Humast*, brother. This time we'll see justice done."

A brilliant moon hung in an indigo sky, illuminating the members of the search party as they huddled less than one mile from the slavers campsite. They spoke in low tones as Frank batted at galnippers the size of dragonflies.

Frank and Kentapoos agreed on a strategy. It would be too noisy to move through the dry underbrush inside the tree line along the road. So Winema would remain with the horses while Frank and Smoke approached the enemy camp from the smooth dirt road. With a head start, Krelatko and Kentapoos would make a wide arc, through the trees, and intersect the road just north of the slavers camp, then move quietly south, putting the slavers between them. Near the slaver's camp Frank and Smoke were to wait for Kentapoos's owl call, signaling that he and Krelatko were in position.

Once Kentapoos felt sure the slavers were asleep, a second owl call would signal all four men to close rapidly on the sleeping kidnappers and disarm them. Since Frank and Smoke would arrive first, they were to check on the captives. If any were awake they were to quietly apprise them of their presence, prevent them from crying out. It was a good plan, but Kentapoos knew from experience that the best plans often went awry.

Smoke made this known with a sneer. "This is foolish. We can easily kill the *boshtin* with arrow or knife, quick and silent."

In the moonlight, Kentapoos's face reflected the calmness he always displayed before battle. "*Kai*. I have agreed to do this Tchmu'tcham's way."

Smoke said no more, but his expression showed disapproval.

Above the trees ahead, the search party saw a wisp of dark smoke from the slavers' campfire.

THREE or four rods from the wagon Frank and Smoke saw no movement. They listened carefully for several minutes. The crackling campfire and one of the slaver's snores offered the only discernible sounds. Smoke was more accomplished at stealthy movement. He crouched and duck-walked to the wagon with all the sound of a sock-footed cat. Frank watched as Smoke carefully peeked into the weathered dray. His body stiffened. He turned from the wagon, fell to his haunches, and blinked at the night.

Frank felt dread form in the pit of his stomach. *God, don't let them be hurt, or worse.*

In a few moments Smoke returned, his face drawn with worry and anger.

"What is it?" Frank whispered. "Are they all right?"

Smoke whispered back, "They sleep. White Loon is not among them."

Frank dropped his head in disappointment, then raised it to look into Smoke's eyes. "We will find her. I promise, we *will* find her."

Smoke's angry expression didn't change. He looked as though he was coiled to strike. His right hand clenched his sheathed knife.

"What about the slavers?" Frank asked.

"One. Under that tree." He pointed toward a large oak. "Asleep."

"That's good luck for us. At the signal we'll get him. Kentapoos can get the other one."

They waited. Crickets and cicadas chirped a symphony of dissonant notes that rose and fell in waves. Suddenly there was a flutter of wings above them, then two soft hoots. Frank looked up, searched for the owl. Smoke sprang to his feet. He let out a piercing cry. His knife appeared like the fang of a rattler. He charged at the sleeping slaver under the nearby oak.

"No—! Shit!" Frank hissed between gritted teeth, and followed Smoke at a run.

Smoke's war cry startled the slaver's eyes open. In an instant he threw off his tattered blanket. He pulled his pistol one second before Smoke struck. Smoke buried his knife to the hilt in the man's chest as the pistol discharged. The slaver cried out. The impact of the bullet lifted Smoke up and back as it punched through his chest and out his back. Screams came from the wagon bed.

The commotion woke the second slaver, sleeping near the campfire. He rolled out of his blanket and came up holding his rifle. Backlit by the bright moonlight, Frank made an easy target as he sprinted toward Smoke's crumpled body. Three shots rang out. The slaver staggered as he tried to look over his shoulder at his assailant. His finger reflexed on the trigger, discharging his rifle as it traversed downward. Frank felt a hammer blow to his right leg. It buckled, sending him sprawling into the dirt.

The slaver moaned, dropped the rifle, and fell sideways, holding his shoulder.

"Frank!"

Frank recognized Winema's voice. *What is she doing here*? Pain stung his leg like the bite of a bullwhip. In a moment he saw Winema's face hovering over him. He wanted to tell her to hide, but his teeth clenched in pain.

"It did not hit the bone. Went through," Winema murmured as she wrapped the wound tightly.

Frank winced and managed to blurt, "Smoke—" and pointed to Smoke's body.

Winema shook her head. "Too late for Smoke. You stay. I must see to the slaver."

Angry over her dangerous presence at the camp, Frank yelled after her, "Where the hell ya think I'm gonna go?" He propped himself up on one elbow. "And what the hell are you doing here?" But she already leaned over the slaver. Frank lay back and bit his lip. "Goddamn it!"

Lodge Woman heard their voices. She yelled from the wagon, "Here! In the wagon! Untie us!"

Frank jerked around. "It's all right, Lodge Woman. It's Frank and Winema!" *Where the hell is Kentapoos*?

Winema approached the groaning slaver carefully, keeping her small Colt trained on his chest. "On your belly, *wochaga!*"

The slaver eyed her pistol. "Aw, Jesus. A squaw. You shot me with that little thing?" She cocked the hammer. He did as he was told. "Help me, damnit. I'm bleedin' to death," he whimpered into the dirt.

Winema tossed him a piece of rope and gestured toward his ankles. She fumbled for the right English words. "Lucky you not hurt my man bad, *boshtin*, or I kill you now." As he finished tying his own ankles, then signed with her free hand. "Over—hands in back."

The slaver turned over and groaned.

"WINEMA!" Kentapoos yelled breathlessly as he and Krelatko arrived from their long sprint down the road. He trained his pistol on the slaver while Krelatko finished tying his hands. "We heard the shots, but we were far up the road. Are you hurt?"

The slaver whined, "My shoulder. I'm dyin' here, damnit."

Kentapoos kicked him hard in the ribs. He yelped. "Quiet, dog, or I will make you into a bitch." Kentapoos's mouth tightened into a thin line. "What happened? Why didn't they wait for my signal?"

In a voice subdued but still strong, she said, "Smoke is *luelótan*." She looked at Krelatko and managed a weak smile. "Lodge Woman and Moonlight are safe in the wagon. Go to them."

Krelatko's face lit bright as the moon as he sped toward the wagon.

Kentapoos looked around anxiously. "Tchmu'tcham. Where is Tchmu'tcham?"

"By the wagon. He is shot but not bad. I must go to him."

Winema treated Frank's and the slaver's wounds. Kentapoos and Krelatko helped her load the slaver and Frank into the wagon bed.

Kentapoos was still angry as he eyed Frank in the wagon. "Why did you not wait for my signal?"

"Smoke was all fired up once he seen White Loon was

missing. An owl up in the trees hooted, and Smoke lit out screamin' for that slaver over there before I could stop him."

The Waterbrash slammed his fist against the back of the wagon. "The fool. Now he is dead and you are shot."

After embracing her friend, Winema asked Lodge Woman, "Are you unhurt?"

Lodge Woman's face was filthy and haggard, her eyes vacant. Winema guessed what had happened, the aura of pain surrounding her friend that any woman could recognize. This wound could not be healed with dressings or ointments.

Lodge Woman's reunion with her husband seemed strained, but Moonlight ran to her father, clung to him like a frightened bird. Krelatko looked at his wife, then at Winema with an expression of hurt and confusion. Winema had guessed it would take time before the family healed. She felt little pity for Krelatko. All this had come to pass because of his self-indulgence.

Winema untied the Shasta children, spoke softly to them. She washed their faces and prepared a meal. The children ate like winter-starved wolf cubs, but Lodge Woman only picked at her meal.

Frank watched Winema hustle around the campsite, cooking, cooing to the children, catering to him and Lodge Woman. Finally she sat down to eat her food. He smiled at her and shook his head. He knew she must be as exhausted as everyone else from stress and lack of sleep.

"What?" she said, pausing between mouthfuls.

"You're amazing."

Her eyes crinkled into question marks. "A-mazing?"

He chuckled, then winced from the sting in his calf. "It means you're the best thing that ever happened to me."

Her face lit up. "You talk too much."

"What of the Shasta youngsters?" Frank asked.

"Kentapoos will take them to Kalelk. They will be adopted by Modoc families." She looked at the youngest Shasta boy sitting next to her, tussled his hair. "Now, they will have new parents and brothers and sisters. They will be *Modokni*."

After the meal Winema and Lodge Woman packed the cooking gear, then Winema walked over to Kentapoos and Krelatko. "I need your help. We must make a sweat for Lodge Woman."

Krelatko looked at her with tired eyes. "Tonight?"

Her eyes flashed with irritation. "*Ih*. Tonight. Can you not see your wife's pain? We must act now before the evil within her grows too powerful."

The Modoc men looked at each other, then at Winema. Grudgingly, Krelatko stood. "*Nent*. Let us get started, then."

His face pinched in frustration, Frank looked at his dusty and weary wife. "Y'all be up half the night doin' that, Winema. Can't it wait?"

Winema shook her head. "She must sweat now and begin the cleansing prayers. There is good moonlight to see."

It took almost two hours to build the domed sweat lodge, build a fire and heat the rocks. The site had to be a healthy distance from the still roaming spirits of the dead men. Using willows tied to form a framework, they covered it with brush and saddle blankets. It took another two hours to locate the proper rocks, build the fire pit, and heat the stones. The orange and lemon flush of dawn lit the eastern sky as the women undressed behind the lodge, wrapped blankets around themselves, then stooped to crawl into the cramped lodge, one at a time. Krelatko acted as firekeeper and, using a forked stick, brought them fresh rocks as needed.

Winema pushed the blanket door aside and said, "Heat all of those rocks. It must be a very hot sweat."

Closing the blanket door, Winema poured a cup of water onto the glowing stones. They popped and snapped, releasing a blistering wave of steam into the tiny chamber. Finally, sprinkling sage and cedar on the rocks, Winema started the first prayer-song.

The two women returned to camp more than an hour after dawn, their skin puckered, their hair wet and matted. They looked tired but more relaxed. There was a glow about them. It was then that Lodge Woman told the group about the manner of White Loon's death.

While the women slept, Frank guarded the slaver, Axel, and kept an eye on the children while Krelatko and Kentapoos took Smoke's body to a clearing Kentapoos had passed through the night before. They conducted the cremation ceremony for White Loon, returning to the wagon around noon with several hares and a pheasant they'd killed on the way back. The group ate quickly and began the journey home.

Despite their rising spirits when they neared home, Frank began to feel apprehensive about his assurances to Kentapoos. *Would* a White jury put the slaver in prison? He desperately hoped he hadn't overpromised.

TWENTY

WINEMA OPENED THE cabin window and breathed the cool sweetness of the soft, fall rain. It had rained all day, helping to suppress the dryness and heat. She heard the sound of his cane as Frank came up behind her, hugged her from behind, then kissed her neck. His hands dropped down to massage her bulging belly. They remained that way, cheek to cheek, watching the shower in silence.

Winema crossed her arms, gathered her husband's arms around her tighter. She sighed. "I have always liked the rain smell."

Frank rested his chin on her shoulder and inhaled. "Umm. I like your smell better." He tickled the ridge of her ear with his tongue, then nibbled at her earlobe.

She shivered and her voice turned husky. "Tchmu'tcham. You know what that does."

He kept nibbling. "Yep. And I know what rain does to you, too."

She turned in his arms and kissed him. The deep kiss quickened her blood. Perhaps it was the rain, or that it had been too long, or both. She felt like a she-wolf in heat. She wanted him *now*. They grappled with each other's clothes like impatient adolescents. She helped Frank to the floor, being gentle with his leg, then removed his trousers. Lifting her skirts, she mounted him.

"I hope we don't get no vis'tors," Frank worried between breaths.

She hushed him with her mouth.

Afterward, as they lay on the floor together, catching their breaths, Frank suddenly looked worried. He propped himself on one arm, felt her belly with his right hand. "I hope we didn't hurt the baby."

Winema looked at him with laughing eyes. "I think not, husband."

He relaxed. "Bet he wondered what all the shakin' was about."

They laughed. The more they laughed the funnier it became, and they rolled on the floor like giggling teens.

When the rain stopped, a light breeze scuttled the clouds across the sky, allowing sun rays to stream through patches of blue. Winema felt a gush of warmth between her legs and she let out an involuntary "*Ai.*"

Startled, Frank said, "What is it, darlin'?"

Her eyes became round as apples. "I think you should hitch the wagon."

They helped each other off the floor. When she got to her feet, Winema's hand flew instinctively to her belly. "*Atui.*"

Frank was in a near panic. "I knew it, I knew it. It's my fault. I shouldn't have—"

Winema inspected her dress. The wet spots were clear. She feigned calmness and squeezed his arm. "It is all right, Tchmu'tcham. It means the child comes. Now let us ready the wagon."

They hitched the slaver's matched bays to the dray in record time, then Frank went to the rear of the springboard to help Winema into the bed. "*Kai!* The ride back there is too damn hard," she said. "I will ride with you on the seat."

Frank shook his head. "It's a damned shame most of the English you're learnin' is cuss words. Ain't proper."

She waved him off. "Here, I will help you."

"Aren't we a sight?" He laughed nervously. "A woman about to give birth trying to help a cripple."

She offered her shoulder so that, using his good leg, Frank could lever himself up onto the seat. He reached down, helped Winema up. He whistled, snapped the reins, and they were off.

They arrived at Lodge Woman's latch in under two hours, surprisingly good time in light of the frequent stops to relieve the pressure on Winema's battered bladder. Her pains were now only a few minutes apart.

Inside her latch Lodge Woman and the midwife—Winema's Aunt Kweelush—examined Winema. "This child is in a hurry. He will be coming soon. It is a good omen." The women shooed Frank and Krelatko out of the lodge and closed the reed door.

The intensity of the pain startled Winema. It attacked in great waves from her back to her pelvis. She had helped with many births, thought she knew what to expect. But this time it was *her* feeling the pain. Yet, as a Modoc, she had been trained from childhood to ignore discomfort, to accept it, even to challenge it if necessary, and she prepared herself for the wearying labor to come.

It turned out there was little need for such preparation. In a few minutes Kweelush was telling her to push. Winema silently prayed to Isees for a healthy son, then pushed with all her remaining strength. It felt so good to push. There was a final pressure in her pelvis, then sudden and wondrous relief, as though she had passed a great stone. She looked down and saw her son in Lodge Woman's hands.

Waves of love she'd never thought possible enveloped her. The covering of blood and patches of white did not mar his beauty. The two friends laughed in giddy excitement as Kweelush cut and tied the sacred cord that bound her to the rebirth of her life, to her line. She had already sewn a fine little pouch to contain the cord, and decorated it with dyed quills. It would hang from the child's cradleboard. She had done this as her mother did before her, and her mother's mother before that.

As Lodge Woman handed her the infant, Winema remembered Frank and asked Lodge Woman to call him in. Frank looked at the baby with awe, as if he did not believe it was real, as if he was afraid to touch it.

Winema beamed, "You have a son, husband."

Frank looked at Winema with worried concern. "Are you all right, darlin'?"

"*Ih*. Now go and tell everyone of our handsome boy." Winema could feel Frank's nervousness and felt it best to assign him some task to keep him busy. Bragging should be a happy task for a new father. In afterthought she called after him. "Tchmu'tcham. Remember, we are not to eat fish or meat for five suns."

Frank's eyebrows arched in surprise. "What? Why not?"

"It could be bad for the child."

"Bad for the . . . How could it be bad for the baby?"

She gave him a look that abided no argument. "It is the way. Would you wish harm on our child?"

He sighed, then left the lodge muttering something about having to live on camas cakes and twigs. Winema looked at Lodge Woman and shook her head. "It is hard to teach White people some things."

Lodge Woman grinned and covered her mouth.

On the second day following the birth, Winema strapped the child into his new cradle board carved by his great-uncle. He fit perfectly, snug with only his cute, round face protruding from tightly laced coverings. Later, Winema removed him from his cradle board and placed him over a basket filled with water. She arranged heated rocks and sprinkled pond lily seeds in the water. The steam gently rolled over him.

"You see," she explained to Frank, "he has his first sweat. The steam purifies our child. The lily seeds, which are light in weight, will make him easy to carry."

On the fifth day the stump of the child's life cord fell away. Winema sewed it into the pouch and tied it to the cradle board. Each morning and evening, as she sang special songs, she lovingly bathed the child in oil made from the lopaqs root to prevent chafing.

"Mmm. How 'bout you use some of that on me some time?" Frank said with a wink.

She grinned and tried to wink back. Still learning this strange facial signal, she tried one eye then the other, but usually both eyes ended up blinking at the same time.

After observing the oil bath, Frank said, "I haven't told you his name."

Winema hushed him with two fingers against his lips. "No! Do not say it!"

Frank looked puzzled. "Why not?"

"It is not time. Tomorrow, the sixth sun after his birth, after sunset. That is when we name him. I told you all this two moons ago. Everything must be done in the proper way to prevent illness or misfortune for him."

Frank sighed. "It sure ain't easy bein' Indian." Again, he left the lodge muttering.

On the evening of the sixth day, all Winema's relatives arrived for the naming ceremony. Jakalunus said a special blessing over the child, then Winema's Uncle Moluks performed the ceremony. It was not an elaborate ritual. That was saved until the boy became a warrior and took his adult name. Moluks named the child Charka, Handsome Boy, much to Winema's liking, for everyone agreed with her that the infant was the most handsome boy child they had seen in many seasons. Except for Winema's Aunt Kweelush, who mumbled something about his light complexion.

Charka's jet-black hair matched his mother's, but his complexion favored Frank's. His face presented a good mix of Frank and Winema: high, wide cheek bones, with Frank's small mouth and extended chin. His large, searching eyes brought the most comments—the color of burnt toffee.

At last Moluks asked Frank what Charka's White name would be. Frank grinned and Winema was sure his chest grew a hand's breadth.

"Jefferson Davis Riddle."

"What does it mean, Tchmu'tcham?" Moluks asked.

"He's named after the great *tyee* of the south."

Moluks smiled. "Then it is a good name." He spoke to the crowd. "A man with four such strong names will no doubt be a *laki* himself—a war chief."

The men yipped and the women made ululating sounds with their tongues. But Winema smiled only half-heartedly. She had other plans for her son, the least of which would be a war-maker. This one would be a peacemaker, a bridge between two races, a man who could walk in both camps, a man who would tear down walls.

Winema smiled down at Charka, who delighted the crowd by burping and spewing his dinner on his great-uncle's shirt.

Twenty-one

Steele and Roseborough
Attorneys-at-Law
Yreka, California

Elisha Steele, Esq.

16th November, 1863
Dear Brother,

It is my hope this letter finds you and Edna in good spirits and health. We were relieved to hear little Mary recovered from the whooping cough. Several children here, alas, succumbed to the dreaded illness.

Winter is almost upon us and the days grow colder. Samantha and Caleb are doing well in school. They rather like their teacher, Mr. Hopkins. We are lucky to have him. He has a fine eastern education.

I am sure you are following the war news. Our prayers are with Mr. Lincoln, but one blanches at the terrible cost. So many of our young men gone.

I have some rather confounding news. I wrote you last that the President had appointed me Indian Agent for the Yreka region, and it could not have been at a more unsettling time.

In your last, you had asked about the current Indian situation. The *Klamaths*, Modocs, and Shastas are again at war with each other, resulting in several deaths and kidnappings. Winema Riddle, the Modoc wife of Frank T. Riddle, came to see me twice last month. She has convinced her cousin, Captain Jack, that peace is far preferable to war. Jack, who is a very affable fellow, is the war chief of the Modocs and the one who must convince the young warriors. Old Chief Skonches has always been a prudent man and has told me Jack, and his counterparts with the other tribes, are the ones we must assuage.

While I have been too busy here in Yreka to visit the tribes, Captain Kelley, commander of the army garrisons in the valley, reported to me that upon his inspection tour he found the tribes so destitute that he distributed ten tons of beef and six tons of flour to them from his own stores. The cause of the destitution is clear: the natural encroachment of the growing White civilization surrounding the tribes. The tribes are too few and too poor to retaliate, so they fight each other for the scarce resources. Then, too, many of the Modocs and *Klamaths* are now in the employ of local ranchers and do not wish to bite the hand that feeds them.

Mrs. Riddle, a woman of sagacity and courage, is becoming well-known and respected among the tribes. She has proven herself to be a persuasive force and an estimable partner in our efforts to attain peace in the region. I would certainly prefer her services over the omniscient Senator Conness (you may recall this windbag from Sacramento when you last visited).

Apparently, the venerable senator returns my good wishes as he has convinced Mr. Lincoln that I am the wrong man for the post. It seems I have been replaced by a Mr. Austin Wiley, of whom I cannot tell you as I have not had the honor of meeting him. Upon Mr. Wiley's arrival, I will advise him of the situation just described, and recommend a treaty be drawn. Both Captain Jack and Mrs. Riddle believe this the best solution, as do I, even though the tribes will most likely be required to cede some of their lands.

I must say that I am in a quandary over the tribes' situation. Although we Americans hold our Constitution dear, the "great interpreters" have seen fit to bend the sacred tenet that all men are created equal, and make random exceptions. As you know, I believe in the literal translation of that great document.

It would seem Mr. Lincoln shares my feelings as he took the courageous step of signing the Emancipation Proclamation. Why he does not recognize the similar plight of our country's indigenous denizens, I cannot guess.

The honorable senator from California is aware of my feelings and has therefore warned the President of my "radicalism." No doubt the noisome discussion the senator and I had in late September concerning citizenship for the Indians served as a catalyst for my short government tenure.

It seems I am rambling, so I will close now, dear brother, on this rather sad note. Only providence can guide events from this point. As you see, "my cup runneth over." Therefore, it looks as though we will be unable to join you for Thanksgiving this year, though we certainly look forward to seeing all of you at Christmas. All our love to Edna and the children.

Your brother, Elisha.

~

Kentapoos squatted by the dead buck's head, placed a pinch of sage in the animal's nostrils, and spoke the game-taking prayer: "Forgive me, brother, for taking your life. You have given it so my family may live." The providential appearance of the buck was no doubt due to Kentapoos's earlier visit to the nearby spring, the one that holds the tears of all deer so that no deer will ever cry in anguish when it is taken for food and clothing.

He stood and stretched. His breath fogged the chilled air as he scanned his surroundings. Fir and pine branches drooped, asleep under the weight of their white winter robes. The season of *witsduk* always brought deep powdery snow to the sacred mountain. Here, he felt closest to the Creator and to the spirit of his father. A distant shriek from above caught his ear, and Kentapoos peered between the branches. There, silhouetted against a patch of sky as blue as Elisha Steele's porcelain, soared brother hawk, the bird Kentapoos had taken as his special guide. Kentapoos knew he was more than a hawk. Smiling, he cupped his hands to his mouth and shouted, "A fine morning, Father! I see you have come to help your son again!"

The proud bird cried once more. His feathered wingtips flirted with the air, then he soared away. Returning to his task, Kentapoos rolled the deer onto its back and started his cut. The warmth of the exposed viscera met the icy air, producing puffs of steam. After dressing the deer and jerking the meat, Kentapoos sat by a small cookfire, enjoying the rich flavor of the liver and heart—his right as the taker of the game. He felt the icy breath of winter against his neck. The warmth from the crackling fire felt good.

A successful hunt and the crisp mountain air usually invigorated the war chief. Except this time, he thought glumly, he had been forced to forage far from *Mowatoc*. It had taken three sleeps to find one buck. Only a few small animals and birds lived close to the overhunted valley, and they had become wise to the way of hunters.

There was much to think about. His recent meetings with Steele and Winema were long and weighty. After the discussions, when he was alone, he felt the world closing in on him, that great change was being foisted upon him faster than he could react. As long as he could remember, the People controlled their own destiny. No enemy had the power or strength to change this. The *Modokni* bowed to no one. Then the Whites came, their numbers were as many as the *juljulius* in summer.

So, for the sake of survival, the People shared their land, their game, and their fish. There *were* good times, he thought. He had learned much from the Whites, and he had made many friends, like Steele and Tchmu'tcham, and some of the ranchers like Fairchild and Applegate. But then there were the others: the Wrights, the sickness-bringers, the ones hungering for Modoc women, the land stealers, the slavers, the whiskey sellers. He had seen Modoc men who, lusting so for the *boshtin* drink, sold their own wives and daughters for it.

Then there was the more pressing problem that increased the pressure, added a sense of urgency. The People were poor. They needed winter clothes. Modoc children cried from empty bellies. Had Captain Kelley not delivered the flour and meat . . . The more Kentapoos thought about it, the angrier he became. He did not like being pushed, and he didn't want the White's charity. This was his land. It had been so since the time of the Old Ones, for countless generations. Why should the People have to capitulate? More and more he felt like a rabbit caught in a snare, the noose tightening no matter which way he moved.

Perhaps this special paper—this treaty, as Steele called it—would stop the waves of ranchers and farmers lapping over the borders of *Mowatoc*. Skonches thought so, of course. He seemed to accept whatever the Whites dealt out. But as Kentapoos thought about it, so did he. It was useless to fight the Whites. They might as well fight the wind that roared from the north in the snow season.

This treaty, however, sounded too much like the other *boshtin* "laws," which could seldom be trusted. Like the law that was supposed to punish the slaver, Axel. Kentapoos had gone to the *boshtin* council house to watch. So many words, but in the end, the eight-man council returned after their deliberations and spoke to *tyee* Roseborough, who then freed the slaver. Roseborough called it a "hung jury," yet no one hung for White Loon's death and Lodge Woman's rape.

Justice they called it. Kentapoos had been angry, but not surprised, and his friendship with Tchmu'tcham had become strained for a while. But that had passed. After the slaver disappeared into the night a free man, life became more difficult around Kalelk. Tetetekus, Cho-ocks, and the others garnered new support as a result, and Kentapoos found himself in the uncomfortable position of defending his friendship with Frank.

Kentapoos sighed, then doused the fire and packed the remaining meat on his horse. He mounted, headed slowly back to Kalelk. The hard part was yet to come—the treaty negotiations. He massaged his growling belly. There was a sour taste in his mouth. Lately, his favorite foods seemed to disagree with him.

FIVE days later Winema and Frank, serving as translators, sat in Skonches' latch with Elisha Steele and Kentapoos. Steele had asked Frank and Winema to attend. With sad eyes, the Yreka lawyer looked across the fire at Chief Skonches. "I thought I should tell you myself, Chief. I am being replaced by a man named Austin Wiley. He will be arriving in a week."

Skonches's left eyebrow cocked, his mouth opened slightly.

Steele continued, "It's politics. We have a new *laki* in Washington, and he wants his own man in the job."

"We will not talk to this Wiley," Kentapoos lashed out. "We trust only you."

Skonches held up his hand as he took another pull on the pipe. He was no stranger to politics—village politics, tribal politics, Indian-White politics. And now, a new set of politics—the freshly negotiated peace with the *Alamimakt, Siastai,* and the *Sot.* Even the distant *Latinkini,* the ones who had killed Kentapoos's father on the far north Deshutes River, had made the long trip for the peace council. For as long as anyone could remember the *Modokni* had been at war with these lesser peoples. It had taken all his skill as a statesman and chief to shake their hands and share the pipe.

Sometimes these things are necessary. With the severe decline of game and fish, the tribes could ill afford warfare. Everyone's attention must now be focused on feeding their own people and dealing with the Whites. A new time had arrived, forcing change upon them like a sudden storm. There were no precedents, no guidance from the old chiefs and elders. He and his council were on their own. And now Steele, one of the few Whites he trusted, was about to desert him.

A cold draft from under the front reed door made him shiver. Skonches took another puff and blew the smoke upward. His eyes leveled at Elisha Steele. "I worry this new man will not understand our ways, my friend."

Steele accepted the pipe. "I will meet with him and tell him all I know. I'm sure it will be fine."

Skonches nodded. "Tell me about this paper the government will want."

Steele cleared his throat. "Well, I don't know much about it, *laki*. But usually the government promises money or goods in exchange for land, and your promise of peace."

Winema, Kentapoos, and Skonches looked taken aback. Skonches said, "Land, they have. We have shared our land with your people, who took it without asking. This land was given to us by *Kemush*. He asked us only to keep and respect it. We, likewise, have asked for no payment. We thought this would satisfy the Whites. Now you say they want more?"

Steele cast his eyes downward. "I don't want to unduly stir the pot, *laki*. Let's wait and see what happens. I could be wrong."

Skonches saw through Elisha's attempt at mitigation. "*Tyee*. We do not know this man, Wiley—what is on his mind, how he thinks. He does not know our people like you do. If we must agree to such a paper, it would be easier to convince the People to do so if they knew *you* had written the paper."

Skonches glanced at Winema and Kentapoos as he spoke. Each nodded in agreement. He shifted his gaze back to Steele. "I think it best if you write this paper for us. Before the new agent arrives. We can give the paper to him and tell him these are our words on the matter. Would you do this?"

The Yreka lawyer studied Skonches's face, then the faces of Winema, Kentapoos, and Frank. He considered the request in silence, then said, "Very well, *laki*. I want to see the best possible terms for your people. I can present the document to Mr. Wiley as your 'attorney of record.'"

Skonches nodded curtly and the two men shook hands.

Steele stood and, with concern in his face, said, "But I can't make any promises, Skonches."

TWENTY-TWO

THE TIME FOR Skonches to present the treaty terms had arrived. The air in the *laki*'s latch was heavy with the smell of smoke and dour men. They sat hip-to-hip in the cramped space. Errant wisps of smoke from the center fire escaped the draft of the smoke hole, causing their eyes to burn and water. Kentapoos's eyes shifted from man to man. Black Wound squinted and set his jaw, his muscles tensed as if prepared to lunge. Krelatko sat to Kentapoos's left, his expression taut. Whusum and Cho-ocks whispered to each other. The *paksh* completed the circle, and all eyes were upon Skonches.

"You risk much, *laki*, bringing a woman into this council. It is foul *lam'etsin*. It will surely bring evil upon us," Cho-ocks warned.

"*Kai.* She earned the right when she was honored with the warrior's ceremony after saving the children at the river," Kentapoos defended.

Hakar twisted his lips into a sneer. "Perhaps all of us should bring our women to council and ask their advice."

"Winema's medicine is strong," Jakalunus retorted matter-of-factly. "She earned her place at this council. Do not forget she killed the *kash* slaver and saved her husband's life. A stronger spirit I have not felt among you."

Black Wound pointed an accusing finger at Winema. "How

do we know she does not bring evil upon us with her moon time?"

Winema's eyes flashed. She was about to point out that many of these men did not speak so bravely when their wives were near, especially Black Wound's wife, but thought better of it.

Kentapoos spoke for her. "Who here would believe Winema would dishonor us in such a way? It is not worth the consideration I would give a louse under my foot."

Black Wound surveyed the faces around the fire. Finding no support other than Cho-ocks, he frowned and sat down.

"Brothers," Skonches began, "you have heard about a paper the Whites want us to make our marks upon. Four suns ago I asked *tyee* Steele to write this paper I hold in my hand. It will mean peace between us. There will be money, gifts, and meat. No longer will our people die from *boshtin* guns. No longer will our women and children cry because they grieve for lost husbands and fathers, or from empty bellies."

Black Wound's face clouded. "And what does our brave war chief think of this?"

Kentapoos's eyes narrowed. "I agree with our chief. More war will bring only death to our People. We are surrounded by the Whites and they keep coming. We grow poorer, they grow stronger. We must find a way to make our living among them. But," he added, "that does not mean we give up our ways."

Black Wound made a short, harsh laugh. "Why am I not surprised? Perhaps our war chief's *boshtin* friends have *ihashed* his mind."

Cho-ocks snapped, "I will make *lam'etsin* against them as I have done against the *Alamimakt*, the *Siastai*, and the *Klamat*. Always have we been victorious because of stronger medicine. We are human beings, after all, while they are not. The spirits have always taken the side of the *Modokni*, and now, with my medicine, we will drive the invaders out!"

"*Heya!*" Krelatko and Whusum chorused in approval.

Jakalunus's mouth hinted at sarcasm. "If the fox cannot

make such medicine, Cho-ocks, surely it would be difficult for the kit."

Hakar appraised Jakalunus with menacing eyes. "Perhaps your medicine has weakened with age, *kiuks*. Perhaps the kit has grown beyond the fox."

Skonches interjected, "Brothers, we are not here to fight among ourselves. If we are weak from within, we surely cannot be strong in our talks with the Whites, who speak with one voice."

Black Wound scoffed loudly. "As do sheep."

Winema enjoyed watching Krelatko's and Black Wound's facial scars twitch in anger. She decided she rather liked the names the miners had given them—Scarface Charley and Black Jim. But she understood them. Cho-ocks was a different matter. There was something reptilian about his eyes—the look of the tortoise, perhaps a snake. She stood. "Our war chief speaks the truth. Our purpose here is to talk like Modocs. The elk herd does not fear the wolf, but the stray elk surely does." She looked at Cho-ocks. "It is true you make strong medicine, *kiuks*. We need your prayers, and Jakalunus's, to make our words on the paper strong."

"*Ih*," Skonches offered, eyeing Cho-ocks. "Even the strongest medicine cannot overcome foolish men."

Kentapoos held up his hand. "Let Skonches tell you of what is in the paper. *Then* we will have something to argue about."

There were murmurs and nods all around.

Skonches recounted the treaty language from memory. "The paper says the *Modokni* will have enough land here in our valley. No Whites will be allowed on our lands without asking. For this we promise not to steal cattle or take slaves. Those who have sold your women to the miners must stop. We will fight no more with the other *mak'laks*. We can still work for Whites on their lands, or as scouts. We can make boats to take people across the river for money. And the soldiers from the fort will see everyone does as the paper says."

Big Knife, an elder of eighty winters, struggled to his feet. "As you know, I usually let the young men do their will. But there is a time for war and there is a time for peace. Even the *sloa* knows to gather her cubs before an approaching prairie fire and find the path to safety. Now is such a time."

Winema watched his eyes, eyes that had looked upon the procession of ages. Knife swept a knotted hand toward the elders at the head of the council. "We guided you through the last seasons in the old ways. We have taught you what we know. Now it is *your* time to guide the People through this fire rushing toward us. It would be a shame to have even one child burned when the path to safety is so clear."

The respected elder's words seemed to douse the tension like cool water on a cookfire. Winema and the young men watched the faces of the remaining elders, who muttered and nodded their agreement. Black Wound and Cho-ocks brooded in silence. Skonches waited for further discussion. There was only a profound stillness as each council member contemplated Big Knife's words. They were about to sign away generations of tradition, a way of life.

Black Wound stood up angrily. "Remember my words, brothers. This is not the end. The *boshtin* will not be satisfied until they have swallowed our lands—every rock, every tree, every blade of grass—and leave us naked and starving like dogs." He swept the mat door aside with such force it tore from its lashings as he stomped out of the lodge.

Cho-ocks jumped to his feet. "Black Wound speaks wisely. Yesterday I saw *tusa'sas*, the joker skunk, behind my latch. It can only mean this paper brings ruin!" and followed Black Wound out of the latch.

Their departure left another lengthy pause in the conversation. Skonches studied each man's face, making eye contact, waiting for further discussion. He knew each of these men intimately. They had fought together, hunted together, smoked together. It was a silent and intensely personal poll.

"*Tchwai*. It is decided, then." The *laki*'s voice was strained. "We have all prayed on this matter. We will sign the paper." He carefully laid the ceremonial *paksh* in its altar near the fire. With moist eyes he regarded Winema and the councilmen. "We are about to enter our final battle, brothers. One we have lost before we began. May we find wisdom in our sweat lodge prayers tonight. *Otwekatuxse.* The council is ended."

◆

THE open window in Elisha Steele's office did little to ease the stifling July heat. Kentapoos, Frank, Winema, and newly elected Judge A. M. Roseborough listened as Elisha read the recently arrived letter from the Superintendent of Indian Affairs:

Office of Indian Affairs
State of Oregon
The Union!

Hon. J. W. Perit Huntington
Superintendent

23d June, 1864
Mr. Elisha Steele, Esq.
Yreka, California

Honorable Sir,
    Mr. Wiley has graciously forwarded your proposed treaty for our consideration. I wish to report that, while we are sincerely grateful for your efforts on behalf of the Indians and our government, the treaty cannot be submitted to Congress in its current form. After the petitioning of several unhappy Siskiyou County constituents, Senator Conness spoke with the President, who concurs that a more equitable treaty be drawn and negotiated by properly appointed representatives of our government.
    In fairness, it is proper for me to explain some of the weaknesses we see in the document you set before us. Firstly, as it is written, the treaty does not compel the Indians to remove themselves from the Tule Lake Basin,

or for that matter, even to remain on a designated reservation. As you know, the lands of Lost River Valley are in great demand by increasing numbers of hardworking farmers and ranchers who deserve to purchase and tend property without the threat of marauding savages.

Secondly, there is no specification of a location and boundaries for a reservation. In light of the aforementioned, your promise of a reservation in the valley is unacceptable to the government and to the people of Siskiyou County.

Finally, since no monies were paid to the Indians for the proposed cessation of their lands, the treaty is not binding upon the government.

The Secretary of War has directed me to present a new treaty to the Indians before the first of November. In this regard, Congress has appropriated $20,000 to cover the costs related to the treaty process. The reservation will be surveyed this summer. I can tell you that it will border on the east side of Fort Klamath and will be called the Klamath Indian Reservation. It will be shared with the Modocs and Yahooskin Paiutes.

Both the Secretary and I wish to extend our deep appreciation for your services as Agent for the Yrekan Region. I look forward to your acquaintance when I arrive for the treaty ceremonies.

Your obed't. servant,

J. W. Perit Huntington

Kentapoos's face contorted as if he had bitten into a bitter root. The small veins in his forehead bulged. Winema's hand flew to her mouth.

Steele let the letter fall to the table and tiredly removed his spectacles. Having received the letter three days earlier, he had already worked his own anger out. "No one is sorrier about this than I. I knew it was a gamble. I was no longer in the position of agent and I had no political base."

"You did your best, Elisha," Judge Roseborough consoled.

"At least you tried," Frank offered with little enthusiasm.

Kentapoos's voice was thick with contempt. "This is a trick, an insult! Now they want *all* our land and to put us on *Klamat* lands. Black Wound and Cho-ocks were right. I trusted too much."

Winema heard more than anger in her cousin's voice. It reflected humiliation. She shared his feelings. A dull ache expanded in her chest. She had refused to believe her people would ever have to give up *Mowatoc*. And to live with the *Klamat*—

She felt tears of anguish forming in her eyes. *Without Mowatoc, there are no Modokni.*

Steele dropped into his chair. "It is a bitter pill, friends, a bitter pill."

TWENTY-THREE

~ DISTANT THUNDER RUMBLED as thick black clouds settled over the valley. Winema went about her chores with little enthusiasm. Part of her was dying. If not for Frank and Charka, she felt sure she would sink into a depthless pit.

As they finished breakfast, Frank struggled to be optimistic. "It'll be fall before the signin' ceremonies, darlin'. Maybe something will come up to change their minds. Steele and Roseborough might convince those fools in Washington that putting Modocs with *Klamaths* is tomfoolery."

Winema didn't respond. She was sick of thinking about it. "Last night I dreamed our villages were attacked by the *Klamat*. A warrior captured me. He said, 'Be my slave or I will cut your throat.'"

"Some choice," Frank said. "Darlin', this ain't the end of the world."

Her mouth curved into an ironic half-smile. "No?"

Frank looked thoughtful. "Elisha says the reservation has its good points. And it'll be nearby, and the tribe will get money and food. They might even build schools there. The People will learn how to farm, maybe learn trades."

Winema scowled. "Let Elisha move to the reservation." Her eyes returned to the now cold surface of her coffee cup. It was obvious most Whites wanted Indian people out of the way, out of sight, out of mind. Others wanted them remade into images of themselves like the carved wooden dolls Modoc fathers made for their children.

First her marriage outside her tribe, then her move to the ranch, now she might lose the remainder of what connected her to *Mowatoc*. She felt as if she had fallen from her horse among a stampeding herd of elk, and she was running among them, realizing she could never keep up and would be inevitably crushed under merciless hooves. While she appreciated aspects of the White world, she was first and foremost a Modoc. No one could take that from her. The blood of her ancestors rushed through her veins like Lost River after the spring rains. This was who she was, who the spirits had willed her to be. She felt it within every fiber of her being.

She leveled her gaze at Frank. "Promise you will never try to make me White."

Frank's eyes widened slightly, his lips parted. Her words cut him to his center. The invisible line surfaced again, like a crack in the earth that shows itself under the stress of freeze or thaw. But this was his wife, not some disapproving villager at Kalelk. She was frightened and heartsick. Frank took her hand in his, looked into her eyes. "I married a Modoc girl, not a White girl. There ain't nothin' I want to change." He seemed to look within for a moment. "I never told you this before, but I think I love you more *because* you're Indian. I don't know how or why . . . I just do." His eyes were almost pleading. "Winema, don't push me away like they do in Kalelk sometimes. You, me, and Jeff are one, and we're gonna lick this head-on, together."

Winema's brow furrowed. "How do you mean—you love me more because I am Indian?"

Frank blushed slightly. "I ain't sure of all the reasons. Maybe that fella that passed through my old camp on Willow Creek one night put it best. I think his name was Miller. He said, 'If an Indian loves you, trusts you, or believes in you at all, he will serve you, guide you through the country, follow you to battle, fight for you, and he and all his sons and kindred will never think of the pay or profit in it.' That's you and Kentapoos and your kin. No righter words were ever spoke."

Winema searched her husband's eyes. Her smile meant to reassure, but it did not chase away her sadness. She squeezed his hand. "And my love for you and Charka is stronger than the tallest tree in *Mowatoc*. But I had to say it once, to get it—" She searched for the words.

"In the open?" Frank prompted.

"*Ih*. I want no secrets between us."

Frank took her hands, pulled her up, and wrapped his arms around her. His voice quavered. "I know this is breaking your heart, darlin'. And it breaks mine to see it. If I could change things, even if it meant making all the White people in the world disappear"—he hugged her closer—"including myself, I'd do it."

Her face rested against his shoulder, and she hugged him hard. The growl of distant thunder grew louder. Jagged forks of lightning speared the earth, and the rain came in torrents.

"Hold me, Tchmu'tcham, just hold me."

That night the thunder cracked and roared like cannon shots that jarred their insides and rattled dishes. Hailstones thwacked the roof and sides of the house, sounding like volleys of grapeshot. Stark, bright lightning flashed their bedroom in the negative.

In the early morning hours the cacophony died away. As Winema lay in the interval between wakefulness and sleep, a dream came to her, a dream unlike any she had ever experienced in its detail and vividness, as if the lightning had permanently seared it into her mind . . .

She was standing in a fog. A milky haze rose from a landscape of glistening ice. The frigid air felt brittle. It hurt to breathe. She shivered as she moved aimlessly through the fog, knowing she was not in the land of the People.

Out of the mist a shadowy form glided toward her. The mist drifted apart and the form took shape—first the head of a man, then the body of *blaiwas*, the golden eagle. He stood as tall as four stacked ponies, yet she felt no fear.

"What is this place?" she asked.

His voice resonated from the four sacred directions—deep, soothing, omniscient. "It is the Above World, child."

"Ahh," she whispered in awe. "Then you are *Laki Yalo*— Sky Chief. You are . . . as the ancestors described." She shuddered and wrapped her arms about her fur coat. "It is so cold here. I shake though I wear winter clothes."

He nodded. "We tire of the cold as well."

"But, tell me, *Laki Yalo*. Why am I here?"

"You are here to witness a sacred event."

He elevated her to him, gathered her close to his soft feathered breast. It was warm and comforting. With partially outstretched wings, he reached into the mist and brought forth a giant stone. Lifting it high above his head, he hurled it downward. The stone struck the ice with the force of a hundred thunderclaps, making a great void in the clouds.

Winema leaned forward and peered into it. Wide-eyed, she drew back, for she saw that she was floating above the clouds. Fearful, she looked again. The villages of the *Gumbatwases*, the *Puskamases*, and the *Kokiwases*, the three bands of her people, could not be seen around Tule Lake, only the-land-of-burnt-out-fires at the south end was visible. And something else was missing from *Mowatoc*, but she could not quite place it.

"Why have you made this great hole in the sky, Sky Chief?"

The great being smiled patiently. "You will see."

He spread his wings to their fullest extent—wider than the sky—and they began to flap. And the wind from the colossal wings beat down on the ice as though someone took the two tallest pines in the forest and flailed them in the air. Winema burrowed farther into his warm down as the ice groaned, then cracked and heaved, and finally burst into massive chunks. When the great feathered wings ceased beating, Sky Chief used their tips to sweep the ice chunks through the hole.

"It is done, Little Swallow. See for yourself."

Again, she looked down through the yawning chasm and gasped. The ice had formed the sacred mountain of *Mowatoc*. Supporting her gently with a wingtip, Sky Chief stepped out onto a cloud, then onto the mountaintop. He then roamed about the mountain, pressing his feather spikes into the ground, dropping earth, then seeds and nuts into the holes. Before her astonished eyes, the earth spread and trees of all types sprouted— maples, oaks, alders, dogwoods, pines, firs—and he named each of them in turn.

Soon the warming sun caused the snow and ice to melt, forming rivulets, then rushing streams. Sky Chief produced a staff, and from it he carved fish shapes, which dropped into the clear waters. As they struck the surface, they turned into darting salmon and tasty suckers. Taking a few leaves from the newly grown trees, he cupped them in his fingerlike feather tips and blew on them. They tumbled and floated into the air, then fluttered to life as birds of every shape and description.

From the remainder of his staff he carved animal shapes. As before, the whittlings fell to earth and transformed into live creatures. This left only the heavy bottom of his staff, from which he carved *lok witem*, the grizzly bear, who would be master over all the others.

At last the weary Sky Chief spoke. "Now *Kemush* and all his helper spirits will dwell on the mountain where it is warmer and closer to the People. In time the People will come here to pray. These great trees will provide shelter, and there will always be game, roots, and berries."

Suddenly Winema felt apprehensive. Why was she, an unimportant *Modokni* woman, selected for this honor, to witness these sacred events? Sky Chief seemed to hear her thoughts. He looked down at her, his expression serious yet gentle. "You must prepare for great change, daughter. The People face difficult times ahead. Peacemakers will become more powerful than warmakers. Seek out Jakalunus and tell him of all you see here. He will answer your question."

She dared to peer up at his wise, powerful face and felt a chill of apprehension.

"Rest now, young one."

Her eyelids became heavy. The iridescent white of the Above World turned as black as the cave of the Old Ones. Then

Sky Chief and the mist faded away like stars at dawn, and only the sacred mountain remained.

In the morning Winema awoke with mixed feelings. While part of the dream left her elated, other parts filled her with concern. She had an urgent need to see Jakalunus about the dream. She shook Frank awake. "Tchmu'tcham. I have had a vision-dream. I must see Jakalunus, *atui*."

Frank opened an eye half-way. "Dream? Now?"

"I will be back by dark."

She kissed him on the cheek, dressed, and headed for the barn.

AT Kalelk Winema found Jakalunus behind his latch, preparing medicine herbs. She stood quietly, waiting for him to speak first. He cocked his head, paused in his work, then continued his task. "Something of importance brings you home, Winema?" He spoke to his herbs, not to her.

"I wish to tell you of a dream, *kiuks*."

"We all have dreams. Most mean nothing."

"This was a vision-dream."

He stood, looked at her. "Why do you think it a vision-dream?"

She expected this question. "Sky Chief spoke to me and told me to ask you its meaning."

His left eyebrow arched as he searched her face. He had always been unreadable to her, his eyes reflecting mystery and wisdom beyond her understanding.

"Come inside."

Winema felt nervous. Other than his wife, few women were allowed inside the holy man's lodge. Jakalunus circled left, around the center fire pit. Winema waited, her good manners preventing her from stepping across it. He sat, then gestured for her to sit. Sitting across from him, she took a deep breath and related the dream.

Jakalunus closed his eyes for several heartbeats, then opened them. "I agree. It is a vision-dream."

The holy man looked at her with what seemed like new respect. "As you have since you were a child, you will take a different path, Winema." Squinting at her, he nodded to underscore his words. "Your dream bears this out. You will be called upon for a task of great importance."

The weight of his words worried her. "What kind of task, *kiuks*?"

"To help the People pass safely through their most difficult time." He reached for his pipe. "That is all I see."

Winema felt rooted to the ground. She waited, hoping for further insight. But the old man merely smoked, his eyes focused on some distant thought. She stood and bowed her head, "*Humast, kiuks*," and left.

Jakalunus took a long draw on his pipe and stared at the closed door. "You have been chosen, Little Sparrow, but I fear the task will prove too hard."

TWENTY-FOUR

≫ ONCE AGAIN THE trees exchanged their coats of green for a patchwork quilt of fall colors, and Sky Chief blew chilly night winds from the sacred mountain. Frank had been right. The four moons preceding the treaty signing allowed Kentapoos and the People to bend to the inevitable. They had argued, accused, and bickered, then realized the inescapable: exile to the *Klamat* reservation, or death.

Over a thousand Indians gathered at Council Grove one mile north of Klamath Agency—Klamaths, Modocs and a small contingent of Yahooskin Paiutes. As a matter of pride, everyone wore their finest regalia, though much of it was frayed and worn from the recent years of want.

The majority of women, and some of the men, wore their basket hats, as did Winema. She had dressed carefully, shunning her White clothes for her ceremonials. She stood out with her *ake snawagas*, the fifty-strand necklace of dentalium shells that draped across her shoulders and chest. She had not worn them since her wedding.

The new shawl of cobalt blue, which she had made herself, draped over her shoulders and arms, the delicate twelve-inch fringe rippling and waving like flowing prairie grass. Her earrings were cut from the inside of clamshells, and round, clear glass beads covered the sinew that attached them to her ears. The beads glinted in the sunlight when she turned her head.

An arbor had been constructed in the center of the grove. Superintendent Huntington and important residents of Siskiyou County sat around a table. The elders and headmen of the three tribes sat on blankets in a half-moon in front of the table. A pipe was passed.

Huntington rose to address the attendees. "Brothers. Today is a grand day. The Great Father in Washington sends greetings to his red children. It makes his heart glad to see you all gathered here together in peace. His heart fills with love . . ."

Kentapoos looked at Winema, who closed her eyes and sighed. To add to the blackness of the day, the superintendent talked to them like children. Huntington droned on, but Winema was watching the faces of her people. Their stoic countenances betrayed no feelings, only their eyes reflected the sadness.

". . . and so today, the ninth of October, eighteen hundred and sixty-four, we will smoke the pipe of peace, bury the hatchet, and take each other's hands as brothers. In payment for your lands, we offer the following gifts: $8,000 in food and supplies for the first five years, $5,000 in supplies for the second five years, and $3,000 for the third five years after this treaty is ratified. The government of the United States will build shops and a lumber mill, and will establish schools to educate you in the agricultural and industrial arts, and in reading and writing."

Huntington laid the treaty on the table and looked out over the crowd. "Now I ask the chiefs to come forward."

So that was it, Kentapoos thought. No negotiation, no request for a fair price for Modoc lands. It was dictated to them.

After they had made their marks on the treaty, the headmen formed two lines, each *Klamath* facing his Modoc counterpart. Kentapoos warily eyed Chief David Allen, who stood opposite Skonches. The chief had taken the name given to him by the Whites. Kentapoos was not surprised. With not so much as a whimper, the *Klamat* had capitulated to the Whites from the beginning.

Huntington continued, "You meet today in peace, to bury the bad past. You are of the same blood, of the same heart. You are to live as neighbors. You can shake hands and be friends."

Captain Kelley laid a trade hatchet on the ground between the two lines of chiefs, then handed each a twig of pine. Two at a time, the chiefs walked up to the hatchet. After laying their twigs upon the it they stepped on the boughs and shook hands. When the last two men shook hands, Chief David cleared his throat. He looked at Kentapoos, then down the Modoc line. "I see your eyes. Your skin is red like my own. I will be the first to show my heart in this matter. We have been longtime enemies. Many of our brave young men are dead. The ground is black with their blood, and our people are melting away like snow."

He gestured toward Huntington. As he spoke his hands and arms moved in symmetry with his words. "We see the White chief is strong and the law is strong. We can be Indians no longer and must take the White man's law. We have made friends. We have washed each other's hands. They are no longer bloody. We have buried all the bad blood and shall not dig it up again."

He looked upward, pointed toward the sky. "God sees into our hearts, and the sun is a witness between us." The chief's arm made a wide gesture toward a towering lone sugar pine near them. "Hear me, my people! This pine bears witness to my words. When you see this tree, remember it is a witness that here we made friends with the *Moadocas*. Let the arm be broken that would harm it; let the hand die that would break a twig from it. So long as snow shall fall on Yainax Mountain, let it stand. Long as the waters run in the rivers, let it stand. Long as the rabbits shall live in the manzanita groves, let it stand. Let our children play around it; let the young people dance under its boughs, and let the old men smoke together in its shade. Let this tree stand here forever as a witness." He folded his arms. "I am finished."

The chief's words took Kentapoos by surprise, as did the sincerity in his eyes. A response was necessary. As a matter of pride he would not be outdone by a *Klamat* chief. Kentapoos whispered to Skonches, who nodded.

Kentapoos began in a soft, hesitating voice. "The White chief brought me here. I feel ashamed that my people are poor. I felt like a man in a strange country without a father, and my heart was afraid." He looked directly at Chief David, his voice strengthening in tone and resonance. "I have heard your words and they warm my heart. I no longer feel a stranger here. Yes, the blood is now washed from our hands. We are enemies no longer. We have buried the past."

Kentapoos's voice now rang with strength and clarity. "I have planted a strong stake in the ground and tied myself with a strong rope. I speak from the hearts of my people, who were once as many as blades of grass. I will not dig up the stake, nor will I break the rope."

Above them they heard the scolding cry of a hawk. All eyes looked skyward. Kentapoos did not have to look. He swallowed hard and winced at his father's bitter rebuke.

~

FIVE days later iron-gray skies hung over Kalelk. Frank and Winema helped load the last of the meager belongings of the Modoc Nation.

Winema looked around. "Where is Aunt Kweelush?"

Frank surveyed the village. "I don't know. She was here a minute ago."

A sad-eyed Wild Girl trudged by. "I saw her by the creek."

As they neared the creek they heard faint sobs. On the far edge of the bank Kweelush wailed as she sat under a tall alder. Slashing frenetically with her knife, she cropped her hair. It hung close to her ears in jagged layers; long locks of salt and pepper cuttings lay scattered around her like discarded memories. Dropping the knife, she wrapped her arms around the tree and prayed to the tree's spirit to let her die—here, in the land of the ancestors. Winema felt as if her heart would fall to the ground. She spoke softly to her favorite aunt as she and Frank gently pried her loose and helped her back to the dray.

Winema was emotionally and physically drained. Once assured Kweelush was seated comfortably in the wagon, Frank joined his wife a few feet away. She was staring into the distance. He put his arm around her, hugged her close.

Winema's voice was almost inaudible. "When I look to the east, I see no dawn. When I look west, I see only darkness."

~

BLACK Wound found Skonches sitting in front of his latch while the chief's wife packed the travois. The *laki* had not slept the night before, his mind assailed by an incessant stream of *what-ifs*. Skonches slowly moved remorseful eyes up to meet Black Wound's scornful stare.

"If you and Kentapoos and the elders had hearts like mine, we would have taken to the war road and driven the *boshtin* from our land. We would have slaughtered their animals like dogs. We would have burned their square houses." His nostrils flaring, his voice grew in pitch and fervor. "The Old Ones grow restless in the caves because their offspring do nothing. We have become a NOTHING-PEOPLE!"

He spit, kicked ashes from the fire onto Skonches's tattered moccasins, then stormed off. The old chief stared at Wound's back a moment, then began to scoop handfuls of Kalelk dirt and cold ashes from his fire into a pouch.

As morning waned, layers of malignant clouds formed above them like great inverted mesas. With a small army escort, the long lines of wagons, travois, horses, and dogs snaked up the dusty road, north, toward *Klamat* country.

Frank drove the team while Winema sat next to her aunt in the wagon bed. As they pulled out of lush forest and onto the plain, the wind picked up. It quickly grew in force. The gusts whipped at them. Dust and grit swept into their eyes and mouths, stinging their faces like swarms of furious bees. It added to the sorrow, the shame—the bewildering punishment.

Deafening thunder pounded the sky followed by claws of

lightning that seared the air, leaving a burnt smell, yet the sky did not weep. Women keened as they held babes close to their breasts. Children cried as they held the hands of baffled toddlers. They all cried, half in grief, half in horror at the terrible anger unleashed by Sky Chief; half in fear that it portended even more onerous reproof to come. Their laments added to the howl of the wind, swelling into an anguished, dissonant chord.

Tears ran shamelessly down Frank's cheeks. "My God. It sounds like the gates of hell."

Winema shook her head. "They are the cries of our ancestors."

Frank slapped the reins and the dray jerked to life. From the wagon bed the two women, their faces blackened with mourning pitch, watched the abandoned lifeless village of their youth disappear behind the bend in the road; the wails resounding in their ears, the bitter taste of dirt upon their tongues.

PART TWO

The Cries
of the Ancestors

"It is the fulfillment of our manifest destiny to overspread the continent allotted by Providence for the free development of our yearly expanding millions."
—John L. O'Sullivan, 1845

They that were brought up in scarlet embrace dunghills.
—Lamentations:4

Bullets don't hurt much. Starving hurts a heap.
—Kentapoos (Modoc), 1872

TWENTY-FIVE

"Yeeeihhhh!" the Paiute chief leaped to his feet, took aim, and fired a bullet through Kankush's shoulder. The Modoc picket staggered but managed to yell the alarm. Yips and war cries preceded a barrage of rifle fire as the raiding Walpape Paiute war party poured both bullets and arrows into Skonches's village.

Skonches dropped his half-finished knife sheath, grabbed his rifle, and shouted orders. He knew very well who the attackers were. *That Sot, Paunina. After women and horses again.* The Walpapes often raided reservation Indians for their government-issue stock and supplies.

As Skonches's wife sprinted away, yelling for the women to follow her, a breathless and bleeding Kankush stumbled into camp. "And where are the soldiers *this* time, Skonches?"

Skonches had no answer. This was the *Sot*'s third raid in six moons. The *laki* called out to Jakalunus. Together, they helped Kankush into Jakalunus's lodge, then Skonches rushed toward the battle sounds. He ran only a few paces before he staggered from the ax-sharp pain in his chest and arm. Bending over, he stumbled to one knee. Since his fiftieth winter the agonizing pains struck more frequently. This time he would have to leave the fighting to the young men.

A bugle tattoo sounded in the distance, and the volume of rifle fire increased.

FORMER local rancher and now *Klamath* Indian Agent Lindsay Applegate rode full-out toward the Paiutes. His Navy Colt bucked three times, the shots whipcracking in the thick humid air. One lucky round smashed into the hip of a Paiute warrior, who folded to the ground, then the six Army troopers and ten *Klamaths* riding with the agent also opened fire.

The Paiutes took cover and triggered well-aimed shots at Applegate and his reservation police. One trooper stiffened in his saddle and fell. A *Klamath* sagged but managed to stay on his horse.

Applegate pulled rein. "DISMOUNT, DISMOUNT!"

Applegate and his men slid off their horses and took cover in the tall weeds and brush, snapping off salvos of rifle fire. Kentapoos and thirty-two Modocs joined the policemen on their right flank. Together they exchanged a withering barrage at the Paiutes. An arrow whispered past Applegate's ear, the fletching nicking his earlobe. "Damn! They're thick as smoked bees." He fired two more rounds, then fell prone to reload. Acrid gunsmoke filled stagnant air.

A trooper on the far left flank yelled, "They set the grass a'fire!"

Lindsay raised his head cautiously, saw yellow flames eating away the tall grass a hundred yards to their front. "Sergeant Casey!"

Casey, twenty yards away and crouched behind a large rock, answered, "Over here!"

"We're gonna roast out here!"

The old sergeant looked around urgently, caught Kentapoos's eye, and motioned with his arm, "Take your men, circle around to their right!"

Kentapoos nodded, jacked another round into his Spencer,

and passed the word. As the Modocs moved out, the policemen
loosed a continuing volley.

The last Modoc in line screamed as a Paiute arrow thudded
into his leg. Kentapoos saw him crumple. He shouted, "Hakar,
Krelatko! Help him!" then led the rest of his men in a flanking
arc.

"BACK, BACK!" Applegate shouted. Crouching and firing,
the policemen started their retreat before the inferno rushing
toward them. Heat waves rippled the air. The firing from the
Paiutes slackened slightly. Casey and his men moved left,
hoping to catch the attackers between them and Kentapoos's
men, but the flames were spreading in that direction as well.
"Sergeant! Move right! Follow those Modocs!"

Casey nodded and passed the word. The men began to sidle
to the right. The fire from the Paiutes was now sporadic.
Kentapoos noticed the significant drop in enemy firepower as
he hurried his men forward. Krelatko had rejoined him, and the
Paiute position was now in sight; Kentapoos signaled his men
to take cover. Ahead, a Paiute leaned out from behind a tree and
fired. The bullet thwacked into a nearby pine, gouging Krelatko's arm with stinging shards of bark. Krelatko stood and fired.
The round bit the tree and sprayed the Paiute with flying debris.
The Paiute cursed, disappeared behind the trunk.

Kentapoos glanced at his friend. "Take two men and scout
ahead. Report to me, then we will make our plan."

Soon Krelatko returned, waving a bloody scalp. "Like
before, they are gone. That last one must have been a deception
while the rest escaped."

Kentapoos gritted his teeth and swore.

＜

WHEN he returned to the village, Kentapoos found Skonches
in his latch, weakened from his chest pain. The older man sat
up with an expectant look on his face. "What of the fire? Must
we abandon the village?"

"*Laki*, the wind sends it away from us."

"You killed Paunina?"

Kentapoos's voice shook with frustration. "No. He escaped again." After two seasons of excuses from the Whites, *and* from Skonches, he had reached a turning point. "I have no more patience, Skonches. We are unprotected in this place. The soldiers do not help us. I say that paper we signed was a ruse to take our lands."

Skonches eyed his war chief patiently. "Applegate has been our friend for a long time. He cannot help it if he has too few soldiers. The government has given us food and clothes—"

Kentapoos waved him off. "Each child got half a thin blanket. Half! The food comes only when we are starving. Where is the mill, the school, the planting tools? The *Klamat* demand half of everything that is ours. They kick dirt on our feet, reminding us each sun we are on their land."

Skonches's eyes narrowed. "*Tyee* Applegate says the council in Washington has not yet signed the paper. They are still poor from fighting the great war in the East. All things will come to us by and by."

Kentapoos snorted bitterly. "Tell that again to the People *O Chief*." He made a sharp, slashing movement with his hand. "I rub out my mark on the treaty. The government has no honor." He drew himself erect as a lance. "I am taking those who will follow back to Lost River, to our home. This is my right since the treaty, when I, too, was recognized as a chief."

Skonches swore and struggled to his feet. "Do not do this, Kentapoos. It will make life harder for all of us. It will bring destruction upon those who follow you."

"Psha! We do not belong in this place. We belong in *Mowatoc*."

The *laki* grasped Kentapoos's arm and spoke in low urgent tones. "*Nent*. So it *is* that the Whites have offered more excuses than goods. But we must show them Modoc words have honor. I made a promise in front of everyone."

Kentapoos locked eyes with him for several heartbeats, then jerked loose from Skonches's grasp, wheeled, and threw the latch door open. He looked back at the elder chief. "We cannot eat promises."

Strain furrowed deep lines in Skonches's face. "Nor will pride and arrogance fill your belly, Waterbrash."

Kentapoos frowned. "I have a greater promise to keep. My promise to the People—as a chief," and he tromped out the door.

~

THREE days later Whitey rode out to the Riddles' to deliver the news. Kentapoos had returned to Kalelk with half the tribe, leaving Skonches and the other half at the reservation. Winema determined to ride to Lost River and convince her cousin to return to the reservation before there was real trouble. Frank opened his mouth to argue, but saw Winema was already on her way to the barn. All he could do was trot after her.

In the barn he helped saddle Skoks. Giving Winema a leg up, he cautioned, "You be careful now, damn it."

She smiled confidently, "*Oka ilagen.*" Her expression turned serious. "I was afraid it was coming to this. Kentapoos has been bristling like a cornered wolf for a long time, yet I have no doubt Black Wound and Cho-ocks, ah . . ." She searched for the correct English word, then made pushing movements with her hands.

"Pushed him?" Frank prompted.

"*Ih.*"

Frank looked out into the barnyard. "Well, I'm as frustrated as he is with the government. In a way I don't blame him." His left hand went to his hip as he massaged the back of his neck with his right. "Still. He signed that treaty. . . ." His voice trailed off as he fiddled with her saddle blanket.

She smiled down at him, patted his hand, then rode out of the barn. Moving her horse into an easy canter, she disappeared down the dusty road.

Frank rejoined Whitey, who watched her ride away, then looked at Frank. "You're a lucky man, Frank." He switched his gaze back to Winema, now obscured by the dust. "Lordy, she reminds me of my Rabbit."

Frank grasped his old friend's shoulder. "If Rabbit was

anything like Winema, Whitey, you were damned lucky to have her—if only for a short spell."

Whitey turned back to Frank. "Hey. I see your beard's all grow'd back."

"Yeah. Winema don't like it much, though. Says it's like kissin' a bear. But I felt kinda naked without one."

Whitey chuckled. "I'm with you, bud."

~

EARLY the next morning Winema rode out of Kalelk toward home. It had been wonderful seeing the old village alive with her people again. After talking with Kentapoos most of the night, she half agreed with his reasoning. She felt his frustration and understood his anger when he found a good part of the valley had been settled, though the treaty was not yet signed by the *tyees* in Washington. This brought the Modocs and the settlers dangerously close together, she had warned. But Kentapoos wouldn't budge.

Frank was shoeing a horse in the barn when she rode up. He walked out to greet her.

Worried and dusty, she dismounted. "He is staying."

Frank sighed, scratched his beard absently. "There'll be trouble. Them settlers are going to get real skittish. They'll start crying to the army."

Winema brushed dust off her dress. "We spoke of this. Jack says the soldiers are small in number. He thinks they are weak-hearted like rabbits."

Frank considered this. "Don't be so sure. What if they try to run him off?"

"He will talk to them. And he has gone to some of the ranches to tell them of his return, that there will be no trouble."

Frank smiled appreciatively. "That Jack. He's a helluva politician when it comes to working with *Whites*." His smile faded. "But he's putting Lindsay in a tough spot now that he's agent."

"*Ih*. He will talk with Casey, too."

Frank grunted and scratched the back of his head. "What I

worry about is Jack bein' able to control Black Wound and his boys. Black Wound is apt to say anything to get Jack riled. I've heard him tell lies that would make a weasel think twice."

～

A week later Frank was tallowing his tack when he heard a buggy pull into the yard. He sauntered out to meet the visitor. A short man dressed entirely in black stepped down from the rig. His vest and cravat matched his frock coat. He strode toward Frank, hand extended. "Hello, neighbor. I am the Reverend Eleazer Thomas, new to these parts. I replaced Reverend Hill, who's been transferred to Salem."

Frank shook the hand hesitantly. The only preacher Frank ever liked was Reverend Hill, a feisty pastor who Frank once watched knock a heckling gambler down a flight of stairs in Hawkinsville. He assumed most men of the cloth resembled the stoic, overpious pastor from his childhood in Shelby County, Kentucky, who seemed to revel in whipping Frank in Sunday School, and who was later caught in the arms of a married church woman. The clean-shaven Thomas's hairline receded severely, stretching his forehead from his eyes to his crown. His bushy eyebrows all but hid his gray eyes, giving him a hawkish look. "Nice place you have here, Brother Riddle. Real nice."

Frank continued to wax the harness he still held in his hand. Frank wrestled between his normally good manners and his discomfort with preachers. He had neither the time nor interest to get into an extended conversation with Thomas.

Winema walked out onto the porch. Thomas noticed her and frowned.

"What can I do for you, Reverend?" Frank inquired.

"Business, I'm afraid, Brother Riddle. I prefer social visits first, but no sooner had I arrived than I was visited by Judge Roseborough."

"Roseborough, huh?"

"Indeed. The judge gave me a list of men living with Indian

women in the county. He said now that the treaty has been formalized, the law states she must move to the reservation, or you must marry."

Frank stiffened. "I *am* married."

"You are?" Thomas's brow knitted in confusion. "Perhaps you married outside the county? I could find no marriage license recorded."

Frank's lips thinned in annoyance. "Didn't need no license. We were married by her father, the chief."

Jeff peeked around the side of the house where he had been playing with his dog, Mutt.

Thomas's beady eyes widened. He mumbled something under his breath.

"What's that, Reverend?" Frank asked.

His eyes fixed on Jeff, Thomas cleared his throat uncomfortably. "I was saying, brother Riddle, the law is quite clear. If you want to remain here with your, ah, wife, you will have to get a license and be married before the eyes of God. In a Christian church."

Winema had now joined them.

Frank's face pinked. "Why, you little popinjay. I had a belly full of your kind back home. Get your ass in that buggy and make dust outta here."

The minister looked flabbergasted. His eyes darted around like a cornered mouse. "See here, Brother Riddle. Surely you don't want your child lost like a heathen?"

"Never you mind about my son. He ain't lost. I know right where he is." Frank grabbed the pastor's arm and hustled him back into his buggy.

Red-faced, Thomas sputtered, "I will have to report this to Judge Roseborough immediately!"

Frank squinted at him. "You do that, Reverend. And make sure you spell my name right. I despise it when folks misspell my name."

"REVEREND Thomas is right, Frank. It's the law," Judge Roseborough intoned as he leaned against his heavy mahogany desk two days later.

"Nobody is going to send Winema to that damned reservation unless it's over my dead body," Frank exclaimed.

Winema grasped his arm. "Do not anger yourself, husband. It will be fun to be married a second time."

Frank looked at her, astonished. "What?"

"I have thought it over. It will be better for Jeff. He is half White, so his parents should be married both ways."

Frank's mouth formed a surprised *O*. Winema seemed perfectly at ease with the idea. "Well, I . . ." He couldn't think of a counterargument. He glanced at Judge Roseborough, who grinned as he shuffled papers on his desk.

Winema shifted her gaze to the judge, then back to Frank. "You respected our traditions. Now I will respect yours."

Frank cleared his throat, squared his shoulders. Squeezing Jeff's hand, he looked down into the boy's big toffee eyes. "Well. For Jeff's sake, we could go along, I guess."

Roseborough looked up and brightened. "Splendid, Frank. Winema is right. It's best for Jefferson."

Frank said, "But I won't be married by that wind-sucking preacher, Thomas. I want you to marry us, Judge."

The Judge considered this a moment. "All right, Frank. I'd be happy to. The law only requires the marriage be solemnized by either an ordained minister or a justice of the peace, one of my additional duties around here." He consulted the large day book on his desk. "How does next Tuesday at ten A.M. sound?"

Jeff looked delighted. "Are you and Ma gonna get married, Pa? Can I come?"

Winema squeezed the boy's other hand, "*Oka ilagen*. It will be fun."

❦

AT 9:45 A.M. on the following Tuesday, Frank and Winema found themselves in Judge Roseborough's office. Winema had convinced Frank to again wear his boiled shirt, a new pair of pants, and new shoes. She wore her favorite blue dress. Jeff wore little knickerbockers and a snug-fitting blue cap with a white bill.

The outer door opened and Whitey peeked in. "I, ah, brung a friend."

Whitey stepped inside. A sheepish-looking Nathan Hopkins, grasping a large bouquet of flowers, followed him in. Hat-in-hand, Nathan approached Frank and Winema. Frank eyed him warily.

The schoolteacher cleared his throat. "I'd like to apologize to both of you. I have acted rudely." He looked into Frank's eyes. "We had too many years together to just throw away, Frank. I hope you will forgive me." Blushing, he looked at Winema. "Oh. These are for you, Winema."

Winema took the bouquet and smiled, then looked at Frank expectantly. Nathan turned his hat in his hand two inches at a time as he awaited Frank's response. Frank studied the toes of his boots for a few moments, then returned his gaze to Nathan. A smile inched across his face as he reached out to take Nathan's hand. "Good to have you back, Eyes."

Whitey slapped his thigh and broke out in his wheezy laugh, "By Gawd, we're back together again. Jist like ol' times."

Whitey's comical laugh broke the tension, and everyone burst into laughter. Jeff giggled and hopped around the room like a jack-in-the-box.

Judge Roseborough finally interrupted. "This is the first wedding I've seen where the celebrating started *before* the wedding."

"You're right, Judge. Let's get this over with and get on with the real celebratin'." Frank chuckled.

Roseborough donned his spectacles. "Now, you have a choice, Frank and Winema. You need two witnesses. Before, you were going to use Whitey and Elisha, here. Do you want to change your mind?"

Frank looked at Elisha. "Elisha, if you don't mind, I'd kind of like to have my two old partners as our witnesses."

Elisha smiled. "Not at all, Frank. Happy to step aside for old friends."

"Only one last detail to take care of," Roseborough interjected. "You'll need a Christian name, Winema, for the license and marriage certificate."

Winema looked at Frank with a blank expression.

Frank scratched the back of his neck, his brow furrowed in thought. "Hmm. I didn't know about that."

Winema asked, "What is a kris-tin name?"

Frank explained that people often used a name of an ancestor or friend.

Winema's face lit up. "My mother's name was Tobius."

Frank said, "That don't sound too feminine, though."

Elisha said, "How about Toby?"

Frank tried it out. "Toby. Toby Riddle." He looked at Winema. "*Domulis wopuku?*"

"I think it is a good name, like my mother's name."

Frank looked at the judge and shrugged. "Toby it is."

The judge completed the forms, then picked up a book and started reading aloud.

The ceremony lasted only five minutes before Judge Roseborough said, "You may now kiss the bride."

Frank's eyebrows jumped in surprise. "That's it?"

Winema elbowed him. "That is what you said at our first wedding. Now be quiet and kiss me."

~

THE wedding party moved to Delmonico's restaurant, where there was much laughter and reminiscing. No sooner were steaks ordered all around than the café's front door swung open and Kentapoos strode in. He hadn't changed his old habits and frequently came to town to see Steele, Roseborough, and his other White friends.

Frank saw him first. "Jack! Over here!"

Kentapoos grinned at the gathering. "*Tyee* Steele told me you were here."

Frank pulled over a chair from a nearby empty table. "Good to see you. Here, have a seat. You just missed the wedding."

"*Ih*. I heard about it." He smiled at Winema. "You look nice in that color, cousin."

Winema beamed. "*Humast*."

Frank leaned over and spoke from the corner of his mouth. "A little dicey, comin' to town right now, don't you think?"

Kentapoos smiled, pulled a piece of paper out of his shirt pocket, and handed it to his brother-in-law. Frank opened it and read:

> Jack, the Indian to whom I give this paper makes a living for himself by farming and trapping and wants me to give him this paper certifying to the fact that he is a civilian Indian and not a wild Indian; that he is an independent freeman entitled to the protection of life, liberty, and pursuit of happiness by the laws of civilization.
>
> > A. M Roseborough
> > County Judge of the County
> > of Siskiyou, and State of
> > California

Frank laughed and slapped Kentapoos on the back. "By God Jack, you should run for office."

TWENTY-SIX

July 1867

AN OPPRESSIVE HEAT lay on the conferees like piled blankets as they sat in the high grass. The rising and falling whir of legions of invisible crickets and grasshoppers provided the only sounds. Lindsay Applegate mopped his forehead with a sweat-stained yellow bandanna. This was his second visit to Kalelk. He had brought his boss, Superintendent Huntington, who constantly slapped at mosquitoes and complained about the heat. Winema, hired as interpreter, sat on Applegate's right.

Kentapoos had drawn a line at the river where a natural bridge of rocks allowed passage into the village. No Whites were allowed across the narrow river, so they sat under a shady copse of alders just off the road. Heavily armed, Cho-ocks, Black Wound, and three other Modocs squatted on either side of their new chief, their faces masks of defiance.

Huntington sighed noisily in frustration. They had smoked and talked with the Modocs for two hours, the conversation moving in circles. Lindsay had forewarned Huntington of this, advising him that Indians reasoned in a circular fashion, as opposed to the linear thinking of Whites. Huntington seemed uninterested in his counsel.

"But, Jack, we're distributing a major portion of treaty supplies today. The treaty was finally ratified," Applegate offered enthusiastically.

"It is too late, *Plaiwash*," Kentapoos replied, using Applegate's Modoc-given name of Gray Eagle.

The superintendent grimaced. "I'm fed up with begging these people, Lindsay." He shifted his eyes to Kentapoos. "It is this simple, Jack. Either you come back to the reservation peacefully, or we force you back."

Black Wound jumped to his feet, his rifle at port. "Like your treaty, blanket-maker, your threats are empty. Send your puny soldiers, and we will show them what Modoc warriors can do."

The rest of the Modocs stood. "*Heya!*"

Applegate, Huntington, and Winema scrambled to their feet. Huntington glared at Kentapoos and Black Wound. "Very well. If it's violence you want, violence you will get."

The officials mounted their horses. From horseback Huntington warned, "And remember. If one White settler is harmed in any way, there will be no quarter given." He slapped his reins and galloped off, followed by Applegate and Winema.

About a mile from the meeting site, Lindsay Applegate moved up next to his supervisor.

Huntington's face was dark. "Just what I expected from those renegades. Violence is all these savages know, Applegate. It appears the newspaper accounts I read while in Denver were correct."

"Superintendent, I've lived out here for twenty years with Indians as my neighbors. Until just now, I can remember only one time I ever heard an uncivil word from one of them. Newspapers never put out a bigger bug-a-boo than this universal fear of Indians."

Huntington looked aghast. "By God, sir. Have you forgotten the murderous wagon train massacres? The Whitmans?"

"No, sir, I haven't. I'm not saying there aren't ornery ones, but for every White man killed, the ghosts of a hundred Indians follow. I've seen it repeated time after time. A White is killed—usually by a road agent or a greedy neighbor—and the account of it fills the land. Telegraphs and printing presses build it up out of all proportion. An artist is called in and he puts the affair before the world in flaming illustrations, and a general cry goes up against the Indians."

The superintendent's face clouded with anger. "I suggest, sir, you remember which side you are on!" He spurred his horse ahead, leaving Applegate in the dust. Lindsay knew then his short tenure as agent was about to expire.

＊

As they rode toward Fort Klamath, Winema pondered the sharp exchange between Huntington and Kentapoos. Part of her wanted to renounce Huntington and stand with her cousin. Another part wanted Kentapoos to return to the reservation and use his skills to better the new way of life.

Living with one foot in the White world and one in the Indian was taking its toll. Sometimes she felt her spirit spinning downward like a wingshot bird. The problem was, she understood both points of view. Sometimes she wished she didn't. In her darkest moments she questioned the prudence of her marriage. She tried to picture whose side she'd take if she had not married Frank—Kentapoos's or Skonches's? Perhaps she should have adhered to Aunt Kweelush's marriage advice: "The otter does not marry the beaver."

The black thoughts unnerved her, and she flushed with shame. How could such ill things enter her mind when she loved Frank and Jeff more than her own life? Had she selfishly forsaken who she was for comfort and convenience? Where did loyalty to her cousin end and her responsibilities to Frank and her chief begin? But as Kentapoos liked to say, this was "up-in-the-air talk." The arguments ran in circles like a pup chasing its tail. It only left her more depressed, more frustrated.

When she returned home, Winema handed her two days' pay to Frank. She was glad to be rid of it.

Frank grinned. "Another twenty dollars. We can sure use it. We could make a helluva living doing this government work if it was steady."

His smile faded when he saw her drawn expression. "What is it, *Ena*?"

Winema unconsciously rubbed her palms against her dress. "I get no pleasure from this money. I feel . . . dirty when I take it."

"Now, Winema, we talked about this. The treaty's signed and the supplies are coming on time. It looks like the *laki* was right, and you feel loyal to him and Jakalunus, remember?"

She nodded without enthusiasm. He was right. This had been her decision—until each time she met with Kentapoos. Then the mental tug-of-war renewed itself.

Frank frowned. "You're not thinking of giving your wages away again?"

Her eyes narrowed. "Our family needs it more than we do."

Frank set his jaw. "We help out all we can, Winema. Hell, half the time they're down here with us. We need that money for planting season, and I need to replace some old tack . . ." Frank trailed off as he watched her face darken.

She felt disappointed in him. "After all this time you still think like a White man. We are rich compared to my people. We grow plenty of food. You sell horses and hides. It is not right we have so much more. They think us selfish, and they are right."

Frank swore under his breath. "Rich? We're barely makin' it ourselves. That's your aunt Kweelush talking, not you."

Winema took a step back. "You used to like my family."

Frank made a frustrated face. "I like your family just fine." He shoved his hands in his pockets. "I could just do with a little less of Kweelush. She never liked the idea of our marriage. Anything White is bad." Frank paused a moment, then. "Not so sure about a couple of your cousins, either, now that I think about it."

Winema glared at him. Her hands flew to her hips. "Who? What do you mean by that?"

"Well, your uncle Moluks and his wife, for example. They come over here and help themselves to our food and beds without so much as a how-ya-do."

Frank bolstered himself for the rebuttal.

"Ha! What do you know about relatives, man-who-deserts-his-own-relations?"

Frank bristled. "Now, how could I have met you if I'd stayed in Kentucky with my parents? Tell me that!"

Winema didn't feel like arguing further. Turning her back, she loosened Skoks's girth strap. The pony blew out and nodded his head as if in appreciation. Winema patted the piebald's neck and gently guided him toward his stall and unsaddled him.

Frank slapped the coiled rope he was carrying against his thigh in frustration. Finally he pocketed the heavy coins and sighed. "So what happened at Jack's?"

Stiffly she recounted the meeting and the mutual threats.

"Damn. It's going to come to trouble, sure as hell."

Winema walked to the small yellowed barn window and stared out. "Perhaps I should be with him . . . when the trouble comes."

Frank's eyes widened. He took her by the shoulders. "Like hell. I've always let you go your own way, Winema, but this time I got to put my foot down. Jack's a big boy, and he's got friends around here. Things still might work out. But if they don't, I don't want you getting shot at. You got Jeff to think about, too."

Winema crossed her arms. She remained frustrated with Frank's attitude about money and family. His priorities seemed reversed. Family and tribe came before individual wants. "We have talked of this before. If we have food, we share it. If we have money, we share that as well."

"Damnit, Winema. You make me sound like Midas. When have I ever refused your family anything? If we went broke and moved to the reservation, we'd be in the same boat as everyone else. With the ranch, we got something to offer."

She had to admit he had a point.

He moved closer. "I've been thinking on this. If we keep hiring on as translators we can stay involved, keep working on Jack. We can help keep the peace, maybe stop trouble before it

starts. Can't you see? Bein' the translator is the best place to be.
You'll be there to calm Jack down if things get hot, make sure
words don't get mixed up. Hell, it's where you can do the most
good!"

Winema heard the words, but she was as distant as the
moon. She was thinking that over the recent months her spirit
had become tainted, her mind confused. Her visits to the sweat
lodge behind the house helped, but the bad thoughts and
feelings always returned like unbidden ghosts.

She was long overdue for a visit to the sacred springs. It was
time for a spiritual cleansing, she thought, time to seek
answers. She cast her eyes downward. "I will think about it."

━━━

EARLY the next morning Winema rode the thirty miles to the
place-where-Kemush-left-his-footprints. She left the road and
crossed a dry creekbed. Ahead lay a broad vista of open
grassland. Far to the east she could see mountains and foothills,
like crumpled butcher paper, against the horizon.

The argument with Frank had left her drained. It seemed
there were no clear answers any more. Life in Kalelk had been
simple; the codes were clear—family, loyalty, respect; who
were friends, who were foes. Life now seemed a confusing
tangle of conflicting loyalties and impossible rules.

Entering the forest, she could see serpentine fingers of
ground mist ahead. The morning sun broke through the trees,
dappling her arms with patches of light and warmth. Just
nearing the springs lifted her spirits. Soon she heard the hiss of
escaping steam, then the familiar smells of wild lavender and
damp moss. Pine scent wafted through the air, beckoning her.
Near the spring she felt an invisible spray mist her face and
arms.

Why had she waited so long? She had not paid close enough
attention to her own spirit, nor to her personal relationship with
Kemush. Too long in the White world, she had spent too much
time on the physical, too little on the spiritual; too much
thought given to the drudgeries of daily life, and too much time

looking for answers from everyone except from Him, who is all-knowing. No wonder she had spirit sickness. She had almost forgotten what her father had taught her, what Jakalunus preached. Her first priority must always be the health of her own spirit. To do this only required looking to the Creator for guidance.

Arriving at the spring, she dismounted and disrobed. The fissure spewed a fresh cloud of steam, and the fine spray tingled her flesh. She walked into the familiar embrace of the warm mist and recalled a story Secot once told her. They had been on a trading trip to the tribes who lived near the great salt water, where her father collected the dentalium shells for her ceremonial necklace. She had been upset and worried about an argument she had had with Wild Girl. Also, they had found no game for three days. Weak with hunger, Winema worried aloud they might starve. Secot had smiled patiently, but said nothing. When at last they stood on the beach, her father pointed to a small island floating an arrow's arc away. A lone gull soared above.

"Little Sparrow. Do you see that island out there with the gull gliding above?"

"*Ih*, Father."

"Grandfather has given that gull a single-mindedness. His mind is not cluttered with unnecessary concerns. When next your mind is muddled with the concerns of life, and your spirit droops like a leaf in the rain, remember this island and the gull. Remember the peace and beauty of the island, and the sea bird's uncluttered mind. Most important, remember that no matter how bad things seem, Grandfather, in all his wisdom and kindness, has never abandoned us. By-and-by, he always provides."

Closing her eyes, Winema allowed her mind to empty, to become as the island, surrounded by a calm sea. She saw herself resting on the cay, a warm salty breeze flowing over her, the gull floating above and she made a silent prayer: *Grandfather. Kemush. Whose voice I hear on the wind, whose breath gives life to the world. I am weak and humble before you. I am but a child who needs your guidance. Remove the clutter from my mind. My people are in trouble, Grandfather. I have prayed, but the spirits are silent. I have relied too much on my own small mind when I should have looked to you. Make me wise that my heart may know my rightful path.*

She took a deep cleansing breath, let it leak slowly from her nostrils. Replaying her argument with Frank in her mind, she reconsidered the possibilities of her role as interpreter. Slowly an idea began to grow, like a pupa in the cocoon of her imagination. Faint words from the past seeped into her mind. Words from Sky Chief, words from Frank, the wisdom of Jakalunus:

"You can help keep the peace . . . it's where you can do the most good."

"The peacemakers will become more important than the warmakers."

"You have been chosen, Winema."

Her eyes popped open. Like dross from a fire, the frustration that had fouled her mind and spirit fell away. It was as if she stood in a room lit by a dim lantern, then someone opened a door and bright sunlight swept into every shadowed corner, washing away the specters of doubt.

"Oka ilagen! THE DREAM!"

She was not a traitor. She was not selfish. She was doing what Sky Chief had foretold, what Jakalunus had interpreted. She looked skyward. *"Humast,* Grandfather! *Humast!"*

Winema threw on her clothes, mounted Skoks, and galloped toward home. The warm summer wind felt cool against her moist skin. Hair streaming behind her, she rode with the carefree giddiness of her youth, her mind uncluttered—focused with the single-mindedness of the gull.

TWENTY-SEVEN

Klamath Indian Agency, November 1869

NEWLY ASSIGNED INDIAN agent Captain O. C. Knapp shook the new Superintendent's hand. "I look forward to serving under you, sir."

The corners of Albert Meacham's eyes crinkled. His mouth, hidden by a full beard, stretched into a wide, congenial grin. "I've heard good things about you as well, Captain."

Meacham's friendly manner belied his misgivings. He knew an agent posting was hardly an officer's choice assignment. As the new State Superintendent of Indian Affairs, Albert had been successful in convincing President Grant to replace military Indian Agents with Quaker ones. Both army agents and politically appointed agents had made a grand mess of the Indian Service. Unfortunately, Washington had yet to find a Quaker agent for the Klamath reservation. Nevertheless, by the grace of God, Albert Meacham was going to bring morality and conscience to Oregon's reservations.

Knapp gestured toward a chair, and Meacham sat. The aroma of fresh-brewed coffee commingled with those of wood smoke and coal oil in the cramped agency office. The veteran army officer walked over to the small stove, grabbed an old glove, and used it to grasp the curved handle of the boiling coffeepot. He handed a cup to his new supervisor and poured a steaming cupful.

The superintendent wrapped his hands around the cup, took a sip. "I think I'm finally starting to thaw out."

Knapp nodded. "The snow came early this year."

Meacham grunted, then smoothed his thin, receding hair. He regarded the thirty-eight-year-old officer carefully. "Tell me, Captain, what do you know of the recent changes in Washington?"

Knapp regarded his boss with narrowed eyes. "As you know, I replaced Lindsay Applegate here at Klamath only a month ago. But I understand you were instrumental in convincing President Grant that the Quakers would do a"—he searched for a diplomatic word—"more efficient job of running the agencies."

Meacham's eyes twinkled. "Quite right, sir. An *honest* job." Then he caught himself and cleared his throat. "That's not to say you, sir, won't do an honest job. I have full confidence in you." Meacham leaned forward in his chair, anxious to get to his point. "Captain, I have completed my investigation of all the agents in the state. Although Mr. Applegate was well-meaning, irregularities still occurred on this reservation. Since both of us are new on the job, I thought it important to clarify my policies at the outset."

Knapp maintained his military bearing, sitting saber-stiff in his chair.

Meacham had given this speech many times. It was a personal crusade now. "I believe the Quaker Policy will rid us of the graft and unspeakable acts of the old system. It is time for modern ideas, for moral men." Meacham smacked his hand on the arm of the chair. "Appalling! Absolutely appalling—the behavior of some of these agents."

"Yes, sir."

Meacham grunted. "Only two weeks ago I interviewed an agent who told me the most propitious way to civilize the Indians was to *wash out* the color. He implied the arranged interbreeding between Indians and Whites until the Indian blood dissolved over the generations. And I discovered he had already implemented this odious scheme!" Meacham's eyes flashed. "Half-breed children running amok, their White fathers unknown; mothers horribly diseased, drunk, or dead."

Knapp shook his head in apparent disgust. "Yes, sir. An abomination."

Meacham stood and began to pace. "By Jehovah, I won't have it! Knapp, we are here to return self-respect to our charges. Educate them, clothe them, make them self-sufficient—bring them out of darkness and into the light of Christianity." He wheeled and stared into the captain's eyes. "And we will do it without lining our pockets, passing off rotten meat, shortchanging supplies, or defiling Indian women. What do you say, Knapp? Are you with me?"

Knapp sipped his coffee. "You're the boss, sir."

"Good! Now, let's see if you and I can convince this Captain Jack to return to the reservation."

Knapp bit his lower lip. "That, sir, might prove to be more difficult than you realize."

The superintendent's jaw set in resolve. "Nevertheless, it must be done. The residents in Siskiyou County are bringing a great deal of political pressure to bear."

"Yes, sir. I've forwarded a few of their letters to your predecessor. To be honest, most of their charges are exaggerated. Jack has kept his people under control down there. Oh, a few cows have disappeared, but in comparison to the problems we're having with Paunina and his bunch . . ."

"I see. Why hasn't the army been successful in moving him back to the reservation?"

"Well, sir, the detachment at Fort *Klamath* is very small. We're spread razor thin. And, we've had other fires to put out. To be honest, keeping these Indians in one place is like trying to herd cats."

"Paiutes and Rogue Rivers, you mean."

"Yes, sir, among others."

"What about the Modocs that *are* living on the reservation?"

"They number around a hundred and seventy. Old Skonches

is their chief—reasonable for an Injun." He eyed Meacham uneasily.

Meacham went on. "How many Klamaths?"

"About twice the number of Modocs. They've always been cooperative. No real problems."

"And what can we expect from Captain Jack?"

Knapp scratched his head. "Not sure, sir. I haven't met him yet. He has a few influential White friends around Yreka. I hear it's his lieutenants—Curly Headed Doctor and Black Wound—who are the belligerents."

Meacham looked amused. "Curly-headed. Where in thunder do they get such names?"

Knapp chuckled. "Names the miners hung on them. Indians work cheap and bring women with them. Curly Headed Doctor is Jack's medicine man, Cho-ocks."

Meacham's frown deepened. "Exactly the kind of thing we must stop, this shameless fornicating with Indian women." He pulled out a White handkerchief, polished the silver head of his cane. "I understand there is some connection between these Modocs and a local rancher by the name of Riddle."

"That would be Frank Riddle. He lives with Jack's cousin. I believe her name is Toby. They have a place on Bogus Creek—about twenty miles from where Jack's holed up. Reliable interpreters, I'm told."

Meacham admired the shine on the head of his cane, then moved his gaze to Knapp. "Well, we'll need them again. I want to go see Captain Jack within the week. I'm sure just a little common sense and straight talk will persuade him."

Knapp eyed his new supervisor dubiously. "Of course, sir."

                        ◀

FIVE days later Superintendent Meacham and Captain Knapp huddled in a council tent near the mouth of Lost River. Outside, a cold wind whipped eddies of snow around the corners of the worn canvas. A small sagebrush fire struggled to warm the interior. Those who were stuck near the outside walls tried to inch their way closer to the heat source, tightly packing the conferees together.

Meacham, his eyes watering and burning from the smoke, sat in front of his eleven-man party, facing Kentapoos across the fire. The pipe had made the rounds four times. Meacham pulled out his watch and flipped the lid for the third time during the past hour. Leaning toward Knapp, he spoke out of the side of his mouth. "Where in blazes are the Riddles? It's almost noon."

Knapp shoved his gloved hands under his armpits. "Probably the weather. But Jack won't talk without them. We'll just have to wait."

The tent door whipped aside admitting a freezing blast of air, and Krelatko. "They are here," he announced.

Dusted with powdery snow, Frank, Winema, and Jeff shuffled into the tent. Meacham stood and reached out his hand. "Mr. Riddle, I assume."

Tiny ice crystals frosted Frank's beard. He shivered, removed his glove, and shook Meacham's hand.

"Miserable weather. I am Albert Meacham, the new Superintendent of Indian Affairs. Thank you for coming."

Frank nodded at Meacham, then he saw Jack. "*Wuk lucee*, brother?" The two friends clasped arms, then Kentapoos embraced Winema.

Jeff shouted in Modoc, "Cousin Kentapoos!"

Winema looked on, proud her son could switch so easily between Modoc and English. Kentapoos's hand flashed to his knife handle. He gave the boy a fierce expression, then growled as he took a fighting stance. Jeff looked delighted and aped him move for move. Kentapoos and his warriors broke into laughter, then Kentapoos knelt down to receive the eight-year-old's excited embrace. "So, you come to your first council, little warrior. You want to see your cousin tame these White men, *ih*?"

Winema knew Jeff was bursting with all sorts of news. He'd not seen his favorite cousin for many weeks. "I can shoot four arrows in the air before the first one lands."

A chorus of approvals came from the warriors. Kentapoos smiled proudly, tousled Jeff's hair. "Ah, you bring warm news on a cold day." Kentapoos nodded toward Krelatko. "Krelatko here could not do that until he was twice your age."

The Modocs exploded in laughter. Frank translated the conversation for Meacham and his party. Winema was pleased. She had guessed correctly. Bringing Jeff helped "break the ice," as Frank put it.

"And Pa says I can shoot the eye out of a mosquito," Jeff blurted. "When will you come and take me hunting again?"

Kentapoos chuckled as he clasped Jeff's shoulder. "Soon, Charka. Now go and sit with your mother and father. We will talk more later."

Jeff looked disappointed, but did as he was told.

Introductions were made and the pipe was passed for the benefit of Frank and Winema. Finally the superintendent cleared his throat. "Jack, I suppose you know we are here to convince you to return to the reservation."

Frank translated, though Winema knew Kentapoos understood exactly what Meacham said. He wanted Frank to interpret the English, and Winema to interpret the Modoc words correctly—with their full intent and meaning. There being little correlation between the structure of the two languages, misinterpretation had caused problems in the past. This they had learned the hard way. And, if Frank should accidentally misspeak, Winema could correct the error.

Kentapoos regarded Meacham for a moment, apparently sizing up the man. "Yes. I know your purpose, but you waste your time, *tyee*. We are happy here in our homeland. We cause no trouble."

Meacham nodded. "I understand you're happy here, Jack, but the treaty—"

Kentapoos held up his hand. "There is no treaty."

Meacham's eyebrows arched. He looked at Frank and Winema.

Frank said, "He feels the treaty was broken, it's no good."

Meacham switched his gaze to Kentapoos. "I'm sorry, but the treaty is in full force. It is a legal document."

This brought a chorus of grumbles from the Modocs. Kentapoos silenced them with his hand. "A treaty," he explained, "is only good when both sides keep their word, *tyee*. The government has broken theirs."

"You are mistaken, sir. The goods are distributed on time, and fairly. We are at peace now, Jack. We are friends."

Kentapoos smirked. "You are new here, *tyee*. Perhaps I need to remind you of what has gone before you. We were promised a mill and schools and farm tools. It has been five winters, yet we see none of these. Yes, we received goods—cloth for one shirt and one pair of trousers for a man and cloth for one woman's dress and one-half a blanket for a child." He paused a moment to let the last statement sink in. "We were promised protection from the Walpapes, yet they continue to raid us and steal our goods and stock. The *Klamat*, our old enemies, treat us rudely. They demand half of everything. You have passed a law that we cannot gamble. Is this how you treat friends?"

The Modocs muttered their agreement.

Meacham appeared unruffled. "I am aware of some of these problems, Jack. I have dismissed the bad agents. Everything will change for the better."

Kentapoos eyed Captain Knapp. "You have sent away our friend, Applegate. We do not know this soldier, Knapp. More reason for us to stay here."

Meacham's jaw tightened. "Be reasonable, Jack. Life can be good on the reservation. I will see to it that we keep our part of the bargain. You have my word on it."

Black Wound sprang to his feet. Anger carved his face with deep slashing lines. "GOOD? I do not see your women selling themselves to the soldiers because they cannot pay the high fort store prices! I do not see your daughters and sons becoming drunks and wife beaters because their hearts have fallen to the ground! We do not take *your* wives and daughters and make whores of them! GOOD?" He spat on the ground.

A muffled snide remark came from the back of Meacham's

men. Frank whipped his head around and glared the man into silence.

Black Wound's words cut Winema to the bone. It reminded her of the shame she felt for all that had happened on the reservation. She had been too busy with her own life. If she had moved to the reservation, could she have done something about it?

The superintendent sighed. His face sagged. "What you say is all too true. I am ashamed of the army's behavior, and offer my apologies. As I said, I have already implemented changes in these directions. There will be no more fraternization between soldiers and your women—Captain Knapp has agreed. There will be no more alcohol on the reservation. No bad meat or high prices. Your women will be treated with respect." He looked directly into Kentapoos's eyes. "Just as your chiefs cannot control some of your young men, we sometimes lose control of our young soldiers. But that is an excuse. I will see to it *personally* that soldiers will be punished severely for their transgressions."

Kentapoos groped the contents of a buckskin bag draped over his shoulder. He produced several sheaves of paper. Handing them to Meacham, he said, "I have papers to prove we mean no harm to the Whites. We can live together in peace."

Meacham took the papers and carefully read each one. They were testimonials from local ranchers and Yrekans such as Fairchild, Steele, and the Applegates as to Jack's character and peaceful behavior. The papers included the pass from Judge Roseborough.

Winema saw Kentapoos appraise the superintendent with a new level of respect. The *tyee* handled the papers respectfully, studying each one. Also, she liked his straightforward approach. He did not try to talk in circles or deny the wrongs.

Meacham handed the papers back to the chief. "I understand you mean no harm. Still, Jack, you signed the treaty in good faith. Your people ceded this land to the United States, received money and goods for it."

Kentapoos grimaced. "I signed no paper. Show me this paper, and we will go back with you."

Winema was unsure of her cousin's motives. Of course there was such a paper and he knew it. But after years of frustration and disappointment on the reservation, Winema knew Kentapoos felt the Modocs had been cheated, and she agreed. Perhaps he was betting the paper had been lost after all this time.

Meacham smiled tightly, reached into his vest pocket, and withdrew the original treaty. He handed it to Kentapoos. Winema saw this man was smarter than Kentapoos realized. He had prepared well.

"That's your mark there, below Chief Skonches's, isn't it?" Meacham prompted.

Kentapoos's face reddened. "That is not my mark." He passed it to Krelatko with disinterest.

Krelatko studied the paper. "Ih, *laki*. That is your mark." He handed it to Wieum, who agreed.

There followed a long, tense pause.

As if in concert with his mind, every feature in Kentapoos's face seemed to shift and resettle. "Very well. I am a man of my word. But I want something in return. I want to settle my people at Modoc Point. You will tell your soldiers to protect us from the *Klamat* and the *Sot*."

Winema smiled to herself. There it was. Kentapoos negotiated well. He never gave up something without getting something in return.

Meacham's face lit up. "Done. Modoc Point is on the reservation." He stood, extended his hand to Kentapoos.

Kentapoos stood slowly. The chief turned and surveyed the faces of his men, then turned back to Meacham. "And you will keep your word about the mill, and the other things."

The superintendent opened his mouth to answer but was interrupted by Kentapoos's raised palm. "Because if you cannot, *tyee*, I will not hold back my men. We will return here for the last time, and we will fight to the death."

Meacham blinked. Straightening his shoulders, he urged his hand forward. Jack took it hesitantly.

As people filed out of the tent, a grim-faced Frank stepped up to the superintendent, spoke quietly in his ear. "Meacham, these people are part of my family. So like Jack, I'll be watchin'."

Meacham looked slightly unnerved, but only for a moment. A wave of relief passed through the Meacham party. They broke into cheers, laughed, and slapped each other on the back. Winema felt a quick stab of fear. She started to wheel around and raise her arms to quell the cheering men.

Cho-ocks sprang to his feet, scowling. "LIES!"

The rest of the Modocs scrambled to their feet and readied their weapons. The air echoed with the clicking of steel springs. A sick feeling spread through Winema. She knew Modoc pride had been wounded by the rejoicing of the Whites on such a solemn occasion. Leaping to her feet, she shouted over the din, "Wait! Wait until I talk!" She moved quickly between the two parties, palming down gun barrels. "Hear me! If you shoot now, we will all be killed."

She looked at Kentapoos. "You have bargained well, cousin. The *tyee* has apologized. He has promised to punish the bad soldiers. You will be able to settle at Modoc Point, farther away from the *Klamat* villages. What can be the gain of our dying here in this cold tent? Who will see to it that these promises are kept if we are dead? Who will see to the feeding of the children?" The guns slowly bowed as she spoke. "Who will be alive to prove what has been promised here?"

She turned slowly as she spoke, her eyes moving from face to face. "I, for one, wish to live to see my son grow to be a strong man. Do you not also wish to see your sons and daughters grow? Do not be selfish, as I have been. Think of the others who depend on you, rather than of yourselves." Winema's upper body shuddered as she jabbed her finger downward. "Let not one more drop of Modoc blood be spilled on this ground!" She pulled Jeff tightly to her. Her voice quavered with emotion. "Have there not been enough broken hearts, enough broken spirits? LET IT STOP HERE!"

The damp wood on the fire hissed and popped. Outside, a piece of loose canvas whipped and snapped in the wind. Men scanned one another's faces, then the ground as all the energy seemed sucked from the tent.

Kentapoos locked eyes with Winema. Quietly he said, "Put up your guns. We leave with the sun."

But Winema saw the dark, threatening faces of Cho-ocks and Black Wound behind him. Black Wound, lingering until the last of the Modocs left the tent, approached Winema and hissed in her ear, "Who are you to speak? You, who has deserted us to live with the Whites. What do you know of our suffering? You are not Modoc. You are *boshtin kash*!"

TWENTY-EIGHT

As soon as the Modocs had retired to the village, Superintendent Meacham approached a short, balding member of his party named Leroy Dyar. "Leroy, I want you to ride up to Linkville and tell Lieutenant Calley to bring his men down here without delay. Tell them to be quiet about it and camp close by, but not out of earshot. I want them here in case of trouble."

Dyar nodded and left.

Winema overheard. She looked at Meacham accusingly. "Soldiers are coming?"

The superintendent adopted a reassuring tone and expression. "Oh, just a precaution, Winema. I plan on a quiet evening and a peaceful departure in the morning."

Winema regarded him a moment. Although she saw no deception in his eyes, she was alarmed and annoyed about the secreted soldiers.

Frank put his arm around her. "I'm sure he's just doing his job." In her ear he whispered, "We'll keep an eye on him."

The Riddles enjoyed a pleasant meal and good conversation with Meacham and his party. Albert told many interesting stories regarding his travels and relations with other tribes in the Midwest and the Plains. Leaning closer to Frank, Winema said, "This one is a good talker. I like what he says."

Frank nodded. "He's been around Indians a lot longer than most. Seems to respect our ways."

Winema grinned. Her eyes danced with pleasure.

Frank regarded her with a curious smile. "What?"

"You said *our*."

Frank massaged his beard. "Guess I did."

Meacham cleared his throat. "So, Winema, how do you like living in the civilized world."

An unexpected tone of condescension crept into Meacham's voice. She should have expected it.

"There is good and bad, *tyee*."

She had adjusted to this quirk in Whites. She supposed some meant well, but it only reinforced her theory as to the White's poor upbringing.

Frank interrupted her thoughts. "We better get some shut-eye, *Ena*. Be a long day tomorrow."

"*Ih*."

Meacham stood, yawned, and stretched. "Good idea. Think I'll turn in, too."

As the group made preparations for bed, Winema watched Frank tuck another blanket around Charka, then whisper something that made the boy giggle. A weary smile tugged at the corners of her mouth. Teasing was an Indian-like attribute of Frank's that she loved.

As she prepared their bedrolls, she reflected on the past weeks. Though White culture had some rough spots, overall she saw many good reasons for White and Indian cultures to commingle. They could learn from each other. But so far, the learning was one-sided. As she lay down to sleep, all she could think of were Black Wound's cutting words—"You are not Modoc. You are *boshtin kash*!"

～

BARKING dogs across the river startled Winema awake. She felt that sudden alertness coupled with the slide of dread she had so often experienced when Kalelk was raided by the *Alamimakts*. Then, galloping hooves, loud whoops, and clanking sabers filled the night air. She grabbed her fur coat and rushed out of the tent, followed by the others. A sun-bright moon hung overhead, casting a ghostly light on twenty rowdy soldiers milling about on horseback, hooting and shouting.

Albert Meacham and Captain Knapp ran up to the young officer in charge. "What is the meaning of this, Lieutenant?" Meacham growled. "My orders were explicit!"

Lieutenant Ephram Calley weaved in his saddle, then tipped his hat. "Eve'nin, Mr. Meacham, Captain," he slurred sheepishly. "Guess we spent too much time at . . ." He scratched his head, then turned to one of his men. "Sergeant Murphy, what was the, ah, name of that grog shop?"

"Keenan's, sir!"

Calley returned his bleary gaze to his superiors. "Yeah, Keenan's, that was it." The shavetail lieutenant tried to sit erect, attempting a more military bearing, but had to clutch his pommel for support. "Anyway, sir, we're here and ready to fight."

Winema couldn't see Captain Knapp's face in the dark, but his tone, while low, was scathing. "You idiot! I—"

Shouts and sounds of whinnying horses from Kentapoos's camp interrupted Knapp's invective.

Frank looked across the river. "Damnit. Now we got trouble."

THE Modoc village leaped into action. There was no mistaking the sound of charging soldiers. Before rushing from his lodge, Kentapoos clasped Green Basket's shoulder. "Stay! The soldiers will not harm you with Winema and Tchmu'tcham here."

Laughs Loud's eyes widened in apprehension. "But where will you go, Father?"

"To the land-of-burnt-out-fires, into the caves. We will make our plans there." He turned to Green Basket. "Join us when you can."

Once outside, Kentapoos shouted orders to scatter, and to meet in the big cave.

Black Wound hurried by, then stopped short. "Did I not warn you?"

Kentapoos scowled in embarrassment. "Get on your horse and ride!"

Situated just south of Tule Lake, the lava beds were a favored hunting ground for the Modocs. Each man knew its terrain like the curves of his wife's body.

≈

WINEMA spent the remainder of the night in Kalelk, working hard at calming and reassuring the remaining Modoc women and children. The following morning she and Green Basket trudged through the snow, across the ice-covered river, and into Meacham's camp. She found the superintendent talking with Frank, Captain Knapp, and Lieutenant Calley. The men huddled around a blazing campfire, warming their hands and bodies with cupfuls of steaming coffee.

Seeing Winema and Green Basket approaching, Frank walked to them. "You all right? It was a cold night."

"*Ih*, Tchmu'tcham," Winema replied.

His eyes shifted to Green Basket. "You and Laughs Loud getting along all right?"

She nodded.

Winema grabbed Frank's sleeve. "I am taking her to see Meacham. She is worried for Kentapoos. She thinks she can talk him into coming back if we promise no harm will come to him. I think she is right. I wish to go with her."

Frank's brow furrowed as he massaged the back of his neck. His gaze shifted to Green Basket, then back to Winema. "You think it's safe?"

"*Ih*. I will be fine."

Frank's mouth tightened into a thin line. "I don't know. . . ."

Winema touched his arm. "They would not dare harm me."

Frank gave in. "All right. But if y'all ain't back in two hours, we're comin' to get you."

Presented with Green Basket's offer, Meacham readily accepted. Within minutes the two women mounted and loped off toward the desolate lava beds. Riding along the high, steep ridge parallel to the beds, Winema stared down at the flat, snow-covered expanse of rock and sagebrush in the valley below. A pale, halberd moon still lolled in the morning sky. She couldn't help remembering the first time she brought Frank and Whitey out here. Whitey had made a face, shook his head, and said, "Next to the Humboldt Valley, that's the forlornest stretch of snagrock and sagebrush I ever seen."

Covering what little color the vegetation had offered, the blanket of fresh snow added to the sense of bleakness. Now, only a wide, flat basin of white interrupted the rough, angry ridges of lava rock. From this height, narrow coulees and fissures, half filled with snow, looked like the dark pencil lines Charka scribbled on paper.

But Winema saw another dimension of this place. It was a source of sustenance for the People, a place fertile with game, and ceremonial sage. It was the home of the cave of the Old Ones, that mysterious place of ancient whispers. And it provided a last refuge for the People in case of overwhelming enemy odds. Here, Modoc warriors could fend off any number of enemies, even *shuldshash* if necessary.

During the ride, Winema glanced at Green Basket and wondered what might be going through her mind. Kentapoos's first wife was eight winters older than Winema. A stoic and proud woman, her mouth maintained a perpetual straight line. A competent wife and doting mother, she kept to herself, preferring Kentapoos's company, or that of Likes-the-Shade, her hand-picked choice for Kentapoos's new second wife. To Winema's frustration, Green Basket maintained a barrier between herself and Winema. Kentapoos had shrugged it off when Winema asked him about it. But he was a man, oblivious to such things.

While Green Basket lacked personality, she wasn't stupid. Shade, at only fifteen winters, was the direct opposite. She giggled and blushed her way through life. She worshipped her husband and was slavishly loyal to Green Basket. It worked out well and Laughs Loud particularly liked it. Shade always let her have her way. They made a close and happy family.

Winema's attention shifted to the dicey trail ahead. Slowly, carefully, the two women picked their way down the side of the ridge, onto the valley floor, past razor-sharp ridges of the dark rock the Whites called basalt, then up the worn trail that wound through the natural pumice parapets, and finally to the caves.

"Ho! *Doly kana*?" a hidden voice shouted.

The women reined up. Green Basket shouted, "It is your chief's wife and cousin, you silly fool! Where do you *think* we're going?"

Bogus Charley, the sentry, begrudgingly allowed entry. Winema and Green Basket found Kentapoos and his council gathered around a small sagebrush fire halfway into the dim, chilly cave. He hustled over as they dismounted. "Where are the other women?"

"At Kalelk. The soldiers found and took the remaining guns. They will not let us go. We are to return to Modoc Point with them."

Kentapoos cursed.

"There is more, cousin," Winema said, then elbowed Green Basket.

Green Basket's face reflected a tired, almost pleading expression. "Come back with us, husband. The soldiers meant no harm. They were crazy from whiskey. Besides, there were only twenty of them."

Kentapoos's eyes widened in disbelief. "Only twenty?" He looked to Winema for confirmation. She nodded.

"Arghh! We are forty-three," he said between gritted teeth. "We ran from such a small enemy?" Again he cursed, then kicked a loose rock. It sailed into the air and clattered down the opposite cave wall.

Winema looked at her cousin with understanding eyes. "*Maklaka ditche hamkuk loke stinas mona gambla otwe.* The White chief talks right. His heart is good. Go with him now."

Wheeling around, Kentapoos stomped to the far end of the cave and stood there. Whusum, Skonches's unfaithful brother, watched him, then jogged over to join him. Winema shivered, hugged herself. The open mouth of the cave created a draft that blew a frigid wind against her back. She and Green Basket shuffled closer to the fire. Winema worried that Black Wound would be here, but he was nowhere in sight. One of the sentries, no doubt. She was in no mood for him tonight.

She felt comfortable, however, with the men huddling around the fire—until Cho-ocks appeared from the cave's darkness, buttoning his trousers. He stopped short when he saw her. Elbowing his way into the group around the fire, he glared at Winema. She glared back, wondering what treacherous counsel he had pressed upon her cousin. His reptile-like eyes penetrated her very spirit. She felt the snake of fear coil in her belly. No doubt he was not the only one of these men who saw her as a traitor, and would kill her if given the chance.

Cho-ocks fingered the handle of his knife, then he slunk away to be with Kentapoos and Whusum. Winema breathed a sigh of relief, then smiled at Krelatko, Lodge Woman's husband. Lodge Woman was with child again. Winema hoped this birth might mellow him enough to settle down on the reservation. Her gaze shifted to young Wieum. The diminutive, sad-eyed man was no warrior. Staring into the fire, he looked cold and miserable. As Frank aptly put it, Wieum was a "home and hearth" man. Forever loyal to Kentapoos, Winema thought his White name, William Faithful, fit him perfectly.

Rising on her tiptoes, she strained to glimpse Kentapoos. He still paced and argued with Whusum and Cho-ocks at the far end of the cave. They gestured at each other with sharp, pointed motions. She worried about her cousin. The Waterbrash was a reasonable man—proud and rebellious, yes—but not prone to rashness. He usually thought things out. He changed, however, when he kept company with Cho-ocks, Black Wound, and Whusum. With them he acted strangely, more distant, harder to reason with. These three were men whose hearts were tainted, men who loved war more than peace. And, whether she liked it or not, men who were influential in council. Kentapoos needed their support as long as he maintained his burning desire to replace Skonches.

Loose rock crunched under moccasined feet, signaling Kentapoos's return. Whusum and Cho-ocks remained in the shadows. The chief took Winema by the arm and walked to a private area of the cave. "Tell Meacham I never wanted a fight. It was the soldiers who made this trouble. We will go back with him if he promises not to tell the *Klamat* I ran from such a small party of soldiers. Tell Meacham to shoot three times into the air if he agrees."

Winema closed her eyes and silently thanked *Kemush*. She was, however, disappointed with the pettiness of her cousin's concern. Pride sometimes dulled his sharp mind.

Green Basket and Winema made it back to Meacham's camp with only a few minutes to spare from the two-hour deadline. Meacham agreed to Kentapoos's demand. Three shots soon echoed across the shadowed vale.

THE trek back to the reservation, and on to Modoc Point was peaceful. Winema and Jeff stayed with her family a few days to make sure things quieted down. They lodged with Aunt Kweelush. The elderly woman was getting on in years and her eyesight was failing.

Frank returned to the ranch. The stock needed tending. Superintendent Meacham returned to Salem. And Captain Knapp holed up in his office like a bear in its winter den, seldom emerging other than for emergencies.

Skonches and his people joined Kentapoos. Almost like old times, it felt good to be back in a village: the familiar smells of the cookpots, the idle gossip, the shouts and laughter of children at story time, and time to chat with Lodge Woman and Wild Girl. Delighted with Winema's decision, Jeff went hunting with Kentapoos, and played with his cousins.

That evening Winema's family packed into Kweelush's

latch. Cold winter nights were made for storytelling, and when
Winema's turn came, Charka led the shouts for the story of
Gaukos and *Kulta*. Winema held out her arm with one finger
extended and swept it over their heads. The children quieted,
and she began. Basking in the warm afterglow of home and
family, she gave the story her best performance.

"To this day," Winema summed up to the rapt audience,
"*Gaukos* travels, and will always travel. You can see *Weketas*,
for *Gaukos* still carries her in his bosom. Sometimes you can
see *Weketas*'s children reclining near her. When *Subbas*, the
sun, comes and *Gaukos* is still in the west, he gets eaten up by
the big-mouthed people, who live on the far side of the lake.
But Weketas always brings him to life, and will do so just as
long as he carries her in his bosom."

The story finished, the adults followed the children, who
were giddy from sitting too long, and rushed outside to see
Gaukos. The winter sky stretched from horizon to horizon like
an endless bolt of deep, blue cloth stitched with shards of
shimmering crystals. *Gaukos* did not let them down. He shone
with a dazzling brilliance, painting the stark winter landscape
with ghostly light.

They watched the stars late into the night, sending puffs of
frosted breath skyward as if exchanging their breath for
Gaukos's light. No one seemed to notice the cold. It had been
a wonderful day of stories, good food, and happy reminis-
cences.

Winema spotted Kentapoos and made her way to him.
"What did the agent say as you rode with him?"

Kentapoos pulled his fur collar closer around his neck. "He
said he will bring us the tools to make logs and rails for our
own skinned-tree houses, and for a council house. Also, he will
bring big wagons, lum-br wagons."

Winema nodded. "That is good, cousin. I trust this *tyee*,
Meacham. I think he will help us."

"Perhaps, cousin. But he is in Salem town and Knapp is
here. I think Knapp wishes to fight us. He is a soldier, not a
blanket *tyee*."

They stood side-by-side for some time, watching the stars, each with his private thoughts. Winema felt reasonably secure for a change. The new superintendent and Captain Knapp seemed trustworthy men. The *Klamat* would be controlled. The treaty rations and money would arrive.

For now, the world seemed a hopeful place again.

TWENTY-NINE

"YOU'RE TWO MONTHS late, Frank. But I'm glad to see you." Nathan Hopkins relaxed his frown and smiled down at Jeff. "And it's grand to see you, my boy, just grand. You are going to like school." Nathan winked. "I can say that because I am the teacher."

Nathan guided Jeff to the front of the one-room school-house, bragging on the recently rebuilt chimney and the two new windows that had arrived from San Francisco just in time for the start of the term. Inside, at the far right of the room, a rust-stained, potbellied stove moaned, straining to heat the room. Eighteen students sat on two rows of benches and gawked at the new boy. Wide-eyed, a blond girl's hand flew to cover her mouth as she reacted to Jeff's swarthy complexion, high cheekbones, and black hair. But a freckle-faced boy with curly red hair donned a friendly grin.

"Boys and girls, this is Jeff Riddle. He will be joining us starting today, and I want all of you to assist him in any way you can."

There was an uncomfortable stillness as Nathan showed Jeff to an empty desk at the right rear. Nathan's eyes narrowed at Seth Wright, a boy with dark stringy hair, sitting one row over, when he noticed him scowl at Jeff.

Having seated the newest student with a reassuring squeeze

of the shoulder, Nathan walked Frank to the back door, his arm
around Frank's shoulder. "He'll be fine, Frank. You'll see." He
winked. "He might even learn something."

Frank frowned as he buttoned his coat. "We'll see, Eyes.
He's here 'cause you'd give me no peace until I brought him."
Frank fixed his eyes on his old partner. "Remember. This is just
a tryout," he said, then put on his hat and muttered, "I never
saw much in schoolin', myself," and left.

❦

JEFF looked at the White faces with a mix of excitement and
trepidation. He had had little contact with White children. His
playmates consisted mostly of Modoc friends and cousins. He
looked forward to new playmates, wondered what they did for
fun, what games they played, what they talked about. Yet there
was that familiar feeling of unease; the way they looked at him.
He knew he looked different. But then he was always the
different one among his Modoc friends.

Jeff thought of the few times when some of the Modoc
children teased him about being White. He had even scuffled
with a couple of the boys over the issue. But for the most part
he felt accepted. Would it be the same here?

At the dinner break the redheaded boy introduced himself.
"Howdy. I'm Isaac Weiss."

Jeff shook the boy's hand.

"So you're new in these parts, huh?" Isaac asked as he bit
into a large red apple.

"Nope. Been here all along. We got a ranch over by Bogus
Creek."

Isaac looked surprised. "Never seen you in town before."

Jeff shrugged. "We don't go to town much."

Isaac nodded and studied his apple, then, "Are you really an
Injun?"

Jeff nodded. "Yep. Well, both White and Injun."

"Gosh. Never had an Injun friend before."

Jeff arched his eyebrows. "And I ain't never had a White
friend before."

The boys looked at each other a moment, then laughed. Isaac stood. "C'mon. Let's go outside a spell. We got ten minutes yet. I'll show you my hideout."

The boys raced for the coatracks next to the door when Scowling Boy jutted out his leg. Jeff saw it too late, tripped, and sprawled onto the plank floor, smacking his chin. The room exploded into laughter. The commotion quickly brought Mr. Hopkins to the scene. He helped Jeff to his feet. "Are you all right, Jeff?"

Jeff nodded as he massaged his chin. He gave Scowling Boy a cold stare. Mr. Hopkins followed Jeff's gaze. "Seth. Did you have anything to do with this?"

Seth feigned surprise. "Me? No, sir. I can't help it if he's clumsy."

Jeff looked at his teacher. "It's all right, Mr. Hopkins. Can Isaac and me go outside now?"

Mr. Hopkins stroked his chin. "Go ahead. But stay close and listen for the bell. Especially you, Isaac. The last thing you need is more tardies."

"Yes, sir," Isaac blurted. "I mean, no, sir," as he and Jeff made for the door.

After the boys inspected Isaac's hideout in a nearby thicket, Jeff asked, "Who is that big, mean kid?"

Isaac frowned. "Seth Wright. Watch out for him. He's big and he's mean."

Jeff pushed his hands into his coat pockets as they walked. "What's he got against me? He doesn't even know me yet."

Isaac took two quick steps and glided on a patch of ice. "He knows you're Injun, and that's all he needs to know."

Jeff looked into the distance. "Well, I'm used to that—bein' different and all."

Isaac said, "Yeah, me, too."

Jeff scrunched his brow in confusion. "You ain't different from him."

Isaac kneeled down to inspect a colorful rock. He worked it back and forth until he extracted it from the winter-hardened ground. "'Cause I'm Jewish."

Jeff looked even more confused. "Jewish?"

Isaac inspected the rock closely. "It's a religion."

Jeff looked over Isaac's shoulder at the rock. "My ma says religion is personal business. Ain't nobody's business what your religion is."

Isaac chuckled. "I like your ma already," then, "Hey! Look! It's gold!"

"Let me see." Jeff scrutinized the rock. "Nah. Just fool's gold."

Isaac frowned. "How do you know? It *might* be real gold."

Jeff shook his head. "My pa was a miner. He taught me."

Isaac looked disappointed but pocketed the rock anyway.

In afterthought, Jeff said, "Bet ya didn't know Mr. Hopkins was my pa's partner?"

Isaac's mouth dropped open. "Noo."

Jeff smiled smugly. "Yep."

They walked on in silence, then Isaac looked thoughtful. "Seth Wright's Pa was kilt by Injuns. They say the Modocs cut off his nuts whilst he was still alive."

Jeff stopped in his tracks. Isaac took two more steps before he noticed his new friend's absence. He turned to face Jeff. "What's wrong?"

Somewhere deep in the recesses of Jeff's mind the name Wright was familiar. He didn't know why, but it was an uncomfortable recollection. He decided it best to say no more about it. To Isaac or anyone else.

By the fourth week of school Jeff was depressed. He missed being outdoors, helping his father with the stock and playing with his cousins when they visited. To make things worse, school had caused him to miss the birthing of a new filly. While Jeff liked Mr. Hopkins well enough, he disliked all the rules, the drills, and being tutored by kids younger than himself. Mostly, he hated sitting still. The other kids were all right. Other than asking silly questions about Indians—some of which shocked him in their absurdity—they kept to their own. One boy asked Jeff if it were true that Modocs were devil worshipers, and one girl was convinced Indians were cannibals. But Isaac was different. Isaac seemed more interested in Jeff as a person and they had become fast friends.

Not soon enough it was Friday again, and three o'clock. Jeff and Isaac scrambled out the schoolhouse door just ahead of Seth Wright.

His breath clouding the cold air, Isaac said, "Hey. Before we head for home, let's play at the hideout for a spell."

Jeff needed no encouragement. He felt cramped up after several torturous hours folded into his oak desk.

"I'll race ya!" Jeff challenged, and the boys sprinted toward Isaac's thicket several hundred yards from the schoolhouse. Jeff, used to racing his cousins, lead by five horse lengths by the time they reached the thicket.

"Man alive. You sure can run," Isaac panted as he bent over and rested his hands on his knees to catch his breath.

Jeff was barely breathing hard. He chuckled. "You gotta be a good runner if you want to keep up with Modocs."

They ducked into the thicket and sat a moment until Isaac caught his breath. Then a curious smile crossed Isaac's lips as he fished in his pocket and produced a corncob pipe. From the other pocket he pulled out a small cotton tie-bag of tobacco and a box of sulfur matches. He arched his eyebrows up and down conspiratorially. "How 'bout a smoke?"

Jeff replied, "Sure. We'll smoke to our new friendship."

Isaac looked at Jeff curiously. "That's a good a reason as any. Mostly it's just that there ain't no grown-ups around to whip us if we *do*."

Jeff made a face. "*Whip* us. Why would they do that?"

Isaac gave Jeff an incredulous stare. "You mean your folks wouldn't whip you if they caught you smokin'?"

Jeff looked taken aback. "Hell, no. My folks would never whip me. Besides, Modocs smoke pipes all the time."

Suddenly Jeff looked alert and cocked an ear. "Somebody's comin'," he whispered. "Did you invite anybody to the hideout?"

Isaac frowned. "Nobody knows about it but you."

Seth Wright's adolescent voice cut through the air. "Hey,

Injun! Come on outta there. We wanna talk to you." Recently Seth's voice had started to vacillate between a child's and a man's and had the habit of breaking into a high falsetto.

Jeff and Isaac looked at each other. Isaac shot out his hand to stay Jeff. "Don't go out there. We can sneak out the back."

Jeff shook his head. "My pa and my uncle taught me to run from no man."

Before Isaac could protest further, Jeff got up and made his way out the thicket entrance. Isaac followed timidly behind. Two other boys from the school, one wearing a shabby, patched duster and the other a ripped tan hat, stood next to Seth. At the age of twelve Seth was a good three inches taller and twenty pounds heavier than Jeff. Stringy black hair framed a face so fair it was almost transparent. He held his hands behind his back and stood with his feet wide apart. It was obvious from his posture, his smirk, and his half-lidded eyes that he was not there to smoke a pipe of friendship.

"We *here* are the Anti-Injun Committee," Seth announced. "We don't want no dirty, scalp-lickin', back-stabbin' Injuns in our school. Especially *grubby, root-diggin'* Modocs." Seth managed to increase his sneer on every adjective.

Jeff stiffened but held his temper. He wasn't afraid of Seth Wright, but neither did he want to cause trouble between Mr. Hopkins and his pa by fighting at school.

Jeff eyed the boy while watching for any hint of movement by his cohorts. "I don't like goin' to school any more than you do. How 'bout we just keep outta each other's way? Ain't no reason for name-callin'."

With a menacing smile, Seth moved closer, his hands still hidden behind his back. "Why, shore. And we can all be ol' friends, can't we, boys?" he said in a syrupy voice as he glanced at his two friends. His head jerked back to Jeff. "Why, maybe I could even take ya home to dinner with me. That'd be *real* nice, wouldn't it, boys?"

Isaac blurted from the thicket entrance. "You leave him alone, Seth. He didn't do you no harm."

Seth looked over Jeff's shoulder. "Well, now. We gotta Jew-boy and an Injun. Quite a catch, huh, boys?"

Shabby Duster and Ripped Hat snickered.

Seth gave Isaac a cold stare. "We'll take care of you in a minute."

Jeff squinted at Seth. "Like I said, there ain't no reason for name-callin'."

Seth shifted ice-blue eyes back to Jeff. "You're right, Injun."

Jeff sensed Seth's sudden movement and stepped back. An ax handle suddenly appeared in Seth's right hand. In a blur, it whooshed down and struck Jeff on the left shoulder, just missing his head. The jolt brought Jeff down to one knee. Isaac yelled and ducked back into the thicket, closely followed by Seth's helpers.

Lightning bolts of pain shot through Jeff's shoulder and neck. He threw himself forward, grabbing one of Seth's legs, hoping to bring him down. But Seth backed away and swung the ax handle down again. It struck Jeff across his upper back, the force sprawling him to the cold ground.

He heard Seth shouting, "That'll learn ya, you stinkin' Injun! This one's for my pa!"

Jeff felt the wind rush from his lungs as Seth's hard-toed boot smashed into his side. Once, twice, three times. Jeff couldn't get his breath. Unbelievable pain shot up and down his back, shoulder, and rib cage. He heard Isaac screaming, "No, stop, ahh!"

Now Seth's voice was in his ear, his mouth only an inch away. "You dogshit Injun. If I ever see you again, I'll *kill* ya. You hear?"

The ax handle came down again. Jeff writhed in pain, then there was darkness.

JEFF was confused. As the fuzziness diminished he saw that he lay on a bed in a strange room. He felt as if he'd been trampled by a team of mules. Every inch of his body ached, especially the back of his head. He could hardly bear to move.

"Thank God. You had me worried, young man."

Turning his head, a tiny woman with orange-red hair swam into view. A concerned smile graced her angular face, which was sprinkled with hundreds of tiny freckles. She looked remarkably like Isaac. With a damp cloth she reached over and gently mopped his face. "I'm Mrs. Weiss, Isaac's mother. You're at our place."

"How'd I—" Jeff blinked several times. "I don't remember how I got here."

Mrs. Weiss neatly laid the cloth over the lip of a porcelain washbasin. "When Isaac was late coming home, I sent his brother, Aaron, looking for him. Aaron found both of you, and so here you are."

The scene at the hideout flashed into Jeff's mind with the vividness of a lightning storm. "Where *is* Isaac? Is he all right?"

"Isaac will be fine. Just a few bruises. He and Aaron rode over to your place to get your folks."

The freckle-faced lady sighed. "As for you, Dr. Wilkins is on his way. I want to make sure you don't have anything broken." She brushed damp hair from his forehead. Her fingers were warm and gentle, and she smelled of flour and blueberries. "You took an awful beating, hun." Her lips tightened. "If I get my way, that Wright boy will be expelled. And his friends, too."

She helped Jeff sit up, fluffed his pillow, and presented a steaming bowl. It smelled wonderful.

"Now you eat this, Jeff. You will feel much better if you get Mamma Weiss's chicken soup inside you."

The soup's aroma started his stomach growling. Mrs. Weiss fed him a spoonful. He had never tasted anything so good.

❦

WINEMA reined up in front of the Weiss house, tied off the lines, jumped down from the wagon, and was onto the porch in a blur of motion. She knocked on the door, but Isaac had dismounted behind her and ran to open it for her. A petite redhead flowed out of a back room, her bony hand extended.

"You must be Mrs. Riddle."

Winema took her hand but was looking around for Jeff.

"Jeff's back here. He's doing fine."

Winema heard Jeff call from behind the half-open door, "Ma? I'm in here, Ma."

Winema rushed into the bedroom and to her son's side. She leaned over and cupped Jeff's hand in her own. "Are you hurt bad, *gaw oonok*?"

"Aw, I'm all right, Ma. It hurts a might when I move around."

But Winema could tell from his face that he was hurting. She couldn't help a swell of pride that he did not complain.

Jeff perked a little. "Ma, Mrs. Weiss gave me this soup. You gotta taste it. You never tasted anythin' so good in you're *en*tire life."

Mrs. Weiss laughed. "Now that's a young man who's welcome at my table any time."

Winema smiled at the White woman. "Thank you for helping my son."

Mrs. Weiss waved her off. "Think nothing of it. I'm sure you would've done the same for Isaac. Please, call me Ruth."

Winema nodded. "I am Winema."

"Glad to know ya, Winema."

Dr. Wilkins arrived and after examining Jeff said to Winema, "That's one tough young'un you have. But I'm afraid that ax handle left some nasty bruises on his back and sides. There's also quite a lump on the back of his head. He has two badly bruised ribs from what I can tell. I gave him some laudanum. He's going to be mighty sore for a couple of weeks. I suggest he get plenty of bed rest for the next few days. No heavy chores or running around."

Winema thanked the doctor. She didn't know what to do about payment. She'd never dealt with a White doctor. "If you come to our place, my husband will give you a horse."

Dr. Wilkins held up a hand. "No, no. That's way too much. I'll see your husband in town next month. We'll settle up then."

He made his good-byes and left.

Ruth clapped her hands together. "Well. I guess Isaac can keep Jeff company while we ladies have a cup of coffee. How 'bout it, Winema?"

Unaccustomed to such hospitality from White strangers— especially from White women—Winema smiled cautiously, then followed Ruth to the kitchen. The Weiss's home was small but immaculate. It was full of blue and red glassware, porcelain figurines, and family photos, many of which were taken in strange-looking places. Winema was attracted to a tall, narrow cabinet with a glass door. It contained a beautiful jeweled goblet and a metal candleholder with nine branches.

Ruth said, "That Elisha cup and menorah belonged to my great-grandmother. They came all the way from Romania." She spoke each word methodically.

Winema understood that it was an important family heirloom, but the terms *menorah* and *Romania* were a mystery. She nodded and muttered an appropriate, "Ahh," then said, "I speak good English, Ruth."

Ruth pinked slightly. "I'm sorry. I just remember how much trouble *I* had with it."

Winema's eyes formed question marks. She had noticed a strange accent in Ruth's speech.

Ruth continued, "We came to this country when I was six. And we only arrived here in California a year ago."

"From the place"—Winema fished for the word Ruth used earlier—"Ro-many?"

Ruth nodded enthusiastically, pleased Winema remembered. "Yes, yes. It is across the ocean."

Winema was fascinated. She'd not met anyone who had come across the great water. She brimmed with questions, but it was rude to flood a new acquaintance with such. She would wait until they knew each other better. Ruth showed Winema to a kitchen chair and poured two cups of coffee. "You know, this isn't the first time we've had trouble with that Wright boy."

Ruth sat across from Winema, secured a muffin tin with a potholder, and began plucking out fat blueberry muffins fresh out of the oven.

Winema frowned. "What was fight about?"

Ruth popped out the last muffin and looked at Winema sadly. "I'm afraid it was about Jeff being Indian."

Winema's jaw tightened as she nodded.

Ruth studied Winema's face as if waiting for something more. Then she sighed and smiled pensively. Her voice dropped, almost a whisper. "Of course." Ruth gazed into Winema's eyes with sudden understanding. "You are not surprised, are you?"

Winema shook her head.

Ruth went on, "It's something he will have to deal with his whole life. It's something Isaac—all of us—understand all too well."

Ruth served her guest two muffins. Winema sipped her coffee, then looked curiously at Ruth. "All of us?"

"Jews." She appraised Winema a moment. "I guess I really mean *you* and us. *Any* of us who are different."

Winema nodded. "Ahh. Like the Chinamen, too."

Ruth arched her eyebrows as if impressed with this thoughtful inclusion. "Yes. Like the Chinamen, too."

Passing a bowl of thick, yellow butter to Winema, Ruth smiled. "Winema, I think you and I are going to get on just fine."

THIRTY

The SEASON-OF-*WITSDUK* waned and the snow began to melt, leaving the grass gray and closely pressed from its long sleep. Kentapoos rose early, anxious to begin the tree cutting. After the morning meal everyone gathered to watch the preparations. The agent had promised to help with the lumber wagons but never came. Men struggled with nervous teams of horses, tangled harnesses, and confounding double trees, delaying their departure considerably. Now Kentapoos was relieved that two of the men had learned to use the gear from their ranch-hand experience.

Since Modoc Point consisted mostly of grassland, the men would have a long ride to reach the place of the tall pines. As they made final preparations to leave, a soldier trotted into camp. Kentapoos and Skonches approached him.

"Cap'n Knapp wanted you t'know the treaty was finally signed in Washington," the beefy sergeant intoned in a rolling brogue. He wore low reddish sideburns and his eyebrows were heavy and as white as cornsilk. "The rest o' your goods and money will be here the first o' the month."

Skonches looked pleased. He thanked the soldier. Kentapoos remained silent, turned and returned to the lumber wagon. The sergeant shrugged and rode off.

Skonches caught up with Kentapoos. "Why do you act in such a way? Finally we will receive what is owed to us."

Kentapoos pulled himself up into the wagon seat, then looked down at Skonches. "They are five winters late." He untangled the traces. "If you think hard, Uncle, you will see the money they promised will be divided among *all* the *mak-laks* here. There will be little money left, *that* you can believe. As for the rest . . . we shall see."

Without another glance at the elder *laki*, Kentapoos gave a shout over his shoulder to his wood-cutting party. He snapped the lines, and the wagon creaked to life, leaving Skonches standing alone.

—

AT the wood-cutting place the afternoon of the first day and the morning of the second went well. Several large stacks of cut rails and planks lay neatly piled on the ground. Around midday Kentapoos heard riders approaching. He shielded his eyes as he squinted at the trotting forms, then frowned as he recognized a large party of *Klamat*.

They were well armed and drove three wagons similar to the Modocs'. Stopping beside the piles, they dismounted and, without speaking, began to load the lumber into their wagons. Kentapoos took a stance, folded his arms, and waited for the *Klamat* leader to approach.

A hard-looking man with a high-crowned hat, sleepy eyes, and a smirk on his face swaggered over to Kentapoos. His right hand rested on the handle of a Navy Colt tucked inside his woven belt. Two belligerent-looking armed guards flanked him. He appraised the Modoc chief with squinted eyes.

"I am Link River Jim. This is my land. You have no business cutting my trees down. This is not your country." He made a sweeping gesture with his hand. "The grass, water, fish, fowl, deer, and everything else belongs to me." The smirk faded and he pointed to the lumber. "I will take those rails." The *Klamat* tapped his chest with his fist. "My agent will protect me and my people."

Kentapoos barely contained his outrage. "Your chief, Allen David, promised we would be left alone."

Link River Jim shrugged. "He is old. Tule Lake is your home. Go there and live, and do what you please."

Kentapoos stood his ground though his grip tightened around his ivory-handled knife. Black Wound, Hakar, and Cho-ocks now joined him. They carried Spencers. Kentapoos returned the *Klamat*'s threatening scowl. "I am not afraid of you, but I promised the agent I would not fight you."

Link River scoffed. The *Klamat* guards cocked their rifles. Black Wound and Hakar followed suit. The seven men glared at each other. Kentapoos did a slow burn as he continued to finger his knife. But he had promised Meacham and Winema he would not fight with the *Klamat*. Turning his back on Link River Jim, he faced his own men. "We will quit for now. He looked at Whusum, now his sub-chief. "You and I will go see the agent, *atui*. The rest of you, return to the village."

Black Wound sputtered, "But what of the wood?"

"Leave it."

Kentapoos turned and eyed the sneering *Klamath*. "We will be back."

On the way to the *Klamath* agency office, Whusum frowned. "You think it will do any good, complaining again to 'Blanket' Knapp?"

Kentapoos looked straight ahead. The creases in his brow seemed more deeply set over the past two winters, as did the crow's-feet etched into the corners of his eyes. "What choice do we have, for now?"

Whusum studied his chief's face. "During the lily seed time, after the *Klamat* drove our women from *Klamat* Lake with rocks and sticks, the blanket man said he would see that we were not pestered again."

Kentapoos only grunted and set his jaw. He was remembering the *Klamat*'s constant slurs and obscenities the People had swallowed over the past months. "Cowards," they had called them. Cowards for abandoning *Mowatoc* when *they* gave up their lands without so much as a whimper.

An hour later they reined up in front of Captain Knapp's office. Kentapoos spilled his story, but Knapp seemed self-absorbed. He half-listened, then looked up from his paperwork. "Move your people up Williamson River a few miles. The *Klamaths* won't bother you there." He made a waving motion with his hand. "Let your rails go, Jack, and move your people. If the *Klamaths* bother you then, I'll attend to them. But don't, by any means, fight with them." His eyes flitted back and forth between Kentapoos and the papers cluttering his desk. "Leave everything to me."

Kentapoos left feeling angry and disappointed. The sight of all those papers, and Knapp's preoccupation with them, revealed much about the man.

Whusum mounted his horse. He twisted his lips into a sarcastic frown. "If Knapp likes the Williamson so much, let *him* go there."

Kentapoos grunted approval. "Whites like Knapp put too much time and trust in their scribblings. Perhaps if the *boshtin* spent that time talking as men, looking into each other's eyes, they would see it was people who make the world work, not papers."

Whusum noised his agreement. "In time, maybe we can train him."

Kentapoos snorted at the joke. "We would starve first."

It had taken Kentapoos years to finely hone his people-reading skills. Perhaps if men like Knapp had the opportunity to observe and participate in the countless council meetings he had, they could begin to deal with Indian people like men. The Waterbrash had a sour taste in his mouth. It continued to grate that such people ruled over him. It was only because of their staggering numbers and resources that they sent him from their lodges like a submissive slave.

Kentapoos tucked away his bitter thoughts. "For now, we will do as Knapp says. Anything to get away from these *Klamat kash*."

They heeled their horses into a lope.

The Modocs could make do if left in peace, Kentapoos

thought. Not all the *Klamat* wished the Modocs ill. But until Chief David could restrain his young men, which seemed unlikely, life would be oppressive on the reservation.

✺

SUNBEAMS slanted through the wavy glass of Winema's kitchen window, bathing her and the counter in its light as she finished arranging the bouquet of fresh mayflowers in an old tin mug. Charka beamed proudly as his mother took extra care in their arrangement, then stepped back to admire them.

Aunt Kweelush watched from her chair at the kitchen table. "Ahh," she breathed, "how big they are this season." She moistened her fingers, dipped them into a bowl of sugar, then slid them into her mouth.

Lodge Woman looked on, smiling. "*Ih*. It foretells a plentiful summer and a mild winter."

Charka managed to stretch his grin another three teeth. Winema glanced at Moonlight, Lodge Woman's daughter, standing restlessly by her mother. Shifting her gaze back to her son, Winema said, "You and Moonlight go and play now. There will be only dry old woman talk in here."

The eleven-year-old looked at Moonlight out of the corner of his eye and grimaced. In English, he whispered, "Maaa. She's a girl."

Winema frowned slightly, gave her head a single sharp tilt. Charka sighed.

Moonlight bubbled, "Come, Charka. I will race you to the creek. This time I will beat you."

Charka's face clouded. "We'll see about that." He sprinted toward the door with Moonlight in hot pursuit.

Lodge Woman chuckled. "It brings back memories, does it not, Winema?"

Kweelush grinned impishly. "Not too long ago it was you and Kentapoos."

Everyone laughed.

"Now it is Frank who chases her," Lodge Woman quipped.

Winema and Lodge Woman laughed, but Kweelush sighed noisily and looked sad-eyed out the window.

Winema feigned a stern expression. "Now, Aunt Kweelush . . ." She hoped to head off any of Kweelush's complaints about Frank.

Kweelush frowned. "You see. Already you disrespect your elders the way the *boshtin* do."

"Respect goes both ways, Aunt. Besides, not all Whites are 'White.'"

Kweelush harrumphed. "If you had stayed with your own kind, favorite niece, you would know differently."

Winema tired of playing the dutiful niece. "*Tchawai.* Then you liked it when your husband was able to sell you to another man for the night? A White man, even." Her tone was more biting than she intended.

Kweelush straightened in her chair, her frown deepening. "It is not a woman's place to question her husband. Besides, you pick the worst example." Her mouth twisted into a half smile as if struck by a sudden, canny retort. "That did not happen much until the *boshtin* brought whiskey to our men. It is that poison water that brings so much grief." She drew herself up, looked triumphantly at Lodge Woman. She made a spitting noise at the floor. "May fleas nest in their eye sockets for that."

Lodge Woman remembered the rape and her husband's addiction to whiskey. "*Nent!*"

Winema bristled. "Aunt Kweelush! I *hope* you do not include my husband!"

Lodge Woman looked apprehensively at Kweelush, then blurted, "Tchmu'tcham is a very good father, Kweelush. The White fathering way is a good one. An uncle and father all in one."

Kweelush shrugged. "That is why the Creator gave children both a father *and* an uncle."

Lodge Woman looked at Winema with a defeated expression.

Winema's mouth thinned into a taut line as she appraised Kweelush. While she respected her aunt, she wanted to stifle this discussion once and for all. "I know how you feel, *gaw pinkuk-fumti*, but I will hear no more bad talk about my husband. He is a good man and he respects our ways. He is a good provider, a good father, and he shares his home and cookpot with his relations. You could ask for nothing more."

Winema's tone and expression brooked no argument. Kweelush's face pinched up like a prune, but she held her tongue.

Lodge Woman took the opportunity to change the subject. "Things are getting worse on the reservation, Winema."

"*Ih.* I have heard. Something must be done."

"What can be done? The *boshtin* will say we have already gotten what was promised us."

Winema's face hardened. "Let them eat their treaty. Either that or allow us to hunt beyond the reservation. There is no excuse for hungry children."

"Then . . . you are for war?"

"And add death to hunger?" She shook her head, sighed, and glanced out the window. "Before I take Kweelush home, I will think of something."

~

KENTAPOOS and Whusum agreed on the new location for the village, five miles north of Modoc Point on Williamson River. As Kentapoos had predicted, the amount of food rations agreed upon five years before had not even lasted the winter. Reservation game was scarce. Husbands and wives bickered. The children cried from hunger.

Early in June, Kentapoos and Skonches were startled to see Winema and Chief David leading a large contingent of *Klamat* up to the village. Skonches walked out to meet them. Though happy to see his cousin, Kentapoos was taken aback. He remained near his latch, watching.

"*Wuk lucee?*" Skonches shouted.

Winema waved back, "*Moan ditch hosoyuk! Domli ditchki?*"

Chief David and Winema reined up and dismounted. The *Klamat* chief grasped Skonches's hand. "A sign of friendship,

Skonches. We have come to take you fishing and to share what little we have."

Skonches turned to shout the good news to his people. "The *Klamat* have come to take us fishing! And they have brought food!" He stood by David and shook his hand for everyone to see, all the time eyeing Kentapoos. "Winema is with them!"

Flanked by Whusum, Black Wound, and Cho-ocks, Kentapoos's expression remained stoic, his arms folded. But curiosity poked at him like a lance point. What was Winema doing with the *Klamat*? And what were the *Klamat* up to?

Several relatives and friends hustled forward to greet Winema as the chiefs retired to Skonches's lodge. She laughed and spoke briefly with each one, finally working her way to Kentapoos.

"What by the names of the *skoksi* are you doing with those *Klamat*?" he asked.

"Doing what you men should be doing. Making peace."

"Ha!"

She ignored the rebuff. "Chief David's people are hungry, too. They want only friendship. They even brought some of their rations to share."

Kentapoos craned his neck. "I do not see Link River Jim and his whelps."

She locked eyes with him. "Of course not. Like our own troublemakers, he does not want peace. Making trouble is more manly." She paused for effect, then let her face relax a bit. "We do not need his kind. If we can bring the majority together in peace, the arrogant fools will have to give in, or be outcasts."

"Tell that to Link River Jim."

"I did."

Kentapoos's face reflected mild surprise. "You did?"

"Last night. I told him, and his pups, that any fool can see the time for quarreling between *mak'laks* is over. That now the *survival* of our race makes us as one. I told him that only the *boshtin* government wins if we kill each other, as there will be fewer rations and blankets for them to buy, and more land for them to steal."

Kentapoos's eyes sparkled as he grinned. "You said all that?" He threw his arm around her and faced his men. "Did you hear what my brave cousin told those 'Paiutes'?"

The men laughed at Kentapoos's derogatory description of the ornery *Klamat*. He looked proudly at Winema. "Again she has earned her name and a place at the council."

＜

AFTER a week of successful fishing and feasting with the *Klamat*, even Kentapoos was enjoying the conviviality and goodwill. Link River Jack and his crew remained conspicuously absent. A good deal of flirting took place among unmarried men and women during the two-week visit. Over one evening meal the topic entered the chiefs' conversation.

"We may soon have some weddings, Allen David," Skonches remarked.

"So it seems." The Klamath chief arched his eyebrows conspiratorially. "One does not shoot into a camp where his relatives sleep."

Kentapoos and Whusum frowned at Skonches. "A little grabbing under the blankets is natural, Skonches, but marriages?" Kentapoos remarked.

Skonches turned serious. "Do you know of a better way? We must live together now. If your young men have your way, we will all be killing each other and there will be no more *mak'laks* on the reservation."

Chief David noised his agreement and took another puff on his pipe. "Spoken wisely, Chief Skonches."

Whusum glared at his elder brother. "Yes, brother. And if you keep that up there will be no more Modocs, only more mouths to feed—half-breed mouths at that."

Skonches eyed his brother, then tilted his head toward Chief David. "Chief David, here, could say the same thing, could he not?"

Whusum shifted spiteful eyes to Kentapoos. "Another of your cousin's peace ideas?"

Kentapoos reddened. "Watch your tongue, Whusum. Tongues that wag too much often get bit."

Whusum got up and tromped off, muttering under his breath.

Kentapoos also stood. He gazed down at the two chiefs. "You need only control Link River Jim to keep the peace, David. Should a *Klamat* and a Modoc choose to marry as a result of the Creator's will, we must accept it. But it should not be forced."

Chief David nodded thoughtfully. He took two leisurely puffs from his *paksh* before regarding Kentapoos with sagacious eyes. "Perhaps the Creator has brought us together here for this reason. Have you considered that?"

❧

WINEMA sat in a hard chair across from Albert Meacham. He seemed to grow more uncomfortable with every tick of the big hand on his new Silas Burnham Perry wall clock. It was obvious he felt uneasy discussing business matters with a woman. She wished she had waited until their horses had recovered from the strange *nebaks*. "Epizootic" they called it. Then Frank could have accompanied her.

The sickness was raging through the farms and ranches of Siskiyou County. Frank forced bottles of fish oil down his horses' throats and bathed them with liniment, but two of their best mares had succumbed to the flulike illness. She worried about Frank and their remaining animals, but her visit here was already overdue. Starving Modocs were more important than sick horses.

Winema strained to appear calm. She had to instill within the superintendent a sense of urgency without losing her temper. "I understand about the treaty, Mee-cham, but something must be done. The People are hungry. They need winter clothing. You must do something, now."

Meacham sighed. "I am as frustrated as you, Winema. I have sent a hundred letters and telegrams to Washington. I have explained it every way I can—so that a five-year-old could

understand it. Those simpletons can say only one thing: "The
treaty has been complied with." He slapped his hand down on
his desk. "Nary a one has ever set foot on a reservation, never
met an Indian except standing in a receiving line when chiefs
are paraded through Washington on goodwill visits. Goodwill.
Ha!"

"You said the prez-dnt wants to do right by us."

"Oh, I think he does. But Mr. Grant is surrounded by buf-
foons and carpetbaggers. They'd sell their own grandmothers if
they could make a profit. And then there's General Sherman."
He looked down his nose. "*He*, my good lady, is no friend of
the Indian."

Winema thought a moment. "Then we should go see the
prez-dnt. I will tell him what is happening to my people."

Meacham's eyes widened. "Well—it's not that simple. To
see the President—you see . . ." He dropped into his chair.

Winema gave him her most determined look. "Is he the
chief of all chiefs or isn't he?"

Meacham studied his desk blotter and drummed his fingers.
The wall clock ticked. Meacham cleared his throat. He studied
her face for several moments, tapping his lower lip with his
finger.

He sighed resignedly. "You have an idea, Winema. I'll see
what I can do."

~

SHORTLY after Chief David's people left, the Modocs once
again began their cutting. By late afternoon of the second day
three hundred rails awaited loading into the lumber wagons.
And once again Link River Jim and his men drove their wagons
in.

Kentapoos was furious. He and his men lined up across
from the *Klamats*.

"Lakilash *stani*!"

"Paiute filth!"

"Your mothers fornicate with dogs!"

The curses flew back and forth. But again Kentapoos

recalled his promise to allow Agent Knapp to handle the *Klamat*. He swallowed bile and held back his men. But if Knapp did not take some immediate action, Kentapoos and his men would silence the thieves forever.

For the third time Kentapoos rode to see the agent. This time he took along Bogus Charley, who spoke good English. On their arrival Captain Knapp's face twisted in annoyance when he saw Kentapoos. Stepping out onto the porch, he closed the door behind him. Kentapoos felt insulted. Now, the agent would not even allow him inside. He swallowed his pride and voiced his complaint.

Knapp's face rearranged itself into an angry scowl. "Damn you, you black son of a bitch. If you bother me any more with your gripes, I'll put you where no one will ever bother you again."

While the viciousness of the words startled Kentapoos, Knapp's attitude did not. He had heard talk about him. The man hated his job and was trying to get reassigned to an army field unit. Kentapoos had predicted correctly. Knapp was a soldier, not a bureaucrat.

Kentapoos stood with his arms folded, a smirk on his face. In English he said, "Bogus, tell this *boshtin* I am not a dog. Tell him I am a man. Tell him we won't be slaves for a race of people who are no better than us. And tell him that if he does not protect us"—He leaned forward and gave Knapp a piercing glare—"*as promised*—we will leave his reservation."

As Bogus translated, Knapp's face turned purple. He shook with rage. "Don't threaten me, you bastard. Get your red ass out of here! And be quick about it!"

Kentapoos said in Modoc, "May vultures dine in your anus."

Knapp looked wild-eyed at Bogus. "Whad' he say, whad' he say?"

Bogus smiled with mock deference. "He said his heart is heavy with sadness that he caused you anger."

Kentapoos cursed Knapp and the government all the way back to the village. He was fed up with the *Klamat*, with hungry children, with their slavelike existence on the reservation. "I have tried it the *boshtin* way. No matter what we do, we end up with dirt in our faces."

Kentapoos arrived at the village in a foul mood when he spotted his sub-chief. "Whusum! We council in my latch!"

Within minutes Whusum, Black Wound, Cho-ocks, and the rest of Kentapoos's council packed into his lodge. The Waterbrash related his meeting with Knapp. Cho-ocks waved his fist in the air. "That horse turd. I will make medicine against him. When I finish, his balls will wither to the size of beans."

"I have a better idea!" Black Wound shouted. "We go and kill him, now! I will cut off his balls before you can shrink them, *kiuks*."

There were shouts of approbation. Bolstered by their support, Kentapoos stood, shoved a fresh eagle feather in his hatband, and jammed the battered officer's hat onto his head. "It is time we leave this place. It is time we go home!"

Word raced through the village. By evening all of Kentapoos's people and three-fourths of Skonches's people wished to leave.

Skonches saw that the People had spoken. Either he could remain on the reservation as chief of the remaining thirty-five starving Modocs, or follow Kentapoos. He chose the latter.

Two suns later, 370 singing and chanting Modocs, along with their travois, dogs, and wagons headed south. They were going home.

THIRTY-ONE

WHEN FRANK RETURNED from a horse-buying trip in Salem and found out about Jeff's beating, he was furious. He paced back and forth in the kitchen shouting at Winema, at the stove, at whatever was convenient. "I'll be Goddamned if I wasn't right. I never shoulda let Eyes talk me into it!" He glared at Winema. "Didn't I tell you? And why didn't Eyes *tell* me Wright's boy was in that school?"

Winema sat at the kitchen table, scooping fresh butter from the churn into a large bowl. "Nathan sent those boys away. He spelled them."

Frank sat down for the third time. "That's expelled, Winema. Christ! That kid coulda broke Jeff's back or worse." Frank shook his head. "A bushwhacker and a coward, just like his old man." He stood again. "Well, that's it. Jeff's done with schoolin'."

Winema smiled to herself. She had decided the same thing but wanted Frank to make the decision. Schools and such were of the White world, the usefulness of which seemed less than practical. Some of the inner workings of the White world remained downright mystifying. Such schools did not teach boys to hunt, to gather food, to defend themselves against an enemy. And they certainly wasted girls' time when they should be helping out at home and learning the skills necessary to be

useful wives and mothers. Besides, she missed having Jeff
close to home all day, and she knew he missed working with
his father and playing with his cousins. She breathed a con-
tented sigh. Her son would be home with her again—the way
it should be.

～

MOTHER *Fol'dum* finally lifted her winter robe and wearily
drifted back to the Northland. Over the winter Winema, Frank,
and Jeff made several trips to the reservation. She was sickened
by what she saw. The People were hungry, poorly clothed, and
morose. They were changing before her very eyes. Too many
had lost their pride. Families bickered and struck their children.
Some, like Kweelush's husband, had become drunkards and
had abandoned their families. Others drifted into mining camps
and sold their pride, or their bodies, for whiskey. Modoc tribal
law of no sex outside marriage had collapsed and fatherless
children wandered about aimlessly. Winema wondered if she,
too, would have lost her pride and spirit had she married a
Modoc man and lived on the reservation.

Steeped in anger and guilt, Winema was not surprised
Kentapoos had given up on the reservation, and she had
confronted Captain Knapp about the conditions. But he only
shrugged and mumbled about Washington. In their last meeting
Winema had accused him of killing her people with promises,
and he had ordered soldiers to escort Frank and her off the
reservation.

When the cheerless summer finally gave way to *Sha'lum*,
and her people were once again quietly residing in *Mowatoc*,
Winema's spirits were lifted. It was time to gather sweet
elderberries along the creek, one of the traditions of the old
days that always brought warm memories. Winema made it a
family event, a day's outing with a picnic lunch. Jeff helped
Frank hitch the team of matched grays, then he and Mutt
chased each other around the front yard while Frank and
Winema loaded berry *wekkis* and their dinner onto the wagon.

Several extra *wekkis* were loaded for berries to be taken to Lost
River.

Mutt noticed the rider first. He stopped his play and barked
a warning in the direction of the road. Frank shaded his eyes
and squinted at the lone rider. By the way the man sat his horse,
Frank was sure he was Indian, but more than that, there was
something uniquely familiar about him. It couldn't be . . .

Frank's mind raced to catch up with his eyes. He jumped up
onto the wagon for a better view, then he waved, whistled, and
shouted, "*KOLA*! JACQUES!"

The rider stood in his stirrups and waved back, then urged
his horse into a trot. Frank laughed, danced a jig in the back of
the wagon, and shouted down to Winema, "It's Jacques,
Winema! It's White Eagle!" He whipped off his hat, slapped it
against his thigh. "I'll be double damned!"

Winema and Jeff stared at Frank with surprised half-smiles.
They'd never seen him so excited. Frank jumped down from
the dray. "You remember. My friend from the wagon train."

"Your Indian friend, Pa?" Jeff chimed in.

"That's the one, son. I thought I'd never see him again."

Jacques trotted into the yard. He wore a blue homespun shirt
with fringed buckskin trousers and beaded moccasins. He
looked down at Frank and smiled. "It is good to see you again,
kola."

Frank laughed, delighted once again at hearing Jacques's
unique mixture of French, Indian, and English. "Well, come
down off'a there and meet the family."

Jacques dismounted and the two friends embraced. Frank
was embarrassed at the depth of his own emotions and had to
fight back tears. Leaving one arm around his friend, Frank
turned to face his family. "Jeff, Winema. *This*," he emphasized
proudly, "is White Eagle."

Mouth agape, Jeff craned his neck to take in all of the tall
fabled Cheyenne. Frank had to chortle. He'd forgotten himself
how tall Jacques was—over six feet, he guessed. Of course his
friend looked older after seventeen years, but Frank was

shocked at the deep worry lines and a veiled sadness in his dark eyes.

Frank tucked away his concerns and introduced Winema. Jacques winked at Frank. "You still have good taste in women, I see." He smiled and nodded at Winema.

Clasping Jeff's shoulder, Frank said, "And this is Charka— Handsome Boy—our son."

Jacques's face seemed to brighten. He squatted down so he could look into Jeff's eyes. "I am glad to know you, Charka."

Jeff gawked at the stranger, then looked at his father. "Holy cow, Pa. He's even taller than you said."

Laughing, Frank queried, "How 'bout you, Jacques? I remember when we parted at South Pass and you were headin' home. You figured your ma would have some filly with marryin' in mind."

Jaques stood. A fleeting shadow passed across his angular face. "*Oui*. She found a good one."

Winema interjected, "We forget our manners, White Eagle. Come into our lodge and eat."

Jeff eyed the beautifully beaded rifle case attached to Jacques' saddle and asked enthusiastically, "Can I help ya carry your gear, White Eagle?"

Jacques smiled down at the youngster. "I would be honored, Handsome Boy."

Entering the house, Frank asked, "I hope you're gonna stay a while?"

"A week or two. Then I must head back to the reservation."

Frank showed his friend to a chair and Winema disappeared into the kitchen. "Reservation?" Frank sighed. "Damn, I guess I didn't think . . . Don't keep up with the papers much." He looked down and shook his head pensively, said to no one in particular, "The Cheyennes on a reservation." Looking up, he said, "No more scoutin' for trains?"

Jacques slowly removed his black, high-crowned hat, straightened the eagle feather in the band, then placed the hat on the table. He ran his fingers through his shoulder-length, black hair, now cobwebbed with streaks of gray. "No, my friend. I will help no more Whites move through my country."

Frank nodded knowingly. Despite Jacques's ties with his Cheyenne friends and family, Frank knew Jacques had enemies back home—fellow Cheyennes who distrusted half-breeds, let alone condone Indians who worked for the wagon trains.

Although Jacques Dubois was half French, he had chosen the Cheyenne lifestyle of his Cheyenne-Sioux mother. He was a proud and honest man and had taken eighteen-year-old Frank under his wing on the long journey along the Oregon Trail. In those days the Cheyennes and the Lakotahs allowed the cloth wagons to move through their country, and scouting was an honorable profession.

By the time Frank showed up, Jacques had made two trips on the trail as a scout. Frank had been fascinated with Indians and latched on to Jacques like a burr on a bear. Jacques was only twenty-five at the time, but had already carried a lifetime of experience and maturity. He had trapped beaver with his father, attended a missionary school, spoke four languages—not including Chinook—and had undergone the rites of passage of a Cheyenne warrior.

As far as Frank was concerned, you could take every lawyer, teacher, and doctor in the whole territory and you wouldn't match Jacques's wisdom and honesty. In fact, there was only one other man that tied Jacques for such lofty admiration, and that was Robert E. Lee.

Winema came into the front room and announced dinner was ready.

Frank grinned and shook his head. "Damn, it's good to see you, Jacques. We've got a heap of catchin' up to do."

The crow's-feet at the corners of Jacques's eyes crinkled as he smiled. He looked at Winema and Jeff, then back to Frank. Almost wistfully, he answered, "*Oui, mon ami*. A heap."

❧

AFTER dinner Frank and Jeff went out to unhitch the wagon team and tend the stock, leaving Winema to entertain Jacques.

She was glad for the opportunity. Jacques studied her as he sipped his coffee. Winema found the situation a bit unnerving, imagined Jacques felt the same. Jacques was both Indian and White. She didn't know how traditional he may or may not be. Being a married woman, should she speak first or wait for him to begin conversation? She decided to ease the tension by speaking first. Jacques must have been thinking the same, for they started talking simultaneously. They chuckled.

Jacques said, "You have chosen a fine man for a husband, Winema."

This put Jacques on her good side immediately. Anyone who complimented her husband had to be worth knowing. "Thank you, Jacques. I am glad you came. It makes my husband very happy. He speaks much of you."

Jacques looked mildly surprised. "After all these years?"

Winema nodded. "Oh, yes. I think it is because of you that Frank and I met."

"Because of me?"

"*Ih*. Was it not you who taught him so much about Indian people—to respect our ways?"

Jacques grinned. "So, it stuck, then?"

Winema scrunched her brow in confusion. "Stuck?"

"Ah. I am sorry. I mean he remembered everything I told him?"

"*Ih*. Because of it he"—She searched for the right word—"im-press my father and me."

"Good, good." His eyes probed hers again as he leaned forward. "Winema. I want to tell you how happy I am that he married a good Indian woman."

"I am glad, too. But why?"

Jacques looked thoughtful for a moment. "You know that Frank and I became friends on the trail."

Winema nodded.

Jacques continued, "He may be White, but his spirit is like ours."

Winema looked at Jacques with new respect. He knew her husband as she did. "You are wise, White Eagle."

Jacques smiled thinly. "I cannot take the credit. Frank is, as the Whites say, an open book. He does not deceive."

Winema covered her mouth and chuckled. "*Ih*. He has still not learned to hide his feelings like you taught."

Jacques chuckled as he started to rummage in his saddlebag.

Winema said, "I was hoping you would tell me about that, and about Fort Laramie."

Jacques removed a long-stemmed clay pipe from the bag. Winema went to the fireplace mantel, retrieved a box of matches, and handed them to him. He watched her as he packed the pipe. "You wish to hear about Sweet Grass, don't you?"

Winema colored slightly, swept some crumbs from the table into a cupped hand, and shrugged noncommittally. "I am cur-i-ous."

Jacques lit the pipe, blew a stream of smoke upward, then gazed at Winema. "It is only natural." He chuckled to himself. "He was so young and green then. And very excitable. He wanted to know everything right now." Jacques leaned back in his chair and puffed reflectively. "Indeed it was *because* of Sweet Grass that he got his first lesson in controlling his face. It was the morning after Frank *knew* the girl; the morning we were to leave. . . .

━

DAWN had come unnoticed to Fort Laramie as iron-gray skies diffused the light, promising a dreary day. Looking for Sweet Grass, Frank found her family campsite abandoned. He stood there, frozen in disbelief. At first he thought perhaps he had found the wrong campsite, but there was no doubt. Her tipi had stood next to the one with the painted otters on the sides. He rushed to Iron Necklace's lodge, and jingled the bunched deer claws hanging at the tipi's entrance. The skin door moved aside, and the pocked face of Jacques's cousin, Iron Necklace, appeared. He squinted at Frank, then motioned for him to enter.

Jacques was there. A woman was stowing his bed robes. It appeared Jacques, too, had found feminine company last night.

Frank's face revealed his worry. "Jacques, Sweet Grass's lodge is gone. I can't find her anywhere."

Jacques raised his eyebrows. In Lakotah, he translated for Iron Necklace and there was a short exchange between the two. Jacques nodded his understanding. "My cousin says Sweet Grass's father runs the Sun Dance next week. The family travels there to make ready."

Frank's spirits spiraled down like a wounded bird. How could she not tell him she was leaving? "Aw, hell," he blurted. Every line in his face showed disappointment.

Jacques watched him, a brief expression of reproach on his face. "Sit here, Frank," he ordered, pointing to a robe next to him. "If you want to be with Indians, you must remember your face is the *miroir* of your soul. We watch a man's face and eyes closely. You must control yourself."

"Why? I'm mad and don't care who knows it," Frank snapped.

Jacques opened his pipe bag and began to load his pipe. An effigy of a bear sitting upright, hewed from red pipestone, served as the bowl. He lit it and took a few priming draws before the mixture smoldered to life. Passing the pipe to Frank, Jacques switched to Chinook. "Here, smoke."

"I don't want a smoke now."

Frank was annoyed that Jacques was using Chinook. He still didn't feel handy enough with it, but Jacques insisted it was the only way to learn.

Iron Necklace sat cross-legged across from them and watched impassively.

"It takes much practice for *wasichus*, but you must learn. You must never give away your true feelings unless you are sure you want to."

Frank frowned as he remembered his pa telling him to stay away from card games because he couldn't keep a poker face. "What's it matter? I'm with friends—you and Iron Necklace."

"Someday you might be with other Indians, and they will watch your face. They will see what makes you afraid, what makes you angry, and they will know your *faiblesse*, uh, weaknesses."

Frank stared at the ground, only half-listening to the advice. He was thinking of Sweet Grass's cheeky smile, her easy laugh, the goose bumps he got when he touched her soft, dusky skin. He fought the idea he would never see her again.

Jacques angled his head toward Iron Necklace. "Look now at Iron Necklace. What do you see?"

Iron Necklace's face was expressionless as a stone.

"Nothin'. But he always looks that way," Frank protested.

Jacques smiled and shook his head. "But sometimes he jokes and plays tricks. You have not seen this. You must earn trust with Indians. They believe in action, not words."

⟵

JACQUES gave a curt wave of his hand, indicating his story was finished.

"You must be raised in our way," Winema observed.

The door burst open and Jeff rushed in, wound tighter than a dollar watch. "White Eagle. Pa wants you to come out and see our herd. I can show you my pony that cousin Kentapoos gave me. He's a beauty!" Jeff looked at Winema. "Ma. How 'bout we have our picnic tomorrow? It'll be even more fun with White Eagle along."

Winema chuckled. "*Oka ilagen.*"

Jeff whooped, then dragged a bemused Jacques out the door.

THIRTY-TWO

On the day of the picnic, wispy clouds, like pulled cotton, floated lazily in a pale blue sky. Open fields teemed with butterflies and fat bumblebees, and the forest was alive with the chatter of buck squirrels and the gobbling of wild turkeys. After a picnic dinner of cold beef sandwiches, sweet potatoes, camas cakes, and succulent elderberries, Jeff wanted to show Jacques some of his favorite spots. As they walked together Jacques listened to Jeff relate Modoc tales about the various landscape features they encountered. He was pleased. The boy was close to the earth and appreciated tradition and storytelling. And he respected the Creator. His parents had taught him well.

They strolled in silence a while, and, again, Jacques was impressed with the boy. Jeff did not fear silence, did not feel every moment had to be filled with banal conversation. After a while Jeff asked, "Uncle? (His mother had reminded him to use the proper title of respect to an adult man). When you were a kid, did other kids make fun of you because you were a breed?"

"*Oui*. Sometimes."

Jeff stopped along the creek, squatted down, and, quick as a finch, scooped up a palmful of wriggling tadpoles. He studied them a moment as the water drained through his clenched fingers. "Does it ever stop?"

"No, nephew. It will never stop. But as long as you are proud of who you are, such words will not hurt you."

Jacques sat down next to Jeff on the creek bank. "Sit and rest yourself." He then removed his moccasins and dangled his feet in the cool water. Jeff shucked his shoes and followed suit.

"Ahhh," Jacques breathed.

"Ahhh," Jeff mimicked.

Jacques smiled. "You see, nephew. We are special, you and I."

Jeff cocked his head. "Special?"

"*Oui.* We are Two Hearts. We understand the world in a way others cannot. We carry the generations of two races within us." Jacques studied the sky a moment. "I think Grandfather knows this road He has chosen for us is a hard one. He tests us."

Jeff scrunched his nose in puzzlement. "Tests us?"

"Grandfather tests each of us in a different way. Ours is that of the Two Heart, the one who must walk two paths. If you are strong, you will be the better for it. My friends, Charley and George Bent—they are also half White—we have talked of this many times."

Jeff mulled this a moment, then, "At least you got some other breed friends. I don't. Sometimes I just wish I was full Modoc. But then I feel bad 'cause I wouldn't have Pa."

Jacques nodded empathetically. "Around the fire in my mother's lodge, or when I am at the Sun Dance, I know I am home, that I am Cheyenne. Then some Cheyenne will call me a White man, try to make my heart bad. But then I remember it is only Grandfather testing my spirit, and I become stronger." Jacques peered into Jeff's eyes. "Because, you see, I know who I am, where I come from. No one can take that away from me. No one can take that away from you." He straightened, placed his hand on Jeff's shoulder, and gazed earnestly at him. "You are Modoc and you are White. Never forget it. Honor it. Teach these ways to your children. Let no man take it from you."

By the time Jeff and Jacques returned to the picnic site, it was time to pack up and head home.

"It's about time," Frank teased. "I thought y'all got lost."

Jacques flashed a wry grin at Jeff. "How can two Indians get lost?"

＊

JACQUES'S visit seemed to pass faster than a bullet. Before Frank realized, almost two weeks had passed. Whitey and Nathan had come out, and there had even been time to introduce Jacques to Jack and some of the other Modocs. It had been a wonderful time—a time of reminiscing, of reflection, of rebonding. And it had been a needed break from the worries about Jack and the treaty problems.

Two days before Jacques was to leave, he and Frank rode over to a nearby butte and camped out. Like the old days on the Oregon Trail, Frank wanted it to be just the two of them. He had worried about the sadness in Jacques's eyes. The way he had first looked at Winema and the way he reacted to Jeff, signaled something bad had happened to his old friend.

The campfire bathed their faces in hues of orange as they talked and smoked after a fine venison supper. Stars studded the night sky like tiny, winking jewels.

"Reminds me of that night we talked out on the prairie, near Independence Rock, don't it?" Frank mused.

"Ah," Jacques replied softly and nodded.

Frank poked a stick at the glowing embers of the fire, then asked, "What ever happened to Sweet Grass?" He chuckled. "I reckon she's married and got youngsters now."

Jacques's expression darkened. "I knew you would ask this. She is dead, *mon ami*."

Frank's face fell.

"She was killed at Sand Creek when the butcher, Chivington, attacked Black Kettle's camp. She and her two daughters. Six winters ago."

Frank was startled by his reaction. Something collapsed inside him. A young girl he knew for only three days—seventeen years ago. How could the shock and sadness be so acute? He couldn't speak for several moments, then, "Why? How . . . how did it happen?"

Jacques peered into the fire. "The Colorado Volunteers needed a victory. So they raided the closest camp—a peaceful camp. A camp that flew both an American flag and a white flag. Mostly women and children were killed."

Jacques absently fingered a small medicine pouch that hung from his belt. "Including my wife and son."

Frank stiffened. "My God, Jacques." A torrent of emotion swept through him, waves of sadness as he now realized what had effected his old friend so profoundly. How hard it must have been for Jacques—being around Winema and Jeff these past days.

"I don't hardly know what to say. It's—it's just too much bad news all at once."

Jacques nodded. "It was a long time ago."

Frank asked, "But where were you and the other men?"

"A buffalo hunt. The army had told us to hunt there, to stay at Sand Creek." His face hardened. "Where we would be safe."

Frank sighed. "I *did* hear about Black Kettle. You talked about him a lot back then. He sounded like a good man."

Jacques laid his hat back down. "*Oui*. The soldiers murdered him. That time it was the woman killer, Custer. Two winters ago on the Washita."

Frank stood and sat next to Jacques. "Lord, I'm sorry, *kola*. So damned sorry." He shook his head. "It's so goddamned unfair."

Jacques rested a hand on Frank's arm. "*Oui, kola*. But such is life, *non*?"

A helluva lot more unfairer for some than others, Frank thought. He wiped his eyes with his bandanna. "You never married again?"

Jacques shook his head. "No."

A soft night breeze rustled the tall grass. Frank filled with sudden inspiration. "Stay here with us, Jacques. We could go into business together. Winema'd feed you good and you could meet a nice Modoc gal, or a Klamath. She could introduce you."

Jacques smiled. "Thank you, my friend. But I have not lived

in the White world since my wife and son passed to the other side. My place is with my people. I must help them through this hard time. You know what life is like on a reservation."

Somewhere in the distance a lone wolf bayed at the shimmering moon. Frank understood. He knew his friend too well; there would be no point in arguing with him.

"Jacques, I think we should build a sweat tonight. We'll pray for your wife and young'un, then we'll pray for your safe return, and for your people. I want this to be the last thing we do together."

Jacques stared into his friend's moist eyes. His voice quavered. "*Washteh*. It is good."

❦

EVERYONE felt blue on the day of Jacques's departure. Frank helped Winema make a big breakfast consisting of fat bacon, cornbread in pone, dandelion greens, wild honey, and fried onions.

After the silent breakfast, they walked Jacques out to his pony, Frank and Jeff helping to carry Jacques's meager belongings. Jacques allowed Jeff to carry his rifle in the beaded case. Then Jacques stopped short as he saw the fine roan mare tethered to his pony. His face lit up as he turned to Frank.

Frank grinned. "She's my best and she's yours. You'll need two mounts for your trip."

Jacques walked up to the mare and stroked her thigh and legs. "*Merci*. She is a fine animal."

"I'd feel a helluva lot better, Jacques, if somebody was ridin' with you. That's a mighty long trip for a man by himself."

Jacques strapped down his saddlebags and made a curt laugh. "I was traveling this trail when you were—how they say—in short pants."

Frank stroked the back of his neck and looked dubious. "Yeah, well, this is mean country for Indians and breeds."

Jeff piped up, "I could go with him, Pa! I could help."

Jacques chuckled, squatted down to face the boy. He clasped Jeff's shoulders. "And you would be a big help, too, my nephew. But I think your mother and father need you more, *oui*?"

Jacques held up a finger. "Ah. Wait." He stood, groped his saddlebags, and produced a roll of tanned buckskin, handed it to Jeff. "Open it," Jacques prompted.

Jeff gently unrolled the buckskin, revealing a magnificent flute carved from cedar. A slideable effigy of a sitting hawk was tied over the main air hole, near the mouthpiece. The wood had been lovingly smoothed to a soft, rich texture. Jeff's eyes became big as pawpaws as he ran his hands over the flute's surface.

"I made it for my son," Jacques explained. "Now it is yours. When you play it, you will think of old Jacques, eh?"

Jeff looked at Jacques with wide and solemn eyes. "*Wash-teh!*"

"Wait," Jeff said as he groped inside his shirt and produced something wrapped in a handkerchief. He handed it to Jacques. "This is for you, Uncle. I made it myself."

Jacques nodded and smiled at Jeff as he unwrapped the cloth. It was a nicely carved wooden horse. "*Sacré bleu,*" he admired. "And what a fine horse it is. As you say in your own language, *humast.* I will keep it with me always."

Jeff beamed. "It'll keep your pony strong for the long ride."

Jacques fished in his saddlebags once again and pulled out two other skin-wrapped items. He laid one on his pony's back and handed the other to Winema. "And this is for you, good wife and mother."

Winema nodded politely and opened the small bundle. "Ahh," she breathed as the gift inside was revealed. Her hand went over her mouth in wonderment. It was a stunning beaded rosette—a white star surrounded by concentric circles of pink, orange and red—a sunset. The rosette was attached to a long, twin-rowed necklace of the tiniest, most delicate polished seeds she'd ever seen.

"Our women make the finest beadwork. It was my wife's. Until you, I found no other worthy to wear it."

Winema cast her eyes downward in humility. "*Humast*, White Eagle. We will miss you."

At last Jacques retrieved the last bundle resting on the pony's hindquarter and handed it to Frank. "And this is for you, my friend."

Frank unrolled the skin.

"Whoa!" Jeff blurted as he saw his father's gift.

Frank lifted the pipe to examine it. Its catlanite bowl was a perfect carved eagle's head. Peyote-stitched beads completely covered the long, straight wooden stem. Several large eagle and hawk feathers dangled from the bowl, stem, and mouthpiece.

"This pipe was given to me by Iron Necklace many seasons ago. It has been blessed in a sacred way and should only be used for ceremony and prayer."

For a moment Frank was unable to speak. He could only stare at the sacred pipe he now held in his hands. It felt warm, vibrant—like a living thing.

"I remember oglin' it in his lodge," Frank managed.

Frank lifted his eyes to Jacques, then the two embraced for a long time. Mounting his pony, Jacques said, "We will meet again, my friends. I know this in my heart."

"Godspeed, my brother," Frank said.

Winema said, "You will be in our prayers, White Eagle."

Jacques smiled at Winema, winked at Jeff, then rode out of the yard and onto the road. Frank, Jeff, and Winema watched him ride away. He stopped once, turned in his saddle to wave, then resumed his journey, eventually shrinking to a speck in the distance, then disappearing into the distal haze.

THIRTY-THREE

Kalelk, Kchil'wifam, 1871

❧ DOCTOR GEORGE, THE Paiute holy man, finished his emotional speech with a stem winder. "And so my brothers and sisters. I bring sacred medicine. From the great holy leader, Yu'yunipi'tqana, the Shouting Mountain, I bring to you a holy dance! Indian people are in danger. It is so because we have abandoned the ways of our fathers. We are not White! Leave the Whites to their ways and leave us to ours." He held up a Bible. "God did not intend us to be White. The black robes taught us about Jesus, the sacred messenger. But many of us knew of him long before the black robes came. Our forefathers knew the Great Spirit *before* the White man was created. We know that after God made the red man he made the White, the yellow, and the black. Each has his part of the world.

"God gave *us* this country. The Creator told the Shouting Mountain these things through a medicine vision. In turn, Yu'yunipi'tqana taught me a sacred dance, the Ghost Dance, and now I teach it to you. We have sent runners to every tribe. They learn of it as you learn of it."

He tied a red and blue cloth flag to a sharpened stick, rammed it into the ground. A white star decorated the upper half. "Let this be our medicine flag. And let these be our sacred rules: Do no harm to the Whites—have nothing more to do with them! Own no cows or sheep or hogs. Do not gouge the Earth Mother with their plows! Throw away everything given to you by the Whites. And eat only Indian foods."

His voice dipped low, forcing his audience to lean forward to hear, then he built to a rousing crescendo. "If you dance as I have taught, your relatives who have passed over will return from the east when the grass is so high," he preached, holding his hand midway between ankle and knee. "Our brothers, the deer, and the other animals who have passed on, will follow behind them! Do these things, my brothers and sisters, and the White man will vanish like frost in the sun!"

The Modocs exploded with trills, yips, and war cries. The drums struck up a steady beat. People formed a large circle, joined hands, and began a shuffling step to their left.

Kentapoos and Winema watched from afar.

Winema frowned. "I do not like this."

Kentapoos shrugged. "It is good for the people to believe in something again. Perhaps the Paiute truly had this vision."

"If he is wrong it will serve only as another disappointment for the People. I am glad he goes back with the sun." She frowned at Doctor George, standing in the center of the circle, his eyes closed as he thrust his hands toward the sky and chanted.

Yet somewhere deep in her gut she almost wanted to believe.

Kentapoos said, "We have been home more than a season and all remains quiet. I think this time the Whites will let us stay." He smiled and gestured with his eyes toward the dancers. "And if not . . ." He shrugged. "We have the Ghost Dance."

Winema shook her head. "No, cousin. The Whites are *not* quiet. Here in Kalelk you do not hear their angry words. While you sleep many plot against you and complain to the government. I worry for you and our people."

Kentapoos clasped her shoulder. "You worry needlessly. I visit Yreka and my rancher friends often. There has been no trouble."

Winema looked at her cousin skeptically. "You hear what you want to hear, Waterbrash. The Whites are angry that some of our men have taken their cows. Others have entered White homes uninvited, demanded money or food, and scared their women."

Kentapoos seemed unworried. "The Whites use our land. We are only collecting rent, as they say. Besides, many of them are our friends and pay us with no complaint."

Not to your face, Winema thought. Her eyes returned to the dancers. She watched with an odd mix of wistfulness and worry. Part of her celebrated the two-year-long return to *Mowatoc* by her people, and the collecting of "rent." And, in the depth of her soul, she wanted to believe Doctor George, at least the part about the returning of the ancestors and the game. But she had lived in the White world too long, and she couldn't shake off the deep sense of foreboding. It hung around her shoulders like a heavy bear skin.

Her eyes narrowed as she watched Doctor George. "The return of our relations and of the old ways is worth dancing for," she muttered out of the side of her mouth. "But if my husband burns up, I will cut that Paiute's throat." That said, Winema mounted Skoks and rode toward home.

THIRTY-FOUR

Fa'lum, 1872

ELISHA STEELE LOOKED thoughtfully at Kentapoos as he finished lighting his meershaum pipe. Judge Roseborough stoked the smoldering pine logs in the fireplace.

"We understand your frustration, Jack," Steele said. "To be honest, things have only been 'quiet,' as you say, because the bureaucracy moves slow and the army's Department of the Pacific is still getting organized. They've got a new general— Canby. He has an impressive war record, and he's bringing in a lot of soldiers fresh from fighting the Apaches."

Kentapoos asked, "These Apaches. They are good fighters?"

"The best, I'm told. Tough as nails."

Roseborough shifted in his chair. "It's our opinion, Jack, that the new state superintendent will act soon. There is just too much pressure on him and the Indian Service."

Kentapoos's jaw tightened. "But Meacham promised us a reservation on Lost River two moons ago. You remember. We met with him and the new agent. Applegate and Fairchild were there. We made a map."

The middle-aged attorney sat on the corner of his desk, puffing on his pipe. "I know, Jack, I know. But Meacham has been replaced by Ordneal, who turned the agreement down.

They want you back on the reservation. That new road between Yreka and Lost River Valley was made for one reason: to entice more settlers. The Whites want to see that good bottom land put to use."

Kentapoos's hands gripped the padded arms of his chair. *Why do they force me . . . ?* "Why is it so hard to give us a little piece of our own land?"

The old judge stood, locked his hands behind his back. "There might be a way, Jack."

Kentapoos looked at him expectantly.

"The only way out of this thing I can see is for you to announce that you've dissolved your tribe, then take up claims like the settlers, and pay taxes."

"Exactly," Steele agreed. "I am of the opinion that the Constitution, the great paper from which we make all our laws, implies that if you pay taxes you become a citizen of the United States."

Kentapoos struggled to interpret the stampede of complex English. He had heard about taxes from Frank and Winema. That was what gave him the idea of collecting them from the settlers at Lost River. Taxes, rent—they were the same. Kentapoos frowned. "Im-plyz?"

"Meaning the great paper could be interpreted to protect an Indian property owner the same as a White property owner," Steele clarified.

Kentapoos's mind moved crabwise in the attempt to grasp the twists and loops of White reasoning. "This sounds like many words only to say what we had asked from the beginning. Respect for our lands."

Roseborough and Steele looked at each other and pursed their lips. The jurist sighed. He seemed to struggle for the right words. "As it stands now, Indians are not citizens of the United States; they are not protected by the Constitution. But, my theory is—"

"Then what are we?" Kentapoos snapped.

The room became still. Outside, they could hear the jangle of harnesses, the rolling of wagon and buggy wheels on Miner

Street. The *laki* continued, "As you have explained the word, how can we not be cit-i-zens in our own land? Only the White man could think up such a thing. We belong to the land. Our forefathers left its care to us long before the Whites came. It is the Whites who are not *cit-i-zens*."

The law-talk men stared at each other, then studied the rug. Kentapoos stood and started for the door.

Jarred from his thoughts, Elisha Steele slid off the corner of his desk. "Will you take our advice, then? Dissolve the tribe and make claims?"

Kentapoos shook his head. "First they tell us to give up our land. Now they want us to give up ourselves. We are Modocs. To give up our tribe is to give up our being." Kentapoos shook his head slowly. His voice took on a low, bitter edge. "We have given up too much already."

Judge Roseborough said, "Going back to the reservation is far better than going to war, Jack."

Kentapoos glared at Roseborough. "Is it?"

The young chief opened the outer door, then slowly he turned back to face his friends. His face was etched with lines of anguish. "My friends, we were dying on that reservation. When your people took away our lands, they cut off our limbs." Kentapoos glared at Steele. "If we disband our tribe, we cut out our own hearts." He thought for a moment, remembering his meeting with Meacham two moons past. "As for staying on the reservation, I will tell you what I told Meacham. Bullets don't hurt much. Starving hurts a heap."

THIRTY-FIVE

State of Oregon
Department of Indian Affairs

DATE: 26 December, 1872
TO: Major John B. Green, Commanding Officer,
First Cavalry, Fort Klamath, Oregon
FROM: Superintendent Ordneal, Washington City

\\MODOC SITUATION MUST BE RESOLVED/ STOP/
GO TO LOST RIVER AND MOVE CAPTAIN JACK
AND BAND OF MODOCS ONTO KLAMATH
RESERVATION /STOP/ PEACEABLY IF YOU CAN,
FORCIBLY IF YOU MUST/ STOP //

Major Green pondered the telegram on his desk. Why would he receive an order direct from the state Superintendent of Indian Affairs rather than through the chain of command? He looked at Captain James A. Jackson. "I wonder if Colonel Wheaton or General Canby know about this?"

The captain shrugged. "Don't know, sir. Colonel Wheaton is ill, as you know, and General Canby is on an inspection tour."

Green frowned, scratched the top of his head. He looked up and sighed. "How long will it take to prepare the troop?"

"I expect a shipment of supplies tomorrow, sir. Another day to gather in some of the men on leave. . . ." Jackson glanced at Lieutenant Calley next to him.

Calley straightened. "Two days at least, sir, to round up all the men."

Jackson faced his boss. "I'd say three days, Major."

"Very well. You leave for Lost River in three days."

Jackson turned to Lieutenant Calley. "Make the necessary preparations, Lieutenant."

Calley snapped to attention. "Yes, SIR. It's about time, sir!" He pivoted in a perfectly executed about-face and marched out the door.

27 December, 1872

WINEMA rode Skoks as if a fire licked at her back. Her mind raced along with the horse. Every minute counted. She needed time. Time to calm Kentapoos. Time for the People to make preparations. She galloped into Kalelk and pulled rein. Kentapoos and his inner council emerged from his latch and hustled to her.

She slid down from the pony, tried to catch her breath. "*Shuldshash* are coming!"

There was an uproar as people crowded around her.

"How do you know this?"

"I have ears at the fort. The soldier chief, Jackson, will lead his men here tomorrow." She grabbed his arm, her face a mask of apprehension. "You must not resist them. If you listen to his words, no one will be hurt. Even better, go to Yainax and join Skonches. You will be safe there."

Cho-ocks pulled his pistol and cocked it. He glowered at Kentapoos. "*Laki! Meki'gam blake'tu.* We will not go! Skonches and his people crept back to the reservation like whipped dogs. Let them! WE will stay and fight."

Black Wound, Cho-ocks, and their minions glared at their chief. Kentapoos watched the three men with pistols warily.

Winema felt a chill. Over the past few weeks she had noticed Black Wound, Cho-ocks, and Whusum had continued to garner power. "If you try to fight the soldiers, you will all be killed," she reasoned. "You could never kill all the soldiers the government can send here."

Kentapoos reluctantly moved his eyes to Winema. "I do not want to fight, and I do not expect to unless forced."

Winema scanned the men's eyes, sighed, then remounted Skoks. Lifting her head and voice toward the crowd, she said, "Take my advice, my people. Return to Yainax and die a natural death with your relations. There is no need to spill Modoc blood here."

There was nothing more to be said. She dug her heels into Skoks and trotted away.

Kentapoos turned to his men. "Krelatko, Slatuslocks, Skietteteko, Hakar! Ride out to Fairchild, Applegate, Dorris, Overton, Boddy, and our other settler friends. Tell them the soldiers will arrive here tomorrow, that they should stay home and no one will get hurt."

That evening the Modoc couriers returned. The settlers promised to stay at home. Kentapoos was pleased. Should there be shooting, it would be only between Modocs and soldiers.

The village dogs growled and fussed all night.

～

As the orange disk rose over the hills to the east, Grandmother Says-No headed toward the river with her *wekkis*. She stooped to dip water, then glimpsed movement across the river—patches of blue and yellow on horseback. Dropping her basket, she scrambled back to the village. "*Ko-idsi boshtinum ho-lalk tchawik sana-holiug*! Wicked White men approach fast wanting a fight!"

The village stirred to life. Dogs barked furiously. The men scrambled to gather horses. But Jackson's horses splashed across the bridge and up to Kentapoos's latch before a defense could be prepared. Jackson and Calley dismounted and approached Kentapoos. Kentapoos heard pistols and rifles cocking behind him. He held up his hand. "*Getak!*"

The captain signaled his men at ease while eyeing the chief. "Jack, we been sent to bring you and your people safely back to the reservation."

Kentapoos's voice was strained. "You ride into my village in darkness and scare my people. Why do you not come to me like a man, in the daylight, when you want to talk?"

Jackson propped his hands on his hips. "I don't want any trouble, Jack. Just gather up your men so I can talk to them."

Kentapoos scanned Jackson's eyes a moment, then called the village men forward. Big Knife murmured to another elder, "This man might want to repeat what Ben Wright did to us. Be ready."

Jackson eyed Kentapoos's pistol. "Now, Jack. Lay your gun on the ground."

Kentapoos gripped his pistol handle harder. "What for?"

"You're the chief. Your men will follow your lead."

"Why do you want our guns? We want no fight."

"It's good you don't want to fight, Jack." He crooked his fingers. "Now just give up your guns and nobody will get hurt."

Frustrated, Kentapoos felt trapped. There were too many women and children about to start shooting now. Slowly he pulled out his pistol, placed it on the ground, then ordered his men to do the same. When Krelatko's turn came, he laid down his rifle, but kept his old cap and ball pistol tucked in his belt.

"The hogleg, too," Jackson said.

Krelatko smiled and pointed to his rifle on the pile. "You got my gun. This pistol is empty."

Jackson's jaw tightened. He looked out of the corner of his eye at Calley. "Lieutenant, disarm this man."

Calley threw back his shoulders, unholstered his Colt, and swaggered up to Krelatko. "Here, Injun. Give me that pistol, damn you, and be quick about it."

Tension charged the air.

Krelatko laughed. Kentapoos held his breath.

"I am no dog," Krelatko chuckled in broken English. "I am man. I not 'fraid of you. If you talk good, I listen."

In one swift movement Calley cocked his Colt and pointed it an inch from Krelatko's face.

Krelatko jumped aside and drew his pistol. The two weapons roared almost simultaneously. A cloud of blue-gray smoke enveloped the two men. Both shots missed.

Women screamed, grabbed startled children, and ran. Calley fired again, but Krelatko was diving for his rifle. The other Modocs followed suit. Another Modoc launched an arrow at Calley, grazing his arm. He yelped and dropped his weapon. Holding his arm, he scuttled about, looking for his mount.

The air ripped apart as the soldiers opened fire. A few Modocs at the rear of the crowd darted into their latches, retrieved bows, and loosed hissing shafts into the disorganized soldiers. There were screams and curses. Horses pierced by arrows whinnied and reared. A bugle sounded.

The Modocs sprinted toward the steep foothills behind them, stopping intermittently to fire at the soldiers to their rear. The bugle sounded again. Kentapoos heard Jackson's voice, "Retreat!" and he fired in that direction, hoping to kill the treacherous *kash*.

They ran for their lives. Women and children led the escape; Kentapoos and several men covered the rear. Suddenly puffs of smoke appeared ahead and to the left, just inside a copse of oaks at the foot of the hills, producing more screams.

Kentapoos, looking frantically about, spotted Cho-ocks and two other warriors. He pointed to the gun smoke. "There! Shoot the *kash*!"

Several other Modocs were already firing into the trees. Kentapoos and his trio joined them. He heard men yelling in the trees. Among others, Kentapoos recognized the voices of Darryl Boddy and Carl Overton, some of the forewarned settlers who had promised to stay home.

Fifteen-year-old Mekadush fell next to her wounded baby. Three elderly men and two elderly women were down, dead or writhing in pain.

"KEEP RUNNING!"

The Modoc men poured all their firepower into the copse, temporarily quelling the settlers' fire.

"TO THE CAVES! THE CAVES!" the chief shouted. He wondered how many heard his directions. His head pounded; his lungs felt ready to burst as he charged through the brush and struggled up the steep slope of the ridge. Bullets buzzed past his ears and whapped into the dirt around him.

The fearsome reality of what had just happened exploded into his mind. Now the Ghost Dance and Cho-ocks's medicine will *have* to work. *Captain Jack* was at war with the United States.

PART THREE

Land of Burnt-Out Fires

About midnight the women began to wail for the dead from the hills. There is no sound so sad, so heartbroken and pitiful as this long and sorrowful lamentation. Sometimes it is almost savage. It is loud and fierce, and vehement, and your heart sinks. . . . Then your soul widens out and you go down with them to the shore of the dark water, to stand there, to be with them and of them, there in the great mysterious shadow of death, and to feel how much we are all alike, and how little difference there is in the destinies, the sorrows, and the sympathies of the children of men.

—Joaquin Miller,
Life Amongst the Modocs: Unwritten History, 1873

The things we admire in man—generosity, openness, honesty, understanding and feeling—are the concomitance of failure in our system, and those traits we detest—shoddiness, greed, acquisitiveness, meanness, egotism, self-interest—are the traits of success. And while men admire the quality of the first, they love the produce of the second.

—John Steinbeck, *Cannery Row*

Listen ye winds to the neighing steeds and clashing sabers, and see the uniformed officers and the brave boys, all with faces turned toward the Lava Beds, going down to vindicate the honor of the State whose soil had been invaded by a ruthless savage foe. The doom of the Modocs is sealed, and war! war! war! is the cry.

—A. B. Meacham, *Wigwam and Warpath*, 1875

THIRTY-SIX

The Boddy Ranch, 28 December, 1872

HAKAR STARED INTO Cynthia Boddy's terrorized eyes as his men crammed into her house. The Boddy homestead was the last in a string between Kalelk and the lava beds. Fourteen dead male settlers littered their trail.

Mrs. Boddy backed into a corner of her kitchen, trying to hide her daughter behind her. "A-are you going to kill us?"

Hakar thought of Kentapoos's standing orders and struggled with the English words, "No afraid. Modocs no fight woman, baby. Soldiers and your man kill Modoc woman, baby. I see your man, I kill him. Now need food."

Mrs. Boddy gave them sugar, flour, and coffee. Hakar nodded and left. He thought of the old woman, Grass, who was too feeble to flee from the soldiers at Kalelk. They had found her charred body curled under a pile of burnt tule mats the following day. The soldiers had set her afire in her latch before returning to Fort Klamath.

It took all of Hakar's will not to kill the Boddy woman.

◄

Fort Klamath Indian Agency Office, three days later

COLONEL Wheaton's face turned from red to purple. His eyelids blinked rapidly. "Fourteen settlers butchered! By God, I'll have the heads of every one of those savages!"

Frank, Winema, Agent Dyar, the Superintendent of Indian Affairs, and Captain Jackson listened intently to the newly assigned area commander. Frank started to speak, but Winema stood first. "*Why* are your people dead?" She glowered at Wheaton and Jackson. "Why are seven of *my* people dead, and thirty wounded?"

Jackson glared back. "And I've got ten dead troopers, six badly wounded. You weren't there. They opened fire on us. We had no choice."

Frank frowned. He knew damn well the Modoc men would never allow gunplay with the women and children around. "That ain't what *we* heard, Captain."

Jackson's eyes flashed. "Who'd you hear from, some old squaw?"

Frank clenched his fists as he moved closer to Jackson. "Like the one you brave boys burned up in Kalelk? We heard you never got General Canby's permission to go down to Lost River."

"By God, sir." Wheaton bristled. "I'll not be questioned by a squawma—" He seemed to rethink his words. "—a civilian. There wasn't time to—"

Klamath Agent Leroy Dyar rose in defense. "Captain Jackson felt the army would lose the settlers' confidence if he didn't take action right away."

The superintendent held up his hands. "All right, enough. We all feel the tragedy of these losses. We have a bigger problem. How do we peacefully return Jack to the reservation?"

Wheaton stood, drew on his high-cuffed cavalry gloves, and placed his hat carefully on his head. "This is no longer an

Indian Service problem, Superintendent. They have molly-coddled Jack for years. Those Indians fired on United States soldiers and murdered innocent settlers."

Dread filled Winema. "*Tyee* Wheaton. I know these lava beds and I know my cousin. I do not think he wants a fight. But if you make war on him there, many of your soldiers will die. Let me talk to him. I will make him see that he must return to Yainax."

Wheaton shook his head. "I have already wired General Canby and expect orders at any moment."

Frank and Winema looked to the new state superintendent for rebuttal. None came. They found themselves missing Albert Meacham.

THIRTY-SEVEN

Yreka Journal, 1 January, 1873

THE MODOCS ARE being gradually reinforced by stragglers from the reservation tribes, notwithstanding the professed friendship of these Indians, and it is also believed some of the Pit River Indians from Eastern Siskiyou are joining them. Some of the soldiers, immediately after the attack, went to Miller's Island and took a view of the Indian camp, where they saw more Indians than usual, which convinced them that the Modocs have been receiving reinforcements from some quarter.

The time of the Oregon Volunteers has almost expired, and they will soon be mustered out. There are about 280 soldiers in the field, and so many are required for escort, standing guard, and other duties, that there are but seventy-five men to do the fighting, being less than the number of fighting Indians.

Should the fight linger on, there may be great danger of an outbreak at the reservation in which case the settlers in the neighborhood would be in great danger of their lives and property.

We learn that three hundred bomb shells and a number of ordnance have been sent for. Bomb shells are something the Indians are not acquainted with, never before having smelt gunpowder in that shape.

The Riddle Ranch, 10 January

FRANK placed a cool cloth on Winema's forehead as she lay in their bed. Fatigue and worry chased each other like dark clouds across her face. "Damn it. Didn't I tell you you'd make yourself sick running back and forth between Jack and Wheaton?"

Charka cast a worried look at his mother. "Ma's gonna be all right, ain't she, Pa?"

Winema extended a fevered hand to grasp her son's. "*Ena* will be fine." She coughed several times, then her eyes shifted to Frank. "You should see the sick ones at the caves." She closed her eyes as if in pain. "So cold and wet . . ."

Frank frowned. "Well, Jack can come out of there any time and go back to Yainax, damn it."

Winema shook her head. "Cho-ocks and Black Wound have convinced him not to trust the Whites. He will not"—another fit of coughing racked her body—"will not come out until he has land in *Mowatoc* like Mee-cham promised."

Frank wrung out the cloth in a pan of cool water and mopped Winema's face. Shaking his head, he said, "Christ. Them caves are a damned sight worse than the reservation ever could be."

She nodded. "I told him about the soldier camps."

"At the Van Bremers' and the Fairchilds'?"

"*Ih.*" Winema rested regretful eyes on Charka. Worry lined his youthful face. Suddenly he seemed aged beyond his twelve seasons. "*Ena*, I heard the soldiers say bad things about our people. They said they would soon 'have Modoc steaks.'"

Frank managed a thin smile. "Not to worry, son. I spoke with General Canby yesterday. He said he thought the snow would bring them out soon, that there'll likely be no shooting."

Charka's concerned expression didn't change. "I'm worried about Aunt Kweelush and Lodge Woman . . . and Moonlight."

Winema squeezed his hand. "I know, *gaw oonok*. We all

worry." Winema glanced at Frank. There was nothing else to say. Charka was well aware of the situation. He was at that difficult age, between childhood and adulthood, where some adult actions made sense and others defied youthful logic. Not too long ago Charka's favored lament had been, "It's not fair." Frank had said he recalled that age, but it had been much easier for him. He did not have to struggle with an "Indian side," nor did he have to bear the sting of being called half-breed, or dirty redskin.

Charka arched his small eyebrows expectantly. "I hope they come back soon. Cousin Jack promised to take me hunting."

Frank and Winema exchanged thin smiles.

◄━

Army Command Tent, 12 January

DESPITE the efforts of an old field stove, the command tent was ice cold. The officers' breath hung in the air as they awaited orders. General Canby straightened his shoulders, flexed his head to the left as if to smooth out stiffness. "Gentlemen, I still believe this will be over before any shooting. However, we must continue as if we've a fight on our hands." He glanced at Captain Perry. "Captain Perry, take your troop and clear the bluff southwest of Tule Lake, then prepare a camp for Captain Ross and his volunteers. They arrive Thursday night." Turning to Colonel Wheaton, Canby continued, "Are we still expecting Major Mason's battalion along with Ross and the two howitzers on time?"

"Yes, sir. They will march down from the Van Bremer camp on Wednesday."

"Very good. What are your plans for Major Bernard's cavalry?"

Wheaton's eyelids blinked rapidly. "Troop G will fight as infantry, sir. They'll attack from the east. As you know, there is no way to get horses through the lava beds. The men are calling it the Devil's Garden."

The officers chuckled.

Wheaton went on. "Dave Hill and his Klamath scouts will attack from the east side of the Stronghold. Major Green will have operational command."

"Very well," Canby replied, then, "I heard Perry and Lindsay Applegate's brother were fired upon yesterday."

"Correct, sir. They were scouting the western bluff. Apparently, a few Modocs were hidden among the rocks down there. No one was hurt."

"There was some wordplay between the Klamaths and the Modocs?"

"Yes, sir. Unlike Lindsay, Jesse's no Injun lover. But he parlays a little of their tongue. He understood the Modocs to invite the Klamaths to join them. Applegate thinks the Klamaths said they might. Then the Modocs switched to English and asked the soldiers to come down and fight."

Canby frowned. "Let's not take any chances. Use McKay's Warm Springs scouts and send the Klamaths home."

~

Oregon Volunteers Camp, Van Bremer Ranch, 15 January

HARLEY Sievers shivered as he cupped a mug of hot coffee in his hands. He couldn't remember when he had been so cold. "I'm sick of all this waitin'. The army sure as hell ain't gonna kill any Modocs with drills and meetin's."

Piney Hobbs swung his arms and danced from one foot to the other, trying to keep warm. "Boy, I hear ya. I got my eye on that big white stallion of Jack's. I'm gonna take him home with me if these generals and colonels ever stop talkin' and start fightin'."

"Suit yourself. I'm gettin' me one of them good lookin' Modoc squaws to do my cookin'. They say the better lookin' ones cook better'n the ugly ones."

Whitey, who had come to the camp to get the latest news, spat in the fire. "You boys is mistaken. Cap'n Jack ain't on open ground now. Even when he was, he gave Cap'n Jackson the worst lickin' a man ever got in this neck of the woods. Now,

Jack's in the all-firedest place in the world. You ever been down there, in the Devil's Garden?"

The men around the fire stared blankly.

Whitey snorted. "I've been there, and I tell ya, it's all snagrock and caves. Ya can't lead a horse through it in a week. Even if ya could, then ya got rock walls with natural lookouts, and all of it on the high ground. Jack and them Injuns know every inch of it. When they're in them caves, you couldn't *blast* 'em out." He made his wheezy laugh. "I'm goin' down just to see the fun."

"Shee-it, old timer," Harley snarled. "You been panning dirt too long. We got 225 regulars and over a hundred volunteers spoilin' for a good fight. Why, Cap'n Ross said we was so eager to get at them Injuns, he worried we'd eat'em up raw if he let us go."

Whitey chuckled. "Cap'n Ross shouldn't fret none. You won't be hard to hold back when the Modocs open fire."

THIRTY-EIGHT

The Stronghold, Lava Beds, 16 January

KENTAPOOS LOWERED THE ancient looks-far glasses and sighed. He turned and stepped down from his parapet. What he saw only reinforced what Winema had reported. It brought a black cloud over him that would not lift.

Back at the main camp the men were gathered around a large fire. The chief stared morosely into the flames and warmed his hands. "We have made a mistake. We cannot win against the soldiers. Suppose we kill them all? More will come until all of us are killed." He cursed. "I never wanted war; I want peace. And some of those men down there are our friends."

Black Wound's mouth curled into a sneer. "How quickly you forget Ben Wright and those soldier *wochagam* at Kalelk. We can expect nothing from these *boshtin*. We may die, but we will not die first. *I* will fight!"

Krelatko shook his head slowly. "At Lost River I was angry, too. My heart was bad. I, too, have many friends among the Whites." He gazed at Wound. "Our chief is right. We cannot stand against them. My wife and children cry to go home."

Cho-ocks's eyes narrowed like gunslits. "Listen to you. You sound like whining women. My hands are already red with *boshtin* blood. I *want* war. These White men cannot fight. The spirits have told me so."

Black Wound and several other warriors mumbled their approval.

"It is the wind you hear, Cho-ocks," Kentapoos rebuked, "not the spirits. And the wind changes direction often."

Cho-ocks scowled, then turned toward the caves. His voice rose so the women and children could hear. "Tonight, I will make medicine that will turn their bullets away from us! We can kill all the Whites that come! Tonight we Ghost Dance! We will force them to return our land!" He turned to Kentapoos. His voice softened to a low, snide pitch. "Then we will have peace."

Kentapoos despaired as he saw the effect of Cho-ocks's speech on the crowd. Lately, the voices of Kentapoos's followers had diminished before Cho-ocks's boasting tirades. He had allowed Cho-ocks to garner too much sway with the people. And now the final vote would come after the dance. The best he could do was try to reach supporters and swayers during the dance and persuade them to his way of thinking.

THE sun dropped below the jagged rim of pumice, then flared behind the high western ridge, causing Tule Lake to darken, then dissolve. As darkness crept over the valley, the Stronghold formed into talons of umber rock, then into shadowed monoliths under the pale moonlight.

His face bathed in firelight, Cho-ocks raised his medicine bundle skyward. "*Kapka, Kemush! Kapka, Isees! Kapka, ditchee skoks! Kapka nanook' kolka ho stinos*! Come all into our hearts! Help us think. Into our eyes to help us see. Into our ears to help us hear. Into our arms to make us strong. Help us to hide from the sight of our enemies. Send killing bullets! Send *lokum skoks* to blind the *shuldshasham* eyes. Make them weak, make them afraid."

A respectful hush fell over the camp. Then, as if punched in the chest, Cho-ocks sucked air between his teeth and blurted,

"Hah!" His eyes grew big as an owl's as he surveyed the crowd. "*Kemush* is here! *Isees* is here! *Ditchee Skoks* are here! I can feel them! Our prayers will be heard. Join your hearts, my people, and with the presence of the good spirits, we will pray for a great cloud to come down and hide us from the soldiers!"

The crowd was mesmerized. "HEYA! HEYA!"

Cho-ocks again raised the bundle. "*Lo'was yanna nanook'ush wal-chot'ka*. Great Spirit, send a dark cloud over these rocks!"

"*HEYA!*"

From somewhere among the rocks, a coyote howled dolefully, and the drum began. A group of women formed a crescent behind the drummers and sang:

> *Mother, come home; Mother, come home,*
> *My little brother goes about always crying,*

The painted dancers formed a circle and joined hands. Cho-ocks and his helpers handed each dancer a sacred peyote button, the cactus medicine that enabled them to see, to understand, to commune with their ancestors—to show the Old Ones the way home.

> *My little brother goes about always crying,*
> *Mother, come home; Mother, come home.*

The dance circle took slow shuffling side steps. Cho-ocks stood in the center, eyes closed in prayer. From time to time he moved inside the circle, wafting sage and cedar smoke on the dancers. There were four heavier honor beats, then the tempo picked up. The dancers moved faster, around and around, their heads arched back.

> *Mother, come home; Mother, come home.*
> *The whole world is coming, the whole world is coming,*

The voices of the seven drummers rose as the women's trailed off.

A nation is coming, a nation is coming,
An eagle has brought the message to the People,
The Father says so, the Father says so.

Boom . . . boom . . . boom-boom-boom.
Honor beats resonated through their breasts. Father Peyote
spread his warm fingers through their bodies, piqued their
senses: visions never seen before, smells never smelled before,
tastes never before as piquant or sour.

Painted half red and half black, Black Wound's face
alternated between ecstasy and rage. He yelped in time with the
honor beats, swinging an old tomahawk over his head. Moving
around the outside of the circle, he jumped and swirled,
swiping the weapon at unseen enemies.

Over the whole Earth, they are coming,
The deer are coming, the deer are coming,

Cho-ocks's high plaintive voice broke through, driving,
prodding, accelerating the beginning of each strain.
BOOM . . . BOOM . . . BOOM . . . BOOM-BOOM-
BOOM.
Woman Watching, Lodge Woman and Kweelush collapsed
to the ground, shaking and mumbling.

King Hawk has brought the message to the People,
The Father says so, the Father says so.

The dancers' faces bore the imprint of their ecstasy. Now
Green Basket and Wild Girl collapsed. The drum, the movement, the words, the peyote, swept away the earthly world,
unleashed frustration, desperation, and sorrow, transforming
them into visions of beauty, of dead loved ones, of the return of
all things good and sacred.

They are coming, all are coming,
Says the Father, says the Father,

The land will laugh,
The mountains will ring,

Cho-ocks was trembling now, saliva foaming around his mouth as his lips formed unintelligible words. The women's chorus lifted their voices a half-step as they shook turtle shell rattles painted with white stars.

BOOM . . . BOOM . . . BOOM-BOOM-BOOM.

Kentapoos chewed one of the hairy, desiccated peyote disks. At first it lay hot and bitter in his stomach. He fought the urge to vomit. But slowly Father Peyote worked his medicine. Kentapoos staggered, then found support against a rock. He felt the medicine warming his belly, caressing his mind.

Slowly the dancers and the drum seemed to fade into the distance as Kentapoos's mind slipped the bonds of flesh. The night sky foamed into a black sea, then burst open like a black flower to allow a gigantic warrior on horseback—galloping, galloping toward him. A great wind rushed before the rider, blowing Kentapoos's old cavalry hat off his head, shoving him against the rocks, compressing his chest and lungs.

The *laki* trembled in horror. Dressed in the old way of a war chief, the ghost rider thundered toward him. Around his head he wore a wide band of feathers. Skins of coyote, beaver, and mink flapped about his shoulders and arms like battle flags. His face was painted completely black, the whites of his eyes flashing through the blackness.

BOOM . . . BOOM . . . BOOM-BOOM-BOOM.

Such anger, such bitterness, such ferocity. It was his father's face. Kentapoos raised his arm to shield his eyes from the raging wind. "*KAI*, FATHER, *KAI*!"

The charging warrior brandished a long rabbit pole with a snare loop on the end.

BOOM, BOOM-BOOM.

Furious eyes pierced like knives of ice. Frozen in terror, Kentapoos watched the snare loop jiggle ever closer. *Move*! he thought. *Run*!

The rivers will sing, the rivers will sing,
Says the Father, says the Father.

He felt the cord snag his neck, felt it jerk tight, cutting into his throat.

"*KAIIIIII*—!"

His scream went unnoticed, overpowered by the simultaneous outcry of Cho-ocks somewhere in the hazy distance—

The drum stopped.

The singing trailed off.

The dark angry warrior shattered into pinpricks of stars.

Groggy, Kentapoos looked inside the circle with haunted eyes. Cho-ocks recovered and was helped to his feet. He rotated slowly, looked into the eyes of each dancer. "You have all seen and felt the medicine of the Ghost Dance. You have spoken with your dead relatives. You saw the Above World and its beauty. You saw the animals returning!"

"*IH! IH!*"

Cho-ocks paused for effect. "BUT DID YOU SEE ANY WHITES?"

"*KAI!, KAI!*"

The holy man climbed a nearby outcropping and looked down on the crowd. "Hear me, my people!" The firelight painted his face in a macabre mask of orange light and shadow. "I have returned from a sacred journey—to the *lokum skoks*. The spirits gave me great power this night. Tomorrow comes the medicine cloud. It will blind the *boshtin* soldiers, AND WE WILL SHOOT THEM DOWN LIKE DOGS!"

"YEEEEE-IH!" Black Wound led the war cry. Waves of yips and ululating trills followed.

BOOM, BOOM, BOOM.

The drum started again. Rattles hissed like angry snakes. Hands joined. More peyote was passed. Their voices rose with greater joy and fervor.

They are coming! All are coming!
Says the Father, says the Father,

My bow is strong; my arrows fly straight,
Says the Father, says the Father.

Bats—shapeless shadows in the night—flitted above on
their way to the valley below as Kentapoos sagged against an
outcropping. The *kiuks*'s medicine was too powerful. Kentapoos knew now the vote would go against him. Slumped like
a man bearing a heavy weight, he staggered toward his cave.
Mentally placing each warrior along the Stronghold's rimrock,
Kentapoos began to outline a plan of defense.

THIRTY-NINE

The Lava Beds, 17 January

THE FIRST LIGHT of dawn came weak and late due to an unexpected thick blanket of fog that hulked over the Devil's Garden. Captain Jackson peered into the haze. "Damn!" He couldn't see twenty yards. Disoriented, Bernard's men had strayed too close to the Stronghold during their dawn reconnaissance five hours earlier. The Modocs had cut down three men, scattering the rest. But Jackson had his orders. There was no going back. He turned and walked into the rousing cavalry camp. Leather creaked, bit rings chinked, horses whinnied nervously, sergeants barked orders, cold men grumbled. Sergeant Kelly brought the captain's horse, held out the line. Kelly knew the captain since he was a young lieutenant. "Beggin' the Captain's pardon, but it's crazy to attack in this blasted fog."

Jackson took the reins and looked around to see if anyone was within earshot. "You're right, of course, Sergeant." He inclined his head toward Colonel Wheaton's command tent. "Blinky says the fog gives us the advantage. It will 'mask our attack across dangerously open ground.'" Jackson mounted and smiled ruefully at the old non-comm. He mimicked Wheaton's demeanor. "'Vigilance, gentlemen! Vigilance!' Those were the colonel's final words on the matter."

The captain heeled his bay and trotted over to his bugler. "Corporal, sound Boots and Saddles."

❧

WINEMA, her eyes red and puffy, huddled in an army blanket inside the command tent. The army was through talking, and she was out of ideas. Frank paced beside her as Colonel Wheaton packed his map case. Wheaton eyed Winema and reasoned, "General Canby thinks all we need is a little show of force this morning. I agree. I figure Jack isn't up for a real fight. He'll surrender and we will all go home. If not, well, your cousin has made his own bed."

Frank looked surprised. "You mean they're going to let Jack off scot-free?"

Wheaton shrugged. "The governor had a conniption when he heard Jack would be sent back to Yainax. He wants to try him for depredations against those settlers." He finished buttoning his greatcoat, turned up the collar. "But that is a political fight between the Indian Service and the state. I'm just a soldier following orders." He nodded curtly and left the tent.

BOOM! BOOM!

Winema jumped. The two howitzers hurled shells toward the Stronghold. Their reports echoed down the valley. A bugle sounded a tattoo. Only yards away they heard Captain Jackson's voice: "FORRRWARRRD!"

❧

AT the volunteer camp, Captain Ross heard the report of the cannons. "There's the signal, boys!" He stood, waved his rifle in the air. "Let's eat'em up!"

Harley's and Piney's rebel yells carried above the rest, and the Oregon Volunteers started forward. The yells trailed off as the men uneasily entered the souplike mist at the bottom of the ridge.

WHAM! WHAM! Shells exploded ahead of them.

"I hope they know when to quit them cannons!" Piney shouted over the din.

"This is crazy!" Harley shouted. "I can't see shit."

Gravy Brooks, a volunteer on Harley's left, said, "I figure if we can't see them Injuns, they can't see us."

Harley's lips twisted cynically. "Yeah, then we *tell* 'em we're coming with them damned bugles and cannons."

The fog enshrouded them now. Harley could barely see Piney to his left. Figures faded in and out like phantoms.

"Aw, Christ!"

"Damn!"

"Son of a—!"

Blinded by the mist, men stepped into crevices, wrenched their ankles, and tripped over rocks. The cannonade lifted and an eerie silence stilled the air. Harley and Piney heard only their own hard breathing against the cursing, stumbling silhouettes around them.

Soon the sun began to burn off the haze. The soldiers and volunteers found themselves scattered across an open plain less than a hundred yards from the Stronghold walls. Harley heard yells and war cries ahead, then an explosion of rifle fire. Bullets buzzed through the air like angry hornets. Screams of pain, curses, and garbled orders filled the air. Two hundred rifles returned fire from the valley floor, sounding like ripping sheets.

"Sonsabitches!" Harley cursed the Modocs in frustration. "Piney! Where are ya?"

Somewhere ahead, Captain Ross's voice cried, "FIRE AT WILL!"

Harley's Sharps slammed against his shoulder as he fired wildly toward the unseen enemy.

"Aiiigh! Lordy, Jesus! Harley, ya shot me!"

Sudden dread poked needle-like into Harley's veins. The fog had burned off in spots, and the Modoc shooters were well hidden behind parapets of rock. Harley's eyes desperately searched around. "Piney! Where are ya?"

Rifle fire from the Volunteers became unorganized and ragged while heavy fire continued from the Stronghold. Captain Ross's voice floated faintly from up ahead, "Retreat, go back!"

Their eyes wide with terror, men bolted past Harley, back toward the ridge camp.

"Look out!"

"Run, goddamnit, run!"

One man rammed into his shoulder, knocking Harley down. He dropped his Sharps as he fell. "Shit!"

Piney's weakened voice floated through the mist, "Help me, Harley."

Harley's heart pounded like the Modoc drum as he clambered to his feet. Forgetting his rifle, he turned and ran with the rest.

IT was easy, picking off the soldiers below. Their bugles and yells gave ample warning. Black Wound laughed and yipped at each round he fired. He shouted insults at the enemy. "Hey, soldier man! Come get me, soldier man! I humped your wife last night, *boshtin!*"

Two blue-coated soldiers and one Volunteer had strayed into the path of Black Wound's rifle. They lay sprawled in the snow below him. The *boshtin* scattered and ran like frightened deer. Thrusting his rifle into the air in triumph, Wound cried, "Yeeeeeih! Yih-yih-yih!"

Fifty-three of his comrades chorused his cheers. Picking his way down the Stronghold wall, he joined the other warriors as they riffled through the dead soldiers' belongings for food, ammunition, and clothing.

"It was as Cho-ocks prophesied!" he shouted to one as he tried on a soldier's fur cap. "His medicine is true!"

The warrior waved. "*Nent!* Not one *boshtin* bullet found Modoc flesh! Not even their big guns can hurt us!"

Another warrior laughed. "The cloud came down and blinded them just as the *kiuks* foretold!"

Modocs scrambled over the field. Several rifles—Spencers, Henrys, Remingtons, Ballards—lay strewn about the valley floor. Black Wound's feelings of elation and invincibility were bolstered by those of his fellows. Not even after one of his singular *boshtin* killings had he ever felt so alive, so powerful.

There was a noise to his left—a groan, then a weak, whining voice.

"Sweet Jesus. Help me, Harley. I'm bad shot."

Wound was on the White man in a heartbeat. The *boshtin*'s eyes opened. Seeing Black Wound, his face stretched in terror. The White man's outcry was cut short, replaced by a gurgle, as Black Wound's knife slashed and blood poured into the *boshtin*'s windpipe.

🙜

The Command Tent

CANBY frowned at Lieutenant-Colonel Wheaton. "Your report, Colonel."

"Nineteen regulars and nine volunteers are wounded, General. The surgeon says two of those won't make it through the night."

"How many killed?"

Wheaton started blinking. He cleared his throat. "Seven regulars and two volunteers are missing."

"Missing?"

The colonel's tone dropped an octave. "Left for dead on the field, sir, or lost in the fog."

Canby flexed his head to the left. "And enemy dead?"

"Unknown, sir."

"I understand Major Green was wounded."

"Yes, sir. The major displayed conspicuous bravery. I will be recommending him for the highest decoration."

"Very well. Is Major Green expected to recover?"

"The surgeon is attending him now, sir."

Canby chewed his lip in thought, then said, "That will be all, Colonel."

Wheaton's brow furrowed as if he was about to add something. He seemed to think better of it, saluted, and left the command tent.

Winema felt sick. Blood had been shed foolishly. Now Kentapoos and the others might die here, or be locked away forever to a *boshtin* jail. And she had no way of knowing which of the Modocs might have been killed or wounded in the attack. Canby turned to her. His deeply lined, beardless face was ruggedly handsome for a man of fifty-six seasons. He had dark blue eyes that were deep-set—melancholy and gentled like those of an old warrior who had seen too much war. They emitted honesty, she thought. She and Canby had enjoyed many long talks over the past cold nights. The star chief was experienced with Indians and respected their fighting skills.

"Well, Toby. Jack surprised me. I didn't think he'd fight. Looks like I'll be needing your services after all."

Winema felt relief wash over her. "No more shooting, then?"

The general cocked his head, leaned toward her. He towered over her. "*I hope*, no more shooting. To be frank, I'm not prepared for a siege against that Stronghold. Not with only two hundred men—less, actually. For those who haven't already deserted, the volunteers' enlistment terms expire on the twenty-fifth." He opened a wood humidor on a rickety field table, plucked out a cigar, then offered the case to Frank. "I want to try to talk Jack out of that Stronghold and back onto the reservation. I'll need your help getting that accomplished." He looked into her eyes. "However, I am also requesting reinforcements from San Francisco."

"What about Colonel Wheaton?" Frank asked.

Canby's face clouded. "He will return to *garrison* duties at Fort Klamath." He emphasized *garrison*.

Winema frowned. "May I speak what is in my heart, *tyee*?"

"Of course, Toby."

She glanced at Frank, then spoke in Modoc. "Do you want to talk to Jack only because you wait for more soldiers, or do you truly want to stop the shooting?"

Frank translated. Canby looked at Winema and smiled. "Still don't trust a Yankee, eh?" He closed his eyes, rubbed his temples. His gaze shifted to Winema. "What do you think Jack wants?"

"*Tyee*, I do not think Jack wants this fight. He said he wants only a little land in Lost River Valley."

The general looked at Frank. "You agree?"

Frank nodded. "General, if he's said it once, he's said it a hundred times."

Canby's face grew serious. "Believe me, I would prefer a peaceful settlement as well. I have ten or eleven dead men already. It will cost a lot more to take that Stronghold. My orders are to put Jack and his people back on the reservation, but I have no authority to negotiate for land."

Frank considered this a moment, then, "Well, then, we got a Mexican standoff. Jack has put himself in a tight spot. He's got to come out of this thing with something, or lose face."

The general unbuttoned the first few buttons of his greatcoat and sat down heavily in his field chair. "Do you think you could convince Jack to powwow with us, Toby?"

"*Ih, tyee*. Yes."

Canby tapped gloved fingers on his field table as his eyes flitted between Frank and Winema. "All right. Tell you what I'll do. I will wire my superiors and suggest the establishment of a peace commission."

Winema brightened and looked at her husband.

"That sounds fair," Frank said. But his face betrayed a lack of confidence in his words.

The general placed his hands on his knees, leaned forward. "Good. But remember. I still have my main mission to accomplish. With the reinforcements, I'll have a thousand men and seven howitzers." He shot Frank a wry smile. "Negotiate from strength. General Bobby Lee taught me that."

Winema saw her husband's smile widen at the mention of General Lee. Canby seemed to know the right things to say.

Winema was a realist. As the daughter of a chief she understood the wisdom of talking peace while preparing for war. Now, they could only wait for an answer from the *tyees* in Washington. And pray.

FORTY

> *Weaha, wea, weyaha,*
> *kaweiha, kaweiha,*
> *ka! ka! ka! weha,*
> *wea, weyaha!*

THE WAR DANCE now usurped the Ghost Dance. Drunk with victory, the Modocs shouted, jumped, jabbing their rifles in the air, pointing and shooting silent bullets at unseen enemies. And there was Cho-ocks, the hero of the day, boasting the loudest, encircled by his admirers.

Kentapoos shared their excitement, but it was fleeting. All day he couldn't shake the feeling he was being watched, evaluated, berated. The vision of his father, the mad warrior rushing at him, snaring his head like a rabbit, loomed large in his mind. The *laki* massaged his throat as he recalled the jerk, then the sudden and violent constriction of his windpipe. A wakeful vision—a medicine vision—offered at least two levels of meaning. Often one meaning was personal, the other more broad. But what *was* the broader meaning of this vision? Did it mean he must fight a war he could not win no matter the result? Or was it a sign of the destruction to come if he did not find a way out? Whichever, there was no need to consult Jakalunus for the obvious meaning of the personal message: death.

An anger as cold as the rocks of the Stronghold erupted suddenly, taking him by surprise. Bitter tears seeped into his eyes. His own father, the man he had worshipped as a child but who never returned his love, who found fault with everything he did, now returned from the spirit world only to mock him once again. Kentapoos tipped back his head and bellowed at the night sky, "FATHER, YOU *WOCHAGALAM WEASH*! YOU *KASH*! NOW WHEN I NEED YOU MOST, YOU COME TO SPITE ME!" Spittle formed around Kentapoos's mouth. "YOUR WORLD IS GONE! WHAT DO YOU KNOW OF MY WORLD?"

The *laki* fell silent. He listened carefully, worried he might have been overheard. But the drum and singers echoed far down the path. He was alone.

Trudging back to camp, he knew his people's happiness would be only a temporary respite. Moving through the swaying bodies, he found his younger wife, Shade. He curled an arm around her and whispered, "Come with me."

At their cave Shade grinned in anticipation. "It has been too long since you wanted me, my husband." She threw her arms around him, pressed her pelvis against his.

He sighed and touched her cheek. "Ah, the fires of youth. I fear the cold has shriveled my desire."

She moved her hand to his crotch. "It is my task to un-shrivel, husband."

Kentapoos gently pushed her away. "I look forward to it." He stroked her hair. "Now, I need you for a more important task. I want you to take my horse and sneak quietly over to John Fairchild's. Tell him I wish to meet with him to talk peace. Ask him to tell Winema this."

In the darkness he could not read her face, but he felt her stiffen.

"Peace? But we are winning."

"Do not argue, Shade. Trust that I know what is best.

Everyone is at the dance, so there are no lookouts to challenge you." He pushed her toward the cave entrance. "Now go."

～

Yreka Journal, 12 February

"*THE country is now in a state of siege. The people that remain in it are forted up safely, but their live stock are at the mercy of the enemy. The Indians, though not numerous, are brave and determined.*

Should they hold out until spring, I have no doubt they will be strongly reinforced from the reservations, and the Modoc country will become the theater of an Indian war for years to come."

Such are the words of Jesse Applegate, father of the Applegate Trail, businessman, family man, and renowned Indian fighter.

Local people do not believe Jack's story about his terrible wrongs at the reservation, and consider his band are just such characters as would not be content with anything but the privilege of living like roving brigands. Besides, it is a well-known fact that Indians generally never live up to treaties.

The new members of the Peace Commission are Jesse Applegate, A. B. Meacham and L. Dyar, all of Oregon, and all connected with Indian reservation which indicates that the administration will never consent to any such humbug notion of giving the Indians a new reservation. The Oregon representatives have played sharp at Washington in getting ahead of the California delegation, and neither California Governor Booth or E. Steele will be connected with the Commission as first proposed.

Meanwhile, this reporter has heard a great deal of complaint about the Army's lack of action. While waiting for the Peace Commission to form, General Canby has turned over command to Colonel Gillem, who has arrived with reinforcements, while the general attends other business. So far, Gillem's main priorities seem to be the creases in men's uniforms and constant drilling. In the meantime, Jack and his desperadoes mill about the countryside in complete freedom, stirring up the other tribes into joining the revolt.

Only yesterday did they attack and commandeer an army supply wagon at Scorpion Point, and the Modocs were instantly resupplied. This being the case, we should not pin our hopes on the commission's first meeting with the Modocs upon Mr. Meacham's return.

FORTY-ONE

Fairchild Ranch, 18 February

ALBERT MEACHAM GESTURED toward Judge Roseborough as he made introductions. "Mr. Dyar, I think you know Judge Roseborough. The judge has known Jack for many years. I have no doubt the judge will prove an invaluable California member of our delegation." He emphasized "California." Californians, of late, fussed that they had no representation on the Peace Commission when the lava beds were on their side of the border.

The superintendent lit his briar pipe, took a few puffs. "You should also know that when General Canby returns, he will wear two hats. He will remain as the military commander in the field as well as serving as a member of our commission. I have been appointed chairman."

The men shook hands cordially. Meacham gestured toward Frank and Winema with his pipe. "And I have retained the services of Mr. and Mrs. Riddle as our interpreters-of-record. Frank will translate our words and Toby will translate the Modoc's words. There'll be no misunderstandings this time."

Heads nodded in agreement.

Meacham went on, "Lindsay Applegate's comment that 'Jawbone is cheaper than ammunition,' is on the mark. For this first meeting I think we merely want to become familiar with each other, perhaps get a sense of what it might take to bring the Modocs out of the Stronghold and onto a reservation."

Winema perked, glanced at her husband.

"*A reservation?*" Frank queried.

Meacham smiled. "Frank, Toby, I think you will be well pleased with Secretary of the Interior Delano's instructions to this commission." He lifted his eyes to address the entire group. "Our first mission is to discover the causes of the war and stop its spread. Secondly, we are to try to find a spot along the coast where the Modocs would agree to go, or some other location should the coast be unacceptable to them. Thirdly, we are not to give orders to the officers; however, we *are* to remind them that violence is to be used only as a last resort."

"Then Jack may return to our old land?" Winema prompted, catching the superintendent with his mouth open as he was about to start his next thought.

His mouth snapped closed. "Well, no, Toby. I meant to say, some location *other* than Lost River Valley."

Damn the twisting *boshtin* words, she thought.

Meacham rubbed his hands together. "Now, Toby has provided me with the current status of things at the Stronghold. By this time, there may be two, perhaps even three, separate factions. Cho-ocks seems to have an equal following to Jack's. Then there's Whusum's people. And now there might even be a third faction. Personally, I find it easier to see it as Jack's people versus Black Wound and his Hot Creek boys. But for the time being, Jack is still the chief." He glanced at Winema. "Is that correct, Toby?"

Winema nodded. "I am worried about these men—the Hot Creeks. You must be very careful when you talk with them. Keep a look-eye on Black Wound, Cho-ocks, and Whusum."

The superintendent smiled, patted her hand. "And we shall, dear lady."

Frank whispered in her ear, "That's keep a 'lookout.'"

Winema closed her eyes and huffed a frustrated sigh,

wondering how she had ever survived without all the brilliant men in her life.

Meacham turned back to the group. "Well, then, I suppose we're ready. Toby, I want to keep my interpreters safe until we know more about the situation up there. So, we need a messenger, other than yourself, to tell Jack we are ready to meet. Who do you suggest?"

Winema thought for a moment, then said, "The woman you call One-Eyed Dixie is camped nearby. She would be willing, I think."

"Very well. Send her out at first light."

Miners Camp on Lost River, 18 February

WHISKEY burned down Kankush's throat and settled hot in his belly. He belched and passed the bottle to Wieum. While on a cattle-stealing mission for Kentapoos they had run across two whiskey traders they had known from the old days.

Charley Harbaugh chuckled at Wieum's grimace, then winked at his partner, Mousehole Smith. "Tastes mighty good after bein' up in them caves for a couple months, don't it?"

Wieum nodded but still held his breath as the burning home brew faded in his chest.

Mousehole said, "You can hunt later. Have another drink."

Kankush passed the bottle to Wieum. "War be over soon," Kankush slurred. "Then we go home to Lost River."

Mousehole laughed. "Sure ya will, sure ya will. And I'll be made chief of all the Injuns in Oregon."

Harley's eyes snapped wide, then he belly-laughed so hard he almost tipped over his chair. Kankush chuckled, then checked himself. He squinted one eye and cocked his head with suspicious interest as the miners eyed each other conspiratorially. Harley grasped Kankush's shoulder like a friend confiding. "You don't think that Canby really wants peace, do ya? I heard tell that the general is pretty smart. I figure he'll try to get you boys all together for a meetin' and then, WHAM! he'll ambush the lot of ya."

The Modocs winced at Harley's sudden sound effect. Mousehole widened his eyes and pursed his lips—the picture of sobriety. "Honest Injun."

Harbaugh continued, "It's a fact, boys. Why, even if ol' Canby don't get you, you can't go back to Oregon. The governor—the big *tyee* up there—he'll hunt ya down and hang ya."

Wieum stood, looked at Kankush. "*Nat keka-istsna*," and the two Modocs made a hasty exit.

Harbaugh closed the shack door behind the anxious Modocs, and the miners burst into laughter. "Did you see that Injun's face?"

Mousehole pounded the table. "Lordy, wouldn't ya like to be there when those two get back to the Stronghold."

Both men could hardly catch their breath. Harbaugh wheezed, "Stupid damned niggers," and uncorked a fresh bottle.

━

The Stronghold, 22 February

HEADED for the meeting with local rancher and friend, John Fairchild, that Shade had arranged, Kentapoos and Krelatko prepared to mount their horses. A freezing rain fell like glass needles, coating the rocks and paths in a treacherous coat of glassy ice.

"*GETAK!*" Cho-ocks strutted into the cave with Black Wound and Skiet-teteko.

"Where are you going, my chief?" Black Wound said with mock respect. "Surely you would not council with the *boshtin* before consulting us?"

Kentapoos was grim-faced. "This is only a first-talk council, to see if we have anything to talk about."

Cho-ocks's voice was as cold as sleet. "What kind of chief are you? Only a Paiute would talk peace when he holds the balls of his enemies in his hand."

Every muscle in Kentapoos's body tensed.

Krelatko stepped to his chief's side. "We had good medicine that day. And the soldiers were few. Soon they will have ten times that number."

The holy man blew out his chest like a bullfrog. "Then I will make ten times the medicine." He glared at Kentapoos. "*Kai!* I forbid you to go."

Kentapoos stared at the smaller man. "You forbid?" Smart politics was cast aside as anger burned in his stomach, worked its way to his throat. Leading his horse, Kentapoos took three long strides, coming nose to nose with Cho-ocks. "You forbid? *I* am the chief, here, not you. *I* will decide when to talk to the Whites. I do not need your permission. I will consult the People at the right time!"

Black Wound took a step back and cocked his rifle.

Kentapoos stiffened. "You are threatening me?"

"You are a fool, Kentapoos. You heard what Wieum and Kankush told us. These talks are another *boshtin* trick. They mean to kill us!"

They were shouting now.

"Fools!" Kentapoos boomed. "If you had ever taken the time to know the Whites better, you would recognize whiskey talk!" He said it with conviction despite a creeping doubt.

Cho-ocks cocked his rifle, aimed it at Kentapoos's belly. "I think maybe the whiskey brings truth to their tongues."

Kentapoos's mind whirled. Had his father ever faced such open revolt? If so, how did he respond? Surely a *strong* chief would not find himself in such a dilemma.

Black Wound whispered into the *kiuks*'s ear. Cho-ocks squinted side-long at Wound as his voice eased slightly. "Very well. Go to your death. But leave your weapons here where brave men can make use of them." He jabbed the rifle barrel into the *laki*'s stomach.

"And if you live," Cho-ocks warned, "and try to come back, we will shoot you down like a dog."

Kentapoos trembled with rage and humiliation. Wound and Cho-ocks became more unstable each day, and Whusum and

Skiet-teteko weren't far behind. They had him, at least for tonight, but somehow, he would get a message to the Fairchild ranch, or to Winema. Time was his new enemy. The Hot Creeks gained support daily while his waned like the winter sun.

~

Yreka Journal

FROM the very first we have considered the Peace Commission a grand humbug and useless expense to gratify a set of mealy-mouthed hypocrites creating such a pressure on the administration to make peace.

Should peace be established by removing the murderers with the other Indians, to another reservation, it may not be long before the treacherous devils will be sneaking back to murder more good citizens. Captain Jack and his lice are a vagabond set, desirous of living like vagrants among the Whites, and stealing whatever they can.

If we believe in the government doing justice to the murdered Whites just as General Crook is gallantly doing with the Apache, so generally endorsed by the sanctimonious peacemongers who feel so good toward the disgusting Modocs, yet despise the Apache, who if anything, are fully as honorable as the Modocs.

The time lost in fooling with the commission could be more successfully employed in whipping the savages, or else the Modocs could be starved out if it takes all winter.

FORTY-TWO

Fairchild Ranch, 25 February

⟋ WINEMA WAVED TO Frank and Charka as she loped Skoks into the front yard. John Fairchild rode at her side. She dismounted and wearily hugged her two men. This was her third trip in as many days to the Stronghold, and she had the expression of a woman who had faced death.

At first Kentapoos wanted to meet in the Lava Beds, but Meacham refused, fearing ambush. So Meacham offered to meet at the ranch, but Kentapoos refused, fearing a trap. Finally Meacham offered to send Winema and John Fairchild to the Stronghold to break the deadlock.

"Are you all right, darlin'?" Frank asked. His hands flitted gently about her torso, as if looking for hidden wounds.

"*Ih*."

Frank threw a blanket around her, escorted her into the house.

"How did it go, John?" Meacham asked Fairchild.

"A bit slippery I can tell you, but Toby stood her ground. Jack agreed to a meeting with myself, Toby, and Judge Roseborough on the twenty-eighth. It will be in the beds, but out of rifle range from both sides."

Meacham straightened and grinned. "That's grand news.

Well done, the both of you." He looked at Winema. "How did you manage to change the Hot Creeks' minds?"

She pulled Charka closer to her. "Jack did it, not me."

Fairchild chimed in. "He convinced them that it was smart to keep the Whites talking until late spring. Then the Modocs could either start the war again or scatter to the mountains."

Meacham smiled wryly. "I admire a smart politician."

Winema sighed, rubbed her eyes.

"What's wrong?" Frank asked.

"I am worried about Kentapoos. I think he has been weakened by Cho-ocks's medicine. A spell perhaps. He is . . . different."

Frank's brow furrowed in concern. "Different?"

Winema shivered and drew the blanket tighter around her, her face revealing both worry and confusion. "I am no longer sure *what* he believes."

＜

Lava Beds, 28 February

KENTAPOOS, Krelatko, and Shade were waiting as Winema, Frank, John Fairchild, and Judge Roseborough walked their horses into the makeshift camp and hobbled them. It was cold and clear, the sky a startling blue. They shook hands all around and huddled around the fire.

"Since you are on our ground, it is proper for you to speak first," Jack said.

Winema turned to her cousin. "We are here to have a good talk with you. We will to stay the night if we must."

A cold smile pulled at Krelatko's lips. "*Ih.* You people might stay here longer than you want."

Winema kept her impassive expression. Krelatko was a big talker, but he was still loyal to Kentapoos. "Krelatko, you would be wise to listen to us. These men are our friends, and I am a Modoc like you. We are here to help you, not to fight you."

Krelatko worked his jaw. "We will see."

Kentapoos gestured to the piled blankets he had laid out around the fire. "Sit. Eat."

Shade passed out jerky.

Judge Roseborough cleared his throat. "Jack, you know me. We've been friends for many years. I am your friend in times of peace or war. You know we are not afraid of your men. As you can see, we are unarmed. We trust you because you are our friends. If you wanted to kill us, you could do it easily. We're placing all our trust in you."

Kentapoos listened soberly. "Your trust is not wasted. You know me. I know life is sweet, but I *will* take lives in self-defense. I cannot hold out long in these rocks against the soldiers with the few men I have. I know that you, Judge, represent the Peace Commission, who intend to make me some kind of offer, but I cannot promise what my answer will be."

Roseborough nodded. "I understand, Jack. Frank and Toby are here to explain some of that to you." The judge nodded at Frank.

"It is good to see you, Jack," Frank began. "I miss our old talks."

Kentapoos smiled glumly. "*Ih.* It is a cold heart that cannot be warmed by talk with a good friend."

Frank nodded. "I am sorry you are in all this trouble, my brother. But there has been trouble all over the world. There are thousands of people living peaceable, happy lives who were once at war. Their *tyees* talked things over and made peace. I think you can reason with these men the government sent. They're good men. Their names are General Canby and Colonel Meacham—the same man that talked to you on Lost River just before you went to the reservation You will all be safe and you will be treated right. Winema and I guarantee it." Frank used Meacham's honorary title of colonel to add further status.

Leaning forward, Frank emphasized his words. "Now, Jack, I want you to make peace. Winema, Charka, and me need you alive and kickin'. So do Shade, Green Basket, and Laughs Loud."

Kentapoos looked at his friend and cousin by marriage, then looked at Krelatko. Krelatko shifted his gaze to Fairchild. "What will happen to the Hot Creeks for killing the settlers in Oregon?"

Fairchild shot Frank a blank look. Frank arched his eyebrows and stroked his beard in uncertainty.

Roseborough cleared his throat. "Well, ah, we can probably keep them out of the Oregonian's hands. Most likely, they'll send them to Indian Territory."

Kentapoos considered this. Sending the Hot Creeks away would make his life much easier. He nodded. "*Nent*. I will meet the commission. Tell them I am willing to hear anything they have to offer if it is reasonable."

Winema took a deep breath, then leaked it out slowly. For the first time in months she allowed a modicum of hope to seep into her.

~

The Stronghold

"MAY those filthy soldiers be as miserable as we," Kweelush snapped as she squatted down on a cold, flat rock before a meager fire. Her lips numbed from chill air, she slurred her words. "We need firewood." She wheezed and hacked between words. "The sagebrush is too green."

Constant cold and hunger made Green Basket's face drawn and pasty. She spoke as she stirred a boiling pot. "The men will bring some when it is safe."

Kweelush hung her head in defeat. "We are not made to live in caves like *lok*. We will die here."

Green Basket spoke in a harsh whisper. "Keep your voice down. You will scare the children."

"Bah! They are young yet. Wait until they are old like me, and their bones stiffen up and ache all winter."

Green Basket ignored her and placed another armful of sagebrush and damp twigs on the fire. Everyone rubbed his eyes and coughed, waving feathered fans and shawls to chase the choking smoke from the cave. Given the choice of freezing to death outside, or suffering the acrid smoke inside, most chose the latter.

The *laki*'s wife was hungry, numb, and tired. And her toes were bruised and sore from running into countless jutting rocks embedded in the cave floor. Dirt sifted its way into their food and water. Her hands and feet ached from the frigid air. Sleep was near impossible. There were fire-tending duties, sick and bored children to attend, snow to melt for drinking water, and food to prepare.

Along with Shade and Laughs Loud, over a hundred of Green Basket's friends and relatives suffered with her, yet the chief's wife felt alone. Kentapoos had become morose and distant. She wondered what Winema was doing—warm and safe in her big house with her White husband. Was Winema a traitor, a coward, or just smarter than the rest of them? Her thoughts moved to other worries, worries about her husband's safety, worries about the growing power of Black Wound, Cho-ocks, and their followers. Since the revenge raids on the settlers, the *boshtin* referred to them as the Hot Creeks, separating them from Kentapoos's followers as the murderers of the fourteen white men. She wondered which posed a greater threat to Kentapoos—the Hot Creeks or the soldiers.

Green Basket shivered, rubbed her stinging eyes, and picked her way to the cave entrance. She snugged the blanket tighter around herself, murmured a quiet prayer, and stared into the bleakness.

FORTY-THREE

Fairchild Ranch, 1 March

    "LUCINDA, THERE IS no argument you bake the finest biscuits in the county." General Canby chortled as he refolded his napkin and placed it neatly on the polished cherry dining table.

Lucinda Fairchild's bourbon-smooth Georgia accent splashed the room. "Why, thank you, General. It's always a pleasure. I hope you will finish your story about that Navajo chief you defeated—Mister . . . oh, I can never remember those primitive names."

"Ah, Manuelito. Actually, that wasn't his Navajo name—"

A commotion in the front room cut off his thought. An excited Lieutenant Calley clomped into the dining room, hat in hand. Excuse me, General, but I think you'd better come outside."

Canby walked out onto the front porch and gaped at the scene before him. Hakar and his eight Hot Creeks stood by their steaming mounts, guarded by three disheveled soldiers.

Canby looked at Calley. "What's this?"

The lieutenant grinned, his Adam's apple bobbing in his enthusiasm. "They say they're here to talk terms."

Canby was dumbfounded. "Well, I'll be damned!"

"They came unarmed, sir."

For a fleeting moment the general creased his brow in suspicion, then made a sly smile. "My strategy is working, Lieutenant. Send a wire to General Sherman informing him that the Modoc war is all but ended. Request instructions as to when and where we should transport prisoners."

The general reentered the front room, rubbing his hands in anticipation. "Well, Meacham, you'll be pleased to know Hooker Jim and his band have just surrendered."

Meacham scrunched his newspaper noisily. "You're joking?"

Canby shook his head. "They're right outside."

Meacham accompanied the general to the front porch. He stared at the Modocs with unease. "Let's get them under close guard until we bring in Jack."

Canby crossed his arms. "I've a better idea. They're unarmed and pose no threat. Let them move about camp, see that we speak the truth when we say we want peace. Calley's guards, here, will see to it they don't escape."

Meacham looked unconvinced. "I don't know, General. I would feel more secure if—"

Canby frowned and interrupted. "Now, Albert," he dismissed, "this is a military matter at this point. I understand these people." He shouted at the corporal of the three-man guard, "Corporal, make doubly sure those men are not armed." Turning back to the superintendent, he continued, "They may be very useful. I may need their cooperation if the Peace Commission is to accomplish its mission."

Albert Meacham frowned, especially when the General said "I."

~

HAKAR was surprised. He waited for the lieutenant to take them under guard, but Calley rode off toward Hawkinsville like a flushed hare. The general disappeared into the house, returned with Meacham a moment, then disappeared again.

Leaderless and hung over, the guards ambled over to a nearby fire to join their friends, leaving the Modocs standing alone.

Hakar looked at Skiet-teteko and shrugged. Slowly they led their horses down into the encampment. It was alive with the smells of saddle soap, horse manure, boiling coffee, gun oil, bacon grease. Other than a few curious stares, no one bothered them.

Hakar whispered to Whusum, "They must think we are *Latinkini* scouts."

"Hey, you!" a gravel-throated voice rang out.

Hakar whipped his head around at the sharp tone.

"Come over here," a *boshtin* in a red shirt drawled, eyes squinted in unsure recognition.

This man was no soldier. The Hot Creeks eyed each other nervously as Hakar moved cautiously toward him.

"You look mighty familiar, Injun."

Hakar shrugged, made the sign that he did not understand. This was often successful in shucking unwanted Whites.

Slowly Red Shirt's eyes widened in recognition. "Shit, you're one of them Hot Creek Modocs!" He yelled over his shoulder, "Hey, Smitty, wasn't you at Lost River with Jackson?"

"Yeah. I was there."

Red Shirt settled his hands on his hips. "You better come over here."

As Smitty strode closer, his jaw dropped. "Son of a bitch, Harley. It's Hooker Jim hisself." He pointed at Hakar. "*He* led the massacres."

Skiet-teteko took a step forward. "Wait. We gave ourselves to General Canby. We are prisoners now."

Smitty scowled. "Is that so?"

Skiet-teteko's mind raced. He threw up his hands. "You see, we have no guns. Calley took them. We go to sergeant now."

Harley squinted. "Yeah? Where *is* Calley?"

Whusum pointed toward the ranch house. "There. Ask him."

Smitty's tight lips relaxed into a wolfish grin. "Well, then, boys, your killin' days is over. The governor issued a warrant for your arrest. As soon as we get ahold of your red asses, we're gonna hang the lot of ya." He leaned forward and spit, spurting a large blotch of tobacco juice on Skiet-teteko's moccasin.

Another White man now joined them. "Yeah, and I'll volunteer to be the hangman—*for free*."

Harley folded his arms and smirked. "I can't wait to see that." He elbowed Smitty. "We best be at the hangin' early if we want to see Jim, here, twitch. There'll be one helluva turnout."

Hakar stiffened, waiting for the men to close in on them. But the White men sauntered away, laughing, the telltale odor of whiskey in the air.

Harley waved, calling over his shoulder, "See you at the hangin', boys."

Once again the Hot Creeks were left to themselves. Either *Kemush* was protecting them, or the *boshtin* grew more stupid each sun. In any case, Red Shirt's words changed everything. Panic surged through Hakar. From their expressions, he could tell the rest of his men shared his fear. Now it was escape or a noose. Actually, it was not death he feared so much, but the horror and humiliation of *hanging* death.

Hakar led his men slowly through the camp. His biggest worry was being recognized by one of the *Latinkini* scouts. They would shoot first and ask questions later. Careful not to call attention to themselves, they mingled in between their mounts so that observers saw only horses' as they moved toward the eastern edge of the encampment, the farthest from the Stronghold. There, pickets were so widely spaced that Hakar could have lead the entire tribe through the gap.

Near the perimeter Barncho spotted an unattended cookfire. A beefsteak sizzled in a skillet. He looked around, and when satisfied no one saw him, unbuttoned his trousers and loosed a healthy stream on the meat.

Hakar had to think fast. He had promised his men special treatment and money if they helped him scout for Canby against Kentapoos. At a safe distance he turned urgently to his men. "You see; I was right! You heard those *boshtin* in the camp. Canby will say anything to get Kentapoos to surrender, then give us all up to the hangmen."

Black Wound clamped Hakar's arm like a bear trap. "You almost got us hanged, you fool," he hissed. "You should have taken my advice and killed Kentapoos. You were foolish to think Canby would make you a chief."

Hakar growled and pulled away.

Not hearing the private conversation, Slolux turned to the others. "Now the *laki* cannot ignore the truth. Canby is a liar. War is the only way now."

Hakar smiled. "Patience, Slolux. Now that Wieum and Kankush have refreshed our cattle herd, we have plenty of food. Would you not rather fight in warmer weather?" He peered toward the Stronghold in the distance. "We will let Kentapoos play with his Peace Council a while longer."

❧

Riddle Ranch, 4 March

TOSSING aside the *Yreka Journal*, Frank shook his head in disgust.

"What?" Winema asked.

He sighed. "Lieutenant Calley got lucky and captured a dozen of Kentapoos's horses."

Winema frowned.

"That ain't all. Canby has been ordered to give in to the Oregon governor. He's refused Fairchild's request of amnesty for the Hot Creeks."

Winema clucked her tongue in frustration. "Do they not understand my cousin's position? Everything they do strengthens Black Wound and Cho-ocks and weakens Kentapoos." She stood, worrying her hands. "Maybe the Hot Creeks are right. The *boshtin* do not want peace!"

Frank studied her. "You don't believe that, Winema."

"Ha!"

"It's politics, darlin'. You can't get around it. Not in the Stronghold, not in Salem."

"Politics!" Winema's jaw tightened. "Fools! They play with people's lives." She flopped into the chair, then immediately stood again. "Can they not see Kentapoos *wants* to trust them while the hotheads do not?"

Frank spoke to the floor. "Well, one thing's for sure. Mrs. Fisher and the other settlers' wives want justice, too."

Winema shot her husband an icy stare. Whose side was he on? Of course she understood Mrs. Fisher's feelings. Seth Fisher was an innocent bystander tending his field. How his wife must despise the Modocs for his murder; how she must see them as bloodthirsty savages, mindless killers. Then Winema's thoughts shifted to the Modocs—how they despised the soldiers and the traitor settlers who ambushed them. She knew all the reasons and excuses from both sides. It was as if she were straddling a gorge, unable to get to either side.

She slammed her fist against the chair arm, "*Kailash*!" This must be what it is like in the place the Whites call hell, a place where you are at war with yourself. For eternity.

~

Fairchild Ranch, 6 March

WINEMA sat opposite General Canby in the Fairchild's front room. A crackling fire in the fieldstone fireplace drenched them with comforting warmth. She concentrated before speaking, remembering Kentapoos's exact words as she relayed them to Canby: "Tell Canby I want everything wiped out, washed out. Let there be no more blood. My heart is sad about those murderers, but I have only a few men and don't see how I can give them up. Will you give up your people who murdered my people while they were asleep at the river? I could give up my horse to be hanged and not cry over it, but if I gave up my men I would have to cry."

The general pursed his lips. "That's all?"

"Yes, General. He hopes you can understand since you, too, are a chief."

"I'm afraid it's not the same thing, Toby."

Winema wanted to argue the point, but the general had been in a foul mood since the escape of the Hot Creeks. He stood abruptly and stretched. "It's late. I imagine you're as tired as I am. It looks like these negotiations are going to take longer than I thought. Let's go ahead as planned. Are you and Frank going out to the Stronghold tonight or tomorrow?"

"Tomorrow, *tyee*. We will con-vince Jack, as you say, to come here, that he will not be harmed or arrested."

"Excellent! I don't know what we'd do without you, Toby."

Winema forced a weary smile. "Be patient, *tyee*." She recalled Frank's words. "Jack is in a loose spot."

The general smiled but didn't correct her. "Manuelito, my dear lady, taught me patience."

The Stronghold, 7 March

SURROUNDED by grim-faced Modocs, Elisha Steele glanced nervously at John Fairchild, standing next to him. Steele paled as he counted sixty-nine angry faces, many of which were unfamiliar to him. "Look, Jack. I came up here because I thought I could do some good. I thought you were going to give up this thing and I could be of some help in your defense."

Whusum craned his neck forward. "You are with Fairchild. We do not trust him. He is the one who told Hakar it was safe to come to his ranch to talk, only so he could be captured and hanged."

Fairchild flushed as he spotted Hakar standing next to Whusum. "That's a damned lie, and you know it!"

The Modocs crowded in closer.

"I should kill you now," Whusum growled.

Hakar and Cho-ocks stepped forward, their rifles cocked and pointed at the peacemakers. "Enough talk. Let us get on with the killing," Hakar snapped.

"*Getak*!" Kentapoos stepped in front of Fairchild. Krelatko stepped between Steele and the Modocs. "I am ashamed. These men have been our friends for over twenty seasons. *Tyee* Steele was a friend of my father's in the old days. We *need* them as our friends."

A hush fell over the crowd. The rest of Kentapoos's followers fell in around Krelatko. Green Basket and Shade moved to their husbands' sides, holding cocked pistols leveled at Hakar and Cho-ocks.

Kentapoos looked at Steele. "Come with us. You will be safe in my cave for the night."

With Fairchild and Steele between them, Kentapoos and Krelatko walked quickly to the cave. It would be a long, cold night.

The following morning, four of Kentapoos's men escorted the harrowed White men safely out of the Stronghold. At the Fairchild ranch, badly shaken, Elisha removed his hat and smoothed back his thick brown hair. "I'm telling you Jack has got himself in one hell of a fix up there. If Krelatko and Jack hadn't stood guard over us all night, we would've been dead men."

Meacham looked concerned. "You say Jack was *pleading* with you?"

Fairchild nodded. "We talked all night. We were too jumpy to sleep. Jack begged us to ask you for some land on Lost River. He said if he could be assured of that, he would bring his people down and surrender *today*."

Elisha hurriedly pulled on his coat. "Jack told me confidentially that Black Wound and a few others threatened to kill the commissioners."

Canby settled back in his chair. "I wouldn't let that worry you, Elisha. That's just Injun puffery." He lit a cigar. "Perhaps you would like to join the commission. Sounds like Jack trusts you."

Steele's hands jerked at his coat buttons. "Not on your life, General. There isn't enough money in the United States treasury to get me out there again. Those aren't the Modocs *I* know." Canting his head, he arched his eyebrows, indicating he expected no argument. "I'm going home. Good day, gentlemen."

Steele stuffed his hat on his head and left.

Meacham seemed taken aback, but Canby calmly studied his cigar. "Interesting, don't you think, that Jack guarded Elisha's safety through the night. That tells you something about the man." He looked at the front door with remorse. "A damned shame. We need men like Steele on the commission. Jack obviously respects loyalty and honor."

Canby appraised Meacham out of the corner of his eye.

Meacham puffed thoughtfully, then withdrew his pipe. "Tried and failed, General. The Oregonians campaigned hard against him in Washington. They're in control. That's why we're having no luck finding a reservation for Jack along the coast. The Oregonians will fight it tooth and nail. Steele, you'll remember, is a Californian *and* friendly with the Modocs." Meacham probed the pipe bowl with a pick. "However, we do have Roseborough, another Californian. The Oregon delegation didn't know his name at the time, and I got him appointed."

Canby looked at Meacham with reluctant admiration.

The superintendent continued, "That's the problem with Washington. They don't understand these people. Indians won't negotiate with people they don't trust." Meacham sighed and inspected his pipe, which had gone out. "But, in this case, I am fast coming to the conclusion that Jack is losing control of those hotheads up there. If we aren't dealing with Jack, I don't believe our Peace Mission can succeed."

FORTY-FOUR

TELEGRAM

DATE: 8 March, 1873
TO: Honorable Columbus Delano
Secretary of the Interior
Washington
FROM: Albert B. Meacham

//BASED UPON RECENT EVENTS, I FEAR FOR THE
LIVES OF THE COMMISSIONERS AT ANY FORMAL
MEETING WITH THE MODOCS IN THE LAVA
BEDS/STOP/PEACE MISSION MAY FAIL/STOP//

TELEGRAM

DATE: 9 March, 1873
TO: Colonel A. S. Meacham
Fairchild Ranch, Lost River Valley, Oregon
FROM: Secretary Delano, Interior Department,
Washington

//DO NOT BELIEVE MODOCS MEAN TREACHERY/
STOP/MISSION MUST NOT BE A FAILURE/STOP/

THINK I UNDERSTAND NOW THEIR
UNWILLINGNESS TO CONFIDE IN YOU/STOP/
CONTINUE NEGOTIATIONS/STOP/CONFER WITH
CANBY/STOP//

TELEGRAM

DATE: 9 March, 1873
TO: General E. Canby
Military HQ, Fairchild Ranch via Ft. Klamath
FROM: General Sherman, Army HQ, Washington

//ALL PARTIES NOW MISTRUST COMMISSION/
STOP/ADVISE YOU TAKE CONTROL/STOP/BEST TO
FIND TWO OTHERS YOU TRUST AND NEGOTIATE
PEACE IN MOST EXPEDIENT FASHION/STOP/
HOWEVER IF INDIANS ARE STALLING I TRUST
YOU WILL MAKE USE OF YOUR FORCES SO THAT
NO OTHER INDIAN TRIBE WILL IMITATE THEIR
EXAMPLE AND THAT NO OTHER RESERVATION
FOR THEM WILL BE NECESSARY EXCEPT GRAVES
AMONG THEIR CHOSEN LAVA BEDS/STOP/
INAUGURATION OF PRESIDENT GRANT ON
FOURTH INSTANT EXCEEDED ALL PAGEANTRY
IN HISTORY OF COUNTRY/STOP/SORRY YOU
MISSED IT/STOP//

FORTY-FIVE

Fairchild Ranch, 10 March

➤ FRANK WATCHED ALBERT Meacham do a slow
burn as General Canby made his introductions. Due to the
flurry of petitions President Grant received from eastern church
groups calling for peaceful negotiation, he had ordered Secretary Delano to "do something." Without consulting Meacham,
the Secretary of the Interior had appointed the newest Peace
Commission member himself.

"Gentlemen, allow me to introduce the Reverend Doctor
Eleazar Thomas, the man appointed to replace Judge Roseborough who, as you know, has cases pending in court. I think Dr.
Thomas brings special insight to our group."

Leroy Dyar smiled at Dr. Thomas. "Well, Reverend, I'm
glad we have a man of the cloth with us. Perhaps you will
provide divine guidance to our mission."

Reverend Thomas preened. "Why thank you, sir. You see, I
feel sorry for these poor creatures, benighted in mind, without
enough of the great principles of Christian justice and power to
recognize and respect the individual rights of others." He shook
his head sadly. "They are a doomed race, hopeless and in
despair, and I feel compelled to help them."

Frank rolled his eyes. He was glad Winema was out of the
room.

Canby gave Thomas a brief look of incredulity.

Meacham cleared his throat and addressed Canby, ignoring Thomas altogether. "That's only what Judge Roseborough *said*, General."

Canby regarded the superintendent with an expression of annoyance. "Inferring what, Albert?"

"I think he quit because he fears this whole thing may get out of hand."

The general eyed Meacham critically. "It's up to us to see that it doesn't." His gaze returned to Thomas. "I understand these people, Reverend. It is common practice for Indians to huff and puff—rattle their sabers so to speak. It is all part of their negotiation strategy. You will be perfectly safe."

Thomas smiled and nodded with half-closed eyes. "No need to propitiate, General. Man proposes, God disposes. He guides my destiny."

Winema flowed into the room with Jeff. Albert Meacham eyed the boy with concern. "Toby, I'm not sure Jeff should go along."

Winema curled her arm around her son's shoulders. "It will be all right. Jeff misses his cousin."

That was one reason, Frank thought. The other was Winema wanted Jeff to remember what really happened here.

"Very well." Meacham pulled out his pocket watch, flipped the cover, and stared at its face with grim concentration. He snapped the cover back into place. "It's time we departed for our meeting. I—ah—prefer to arrive before Jack."

⟵

The Lava Beds, later that day

HEAVY clouds masked the sun, bringing a damp chill to the air. Kentapoos grinned as he saw Charka waiting at the peace commissioner's camp. Charka ran to hold the bridle as his elder cousin dismounted. Krelatko and six others accompanied their chief. Frank, Winema, and the commissioners stood around a sagebrush campfire several paces away.

Kentapoos smiled broadly at Charka, rested his hand on the boy's head, and spoke in Modoc. "So, you have come to see your cousin Kentapoos. I am glad to see you, little cousin."

"*Ih, pusuep.* I have missed you." Charka signaled toward the commissioners with his eyes. "Now the preacher man has joined them."

"Eh?" Kentapoos frowned and peered at Reverend Thomas.

Frank and Winema joined them. "You look tired and thin, Waterbrash. You are not eating enough," Winema scolded as Frank and Kentapoos shook hands.

Kentapoos managed a weary smile. "With you, Shade, and Green Basket worrying over me, nothing bad could happen to me."

"Don't forget *me*," Charka broke in.

Kentapoos chuckled, tousled the boy's hair. "Never." His expression hardened as he jerked his head in the direction of the commissioners. "Why is that Sunday doctor with them?"

"He takes the place of *Tyee* Roseborough, who quit the council," Winema replied.

Kentapoos's brow furrowed. "Quit? Why?"

"He believed the council a waste of time, that nothing would come of it." Her face pinched in concern. "He worries, as I do, that Black Wound or Cho-ocks have taken over."

Kentapoos shook his head, shaken by the news. "First, Steele, now Roseborough. My friends are deserting me." For a moment he looked south toward the Stronghold, then Winema's comment struck home. His eyes narrowed. "I am still chief. Come. Let us see what Meacham says."

Meacham and Kentapoos shook hands, then Meacham introduced Reverend Thomas. Kentapoos ignored the preacher's outstretched hand. "Why is this Sunday Doctor here? I do not trust such men who tell us our ways are bad."

"Easy, Jack," Canby placated. "Dr. Thomas has your interest at heart. He's a good man."

Kentapoos's eyes flicked to Canby. "How long have you known him?"

The general seemed caught off-guard. He glanced at Meacham, who smiled slightly and studied the sky. Kentapoos made a short, harsh laugh and sat down. Thomas's face flushed as he hunched by the fire.

The chief went directly to the point. "I want my horses back. You had no right to take them."

Meacham looked at Canby.

The general cleared his throat. "They are well cared for, Jack. We will return them as soon as you surrender."

The *laki*'s jaw tightened. "Then I will send my wife to see that your words are true. You will let her see our horses?"

"Yes."

Kentapoos continued, "Because you stole our horses and brought more soldiers, my people are suspicious. We need more time to consider what we must do. But I will promise you this. We will not be the ones who fire the first shot."

"We agree to do the same as long as these peace councils continue and your men behave themselves," Canby replied.

Kentapoos regarded the general closely. "I want to tell you that my word is good." He picked up a rock. "Solid as this rock. You will see that for yourselves." He dropped the rock. "But if you live up to your word, I will be surprised. It will be the first time a White chief kept his word with us."

Canby laughed. "You shall see, son. You are entering an agreement with a man."

"We shall see, *tyee*. But the theft of our horses and the arrival of more soldiers has hardened my men's hearts. Your lips speak peace, but your actions speak war. And you have not yet told us where we might go to live."

Albert Meacham leaned forward. "Jack, I want you to know I have been looking into a place for your people. You will not have to return to the Klamath Reservation, that I can promise."

"We want no place other than Lost River. If you will only give us a little land there, we will be happy and all this will be over."

Meacham shook his head. "I'm sorry, Jack. That's impossible. The White people's hearts have turned against you there."

Kentapoos sighed and stared into the distance. A dull ache started in the back of his skull. He dreaded going back to the People empty-handed. Each passing day brought more sour faces, more looks of contempt. He regarded Canby with frustrated contempt. "I will talk to my people again. I will send a messenger when I am ready to talk more." He stood abruptly and gave Meacham a hard stare. "But you have given me little to take back."

FORTY-SIX

The Stronghold, 15 March

"KENTAPOOS!" WOMAN WATCHING bellowed at Kweelush. They glowered at each other as they circled around a bare spot on the cave floor.

"Do not insult my family, witch! Daughter of a whore! Find your own place!"

Kweelush grasped Woman Watching's hair and pulled with all her strength.

"Aiieeeeee!" screamed Woman. She flailed madly at her tormentor. *"This* is my place, you wrinkled hag!"

They pulled, huffed, and struggled with each other, trying hard not to lose their footing on the sharp, jutting rocks of the cave floor. Kweelush loosed a hard blow to Woman's rib cage. Woman cried out and twisted her body in response. She bellowed in hot rage, "I will put a spell on you! Your face will rot before your eyes!" Seeing an opening, she stomped on Kweelush's foot.

"Yiiiii!" Kweelush hopped on one foot, but held on to Woman's hair with one hand, a handful of her dress with the other.

A large group of women gathered around. Their faces hot with the anticipation of a fight as Woman and Kweelush played out their pent-up rage and frustration. They were all sick of the cold, sick of ill children, sick of the caves, and sick of the men. They all wanted to lash out at someone, at some*thing*.

"YOU SMELL LIKE BEAR SHIT!" Woman yelled, then spit at Kweelush's face. The spittle missed its mark, clung to her hair.

Kweelush kicked Woman in the shin, then yanked downward on Woman's hair. Woman screeched, felt for her leg, lost her balance, and fell forward on her face. Kweelush quickly sat on her, sharp rocks jabbing into her belly and chest. Woman let out a tremendous "oompf" as the air rushed from her lungs from Kweelush's considerable bulk. She lay there, gasping for breath.

Kweelush's substantial chest heaved from exhaustion. Between breaths she gasped, "Are you . . . ready to . . . give in?"

Bitter tears welled into Woman's eyes. She pounded the cold dirt with her fist in pain, frustration, and weariness. Finally she nodded and managed a weak, "*Ih.*"

"Take back what you said about Kentapoos!"

"I, I—"

Kweelush shifted her weight. There was an ominous "crack" from Woman's back.

Woman Watching croaked, "*Getak!* I take it back."

Kweelush smiled in satisfaction. She would keep the small, rock-free circle of cave floor for her very own.

FORTY-SEVEN

The Lava Beds, 27 March

FRANK AND WINEMA rode toward the battle-worn army field tent. It sat lopsided on the rocky plain that stretched out flat, midway between the Stronghold and the south shore of Tule Lake. A brisk spring breeze rippled the tarpaulin like a hovering ghost. The sky was gray and overcast. The smell of rain sweetened the air.

Another fruitless meeting with Kentapoos, Whusum, and Krelatko four days prior left both sides tense and frustrated. And now, despite Winema's pleadings, Canby had moved his soldiers closer to the Stronghold to "increase the pressure on Kentapoos." Today, she knew, the two opposing chiefs were determined to push their causes hard.

From the horses around the tent, they could tell Jack and his men had arrived. They dismounted, hobbled their horses, and entered the tent.

"Sorry we're late, Mr. Meacham, General. We had some chores to finish up," Frank said.

The commissioners sat in a small circle with Kentapoos, Whusum, and Krelatko. Two warriors hovered behind their chief, their eyes cold and watchful like snakes watching a bird.

Winema, between Canby and Meacham, faced Kentapoos. This left no sitting space for Frank. He moved toward the opposite side, brushing against Hakar.

He wheeled on Frank. "Get out of my way!"

Winema's eyes flashed. "*Getak!* Behave yourself, Hakar. Act like a man."

Kentapoos glared at the warrior. "Enough of that."

Hakar glowered at his reprimanders, then laughed and stepped aside.

Kentapoos looked at General Canby and continued their interrupted conversation. "General, we can make peace quick if you will meet me halfway."

Canby's eyebrows pinched together in annoyance. "Jack, I want you to understand that you are not to dictate terms to me."

"And you should not dictate to me. I am not your prisoner or slave. I only ask you for a reservation near Hot Creek, or near the Fairchild ranch."

Canby blinked. He glanced at Meacham, who also looked mildly surprised. "Jack, you know I can't do that."

Kentapoos launched himself to his feet, his face a mask of torment. "Then give me these Lava Beds for my home!" His mouth twisted in anguish. "No White man will ever want such a place fit only for jackrabbits and coyotes!"

Winema closed her eyes tightly. The irrational desperation of his request brought an ache to her chest. The land-of-burnt-out-fires offered no trees or shelter, only rocks and sage. No one would want to live here.

Albert Meacham looked up at Kentapoos. "Neither the General or I can promise you any place until we make peace."

"How? How will we make peace? I will not agree on anything you men offer until you agree to give me a home in my own country!"

Reverend Thomas spoke in a calming tone. "Sit down, Jack. Let's talk this over."

Kentapoos glanced at Winema, then half-heartedly sat.

Thomas continued, "Jack, you could never get along with the Whites in this country because of the blood spilt here by your people."

Whusum broke in angrily, "I thought we were not to mention what happened in the past. Only to talk of peace."

Thomas closed his eyes and shook his head as if in grief. "What took place will never be forgotten."

"If that is the case, we will never make peace, nor would we be safe in *any* country," Kentapoos replied.

The general cleared his throat. "Listen. You Indians have got to come under the White man's laws. Our law is strong and straight."

Whusum made a dry, short laugh.

Kentapoos shifted his gaze to Canby. "All I want is your promise that you will give us a home in this country."

Meacham shook his head. "It won't work, Jack. There will always be trouble here."

Canby chewed the inside of his lip, then, "I'll tell you what, Jack. You get your people together and come out under a flag of truce. You are protected under a white flag."

Kentapoos scoffed. "When I was a young man, a man named Ben Wright called forty-five of my people under the white flag."

The general stared straight ahead, his face impassive. Meacham searched his boot sole.

The chief continued, "How many do you think got away with their lives?"

Silence.

Canby said, "That was wrong, Jack. A cowardly act. But *I* am not Ben Wright."

Kentapoos nodded. "Your people at Yreka did not say it was wrong. They gave him a big dance that night, called him hero."

Canby sighed in frustration. "We have told you. We are different men. We want to help your people."

"If you want to help us, give us land here. We will harm no one."

Agent Dyar's face reddened. "Damnit, Jack. How many times we gotta say it? Stop asking for land we can't give."

Black Wound sneered at the agent. "Then send us those who *have* the power." His eyes shifted to his chief. "Why do we waste time with men whose only power flows from their anuses?"

Winema censored the second half of Wound's question.

Thomas held up his hand, his face painted with confident piety. "Brother Jack, let me say something here. God sent me here to make peace with my brothers. We are going to do it. All we need do is trust in God."

Kentapoos regarded the Reverend seriously. "I may trust God, but what good will that do me? I am sorry to say I cannot trust these men in the blue cloth and brass buttons."

The general dipped his shoulder, jutted out his jaw. "What the hell have these brass buttons ever done to you, Jack?"

"They killed our women and babies," the Waterbrash snapped.

Canby shot back, "Did your men not kill innocent settlers?"

Kentapoos chafed, "They were not innocent. They fired on my people at Lost River."

Winema grasped the general's arm. "*Tyee*, do not get angry. You cannot make peace this way. Jack, you, too. Be a man and hold your temper."

Canby and Kentapoos glared at each other for several moments.

The general relaxed his shoulder, angled his head sharply upward as if to stretch a cramped muscle.

Kentapoos seemed lost in thought for a moment, then, "You say we are not to have a home in our country because we killed those settlers."

"Yes," Canby answered. "You see, the settlers would never treat you right. But if you gave up your men who murdered the settlers, we might make arrangements so you could stay here."

Kentapoos's mouth formed a menacing smile. "So that's it." He leaned forward. "Tell me, General. If I were to do that, would you give up your men who murdered our women and children at Lost River?"

Canby chuckled. "Why, Jack, you have no law. Only one law can live at a time."

The general had an annoying habit of laughing at the wrong time. The *laki* eyed the general warily, then touched Canby's knee. "I will make a deal with you. I will give up my men who killed the settlers and let them be tried by your laws if you give up your men and let them be tried by our law."

The general shook his head. "Our men who killed your women and children did it in time of war."

Meacham made a show of pulling out his watch and flipping the lid. "It's—ah—getting late. I think we had better quit for the day. Maybe in our next council we will be able to come to some terms."

Canby shot him a hostile look.

"Psha," Wound noised. "There can be no terms until you move your soldiers back. Any fool can see they are here to attack us."

Reverend Thomas stood and placed his hand on Wound's shoulder. Wound scowled, shook it off.

Thomas was undaunted. "Brother Jim, don't be frightened. The soldiers will not hurt you."

Wound looked the preacher up and down with disdain, then spoke in English. "Oh, I am not afraid, Thomas. *You* are the one who should be afraid."

Canby stood, squared his shoulders, and straightened his blouse. "Let us know when you're ready for our next council," he stated abruptly, then ducked out of the tent.

TELEGRAM

DATE: 28 March, 1873
FROM: Secretary Delano, Interior Department
TO: A. B. Meacham, President of Modoc Peace
Commission, Yreka, California

//ALL PARTIES UNSUCCESSFUL IN LOCATING
NEW RESERVATION FOR MODOCS IN OREGON OR
CALIFORNIA/STOP/ONLY ALTERNATIVE IS
INDIAN TERRITORY/RECOMMEND YOU
CONVINCE MODOCS OF VALUE OF WARMER
CLIMATE/STOP//

FORTY-EIGHT

The Stronghold, 27 March

WHUSUM AND BLACK Wound gathered their followers at Whusum's cave as hues of oranges and pinks painted the western edge of the sky, and the sun slipped behind the horizon. Whusum's face was grave as he faced the large crowd.. "Our chief has become an old woman. I have been trapped and fooled by the Whites too many times. I do not intend to be fooled again. You all see the aim of these peace men. They are on stalling us to allow more soldiers to arrive. When they think there are enough, they will attack."

He surveyed the darkening faces. "Now I want to hear what you feel."

Black Wound moved to Whusum's side, turned to the crowd. "You see things right, brother. I say kill them before they kill us. I say the next time we meet with the peace men, we kill them. When their chiefs are dead, their warriors will scatter like birds." He raised his rifle into the air. "All who agree, stand by me."

Whusum, Hakar, Cho-ocks, and forty-two others stepped forward. But several stood their ground.

Wieum stepped from the shadows. "*Kai*, you are wrong. Kentapoos is our chief until the People vote otherwise. We must not decide such action without him."

Black Wound's face clouded. He opened his mouth, then shut it, the trace of a knowing smirk on his lips. "Go fetch him, then."

Wieum returned with Kentapoos, who studied the men's faces, then hopped up onto a large rock. "I do not know all that you have discussed. But I can say that I will have a hard fight ahead in the coming councils. My aim is to save those of you who killed the settlers and to win us a piece of land in our own country. All I ask you to do is to behave and wait, and do nothing reckless. At worst, we may be forced to return to Yainax and join our brothers and sisters who have returned there. They live in peace; can we not?"

Incredulous, Whusum snorted, "Back to Yainax? Back to where we started?"

"Only if we have to—to save the women and children," Kentapoos replied. "But my plan is to hold out for a reservation at Hot Creek, or right here. When they see I insist on one or the other, they will offer us Yainax. Then I will accept with the understanding I take *all* my people." He stared intently at Black Wound. "*None* of us are to be tried for murder." He swiveled his body, making eye contact with each listener. "My people, depend on me. With your prayers I will get us through this."

Livid with condemnation, Black Wound shook his rifle in the direction of the valley below. "Are you blind? Can you not see more soldiers arriving every two or three suns? You did not see the big bullets we saw in the soldier camp. They are as big as your head! The peace men intend to make peace by blowing our heads off with one of those guns. I say again our only chance is to kill their chiefs."

The crowd buzzed approval.

Krelatko jumped in. "And if that does not stop them?"

Black Wound gave Krelatko a cold stare. "Then we will fight to the end. If I had my way, the peace men would have been killed *long* ago, before so many soldiers came!"

Other voices shouted from the crowd. "He is right!"

"Listen to him, Kentapoos!"

"*KAI!*" Kentapoos barked, his voice crackling with anger. "I cannot do what you ask. You are not thinking straight." He jumped from the rock, started for the cave entrance.

Black Wound caught his arm. "You *will*! You will promise to kill Canby next time you meet."

Cho-ocks jumped in. "*Ih*, and Whusum says he will kill Meacham."

Kentapoos glared first at Cho-ocks, then at Black Wound. "You have eaten too much peyote, my friend. I *will* not do this." He shook off Wound's grasp and turned to the crowd. "Go to your families now. I am finished with this talk."

Rifles cocked behind him. Black Wound grabbed Kentapoos's arm again, brandished a knife. "You will do it or you will die here."

FORTY-NINE

   KENTAPOOS BLINKED. HE stared at Wound for several heartbeats, then faced the brooding crowd. Feeling a sense of bewildered disappointment, he spoke softly, almost pleadingly. "Why? Why do you want to force me into such a cowardly act?"

"Cowardly?" Whusum flourished his knife, the blade winking in the moonlight that slanted through the cave entrance. "It will be a brave thing to kill the Star Chief in front of his men. You will show them you dare to do anything when the time comes."

Black Wound closed in. "And there is revenge. Have you forgotten how Ben Wright murdered our chief, *your uncle*, at a peace council?"

The crowd murmured appreciation for Wound's recollection.

The *laki* swallowed. He felt the pressure, a squeezing sensation around his chest, a knot of wet hemp twisting in his belly. He was losing control. Only fifty-three warriors and their families now remained at the Stronghold. Over the past three moons, others had given into cold and hunger and trickled slowly back to Skonches at Yainax. If only the commissioners had given him *something*. He felt like a weary hawk circling an endless body of water. Eventually his wings would fail, plunging him into the depths. The *laki* backed toward the cave entrance. "I—I have to think. I cannot—"

The crowd moved, squeezed in.

"*You will!*" Black Wound tripped Kentapoos. Kentapoos fell on his rump. Cho-ocks stuffed a woman's bonnet on the *laki*'s head. Whusum threw a shawl over his shoulders. Voices lashed from the crowd, cutting like whips:

"Woman!"

"White man!"

"Squaw!"

"Coward!"

Krelatko cried, "*KAI!*" He rushed toward Kentapoos's side only to be held back by Hakar and Whusum. Black Wound leaned down, nose to nose with Kentapoos. The *laki*'s mind swirled. Wound's face shimmered like a reflection in a pond, then transformed into the blackened face of his father—the dark warrior. The face hissed, "You are no Modoc. We disown you. Lay there, fish-hearted woman."

Kentapoos squeezed shut his eyes, then reopened them. Wound's face reappeared. The *laki* realized his own voice had no more than the effect of a mouse among a den of wolves. While he had brooded and planned in solitude his detractors had solidified their base. How could he fight the *boshtin* army *and* his own tribe?

He flushed, naked in the spotlight of his own humiliation. "*Nent!*" He stood, threw off the shawl and bonnet, and surveyed the angry faces. "If this is what you truly want, I will kill Canby!" His head began to pound. A sour taste came to his mouth. "Though I know it will cost me my life." He glared at Hakar and Whusum. "*And* yours."

Kentapoos picked up his cavalry hat, brushed the dirt from it. The eagle feather had snapped. The Waterbrash inspected it reverently, then narrowed his eyes at Wound and the others. "But I say it is coward's work!"

Replacing the hat upon his head, he stalked out of the cave, the upper half of the broken eagle feather drooping in dishonor.

~

The Stronghold, 30 March

KENTAPOOS had ample time for introspection. Three days of heavy winds and rain confined everyone in their caves. On the evening of the third day after the humiliating shawl incident, he called Wieum and Krelatko to his cave. They shared the pipe for several minutes without speaking. Nearby, Laughs Loud giggled as she shared secrets with her two visiting cousins. Green Basket, Shade, and Lodge Woman talked quietly as they did what they could to patch old baskets.

Kentapoos broke the silence. "I do not want to do this thing they ask. I disagree with Wound and the others. I do not think Canby a treacherous man." He looked expectantly at his friend. "I am interested in your thoughts, Wieum."

Wieum nodded somberly. "*Lockaa gewo*. Call a council, my chief. Take your question to *all* the People. You have only heard from noisy ones. I will see to it that the People will hear what you have to say."

Krelatko said, "Do it tomorrow when it is light, so they can look into your eyes."

Kentapoos puffed thoughtfully on his pipe. His friend's reassurance warmed him. "*Nent*." He offered a tired smile. "*Humast, geo' sut'walinai*."

Morning brought clear skies and warm sunshine. As promised, Wieum and Krelatko acted as camp criers, gathering the People at the dance ground. During the night the two had moved from cave to cave, counseling the nonaligned men to hear their chief's words.

Kentapoos stood before them, knowing this was his last chance to stem the tide moving against him, for now the People stood at the crossing of two trails. One trail led to death, the other to life. It was here and now, when his confidence had all but ebbed away, that he must make his most persuasive speech.

The *laki* folded his arms across his chest, dropped his head in deep thought. There was no sound save a quarrel of crows cawing farther down the valley. Lifting his head, Kentapoos gazed at his people. Seated on rocks and blankets, their faces reflected a patch quilt of emotions. They were tired, gaunt faces, few looked hopeful. Some avoided his gaze and looked at the ground.

"My people, I feel I am lost among you. I feel like a man banished from his friends and kin. I am almost ashamed to address you, for I fear my words may be cast to the winds. But I must try because," he emphasized each word carefully, "from now on our lives depend upon our actions.

"First, I must remind you that life is sweet and love is stronger than hate. It is true that a man must fight to save his life, or to win his heart's desire. But we know a man must be right before he kills. Only then is he justified in what he does in the eyes of the White man's laws. But this is *our* law, also. My people. Let us love life. Let us not walk willingly into the jaws of death, because this is what we will do if we follow Wound's and Cho-ock's road. Death, my friends, comes soon enough."

The *laki* paused for effect. From the left side of the crowd, the Hot Creeks glared at him. Kentapoos shifted his gaze to more accepting eyes, finding Green Basket, Shade, and Laughs Loud. His daughter's intent eyes glistened with pride, and there he concentrated his gaze, drawing new strength from it.

"By and by, the Great Father will call each of us away from our loved ones. Can we think of this without feeling sad? It is the nature of men to mourn the loss of a loved one. Therefore, let us not cause the soldiers to send us crying to Yainax with the bodies of killed relatives. Let them not repeat what they did to us at the fight at Lost River, because I can assure you, my people, if I kill Canby, the Whites will rise up against us like never before and all will be lost."

He fixed the Hot Creeks with supplicating eyes. "My old friends. If the soldiers attack us we can fight better, stronger and braver, because we will be fighting in self-defense; for what is ours. But remember that the peacemakers promised not to attack while the talks continue. As a man, and as your chief,

I have promised there would be no act of war committed on our side."

He stretched out his arms in an attitude of inclusion. "My relatives. Let me show the world 'Captain Jack' is a man of his word." Dropping his arms, he eyed the Hot Creeks once again. "My brothers, you made me promise something a few nights ago that I am sorry of. Do not hold me to it! I ask you this because of the love I have for you all. If you hold me to what I said in passion, we are doomed."

His eyes swept across the main body a last time, his shoulders pulled back, hauling up the final remnants of what persuasiveness and commitment remained within him, and cautioned, "Think on this, my people! Pray on it! Then advise me of your decision." He looked at them for several moments, searching their eyes for some spark of concession. "I am finished."

Whusum stepped forward, his face reflecting the bitterness and hurt of a man betrayed. "Why did you not speak this way when we were at the reservation? Perhaps we would have listened. Now you know yourself it is too late. We hold you to your promise. You *must* kill Canby!"

Kentapoos's face pinched in frustration. His speech was his best and most persuasive. It *must* have had an effect. But now Whusum was forcing an immediate decision. Kentapoos scanned the crowd for empathetic faces, but there were none. A sudden jolt of bitter anger surged through him. Let them have their vote—now. "*Tchawai*! All in favor of me killing the noble Canby, stand!"

Slowly people rose to their feet. Some stood, quick and defiant, their eyes snapping. Others rose sheepishly, only after seeing others stand. Each rising body sent an invisible arrow into Kentapoos's heart, and with each, a small part of him died. More people stood until only twelve remained seated. He watched in disbelief, then in grief. The People had spoken.

With immense sadness, Kentapoos said, "*Nent*. I see you do not love life, nor anything else. I will do what you ask, then. But not tomorrow." His eyes flashed in warning. "First I will ask Canby many times for a home in our country. Only if he refuses—and only then—will I commit this cowardly act." He raised a trembling finger. "But if he comes to my terms, I shall not kill him. Do you hear?"

A few voices murmured, "*Ih*." Most hung their heads, whether in shame or just plain weariness, he did not know. Ignoring his lightheadedness, and a weakness in his knees, Kentapoos stepped down from his rock pulpit. He walked stiffly to the small grouping of family and friends who stood nearby, and together they disappeared into his cave.

FIFTY

The Stronghold, Wednesday, 9 April

WINEMA APPROACHED THE lookout cautiously. Each visit became more dangerous. She knew the Hot Creeks saw her as a traitor. Her diminutive Colt Pocket Model felt reassuring, its contours pressing against her belly. She breathed relief as she reached the outcropping of the Stronghold and recognized Krelatko. He waved and she returned the gesture.

"The *laki* is sick," Krelatko forewarned.

Winema felt a twinge of worry. "What is wrong?"

"It is only camp sickness. Everyone has had it. A bad cough and his throat is sore."

They found Kentapoos in his cave, wrapped in blankets, tended by his two wives. Green Basket was tipping a steaming cup against his lips. He drank, grimaced, then noticed Winema.

Sitting up he managed a sickly smile. "*Haggi*, Little Sparrow. You see, I am old and sick."

His voice was raspy. He coughed several times.

Winema managed a wan smile. "You will never be old, Waterbrash. But I have seen you look better."

"You should have"—he coughed twice—"seen me yesterday."

"*Waquset*. Because Canby wants to talk in two suns."

Kentapoos nodded. "I will be ready."

Winema sat by her cousin and sighed. "Cousin, look at you. Look at your wives, your people. They are tired and sick. I know Canby and Meacham. They will not give in. We will never get our land back." She laid her hand on his shoulder. "You have made a brave effort, Waterbrash, but I beg you— before the Hot Creeks do something bad—take Canby by the hand and return to the reservation. *There* is where the fight is."

The *laki* cleared his phlegmy throat and winced. "At the proper time, Winema." He looked around as if to assure he was not overheard. "I have a plan; I know what I am doing. We may end up back at Yainax, but not without a last effort to get our own land."

Winema squeezed his shoulder, spoke in an urgent whisper. "*Ih.* You must agree to Yainax. I have heard talk in the soldier camp. They are talking about sending you to 'a warm place.' I do not like the sound of it. I feel it is very far away."

Fear flashed across Basket's and Shade's faces.

"How far?" Shade asked.

Winema compressed her lips and shook her head.

"*Kash!*" The *laki*'s outburst caused another coughing fit. "I should have known they were up to something."

"*Kai,*" Winema argued. "Meacham is doing his best."

Kentapoos's face darkened, his eyes squinting in accusation. "Whose side are you on?"

Winema's hand flew from his shoulder as if it were on fire. "I expect such a question from Cho-ocks or Black Wound, but not from you." She stood abruptly. "I am sick of that question! I am sick of this place!" Frustration and anger consumed her. "I am sick of men who think with their balls, not with their minds!" She flung her shawl around her, wheeled, and left the cave.

Winema despaired as she wound her way through the Stronghold and down onto the valley floor. Was there nothing she could do or say to stop this madness?

Near the outer edge of the Stronghold, Wieum stepped from behind a rock, startling her. Raising his finger to his lips to signal quiet, he moved to her side. "Cousin Winema. Tell the peacemakers all will die if they meet with Kentapoos at the next council."

A sick feeling churned Winema's gut.

Wieum continued, "If there is war, would you care for my little girl at Yainax?"

Winema regarded Wieum sternly. "Who is behind this? Wound? Whusum?"

"*Ih*, but there was a council three suns past. Almost all the people voted against the *laki*."

Winema shut her eyes tightly. Why hadn't she been there? Her mind raced. She would have to convince Canby to postpone the council. Grasping at desperate schemes, she wondered if she could bring relatives down from Yainax to plead for reason? Perhaps Skonches could come down and make a plea. Perhaps Steele and Roseborough . . .

She looked down at Wieum. "There will be no war. You must convince Kentapoos to stall the Hot Creeks. Go quickly! Tell them he is too sick to meet with Canby."

Wieum tugged at her hem. "But if there is war—my daughter—"

Winema appraised her cousin sadly. "*Ih*, Wieum. Your daughter is always welcome in our lodge."

Wieum looked relieved and let go her hem. She leaned down, squeezed his shoulder, then dug her heels into Skoks and galloped toward the command tent.

~

ON her return, Winema met Frank and Charka at Colonel Gillem's tent.

"Christ!" Frank exclaimed after Winema shared the somber news. "Do you believe Wieum?"

Winema arched an eyebrow, intimating the answer was obvious.

Frank nodded. "Yeah, I do, too. Wieum's a straight shooter." His jaw tightened. "What the hell's got into those people? Have they gone crazy?"

Winema looked at her husband coolly. "Maybe you would, too, if you lived in a cave with Cho-ocks and Black Wound all winter. You would not know *what* to believe."

Frank sighed and shoved his hands in his pockets. "You got a point."

Winema took his arm. "Come. We must tell Canby and Meacham."

They found the president of the Peace Commission lounging in his tent. Albert Meacham was in good humor. "Well, Toby, I hope you brought Jack to terms today, and we can all go home."

Seeing her face, his smile faded. His gaze shifted to Frank. "What's wrong?"

"You got to cancel that meeting," Frank said. "They're fixing to kill the lot of you at the next council meeting."

Color drained from Meacham's face. "Who told you that?"

"Wieum told her. Just outside the Stronghold. We believe him and so should you." Frank went on, "Winema's as good as dead if the Hot Creeks find out she spilled the beans. I'm trustin' you to keep her name out of this. I'll want the other commissioners' promises, too."

"I understand, Frank. I'll send for them immediately."

In a few minutes Agent Dyar, General Canby, and Reverend Thomas joined them.

Winema gazed into each man's eyes. "My friends, I must tell you something that hurts my heart. But I must have your promise never to tell any of Jack's people how you heard it. My family's life and my husband's life would be put in great danger."

Canby, Meacham, and Dyar promised with solemnity.

Reverend Thomas clasped his hands in the attitude of prayer. "Sister Toby, as a humble servant of God, I could never betray your confidence."

"Very well," Winema said, reassured. "You are my friends. I do not wish to see you hurt. I want no blood spilled here, White or Modoc. You must not go to the council on Friday. The Hot Creeks plan to murder all of you. Kentapoos can do nothing. I was told this by a relative I trust. Believe it if you value your lives."

General Canby produced a cigar, bit off the end, and spit out the dross. A polite smile crossed his face. "Toby, what I believe is that your relative has too much imagination. That destitute handful of Modocs dare not kill us in broad daylight—in front of a thousand soldiers."

Thomas added, "I trust in God to protect us. He would not allow it."

Dyar and Meacham huddled together, spoke among themselves.

Frank scowled at the minister. "Gentlemen, I know these Hot Creeks. Toby and I have been up there. We seen what's going on. Mark my words, if they've decided to kill you, they'll do it. If you go to that meeting Friday afternoon, you'll not see sundown."

Worry lined Albert Meacham's face. "Leroy and I agree with Frank, General. We best postpone the council and think this thing through."

Canby drew on his cigar thoughtfully, then curtly waved it in the air in dismissal. "We'll see in the morning what can be done. I'm turning in." He gave a quick nod, almost a bow, to Winema. "Good night, dear lady." Addressing the others, he said, "See you in the morning, gentlemen. Bright and early."

Winema watched Canby leave. Despite his annoying overconfidence, she had learned to like the man. Indian or White, a warrior was a warrior. Something within convinced them of their invincibility. It occurred to her how similar Canby and Kentapoos were—both committed men who did what they felt best for their people. But Canby was a seasoned chief. How a man who had spent so many years with Indians could be so blind baffled her. She hoped sleep would clear his head.

FIFTY-ONE

 Two Modocs arrived at Colonel Gillem's camp at midmorning to make arrangements for Friday's council meeting. Reverend Thomas, on his way to Meacham's tent, spotted them hobbling their horses.

The Reverend sported a wide smile. He had met them only once and recalled their miner names. "Good morning Boston, Bogus." He clasped a hand on each man's shoulder like old friends. "What is this we hear, that you folks want to kill us? Don't you know we are your friends?"

The Modocs eyed each other. Bogus Charley said, "Who told you this?"

"Frank Riddle's squaw, Toby."

Bogus frowned. "She lies."

The Reverend's expression turned smug. "Lied? Well, mistaken perhaps. That's why I asked you."

Boston Charley removed his horses' hobbles and started to mount.

Thomas's smile transformed into a look of surprise. "Hey, where are you go—"

The Modoc quirted his horse to a gallop and raced toward the Stronghold.

Bogus shrugged. "We see Meacham now."

They turned to see the Riddles and General Canby approaching. Bogus met all with a friendly smile and shook everyone's hands, then all sauntered over to the mess tent. An early lunch was served by Canby's mess staff. The meal conversation was relaxed. Neither Bogus nor Thomas mentioned their earlier conversation. Then, outside, they heard a horse gallop in. The frowning warrior strode into the tent and eyed Winema. "The *laki* wants to see you, *atui*."

All eyes darted toward Winema. A wisp of concern passed across her eyes, then vanished. "Very well. I will go."

Frank's brow furrowed.

She touched his arm. "It is all right. Perhaps Kentapoos is feeling worse." She left the tent and headed for her horse with Frank at her side.

Meacham turned to the warrior. "What does Jack want?"

"He wants to see why Winema lied."

Meacham glanced at Canby, who shared his perplexed expression.

The superintendent turned to Boston Charley. "Lied? About what?"

Now it was the Boston's turn to look confused. "About why she said we will kill you next council."

Meacham's face turned pale as tallow. His eyes shifted angrily to Thomas, then back to Boston. "Who told you that?"

Boston canted his head toward the tent flap. "The Sunday doctor—Thomas."

"Sweet Jesus!" Dyar exclaimed.

Meacham rushed past Boston and out of the tent. He saw Winema mounting Skoks, Frank holding the reins.

"Winema, Frank! Come in here a minute!"

The Riddles reentered the tent with questioning expressions.

Meacham relayed Boston's information, warning, "It's too dangerous for you to go. If Jack wants to see you, he can come here."

Frank's face flushed with anger as he glowered at Reverend Thomas.

General Canby stepped closer. "No." He looked at Winema. "I want you to go, Winema. This is your last chance to convince Jack to give up and make peace. Tomorrow must be our last talk."

Winema nodded. "*Ih*, I will go. I will do most anything to end this peacefully."

His chest and shoulders heaving, Frank turned on Thomas. "Thomas, you lied like a yella dog last night when you promised my wife you would keep quiet. Now Jack has sent for her and you're the cause of it."

Thomas's face flushed. His breathing quickened as though the air inside the small tent had suddenly thinned.

Moving within breath-smell distance, Frank's dark eyes drilled into the preacher. "I'll tell you this, Reverend. If my wife ain't back by sundown, I'll be at your throat like a dunked wildcat."

The Reverend appeared flustered. He threw up his arms in indignation. "Brother Riddle! You should get down on your knees and pray to Almighty God for forgiveness!"

Frank's eyes flashed hostility. "Preacher, you could get down and pray the caps off your knees, and even *then* God wouldn't see fit to forgive *you*."

~

WINEMA pushed aside the front flap and stepped outside. The brisk April air brought welcome relief from the man-smells of the aging canvas. She pulled her wool shawl tighter around her shoulders as the cool wind- fluttered her dark wool skirt. Closing her eyes, she inhaled deeply. She understood Frank's anger and loved him for it. As for Thomas, she felt the foolish Sunday doctor understood neither the *Modokni*, nor the danger he had put her in.

She found Skoks lazily sniffing at a clump of sagebrush and let her hand brush across his withers, sliding it gently to the side of his neck. Skoks nickered, nervously jibed backward. Despite her gnawing fear of what lay ahead, Winema mounted him and headed toward the Stronghold.

Moving the pony ahead at a walk, she gazed at the sacred mountain, its peak capped with a fresh snow. Sky Chief's words echoed in her mind:

You have been chosen, Winema . . . The peacemakers will become more important than the warmakers. . . .

Despite the final vote at the Stronghold, Winema felt she could somehow turn the tide. She scanned the landscape, and other memories flooded her thoughts. This stark, rocky land was once a happy place, a place of worship and sustenance. The binding connection with the Old Ones was near—the spirit cave where the ancestors painted ancient messages on torch-blackened walls. She could feel them. In the cave she had often heard their furtive whispers. Glancing skyward, she thought, have you abandoned us now that we fight among ourselves? Perhaps this is why you are silent. Hear me, Old Ones. Tell me what to do, what to say.

Winema listened for their voices, for their counsel. But only the perpetual wind that blew across the arid rock and sage answered, and the beds seemed suddenly lifeless, a place of portending death.

Abruptly her saddle slid to the left, giving her a momentary feeling of weightlessness. She gasped as she tipped left and the river dream roared unbidden into her mind with stunning vividness. She felt the sickening roll of the canoe as it careened through roiling water, toward a mad roaring whirlpool. Paddling furiously, desperately, she looked behind her. But this time it wasn't Frank who shared her canoe, it was Kentapoos.

Winema mouthed a small cry. The saddle had stopped its slide. She swung off quickly and inspected it. The cinch strap had loosened. Resetting the saddle, she snugged the cinch strap. Peering ahead she made out a large group of warriors gathering to meet her. Her fingers moved unconsciously to the Colt jutting from her belt, then to her medicine pouch tied to her belt. As she gazed at the warriors a great sadness washed over her. She had grown up with these men. She was related to many of them. They, with their wives and children shivering just beyond in the cold and lifeless caves, were her people.

Remounting, Winema straightened, took a breath, pushed back her shoulders, and heeled Skoks ahead. Her heart told her this was the last chance to forestall disaster. She moved ahead, fortified by Sky Chief's and Jakalunus's prophecies. Cupping her medicine pouch, she prayed softly, "Help me to persuade them, Grandfather. Give my words new power, new meaning, Sky Chief. And bring me safely back to my son and husband."

She would not show fear. In fact, she chided herself for feeling fear. Then she saw Kentapoos, emerging from behind the warriors, walking purposefully toward her. His expression sent a shiver up her spine.

FIFTY-TWO

WINEMA MOVED SKOKS up to Kentapoos at a slow walk. She slid off, tied the reins to a sagebush and faced her cousin. "Well, here I am. You are feeling better?"

Kentapoos's face was sallow, deeply etched with worry. He looked like a man who bore a giant boulder upon his shoulders. Tiny blisters of perspiration dotted his forehead and upper lip. "Never mind that," he said. "I understand you told the peace men we are to kill them tomorrow."

Cho-ocks, Wound, and Whusum moved up directly behind the *laki*.

With her face a mask of practiced indifference, Winema said, "*Ih*, cousin. I warned them."

Kentapoos stiffened. Fear bloomed in his face. Obviously he had wanted her to say the opposite. It saddened her to see him like this—pushed to the edge. She spoke to Kentapoos but loud enough that all could hear. "Tomorrow, will you shoot Frank and me, too?"

Kentapoos ignored the question. "You must tell us who"—he looked nervously to each side—"who told you this."

Winema looked into his eyes. "I had a vision-dream. The spirits told me. And they never lie."

"Do not play with me, Winema. Not today."

She folded her arms against her chest. "Do you deny that you intend to kill the commissioners?"

He grew impatient. "Whoever told you that is a liar. Now tell me who told you. No more foolishness."

Whusum cocked his rifle with a flourish.

Bowel-loosening fear squeezed Winema's gut. She knew she was within heartbeats of death. Sidestepping right, she yanked out her pistol and hopped up on a jutting boulder. "Now listen to me! I am a Modoc! Every drop of blood in my body is Modoc! Yes, I told the peace men of your cowardly plot. I did not dream it. One of your own men told me, but I will not betray him."

Striking the pistol against her chest she parried, "Shoot me if you dare! I have a husband and son whom I love, but I am not afraid to die. Not if you are about to shame me and all Modocs by this—this—act of coyotes."

Whusum, Cho-ocks, and Wound leveled their rifles at her. Winema blinked into the rifle bores. She felt herself trembling, but forced her voice to be strong, unwavering. "Go ahead! Shoot me! But one of you will fall by my pistol before I fall. Then the soldiers will avenge my death." She glared at Cho-ocks, Whusum, and Wound. "They will wipe you out!"

The warriors' faces darkened as her words hung in the air. Kentapoos watched Winema intensely for a moment, then suddenly, he rushed to her side, his face imprinted with a mixture of pride and sudden courage. "I will die with this brave woman!"

Eight other warriors moved to join them. For the moment the Hot Creeks looked unsure of themselves. Kentapoos turned to Winema but spoke so all could hear. "My brave cousin. You are a true Modoc; you have proved it today. But you were told a falsehood."

He eyed her from the corner of his eye while maintaining a watchful gaze on the Hot Creek leaders, his expression advising her to disbelieve his words. "No harm will come to the peace men if everything goes right. Tell them six of us will meet them at the agreed-upon place tomorrow, unarmed. Tell them nothing will happen if they talk sense to me."

Kentapoos glared at the Hot Creeks. "Now my cousin will return to the peace camp—unharmed."

The air was sap-thick with tension as Winema stepped down from the rock and mounted Skoks. She could all but feel knives shooting from the Hot Creeks' eyes. Turning Skoks away, she held her breath, waiting for the sharp report, the impact of bullets against her back. But none came.

Winema contained her emotions until she was halfway back to the army camp. Then tears of relief mixed with grief cascaded down her cheeks. She had failed and almost lost her life in the effort. Her body trembled uncontrollably from what almost happened.

Slowly, as she picked her way across the ridge, her breathing returned to normal. Kentapoos's face told her everything. Despite the courage he displayed as he stood with her on the rock, he was no longer *laki*. The Hot Creeks' plan would run its deadly course. Unless Sky Chief interceded personally, the interpretation of her vision had proven utterly false.

～

"CONGRATULATIONS on your safe return, Toby. Tomorrow we'll see what Jack will do," General Canby intoned upon her return.

"Take my word, *tyee*. Do not go," Winema beseeched. "They will kill all of us if we go. They are sure the soldiers will attack them as soon as they get orders from Washington. They are desperate men, *tyee*." Her tears returned. "For the sake of your family, for all of us, heed my warning."

Canby smiled warmly. "I thank you for your concern, dear lady, but as a soldier I must go where duty dictates. I have to go to that council."

Meacham cleared his throat. "We don't have to meet Jack tomorrow. Toby gives good advice."

Canby laughed. "Meacham, Toby has you scared. If you don't go, I'll meet them alone. These Modocs are not fools, Albert. They won't try to kill us only half a mile from our

camp, and in plain view. Besides, they still believe they can
negotiate their land back."

Frank looked grim. "General, if you're that fired up about
going tomorrow, I want to talk with you and Colonel Gillem
before we go."

～

WINEMA and Frank trudged to the tent erected for them near
Meacham's. Frank plopped down on the cot. Leaning his
elbows on his knees, he massaged his face tiredly. "God, let it
be over tomorrow—peacefully."

"Unless Canby gives Kentapoos land in *Mowatoc*, it will not
end peacefully. Can you not get Meacham to con-vince Canby
not to go tomorrow?"

"Oh, I've tried," Frank retorted, "and *he's* tried. Canby is as
stubborn as Jack."

Frank, looking as if he'd just made a difficult decision,
stood. "Winema, I'm going to tell Canby to go out there with
some armed troopers. We can't go out there naked."

Winema gazed into his eyes several moments, then looked
away. She felt drained. And she was out of solutions.

～

FROM the ridge line east of the Stronghold a coyote yipped
twice, then cried out his loneliness in a full-throated bay, the
voice of some ancient soul drifting sorrow across the valley
floor. Asleep in his tent, Canby's eyes popped open. He sat up,
his field cot groaning from his weight. His breath clouded the
damp air. He had been dreaming of his capture of the Navajo
chief, Manuelito years ago on the windswept desolate plain of
Bosque Redondo, and a chilling feeling of déjà vu swept
through him.

◆

Command Tent, The Lava Beds, 11 April (Good Friday)

ALBERT Meacham shifted nervously on his stool, pen poised in hand. He stared at the blank sheet of paper on the dusty, gouged field desk for several minutes. Finally he wrote:

> My Dearest Julia,
>   You may be a widow tomorrow, but you shall not be a coward's wife. I go to save my honor. John Fairchild will forward my valise and valuables, which includes $650 for you. The chances are all against us. I have done my best to prevent this meeting. I am in no wise to blame. Yours to the end.
>
>   Alfred

Frank and Winema slept late. They had been up all night, discussing the looming council. The discussion moved in loops; every option became a slippery slope. Opening the tent flap, they were greeted by a cornflower blue sky and a brilliant sun—brighter than it had a right to be, Winema thought as she headed to Meacham's tent.

At Canby's tent Frank found the general making preparations to leave for the peace tent. Frank placed the tips of his fingers on the general's desk. "Hold on, General. I want to have that talk with you and Colonel Gillem."

Canby looked up from his paperwork. "Ah, yes. I remember."

They walked over to the officers' mess tent. Inside they found Gillem and his entire staff just finishing dinner. A watchful lieutenant called attention.

The general's voice carried across the mess. "At ease, men. Mr. Riddle wishes to talk with you in regard to our council with the Modocs today." He turned to Frank. "Go ahead, sir."

Frank looked at Canby incredulously. Address the entire staff?

Canby folded his arms and smiled. "Go ahead."

Frank looked at the curious faces and swallowed. What he was about to say was meant for the general and Gillem, alone. "As y'all know, we are meeting Captain Jack and his men in council this afternoon." Frank turned to Canby. "For the record, General, I want you to know we go against my warnings and against my wife's warnings. We've warned the commissioners time and again of the danger. I think there's a damned good chance they will be killed today."

The mess broke out in a flurry of side conversations.

Canby raised his hand for quiet. "Is that all, Frank?"

"Ah—no." Frank looked at Canby with unease and cleared his throat. "My wife and I done our best to prevent this council. We gave fair warning and y'all heard it. That's all I got to say."

Canby smiled curtly. "Well, brother officers, I bid you all a last farewell. From what Riddle says, this is my last day." Canby chuckled as he gave Frank's shoulder a fatherly squeeze. Nervous chuckles rose from the crowd of officers.

Frank and the general left the mess tent and headed toward the peace tent. Frank was fuming. He felt like a fool. "Look, General. If I was you, I'd take this seriously and bring ten or twelve armed troopers with us. That would make them Modocs think twice about ambushin' us."

Canby looked shocked. "Absolutely not."

The general stopped short, his face betraying he had remembered something. He excused himself, walked to his tent, and returned with a box of cigars. They continued their half-mile walk to the peace tent. On the way, the general whistled *The Girl I Left Behind Me*.

WHEN Winema emerged from Meacham's tent, Jeff was waiting for her. He had a grim look of determination on his face. "Ma, if anything happens to you out there, I'll—I'll kill them all. I swear." He rushed to her, hugged her hard.

Winema bit her lip, struggling to maintain a calm composure. She kissed the top of his head, then gently pushed him back. Holding his face in her hands, she lost herself for a moment in his dark, innocent eyes. "Don't you worry, my handsome boy. Mother will return unharmed. And Father, too."

She didn't have the heart to tell him she had already discussed his future care with Uncle Moluks should she and Frank not return.

～

ARRIVING at the peace tent, Frank and Canby found Kentapoos and his men patiently waiting. And armed.

Frank stiffened. "General, what'd I tell you? The agreement was we'd all be unarmed. There's nine of 'em. If we're smart we'll make dust out of here right now."

Canby squinted toward the peace camp in the distance. "Most likely even Jack found it hard to disarm Indians." His voice was flat, but for the first time his expression revealed a twinge of concern.

The Modocs seemed in an unusually good mood. When Winema arrived on horseback with Agent Dyar, Albert Meacham, Dr, Thomas, and Boston Charley, they found Canby and the waiting Modocs smoking the general's cigars, laughing and joking. Winema tried to make eye contact with Kentapoos, hoping for some reassurance that he had changed the Hot Creeks' minds, but he avoided her eyes.

Pointing out the pleasant weather, Kentapoos asked Canby if they could continue the meeting outdoors. Canby agreed and blankets were spread. Kentapoos sat opposite Canby, Whusum faced Meacham, Boston Charley faced Thomas, Bogus Charley sat across from Winema, Black Wound faced Frank, and a warrior called Hooker Jim sat opposite Dyar. Another warrior, Slolux, and Hakar stood disconcertingly to the rear of their tribesmen, the telltale bulges of pistols behind their shirts.

The general opened the meeting. "My friends, my heart is glad today. I feel good *because* you are my friends. We will do good work here. You will see that I am ready and willing to help you." He addressed Kentapoos. "Jack, I know you are a smart man. That is why I know you want to make peace. It is bad to fight. As long as you live in these rocks, you will be looked upon as a bad man. The Great Father in Washington said, 'I will not let Captain Jack live in the lava beds. He has been in trouble with my children. I will have to find him and his people a new home, a good home where he won't have any more trouble.'

"Jack," he droned on, "the Great Father says he has got many, many soldiers. He will make you go. He sent me, Dr. Thomas, and Meacham, here, to talk good to you and to make peace. You do what I want you to do and the soldiers won't shoot. But if you act mean and won't listen to us, the Great Father might say, 'My soldiers, go into the lava beds. Make him come out.'"

The general leaned slightly forward. "Jack, even if you killed all these soldiers, the Great Father will send more. You cannot kill all of them. So the best thing you can do is come out of these rocks with me. I won't let the soldiers hurt you. What I say is the law, and the White man's law is straight and strong." The general slapped his hands on his thighs. "What do you say? I want you to talk like a man. Use sense this time."

Kentapoos listened closely to Canby's speech, his impassive face betraying his true feelings only once with a brief frown. He peered into Canby's eyes. "*Tyee*, you speak of the Great Father in Washington. He may be your father, but he is not mine. His law is as crooked as this." Using a branch of sagebrush, he scratched a twisted angry line in the dirt. "Less than one moon ago you made a promise that you would commit no act of war as long as we held these councils. *I* have committed no act of war on my side, have I?"

The *laki*'s speech became strained and clipped. "You moved your army from Fairchild's ranch to Van Bremer's, then stole my horses. You promised to give them back, but you have not. Then you brought in more soldiers and the log guns that shoot bullets as big as my head. You brought all of this right under my nose. Does that look like peace? Is this your 'straight law'? You have broken your word. You say I am smart, yet you treat me as if I had the mind of a bird. How can you expect me to believe you? If a man goes back on his word one day, he will do so on another."

Agitated now, Kentapoos made sharp, slashing movements with his arm. "Take away your soldiers. Take away your big guns, then we can talk peace. Either do that or give me a home at Hot Creek or Willow Creek."

Canby opened his mouth, but Kentapoos interrupted. "Do not tell me of some beautiful country way off. God gave me *this* country; he put my people here first! I was born here, my father was born here. I want to live here. I allowed the White man to share my country. I have tried to live peaceably and never asked any man for anything. Hot Creek or Willow Creek is good enough for me."

He leaned forward, beads of sweat now visible on his brow. "I want to tell you, Canby, we cannot make peace as long as these soldiers are crowding me. Promise me a home somewhere in this country—promise me today. Though your word is not much good, I am willing to take it."

The *laki* gestured toward Meacham and Thomas. "These men will make your word stronger if they promise with you." He sat back. "*Now*, Canby, promise me. I want nothing else. *Now* is your chance."

Canby chewed on his cigar with machinelike precision as Kentapoos spoke. From time to time he shook his head in disagreement.

Hooker Jim stood, walked to Meacham's horse, and took the superintendent's overcoat hanging on the saddle horn. Looking at Meacham, he slipped on the coat. With quick, jerking motions, he buttoned it up and walked around the conferees. Puffing out his chest, he bragged, "I am Meacham now."

Meacham removed his hat and offered it to Hooker, saying, "Here, Jim. Take my hat; put it on. *Then* you'll be Meacham."

Meacham's attempt at humor only added to the tension in the air. The commissioners laughed nervously.

Hooker twisted his lips into a cold smile. "I will get that hat pretty quick, no hurry. Hat will be mine by and by."

Kentapoos made direct eye contact with the general, then

spoke in clear, measured tones, "Canby, do you agree to what I ask of you, or not? Tell me. I am tired of waiting for you to speak." Slolux and Hakar moved their hands inside their shirts.

Meacham paled and stage whispered, "For God's sake, General, promise him."

Canby shook his head. "I cannot. We've been through this before."

Kentapoos sagged slightly, then stood, walked behind Meacham's horse. Winema felt cold tentacles of fear tighten around her chest. Meacham was saying something to Whusum, but Winema was paying attention to Kentapoos.

Whusum leaned forward threateningly. "Give us Hot Creek, Meacham. Give us Hot Creek now!"

Rivulets of sweat rolled down Meacham's face. His voice trembled slightly. "I, I will ask the Great Father in Washington for you—do everything I can, but . . ."

Kentapoos had returned from the horse and now stood in front of Canby. Before Winema could interpret what Meacham said, Kentapoos pulled his pistol and barked, "*Otwekatuxe!*"

Canby raised his face only to stare into a barrel. He froze, the blood draining from his face.

To Winema, everything started to move at half-time. Everyone seemed glued to their positions, watching Kentapoos as if he were on a stage, his face a mask of grief, his pistol barrel six inches from Canby's face. His hand shook. The hammer fell. The cap made a muted pop.

A misfire.

Frank and Winema started to get up. Kentapoos cocked the hammer and pulled the trigger again.

FIFTY-THREE

THE REPORT SOUNDED like a cannon in the tranquil air. The bullet smashed into the general just below the right eye. His head jerked back, yet somehow, he scrambled to his feet, stumbled toward his camp.

Kentapoos slumped; his head hung like a condemned man's. Simultaneously Boston Charley leveled his pistol at Reverend Thomas and blew a hole in his upper chest. Thomas groaned, fell backward, caught himself on his left hand, and held up his right hand. "Don't shoot me again, Boston, don't shoot." He looked heavenward. "Angels and ministers of grace defend us!"

Albert Meacham drew a derringer from inside his coat, pressed it against Whusum's chest and pulled the trigger. Nothing happened, the hammer only half-cocked. Whusum fired at Meacham twice. But Meacham was sidling to the right, getting up. One round perforated the superintendent's lapel, the other his sleeve.

The glue that affixed the commissioners and the Riddles to the ground gave way. They all ran. Black Wound tripped the wounded general, who sprawled to the ground. Wound pounced on Canby's back and, grabbing a handful of Canby's hair, jerked the general's head back, and slashed his knife across Canby's throat, opening a gash of spurting blood.

Boston shoved Thomas to his back. "Well, preacher man. Why don't God help you now, eh?" His face transformed into a hideous sneer. "Your medicine is weak and pitiful."

Thomas covered his face with his hands and sobbed, "Oh, Lord, have mercy on my sinful soul."

Bogus Charley calmly walked over, put his pistol to Thomas's head and pulled the trigger. Blood and brain matter sprayed onto Bogus and splattered Boston.

Whusum cursed as he aimed at the running Meacham and fired again. The pistol bucked. Meacham yelped, grabbed his left shoulder, but kept running. Whusum aimed again, but Winema was suddenly there. She slammed her fist down on his arm. He cursed her, "Out of my way, woman!" and aimed again.

"You fool!" She began pounding on his back. "Spare him! He is your friend!"

Winema swung with all her might, striking Whusum in the chest. He staggered, caught a rock with his heel, and fell.

The other Modocs continued firing at Dyar and Meacham as they ran.

Frank rushed in, grabbed Winema's arm. "C'mon, damnit! We gotta get outta here!"

She resisted.

Whusum yelled, "Beware, woman. I may forget who you are."

Her face purple with rage, Winema shouted, "Kill me if you can, you coward!"

Meacham stumbled, fell behind a protruding boulder, and prepared to shoot at Whusum. Winema saw him thrown back when a bullet appeared to strike him in the forehead. She was amazed to see him recover and fire at Whusum. The bullet smashed into Whusum's leg, knocking him off balance. His left arm windmilled as he crumpled to the ground.

Another bullet hammered into Meacham's arm, sending the derringer flying.

Hakar and Barncho suddenly appeared, armed with rifles. To Winema's left she saw Hooker chasing Dyar across the plain. He fired several times, but Dyar was too far ahead. Hooker gave up and turned back to the peace camp.

Frank screamed at her, "*Now, damnit, now!*" He yanked her arm, pulling her along. They sprinted toward Winema's horse.

Barncho was trying to mount Skoks, who shied away. Winema rushed him, caught the warrior's coat, pulled him off. He hit the ground hard.

"YOU *WOCHAGA*! You will not take my horse."

Frank rushed the warrior, but he scrambled to his feet and cracked his rifle barrel over Frank's head. Frank staggered, then slumped to the ground, stunned. The Modoc swung the rifle in the opposite direction, catching Winema between the shoulder blades. The blow knocked her to the ground.

"*White whore!* I will leave you among your dead brothers if you try that again!"

Again he tried to mount Skoks. Winema grabbed a rock and scrambled to her feet. She slammed the stone against the back of his skull. He grunted and sagged.

"Coward! You will not take my animal while I am still alive!"

The warrior staggered, then recovered and raised his rifle. "I'll kill you, then!"

"No, you won't." Kentapoos's voice came from behind Winema, his pistol pointed at the warrior's back. "If I did not need you for our war against the soldiers, I would blow your head off and leave you here to rot. If you ever threaten my cousin, I will kill you." He cocked the hammer. "Hand those reins to Winema."

The warrior's face twisted in anger, but he handed Winema the reins. With a last defiant look at his chief, he stalked away, leaving Kentapoos and Winema alone.

The *laki* looked down at Frank. "Is he hurt bad?"

Winema kneeled by her husband, helped him to a sitting position. "He will be all right."

Kentapoos's face relaxed in relief. "*Waquset.*"

Furious, Winema snapped at her cousin. "What do you care?"

The *laki* let out a long sigh and looked into the distance, then brought his gaze back to Winema. "I have thrown my life away today. I did something I thought I would never do. I killed an unarmed man. I know I will be avenged by his soldiers, but when I fall there will be bluecoats under me. Tell Gillem he can find me up there." He pointed to the Stronghold. "Not in the mountains. I will be in my camp with my people. I am not afraid to die."

Winema started to speak, but he stayed her with a gesture of his hand. "I have committed a great wrong, I know."

Out of the corner of her eye, Winema saw Boston Charley preparing to take Meacham's scalp. "*KAI!*" She ran over to him screaming, *"KAI! Do not dishonor this good man further! Is it not enough that you have murdered him?"*

Boston went about his work without looking at her. "He will not feel the knife."

He proceeded to cut a gash from Meacham's left ear to the center of his forehead. She yelled again, but he ignored her.

Then a desperate idea struck her. *"Soldiers are coming!"* she bellowed.

Boston jerked upright. "Huh?"

Winema shouted again, *"Ut'nah shuldshash kep'ko!"*

The Modocs panicked, sprinted to their horses, and rode for the Stronghold.

Winema returned to her husband. He was leaning against Skoks, still dazed. She took him by the arm. "Come. We must see if Canby is alive."

They found the general lying faceup. He had been stripped. The grotesque gash in his throat oozed blood into a widening dark stain of soaked sand. Winema knelt by him, shooed away flies from a small puffy hole under his right eye. "My poor friend. If you had only listened."

She straightened his legs and folded his arms across his chest. She wiped away a tear with her sleeve. They moved on to Thomas, and she laid him out similarly. Finally they went to Meacham's body. She wept as she used the hem of her dress to wipe blood from his eyes and mouth, then stopped suddenly. Meacham's lips moved.

"He is alive! He is alive!"

A company of soldiers was just galloping in.

Frank's jaw dropped. "Christ. I cant' believe it. I'll stay with him. You ride back for help."

Accompanying the soldiers back to camp, the preceding scenes flashed through her mind. She replayed Kentapoos's shattered expression as he pulled the trigger. The misfire that hung time in the air. Bodies, white like the bellies of fish, lying among the pumice and sage. It all happened in seconds. Seconds to snuff the lives of an overzealous minister and a decorated Civil War general. Seconds to destroy 150 Modoc lives. Seconds to nullify a prophecy.

FIFTY-FOUR

Colonel Gillem's Tent, 14 April

➤ COLONEL ALVAN C. Gillem stroked his long, dark beard thoughtfully as he faced his field commanders. He was pleased with their new plan of attack on the Stronghold. "That should do it, gentlemen. Any questions?"

There were none.

"Very well. You have heard the Modoc drums and their howls of celebration up there." His lips tightened. "Little do they know they have awakened a terrible enemy—the United States Army—with a vengeance."

He scanned their faces. "May God go with you. And let our battle cry be, 'Remember Canby!'"

Outside the command tent the troops drank toasts to each other and sang lustily:

> *Then stand by your glasses steady*
> *The world's a round of lies—*
> *Three cheers for the dead already*
> *And hurrah for the next who dies!*

~

The Lava Beds, 15–16 April

THOOMP. THOOMP.

Two newly arrived, mule-mobile Coehorn mortars belched fizzing half-pound balls at the Stronghold. Howitzers on the opposite ridge echoed the mortars. Muzzle flashes and shell bursts lit up the night sky like a giant flash pan. The bombardment continued all night.

On the morning of the sixteenth, bugles blew, and Companies E, K and M started their advance, moving cautiously through the sage, maintaining voice silence. A few local volunteers joined the soldiers, including Harley Sievers. By ten A.M. they passed the site of the peace tent, within a half mile of the Modocs. They maneuvered right and linked up with two companies of the Twelfth Infantry at the northwestern edge of the Stronghold. Together, they were to punch a hole in the Modoc defenses.

Steeled with righteous indignation over the death of Piney, and now of General Canby, Harley stalked past the peace camp where the general had perished. Only circles of sand stained black from three-day-old blood remained.

Closer—they were definitely within rifle range now, and the absence of rifle fire from the Stronghold was nerve-racking. What were the savages waiting for? Maybe the artillery did its job. Harley kept his eyes fixed on the top of the Stronghold, scanning for movement. Then he stubbed his toe on a jutting rock.

"Son of a—!"

He fell forward. His finger jerked. His Sharps boomed.

The shot echoed down the still valley. Whoops and ululating cries rose from the Stronghold. A handful of well-placed Modoc snipers opened up, pinning the troops down.

Harley dived behind a small rock that offered little cover, then glanced at the trooper next to him. The fool wore a huge, multi-colored peacock feather in his hat—an excellent target.

A bullet skeened off a nearby rock. "Peacock" ducked his head, held on to his hat. "They got us pinned!" Peering around a rock, he gasped. "I'll be gawdamned! Two of them snipers is women!" He shook his head. "*Women* holdin' off the damned *U*nited States Army."

～

"BACK! BACK!" The order came from the right flank. A bugler sounded retreat.

Peacock cupped his hand, shouted at Harley, "That's it! Let's go!"

There was no answer. Another round ricocheted off a rock with a high-pitched whine. Peacock belly-crawled over to Harley and poked him. "Let's go, bud. They said fall back."

Harley lay facedown, as still as a stone.

"Hey." Peacock rolled Harley over.

What was Harley's right eye was now a reddish-black hole the size of a quarter. Dark blood pooled in the eye socket and dribbled down the side of his face.

Peacock recoiled. "Damn!" He fired once more at the snipers, jumped to his feet, and ran.

The troops, Peacock included, attacked again and again only to be repulsed by a deadly wall of Modoc gunfire. He watched mule ambulances carry dead and wounded back to camp all day, their makeshift, mounted couches rolling and yawing precariously. By nightfall, however, Peacock learned the army had gained ground on the east side of the Stronghold and now controlled all access to the lake.

～

The Stronghold, same day

AFTER the army retreated, snipers Kweelush and Wild Girl prepared a venison stew at Krelatko's cave. They laughed nervously about the fleeing soldiers. When the army did not attack after the assassinations, Cho-ocks had declared his prophecy had proved true—the Modoc warriors remained invulnerable, bulletproof. He led a victory dance around the medicine flag, now festooned with Canby's and Thomas's scalps.

When no attack came the third day, even Kentapoos had started to agree: their chief killed, the soldiers were confused and frightened, yet Kentapoos's warning had proved accurate. The soldiers hadn't run home like frightened deer. They had stayed. And attacked.

Kweelush stopped stirring the pot to inspect the ipos roots Wild Girl was chopping.

"*Kai*, young one. Smaller chunks. They cook faster."

Wild Girl frowned and mopped her forehead. "I am tired, Kweelush."

Kweelush sighed and took over the stirring. "Have you told Wieum about the baby coming?"

Wild Girl's face lit up. "I tell him tonight."

"Ahh." Kweelush smiled.

They looked up as two teenage boys, Slow Eyes and Gets Lost, entered the cave bantering noisily. Gets Lost carried what looked like a black *dasi*, but he obviously strained from the weight of the object. A rock?

"Look! Look what we found!" Gets Lost heaved the object onto a knee-high rock ledge. Curious, Wild Girl and Kweelush moved closer.

"It is one of the big bullets the soldiers shot at us," Slow Eyes observed.

Kweelush's brow furrowed as she eyed the evil thing.

Slow Eyes produced a hatchet taken from a captured army packhorse. "We will discover how it works, and our names will be sung by the warriors at the dance tonight!"

He brought the hatchet down on the ball with a clank. The vibration ran up his arm and he yelped. Everyone in the cave now inspected the ball, except for Kweelush, who maintained a cautious distance. The blade left but a puny scar where it struck the ball.

The two women took a step back. Kweelush made a low sound of wariness.

Gets Lost said, "Here. Let me try." He turned the hatchet and struck the ball with the heel. *Clank!* This time a few sparks flew from the point of contact.

"Ahhh," said Slow Eyes.

Gets Lost grew excited. "Look, there is a hole on this side."

The boys rotated the ball so the small, round hole would be directly under the hand ax.

Kweelush and Wild Girl looked at each other, then Kweelush said, "Boys, I do not think——"

But Gets Lost was already swinging the hatchet down. Kweelush saw an arc of bright light, then only darkness.

≈

As Kentapoos and Wieum walked toward the cave, there was a flash, then a muffled boom that shook the earth beneath them. A great cloud of smoke and dust gushed out of the mouth of the cave, throwing small rocks and chips like pieces of hail. People came running from all directions.

Kentapoos felt the crawl of horror. Coughing and choking, he and Wieum made their way into the dust-choked cave. They found only body parts of the two boys. Wild Girl lay on top of Kweelush. The force of the blast had ripped the clothes from their bodies. Their flesh was mangled and torn as if attacked by an angry bear.

Wieum groaned, fell to his knees beside his wife's body, and began the high, plaintive death song.

Outside, Kentapoos related the sad news. Standing nearby, Krelatko looked sick. "What kind of medicine is this?" he bemoaned to another. "The soldiers can now shoot the big bullets into our caves?"

Wham! A mortar shell made a direct hit on the main council fire throwing fiery brands in every direction. Shock and fear brought cries of terror. Babies bawled. People huddled near Krelatko's cave a safe distance away.

Krelatko shouted, "Cho-ocks's medicine has failed! It was all a lie! Now we are punished for killing the commissioners! Our chief was right!"

Wieum, who had just joined them from the lake side of the Stronghold, added, "*Ih,* and the soldiers block the lake. There will be no more water!"

All eyes shifted to Cho-ocks and the Hot Creeks who huddled together sullenly. Krelatko duck-walked to Kentapoos. "Tell us what to do, *laki,* and the People will listen."

Cho-ocks inflated and stepped forward, one arm waving. "*Kai*! My medicine—"

The crowd shouted him down.

Kentapoos's heart soared, but only for a moment before he felt the heavy hand of responsibility rest once again on his shoulders. He thought of Wieum's words. They could not stay in the Stronghold without water.

Kentapoos turned back to Krelatko. "How many bullets do we have?"

"Perhaps thirty a man, *laki.*"

Kentapoos stood to shout above the din. "I want you to listen to my words! We cannot fight the soldiers without bullets and water. And now their medicine has strengthened such that their big bullets can reach into our caves. We must escape after dark and go south, into the back country."

No voice raised in argument as he surveyed the ragtag remnants of his people. "Go to your caves quickly now and prepare to leave. Unmarried men gather around me."

Only ten unmarried men clustered around the chief. He appraised them somberly. "Brothers, it will be up to you to protect our escape. Who will accept this honor?"

They responded in unison. "*Tchwai!*"

Kentapoos smiled. "*Waquset.* After dark we will build up the council fire bigger than ever. Then I want you to spread out along the walls. Make much noise. The soldiers must think we are here all night."

He drew a hasty map in the dirt. "When the great star of the North reaches here, sneak out and meet us at Horse Butte. You know the place?"

The men nodded.

Wham! Another log gun shell hit less than a hundred strides away. The men ducked and covered their heads as sand and rock rained about them.

Kentapoos regarded his young men proudly. "May the Old Ones be with you, my brothers."

FIFTY-FIVE

The Stronghold, 18 April, late morning

"THEY'RE GONE, SIR," the breathless, paunchy corporal reported. "Only two old squaws and two old men was left."

Captain Jackson was red-faced. He had led a brilliant charge against an empty Stronghold. The best he could do now was to pump the old wretches for information.

"Bring them to me."

The corporal removed his kepi and scratched his head. "Well, sir, the boys, they, uh, got a little excited. They shot 'em."

Jackson threw his hat on the ground. "Damnit!"

"But we followed Jack's trail a'ways." He pointed south. "Down yonder. Looks like an old deer trace. I reckon they're headed for the mountains. They sure were quiet. We didn't hear a thing." He shook his head. "Imagine, movin' all them Injuns, squaws and their nits, and at night—"

Jackson made a sarcastic face. "Spare me your admiration, Corporal. Get McKay up here. I want those Warm Springs scouts on their trail—*now*."

The corporal snapped to attention. "Yes, sir. Right away, sir. Usin' Injuns to catch Injuns." He winked at the captain. "Yes sir, that's what the general would'a done, by God."

Jackson's eyes flashed at the verbose enlisted man. "Shag ass, Corporal!"

∽

THAT night the bodies of the four elders were scalped, then decapitated. Soldiers played kickball with the heads for the next two days.

∽

The Riddle Ranch, 19 April

FRANK shook his head. "It just upsets you, Winema."

Winema's face hardened. "Never mind. I want you to read it to me. It has been many days, and I do not know what is happening."

Frank sighed in resignation. "All right, all right." He opened the *Yreka Journal* to an article entitled, "The Fighting at the Lava Beds. Third Day's Fight," and began reading:

" 'Headquarters, Lava Beds, April Seventeenth—Today has been very eventful and full of terrible fighting. About nine P.M. last evening Jesse Applegate arrived by boat from the other side and reported that the shells had done great execution in the Modoc camp. One shell fell in a big crevice, and instantly the rocks were swarming with them. Everyone was in good spirits this morning, believing the Modocs would be dislodged by night.

" 'At seven A.M. I left camp for the front with Mr. Ticknor and General Gillem's orderly. Some Modocs opened on us at 300 yards range. About 150 yards behind us was Fox, the *Herald* correspondent, and Surgeon Eldridge, mounted and armed, who dodged behind a bluff. About 200 yards behind them was young Eugene Hovey and Sam Watson, citizens of Yreka. They had four horses to be used in taking out the wounded. They were behind at the curve of the rocks, and the wind blowing strong, caused them to not hear the shots. When they neared the curve, Modocs opened on them, and the Hovey boy fell. Later in the day when forces came back, Hovey's body was recovered—'"

Frank shut his eyes. "Christ."

Winema's face went from sad to startled. "What? What?"

Frank regarded her with rueful eyes. "It says the Hovey boy was 'disemboweled.'"

He translated the word for Winema. She closed her eyes and hung her head.

Army Field HQ, *the following day*

A dusty Donald McKay, the half-Cayuse leader of the Warm Springs scouts, entered Colonel Gillem's tent. He was a small slim man, dark skinned, with medium-length black hair, a scraggly, drooping mustache, and a permanent frown.

"Found your Modocs, Colonel. Camped on Horse Butte."

Gillem was delighted. "Excellent, McKay, excellent. Tell Captain Jackson to prepare his troop to overtake the enemy."

McKay nodded and left.

The colonel's face lit up as he turned toward Major Green. "We have them, Major. Have Companies E and F secure and hold the Stronghold. We don't want the Modocs slinking back in there."

A half mile south of the Stronghold, Captain Jackson was pouring a cup of coffee when he heard distant gunfire. He darted out of his tent and found Lieutenant Calley and several men staring at a group of Modocs standing on a rise a few hundred yards to the southeast, safely out of rifle range. Their voices carried clearly across the wide gully between the two ridges.

"Ho! Big gun men! Why don't you shoot?"

The Modocs laughed and whooped. Four of them made a mock march forward, kneeled, placed their rifle butts against the ground and fired them like mortars. Another Modoc bent over, lifted his breechclout, and exposed his buttocks. His colleagues delighted in his antics and roared in laughter. Arm in arm, two Modocs danced around in a parody of a quadrille sometimes held by the soldiers while encamped.

"Hey!" a soldier yelled to no one in particular, pointing toward the lake. "They got to the lake, got their water while we was watchin' the show."

Jackson raised his field glasses in time to see four Modocs by the lake. Three were already mounted, the last man filling a bladder with water. "Son of a—What's Gillem doing down there? Is he blind?"

～

Twelve Miles South of the Stronghold, 26 April

BY noon it was a balmy spring day. Sunlight slanted through breaks in thick clouds. Enjoying the peaceful interlude of the past two days, Kentapoos rested on a high rocky butte, surveying the landscape. Here the volcanic activity that produced the lava flows laid down mysterious patterns of cinder buttes, sharp outcroppings, and round chimneys protruding through multiple layers of lava flows.

The area was replete with game. Animals had migrated to this end of the valley to escape the war. The people had full bellies, for now.

Movement below caught Kentapoos's eye. Raising his looks-far glasses, he spotted Captain Jackson leading a patrol toward Deer Butte. Strapped to one of the mules was a small "log gun." Obviously the soldiers planned to place the gun on the butte, an act Kentapoos could not allow. The Modoc camp would be in easy range of the big gun.

～

CAPTAIN Jackson turned in his saddle to watch Harold Sickle, a camp sutler, galloping toward them. When the old man reined up next to Jackson, the captain looked annoyed.

"Sorry I'm late, Cap'n, but that damned squaw of Riddle's ran off my horse."

Jackson spit without taking his eyes from Sickle. "Why'd she do that?"

"Didn't want me to go. Said she did it for my wife's sake."

Jackson snorted and the men laughed. "All right, we got to rest these horses. They're still draggin' their asses from epizootic. Calley, you come with me and Sergeant Kelly up to the butte. Ought'a be a good place to set that mortar should Jack move through here."

•

HAVING slunk to within a few hundred yards of the troopers, Kentapoos and ten men watched Jackson, Calley, and Kelly climb the butte. Kentapoos scanned north along the ridge, behind Jackson. To his amazement the troops dismounted and settled down to a meal even though they were within an arrow's arc of their quarry.

The *laki* smiled, shook his head, and looked at Krelatko. "The fools are eating. And they have posted no guards."

Krelatko's mouth fell open in disbelief. "*Kaaii.*"

"See for yourself," and Kentapoos gave him the looks-far glasses.

Krelatko peered through the eyepieces and chuckled.

Kentapoos got up into a crouch. "Come, I want to get closer." He looked at Hakar. "You and your men stay here and cover us."

Making a wide arc, Kentapoos and Krelatko scampered to a thick stand of desert mahogany, only a hundred strides from the unsuspecting troopers. They watched one trooper remove his boots and socks and begin clipping his toenails.

Suddenly two shots rang out from across the draw, startling Kentapoos. Hakar and his men apparently couldn't resist such easy targets. The *laki* saw Captain Jackson and Lieutenant Calley duck, then run toward the soldier camp.

The Hot Creeks opened up with everything they had. The soldiers shouted, grabbed their rifles, and scattered, seeking cover and returning fire. Then Kentapoos and his ten men opened up, catching the troops in a deadly L-shaped ambush.

Jackson stood to rally his men, but his orders were cut off midsentence. Hit four times, his body twisted and jerked like a marionette, then crumpled to the ground. Krelatko saw Calley running for his horse. He took careful aim and pulled the trigger. The bullet struck Calley in the chest. He reeled backward. A second round, from the Hot Creeks, smashed into his hip, lurching him forward. Krelatko fired again. The round pierced Calley's neck. Bright blood spattered down the front of his shirt and he collapsed.

The soldiers' horses panicked, bolted toward the main camp at the Stronghold.

Sergeant Kelly reared his head from a crevice and shouted to his men, "Follow me!"

Kelly and twenty soldiers, firing and maneuvering, found refuge in a hollow. Four Modocs captured three of the packhorses which were weighted down with cartridge boxes. They whooped as they scooped them into pockets and possibles bags, then ran to distribute the rounds among their comrades.

As the sun rolled behind the western horizon; the Modoc fire ebbed, then stopped. Forty-one blue-clad bodies lay strewn along the top of the ridge and rimmed Kelly's hollow.

Kentapoos gave the signal to cease fire and led his men back across the draw to hook up with Hakar. "That is enough for today," he said, patting Krelatko on the shoulder. "We had a great victory, but we must save our bullets for tomorrow."

Krelatko grinned and called to the remaining soldiers, "All you men that ain't dead better go home! We don't want to kill you all in one day!"

The Modocs laughed and hooted as they rode down the ridge.

FIFTY-SIX

~~ COLONEL GILLEM COULD scarcely believe the courier's report. Twenty-eight men dead, thirteen wounded— more killed in three hours than in the entire five-month campaign. If that wasn't bad enough, a chilly wind now gusted in from the north. The temperature plummeted, and cold rain began to fall.

Around midnight the rain transformed into a relentless, driving snow. The wind howled and whistled through rock canyons and pumice chimneys. Wounded soldiers moaned and shivered under thin blankets as they struggled along the four-hour trek back to the Stronghold.

On the twenty-eighth General Jefferson C. Davis, General Canby's replacement, arrived at the beds. After a personal inspection and interviews with the field and staff officers, the angry general called Gillem to his tent and relieved him of command.

~~

Captain H. C. Hasbrouck's Camp, Dry Lake, Friday, 9 May

THE sun sat fat and red on the lip of the escarpments. Unearthly humanoid figurines of stone stretched long, macabre shadows across the lava flows. Kentapoos had kept the soldiers' movements under surveillance all day. The fact that McKay and his scouts were with them worried him. The soldiers were certainly moving in the right direction, thanks no doubt to that breed McKay.

Kentapoos knew he must find a way to strike the enemy before they got too close to the Modoc camp. He would not be able to defend the People long under a direct attack from such a large, well-armed force. Not with only forty-three warriors, including four or five women fighters, and over a hundred other women and children slowing him down. He was not worried about the soldiers' capabilities under a surprise attack. They had run like deer each time he had fought them. But he would need both surprise *and* good medicine to destroy the *Latinkini* scouts.

The *laki* looked skyward, searching for the hawk. Surely his father's spirit would look favorably upon him if he killed the *Latinkini*, for it was they who took his life.

Dusk turned into a moonless and foreboding darkness. Gathering his men a half-mile from the sleeping soldiers, the *laki* dispersed them in a crescent-shaped ambush formation that would force the soldiers' backs against a muddy, alkalized lake bed. Squatting down next to a large sagebrush, his nerves worn raw, he awaited dawn.

◄━

JUST before dawn the army pack train boss heard his dog growl. He sat up and listened. Nothing, except snores and the soft crackle of campfires. It was cold and dark. The boss shivered, yawned, and pulled his blankets around his shoulders.

The dog growled again, long and low and menacing.

The boss rubbed sleep from his eyes. A sliver of gray light oozed over the eastern horizon and he could just make out the outlines of nearby vegetation rising above the ground mist.

"YIH! YIH! YEEEIH! The stillness exploded with blood-curdling whoops, the whipcrack of rifle fire. Horses whinnied, bucked, and stampeded to the east. Dogs barked savagely. Men shouted, staggered about the camp, yanked from deep sleep into blood-pumping awareness, then into cold panic.

The soldiers bolted toward the lake. Three were immediately cut down. A few clumsily tried to return fire while running backward, and two more fell. The Modocs came on at a dead run, yelling and firing. Dressed in General Canby's blouse and hat, Kentapoos led the charge.

Thoughts of the recent "Jackson Massacre" rushed through Captain Hasbrouck's mind. It would not happen to him!

"Officers, rally 'round me!"

He swirled his cavalry sword in the air. Steeled by the captain's courage, the officers and non-comms rallied their men, preventing a rout. One lieutenant took several men and circled to the Modoc's left. Hasbrouck led a charge of fifteen men toward a clump of rocks containing a group of Modocs.

Two more soldiers screamed and fell. Charging troops fell prone and maintained their fire. The crash of the gunfire was deafening, and acrid gun smoke hung low in the dew-heavy morning air.

❧

At the rock pile Krelatko was startled to see soldiers charging him. Uncertain, he paused, causing his men to hesitate. The trained troops seemed to sense an opening. They scrambled to their feet, renewed their advance.

"Aiieee!"

Krelatko ducked, glanced at Kankush next to him. But Kankush was on the ground, face up, eyes wide and staring. Dark blood seeped from a gaping hole in the center of his chest.

❧

Kentapoos jerked his head around to his left. Somehow the *Latinkini* scouts had flanked him. He winced as he realized they must have found his stolen packhorses if they came from that direction. Looking to his right, he glimpsed Krelatko retreating under close attack.

"*Getak!*" the *laki* shouted. "Back!"

An hour later the warriors straggled back to camp in a sullen mood. Everyone was disappointed at the ominous turn of events. As people gathered around to get the news, Hakar pointed at Kentapoos. "If it were not for him, Kankush would still be alive!"

After the disheartening failure of the attack, it took very little to push the *laki* over the edge. He pointed back. "Your foolishness cost us our packhorses and ammunition!"

Seven moons of cold, hunger, loss, and desperation boiled over like a cauldron. The crowd joined the confrontation, wives taking the sides of their husbands. Bickering, accusing, and shoving went on for an hour.

Kentapoos once again felt the ominous loneliness of failure.

"Kentapoos brought us to this!" screamed Cho-ocks. "Even his father's spirit pisses on him from the sky. His medicine is less than weak—he *has* no medicine!"

Shade lunged at Cho-ocks, "*Kailash stani!*" and she spit on him.

Cho-ocks's wife leaped at Shade, fingers clawed and extended like a swooping vulture. They scuffled across the dirt, scratching and grunting. Kentapoos and Krelatko surged forward, pulled the brawling women apart.

Kentapoos's chest heaved from the tension and exertion. The hatred and viciousness in the women's sunken eyes alarmed him. His arms trembled with rage as he leveled his rifle at Cho-ocks. "I want you gone from my camp!" His lips twisted in disgust as he peered at Skiet-teteko. Take these 'Hot Creeks' with you! *Atui!*"

Shouting and bickering exploded again. The crowd moved inward, yelling more accusations at their chief. Kentapoos raised his Sharps and pulled the trigger. The blast startled the crowd into silence.

He glowered at Black Wound. "If you people think I caused Kankush's death, shoot me! Now! Here!"

No one spoke.

"I will return your fire, I promise you! For I know I will die fighting. Here or against the soldiers, or on the gallows—it matters little to me now."

He waited for a response. When none came, he continued. "Kankush died a warrior. He deserves our honor, not our quarreling."

Black Wound yelled, "I will stop your talk, coward!" and raised his Henry.

Wieum grabbed the barrel, jerked it downward. "*Kai*! You got what you wanted. You wanted to shoot soldiers all the time. Our chief wanted peace. There are plenty of soldiers left. If you want to shoot something, go out and shoot *them*."

Black Wound stared at Wieum, then yanked his rifle from Wieum's grip. His voice was low and mean like a hatchet. "I quit my chief. I despise him. I am through with him," and he wheeled and pushed his way out of the crowd. Hakar, Bogus Charley, Skiet-teteko, and Cho-ocks followed.

The crowd's attention shifted abruptly to the distant *thoomp, thoomp* of log guns. The soldiers had found them.

"*Run!*" Kentapoos yelled just before two shells exploded eighty strides from their camp. A bugle sounded faintly in the distance.

"THEY'VE FOUND US!"

"SCATTER!"

"TO THE MOUNTAIN!"

With practiced efficiency the camp emptied in minutes. Groups of twenty and thirty Modocs scattered south, southeast, and west.

When the soldiers rushed into the camp they found only phantoms.

FIFTY-SEVEN

The Fairchild Ranch, 25 May

MAJOR GREEN PUFFED excitedly on his cigar as Hasbrouck made his report. John Fairchild and two other officers listened intently. The captain was filthy and haggard. He hadn't shaved or bathed in three weeks.

"They scattered every which way when we pumped the mortars into them. We chased them for a couple of weeks. Every time we got close, they scattered into smaller groups. It was like tryin' to grab a handful of minnows; they'd just squiggle away. Finally we caught up with this group we got under guard outside. Seventy five of 'em."

"Excellent, Captain. I imagine your men are worn out. You've had a helluva chase." Green clapped Hasbrouck on the shoulder. "We'll get the stragglers eventually. The Modocs are finished. It's just a matter of time, now."

The front door swung open. Hakar, Skiet-teteko, Krelatko, and one other Modoc walked in, their rifles hanging loosely at their sides.

Fairchild and the officers jumped up and started for their guns.

Krelatko, who spoke the best English, held up his hand. "No. We are finished fighting. We are tired. Our women and children are hungry. We came to see *you*, Fairchild."

Krelatko gave a command, and the Modocs laid their rifles on the floor. "You are our friend, Fairchild. You know me. I never lie."

Fairchild nodded, though warily.

Krelatko stepped closer to Major Green. "We are done fighting, *tyee*."

He removed his gunbelt and handed it to the major. The others followed suit.

Green immediately sent for General Davis.

The stocky, heavily whiskered Davis swept into the room followed by a bevy of majors and colonels. He eyed the four Modocs now manacled and sitting on the Fairchilds' dining chairs. They looked worse than Hasbrouck. They looked like reprobates from the Stone Age. Their clothes were filthy and tattered, their faces gaunt and deeply lined, their cheeks blackened with pitch in mourning, their eyes dull and lifeless.

Davis smirked, removed his gloves and hat, placed them carefully on a reading table. "Well. How do you do, boys? I am glad to see all of you. You gave us a helluva chase." His smirk faded. "Now where's the rest of your people?"

Krelatko smiled back. "We are tired, *tyee*. Not sure where Jack is. Him, Whusum, maybe fifteen others go way off." He gestured toward himself and his three colleagues. "We fight no more—give up our guns."

Davis stroked his beard thoughtfully, then smiled broadly. "So, you want to quit fighting. I am glad." There was a glint in his eye as he shot a look at his staff. "No doubt you're hungry. Come, we'll get you something to eat."

The Modocs nodded hungrily. They hadn't eaten in two days. As they stood, the general looked as if he had been struck by another thought. "But before we eat, I have an idea to discuss with you."

The Modocs eyed him with wary expectation.

Smiling, the General looked at Hasbrouck and gestured at the manacles. "I think we can dispense with those, Captain. I don't think our guests will be causing any trouble."

Hasbrouck blinked in surprise, then removed the cuffs. He

backed away after the last one, making a face. "I hope I don't smell as bad as this bunch."

The general glanced at Fairchild, who bit his lip and studied the ceiling.

Shifting his gaze back to the Modocs, Davis intoned, "How would you boys like to be free men, have plenty to eat, and maybe a little money to boot?"

The Modocs looked incredulous. They spoke hurriedly to each other in Modoc.

Hakar said, "He wants us to help capture Kentapoos. Why not? We have lost the war."

Skiet-teteko nodded. "*Ih*, maybe we can save the rest of the People. As it is, they are eating their horses. The soldiers will catch them any day now."

Hakar frowned. "It would serve Kentapoos right."

Krelatko said nothing. His shoulders sagging, he stared at the ground.

Hakar looked at the General. "*Ih*. Yes, we will do it."

Willow Creek Canyon, 3 June

KENTAPOOS made one last try at cheering his daughter. A scrawny, listless Laughs Loud hadn't spoken three words in as many days. He just wanted to see her smile again, hear her silly laugh.

He tossed the *dasi* toward her. "Go ahead, Laughs, kick it."

Listless, Laughs looked at him from sunken eyes. They fixed on the ball, then shifted back to Kentapoos. She coughed, a harsh, rasping sound, then sighed and remained sitting on her rock.

Wieum trotted into camp. "*Laki*. Krelatko and Bogus are here. They want to talk to you."

Anger shot through Kentapoos. He knew all about Krelatko, Bogus, Hakar, and Skiet-teteko. They had been observed surrendering at Fairchild's ranch. He picked up his rifle. "Bring the traitors here."

When the two men faced him, the *laki* spit on the ground in disgust. "So, do you come to talk or fight? I hope it is to fight, because that is what I am ready for."

Bogus looked insulted. "Is that the way to treat your own? Am I a stranger or a dog? I have no time for such foolishness."

"Do not play with me, Bogus!" Kentapoos snapped. "I know you have turned against me for money. You are no better than the trickster coyotes that shit in these valleys. Now what do you want?"

Bogus's jaw tightened a bit. "You should be glad that Krelatko and I have not left this work to the soldiers. You know they would shoot you down like rabbits. Why do you treat me in this way? Did I not show you how a Modoc could fight for his rights? I left you as a friend and I have returned a friend."

Kentapoos spat again.

Bogus ignored the insult. "I am here on your behalf. I do not want my chief shot down. You can live if you do the right thing. Give up your gun and go with Krelatko and me to the soldiers' camp. You will get justice." He gestured with his hand. "Look at us. We gave up and we are unhurt. They fed us well and gave us clothes."

Kentapoos moved closer. Feeling the deep pain of betrayal, he locked eyes with Krelatko. "I have heard enough. You intend to buy your freedom by delivering me to the soldiers. *Wochagam!* All of you! I will die by my own hand before I see you sing your victory song at my capture."

"And then *I* will kill you, filthy traitors!"

Bogus and Krelatko wheeled to find Woman Watching leveling a rifle at them.

"Soldiers! Soldiers coming!" four women screamed as they ran toward camp. Kentapoos's men ran to the top of the bluff. Soldiers dotted the countryside below, scrambling up the sides of the bluff. Several of the Modocs opened fire. The soldiers returned it five fold.

Bogus took advantage of the confusion and tackled Whusum. Kentapoos hurried his family toward a dense growth of willows. Woman Watching rushed toward a high ridge.

The soldiers poured over the bluff, encircled the camp, and easily captured most of the exhausted Modocs, including Whusum and Black Wound.

Woman Watching ran along the bluff, firing, screaming at the soldiers, then firing again. "You *Kash*! Leave us alone! *I despise you!*"

Her screaming reached fever pitch; spittle flying from her mouth. She kept firing, cocking, firing, cocking. Two soldiers jerked and yelled, then fell under her bullets. Every soldier's attention was on her now. A fusillade of rifle fire raked the top of the ridge.

"Leave us in peace!" She fired again. "You Miserable dogs!"

Tiny puffs of dust from impacting bullets flew around Woman's feet as she ran. Another volley, and another—all missed their mark.

Black Wound watched with the others from below. He smiled pridefully, thrust a closed fist into the air. "*Heya! Heya!*"

Then all the Modocs took up his yell and whooped encouragement. The women filled the air with high trills. It was as if Woman Watching was an icon—the embodiment of revenge for the years of ignominy and heartbreak.

Her aim was wild now, most of the shots striking the ground or passing far over the soldiers' heads. As if mesmerized, the troops stopped firing and watched her rave, run and shoot.

"Kemush will strike you down! This is our land! Ourrrrss!"

Her hammer now clinked over and over against an empty chamber. She stumbled to a stop and looked down at them, her chest heaving, her eyes wild, like a cornered animal. Sweat-soaked hair matted her face. For several moments they stared at each other, Woman and the soldiers. Then a sharpshooter raised his rifle, aimed carefully, and fired. Woman Watching stiffened, staggered a step to the side, then pitched over and rolled down the embankment several times in a swirling cloud of dust, finally thudding against a jutting boulder. The camp fell silent.

A coyote yipped from a nearby butte, then bayed a lonely

refrain, and dusk swept long shadows across the pumice outcrops.

~

HAKAR and Bogus led a squad of soldiers toward the willow thicket where Kentapoos and his family were hiding. Hakar turned to the soldiers. *"Heh tuk gatt kai duks ah yudah tuk."*

Bogus translated, "Stay where you are and no shooting."

After a moment Green Basket, Laughs Loud, and Shade crawled out and walked toward the soldiers, their heads held high. Then a dark form bolted out of the willows and scampered north.

Hakar's eyebrows jumped. *"Haggi!"* and pointed to the blurred movement. "It is Kentapoos. He is getting away!"

Sergeant Kelly shouted orders and the trap closed. "*Alive*, men, the general wants him *alive!*"

Eight cavalrymen charged toward the *laki*. They rode him down in seconds. Kentapoos tripped in the darkness, fell face first into a clump of sagebrush. Five of the troopers jumped from their horses and converged on the chief, who lay panting and mumbling under their weight. He pounded his fist against the ground and fought back bitter tears. He was out of breath. Out of strength. Out of time.

Captain Hasbrouck looked at his Warm Springs scout. "What's he mumbling?"

The scout leaned down, listened, then rose with a puzzled expression. "He say, *akroh, akroh*. Father, father."

PART FOUR

A Pound of Flesh

A man's mind is a dark mirror.

—Old Gaelic saying

FIFTY-EIGHT

Fort Klamath, 5 July, 1873

OUTSIDE, THE SKY was achingly blue. It was shortly after ten A.M., and a searing sun leached waves of suffocating humidity from the ground. Local citizens, brows furrowed, arms folded in expectation of swift justice, filled the chairs and benches in front and in the center of the room. A few curious Klamaths and Modocs from the reservation sat together at the back of the room, including Hakar, Skiet-teteko, and Krelatko—the men who had thrown a woman's shawl over Kentapoos and called him a coward, then betrayed him.

Other tribesmen stood along the back wall and spilled out the door and into the yard, tight against each other, ears cocked, straining to hear the enigmatic words of the *boshtin* law-talk.

Major Curtis sat at the north end of a long narrow table. At the south end sat Lieutenant Colonel Elliot, the prosecutor, and his two assistants, all in dress uniform. To the right of the officers, Kentapoos, Whusum, Black Wound, and Boston Charley sat grim-faced on a bench, their legs shackled, their wrists chained. Sitting on the floor next to Jack were Barncho and Slolux, also chained. Having posed for photographs earlier, the warriors' hair was cut short into bowl-cuts, and they wore army-issue shirts and new blue jeans.

Frank and Winema sat behind the military Judge Advocate, Major Curtis. At the north end of the room stood a file of cavalry soldiers, their freshly cleaned rifles reeking of gun oil, polished bayonets gleaming. Everyone sweated with equanimity. Flies buzzed about in a languid stupor.

Winema jumped when Major Curtis slammed his gavel on the pine table, the loud whack reverberating through the front room of the guardhouse. "This commission will now come to order."

Winema and Frank were sworn in as official interpreters of the court. Major Curtis, with Frank interpreting, asked the prisoners if they had counsel. Each replied they had been unable to procure any while imprisoned. Of course, no such services were offered, Frank thought, and neither Elisha Steele nor Judge Roseborough had replied to Kentapoos's messages.

"Very well," Curtis said, ignoring the implication. "Mr. Belden, will you please read the charges and specifications."

The court recorder adjusted his spectacles and cleared his throat. "Charge first: murder in violation of the laws of war. The specification in substance was the murder of General E.R.S. Canby and Dr. Eleazer Thomas. Second charge: assault with intent to kill in violation of the laws of war. Specification, second: assault on the commissioners—attempt to kill A. B. Meacham, F. T. Riddle, and Toby Riddle, interpreters, in the lava beds, the so-called place situated on the margin of Tule Lake, California on the eleventh day of April, 1873, to which the prisoners severally pleaded to all charges and specifications, not guilty."

Curtis remained stone-faced. "Thank you, Mr. Belden. Colonel Elliot, you may call your first witness."

Colonel Elliot nodded to Curtis. "I call Mr. Frank Tazewell Riddle."

Frank looked at Winema. She squeezed his hand, then he made his way to the witness chair.

Colonel Elliot straightened his blouse. His face was flushed. Sweat stained his blouse around his armpits. "Mr. Riddle, were you present at the meeting of the commissioners and General Canby, referred to in the charges and specifications just read?"

"That's right."

"Were the prisoners at the bar present on that occasion?"

"They were."

The prosecutor continued his line of questioning, and Frank retold the events leading up to the assassinations and shortly thereafter. Elliot then called Winema to the stand.

All eyes were on the "Woman Chief," as Meacham had named her. She stood, proud and erect, and took her seat at the stand.

"Toby, who told you the Indians were going to kill the commissioners that day?"

"Wieum—William Faithful."

"How long before the meeting did he tell you this?"

"Maybe eight or nine days."

"What was done with the bodies of Thomas and General Canby?"

"They—stripped them. Slolux took Dr. Thomas' coat."

"Toby, do you have anything to add to your husband's testimony?"

She shook her head, then caught herself. She signaled Frank with her eyes, and he translated for her. "Yes. I have something to say. I say that all this would not have happened if you would have given Jack even the smallest piece of land in the valley, a place that was our own. At the end Kentapoos said he would even settle for the land-of-burnt-out-fires. That land is good for nothing. No Whites want it. He was willing to live in caves and hunt rabbits in the sagebrush, but the government said no. Jack did wrong, yes. But the wildcat is only dangerous when cornered."

She stood and pointed toward the back of the room, toward the four traitors. Her voice trembled as she glared at them. "And those dogs back there helped! You gave him no way out, no way to save his honor, his respect." She turned back to the judge. "I ask you to think of this when you meet in council to decide his punishment." She waved her hand. "*Otwekatuxse*. I am finished."

———◆———

WITH Winema interpreting, the defendants were questioned the following day. The room filled to capacity. People batted away flies with folded newspaper fans. Two small windows on either wall did little to assuage the stifling ninety-degree heat. Sweat dripped from the tip of Major Curtis's nose as he conferred with his aide. In the rear, the few Modoc spectators that made it inside spoke quietly among themselves. A Seth Thomas grandfather clock on the west wall gonged, and with military precision, Major Curtis's gavel struck the table on the tenth chime.

Skiet-teteko, now a witness for the prosecution, was sworn in.

"What part did you take in the assassination?"

"I was running and shooting at my friend, Riddle."

This brought chortles from the spectators.

"Did you try to hit him?"

"I did my best."

A low murmur, mixed with a few more chuckles, erupted from the spectators. Major Curtis tapped his gavel and the crowd quieted.

"Did you know that Canby and the others were to be killed?"

"*Ih*. The Indians had a talk the night before."

"Who talked?"

"Most of them. The two chiefs were talking."

"What two chiefs?"

"Kentapoos and Whusum."

"What did you hear them say?"

"I heard them talking about killing the commissioners. I didn't hear who was going to do it."

"What Indians were at the meeting on April eleventh when Canby was shot?"

"Whusum, Kentapoos, Cho-ocks, me, Black Wound, Boston, and Hakar."

Skiet-teteko was excused and, in turn, Boston Charley and Hakar were called. Each was truthful in his account of the planning and execution of the assassinations. Finally Wieum was called, who recounted his warning to Winema regarding the assassinations.

A sudden disturbance in the back of the courtroom interrupted the proceedings. The crowd blocking the door parted, and Albert Meacham entered. Several women gasped and covered their mouths. Using a cane, he walked awkwardly, like a stroke victim. His face was badly disfigured, his left eyebrow partially destroyed by the bullet's entrance wound, a much larger piece of fleshy scar tissue stretching across his right eye, the exit wound. The top of his right ear was clipped off and discolored. His pallid face and sunken cheeks added to his enfeebled appearance.

Jack's lips thinned and he looked at the floor. Whusum, Black Wound, and Boston looked at Meacham as if he were a ghost. Judge Curtis gaveled for order. Colonel Elliot dismissed Wieum and called Albert Meacham to the stand.

"Mr. Meacham, are you feeling up to testifying today?"

Meacham covered a cough with his handkerchief, then mopped his brow with it. His hand shook noticeably. "Yes, Colonel. Thank you for your concern," Meacham responded, his voice as weak as a child's.

"What position did you hold in the late war with the Modocs?"

"I was appointed by Secretary Delano as chairman of the Peace Commission."

"Please state what happened leading up to the assassinations."

"On Thursday, Boston Charley made several propositions. They were accepted by Dr. Thomas, and we made an agreement to meet Captain Jack and five unarmed men at eleven o'clock. All parties were to be unarmed at the council tent on Friday."

"Did Dr. Thomas present it to you officially?"

"Yes. I—I told Dr. Thomas that if occasion required my presence in any business, he was to act in my capacity as chairman, and as"—he winced as if in pain and mopped his face once again—"as acting chairman, he made the arrangement and so notified me."

"Why not General Canby, or Colonel Gillem?"

"I, ah, thought it better to maintain civilian control of the commission as originally designed."

"After that what followed?"

"I protested against holding the meeting, but subsequently yielded to the opinions of General Canby and Dr. Thomas. Mr. Dyar and I dissented."

"Were any of the commissioners armed?"

"Not that I know of."

"Thank you, Mr. Meacham. You are a brave man, sir. You may step down."

A soldier brought a chair and seated Meacham near the front.

Lieutenant Colonel Elliot pulled at his collar as if to vent the heat from his body. "Your honor, the prosecution rests."

Judge Curtis said, "Very well, Colonel." He turned toward the defendants. "Captain Jack. You may make a statement at this time if you wish."

Kentapoos hesitated a moment, then stood. He looked down at his leg irons, then looked impatiently at Winema and Frank. *"Kasker nu nen hankochs gen wad-e te sho lo tunko."*

Winema translated to the court, "I cannot talk dressed in these irons."

"You will have to, Jack. They aren't coming off," Judge Curtis said.

The corner of Jack's tightly closed lips twitched once, then he straightened and looked at the court defiantly. He continued in Modoc, with Winema translating.

"When I was a boy, I had it in my heart to be a friend to the White people. I was a friend to them until a few months ago.

What was it that turned my heart?" He glared toward the back of the room, at the Hot Creeks.

He nodded toward the back of the room. "Some of these men are here today, free men, while I am in irons. You White people did not conquer me, my own men did. Some of my men voted to kill the commissioners. I fought it with all my might. I begged them not to kill unarmed men. What did they do? They threw me down, put a woman's hat on my head, and called me 'Woman! Woman! You may not lead us anymore! You will die by our bullets, not the soldiers'.'

"What could I do? My life was at stake no matter what I did, so I agreed to do the coward's act." He paused a moment, then, "I am not afraid to die with my hands tied behind me. I once thought I would die on the battlefield, defending my rights and home. If I had known what these traitors were up to, we would not be here today. I would have died a warrior's death." He nodded toward Hakar, Skiet-teteko, Boston Charley, and the others watching calmly from the rear. "The men I speak of are now here, free. They fought for their liberty with *my* life."

Jack looked out at the spectators. "You people have driven us from mountain to mountain, from valley to valley, like we do a wounded deer. The Indian has little, yet you want it all. If the White people who killed our women and children had been tried and punished, I would not have thought so highly of myself and my men here. Where is this justice you speak of? You shoot Indians any time, be it war or peace. Can you tell me where any man has been punished for killing a Modoc in cold blood? Ben Wright killed many of my people, among them Toby Riddle's father—my uncle and our chief—Secot. That, too, was at a peace talk. Were he or any of his men punished? No, not one! He and his men were *civilized* White people. And other civilized White people at Yreka made a hero of him for murdering innocent Indians.

"Now, here I am. Killed one man after I had been fooled by him many times. The law says 'hang him.'" He silently studied the crowd. "I see in your faces you are tired of listening to me. Perhaps you think I lie. But I tell the truth." He looked toward the rear of the room where a small crowd of young Modocs had squeezed in. "I feel for the welfare of my young boys and girls. I hope you will not ill-treat them on my account, for they cannot help what wrongs I did. I hope the White Father in Washington will give them a good home and start in life. If the government will give them a chance, they will prove themselves."

Kentapoos turned so that he could face the court and Frank and Winema. "So now I quit talking. In a few days, I will be no more."

He sat down and stared straight ahead, his face now unreadable. Only a few scattered coughs, and the *fwapping* sound of newspaper fans, broke the silence. Winema wept quietly. She wept for Jack, for General Canby, for Dr. Thomas. For her people.

~

ONLY minutes after the final gavel, Judge Curtis and his staff filed back out of a side room and took their place at the head table.

"The defendants will rise."

Winema interpreted and the Modocs rose slowly, their chains and manacles rattling the still air.

Colonel Elliot stood and peered at the defendants. "This court finds you—Captain Jack, Barncho, Black Wound, Skonches John (Whusum), Boston Charley, and Slolux—guilty of the murders of General Edward S. Canby and Dr. E. Thomas, and of the attempted murder of Agent L. Dyar and Colonel A. B. Meacham. The sentence of this court is that you be hanged by the neck until dead. May God have mercy on your soul."

The gavel slammed. The Whites exploded in cheers and whistles.

Winema slumped in Frank's arms.

FIFTY-NINE

Fort Klamath Guard House, 2 October

~ KENTAPOOS WAS NOT allowed visitors until the day before his hanging. Frank and Winema arrived at the guardhouse midmorning. Entering the orderly room, Frank removed his hat and turned it anxiously in his hands. "I guess I'll go in first, *ena*. I—I got some things I gotta straighten out with Jack."

Winema nodded somberly and touched his arm. He nodded to the young private, who escorted him to the rear cells.

As she took a seat on a bench outside the jail door, Winema gathered her strength for the final goodbye. Like tendrils of smoke, old memories curled into her mind: when she and Kentapoos were children, how they played together, how he had fawned over her, protected her. How proud she was of him, and how proud he was of himself, the day he had earned warrior status. On that night Secot had held the warrior ceremony and tied the hawk feather to his nephew's hair. At eight winters she thought she was in love with her brave, handsome cousin.

Then he came to her at the circle and asked her to accompany him in the honor dance. There they were, just the two of them, leading the procession, the deep rectangular drum throbbing a steady beat. Each beat echoed back from *Kaela Ena*, through the soles of her moccasins, into her legs, resounding in her chest. She looked up into her cousin's face, beaming with Modoc pride, and she felt a special bond. . . .

～

KEYS chinked and clanked as the private opened the cell door and Frank walked in. Kentapoos's face was sallow, but he managed a wan smile. Frank sat down across from him at the small square table.

Kentapoos's brow knitted in concern. "How are you, my brother? And how is my little cousin, Charka?"

Frank stared at him for several moments. He had so much to say, yet, now that he faced Jack, words eluded him.

"Fine, everybody's just fine."

Kentapoos nodded and smiled, leaning back in his chair. "I am glad to see you. I have had few visitors."

"Are they feedin' you well?" Frank asked.

Kentapoos's mouth formed a half-smile. "*Ih.* You know how I like *boshtin* cooking."

Frank drummed his fingers on the table, gathering his thoughts.

Kentapoos asked, "How are my wife and son?"

Frank shifted nervously in his chair. "How would you expect? Them knowing you'll be hanged tomorrow."

Jack's smile strained. Outside, they heard hammering. Frank could restrain himself no longer, and the words finally gushed out. "Why, Jack? Why in God's name did you do it?"

Kentapoos shook his head slowly. He spoke in measured tones. "Still you do not learn from us. God did not make me do it, Tchmu'tcham."

"Don't play with me, Jack."

There was a tense flicker of his jaw muscle, then Kentapoos's expression softened. "I am a *laki.* You know I must abide by the will of my people."

Frank's frown deepened; his face flushed, his voice rose, "Damn it, Jack! You're a smart man. You had to know it was wrong to murder those men. *I* told you, *Winema* told you, *Meacham* told you—people you trust—that Canby was decent and there was no trickery. Christ! Who did you need to hear it from—God?"

Kentapoos's face remained placid. "You are not Modoc. I do not expect you to understand."

"Don't play noble savage with me. You're talkin' to family, now." Frank paced, rubbing the back of his neck, months of pent-up frustration erupting like infected sores, the scabs suddenly scratched away. "What galls me most, Jack, is that you put Winema in danger. I can't forgive you for that."

Kentapoos's face pinched. "I cannot forgive *myself* for that. Wound, Hakar . . . all of them agreed you and Winema would not be harmed, as I had ordered."

Frank was stalled a moment. Then thinking about Black Wound and Hakar, the anger returned. "That's just what I mean. Those sons-a-bitches lied to you. *They're* the ones you put your trust in, not Winema or me."

Anger, frustration, and grief continued to gush through Frank as though a dam had burst. He grabbed his chair and threw it behind him. It skidded along the floor, crashed into the wall. "Goddamnit, Jack! Look at yourself, sitting here in chains. Look what you done to Winema, to Chief Skonches, to your family! To yourself!"

Kentapoos looked sidelong at Frank. "To you?"

"Yeah, *to me*, goddamn you!"

Frank leaned over the table, nose-to-nose with his dearest friend. "I trusted you. I believed in you. *Canby* trusted you."

"And I embarrassed you in front of your White friends."

Frank was stunned. The remark cut like a knife. He grabbed Jack by his shirt, pulling him partially off the chair. "Damn you, Jack. I should strangle you right here with my bare hands."

Kentapoos remained motionless. Frank stared into his eyes. Did he see a tear welling?

The door opened and a soldier looked in. "Trouble, Mr. Riddle?"

Frank, trembling with emotion, let go Jack's shirt and straightened. "It's all right, Private."

The soldier backed out, closed the door. The two men eyed each other uneasily. The hammering outside seemed to grow louder.

Kentapoos sagged in his chair. "I . . . did not mean that, Tchmu'tcham. Perhaps it would be better if you *did* kill me. Better to die at the hands of a friend than hung like meat in front of my people . . . in front of my wives and child."

Frank backed away. He felt drained as he looked at his old friend. He had no more words. "*Kemush* be with you, my brother."

Kentapoos looked at Frank with glistening eyes. "And with you."

Frank signaled the guard. The door opened and he walked out.

❧

FRANK emerged from the interrogation room, snuffing out Winema's reminiscence. She saw the sorrow, the strain in his face. He shook his head, then walked out the front door.

The guard let Winema into the small, stark room. She stood near the door, suddenly unsure of what to do. Deep lines were carved into Kentapoos's face, his eyes marbled with red. Yet he maintained his proud bearing.

Smiling wanly, he stood. The raspy scrape of his chair against the plank floor echoed in the near empty room. His leg chains clinked as he moved toward her. They embraced. And the tears came. She thought she had no more tears, but they flowed as if the sacred springs welled within her. Her body shuddered with each sob. Kentapoos held her, let her cry. When the sobs subsided, he gently pushed her back and wiped the tears from her face with his thumbs.

"So many tears our women's eyes have shed." He squeezed her shoulders. "You must be strong, Little Swallow—for your son and your husband." He looked into her eyes. "For the People."

He hadn't called her Little Swallow in a long time. She shook her head. "Oh, Waterbrash. How did it come to this? Why didn't you listen to us?"

"What is past, is past, cousin. There is no use dwelling on it. You know it is not our way. My life is finished, but yours will be full."

Kentapoos eyed the guard's door, leaned closer to her ear. "I would ask you to do something for me."

"*Oka ilagen.* You know I will."

"I want you to see that Green Basket, Shade, and Laughs Loud are treated well. I have heard they are to be sent away. Ask Meacham to see that my daughter returns one day to *Mowatoc*, to be near the bones of our fathers. Also, I want you to see that my body is burned at Yainax, in our way. Will you do this?"

Winema felt a crushing sensation in her chest. She didn't know if she could accomplish these things. The army still fumed over Canby's death. They no longer listened to her or Meacham.

Kentapoos squeezed her shoulders again and spoke in low urgent tones, his eyes pleading. "Winema, don't let them desecrate my body. You know if I am not burned, and the ceremonies not done properly, my spirit will not rest." He squeezed harder. "They have taken my home, my land, and my life. Do not let them steal my spirit as well. Do not let them take that last measure of me."

She moaned softly.

"Promise me," he said, his jaw tightening.

She nodded, and her head and shoulders sagged from the weight of her promise.

His voice was suddenly husky. "Now go, Little Swallow. Help our people. I will always be with you."

The guard's key rattled in the lock. Squeezing Kentapoos's hand, Winema said, "I will pray for your spirit, Waterbrash. May *Kemush* watch over you, and may—may your journey west . . . be . . ." She couldn't finish.

The afternoon sun had moved low in the sky. The window

bars cast jagged shadows across the plank floor as she turned and walked quickly from the room.

Outside, the day's warmth collided with a cold front from the north, making the sky soupy with clouds. Distant thunder growled. The rain began with scattered drops the size of half dollars, splattering against the roof heavily like spent rifle balls. Then it grew to a groaning roar.

After a while the drops diminished in size and speed, and the sound of their impact with the forest became a gentle steady sigh, as if after one, final anguished effort, the exhausted spirits had acquiesced to the inevitable.

SIXTY

Fort Klamath, Friday, 3 October, 1873

EARLY MORNING CAME amid a golden haze, then blue skies and a soft fall breeze. Frank and Winema stood by Skonches, watching a squad of soldiers herd the "renegade" Modocs into the courtyard. The army finally issued them new clothes, replacing the lice-ridden rags they had worn for months.

Winema rushed to her friends and relatives, trying to speak soothing words, words that fell flat before she even spoke them. Toward the back of the crowd, they spotted Green Basket and Laughs Loud. She and Frank joined them, embraced for a long time.

Winema's eyes searched the grounds. "Where is Shade?"

Green Basket's face sagged, her eyes distant and lifeless. Winema felt her trembling through her wool shawl.

"Hiding," she mumbled. "Charka?" she asked.

"With friends," Winema answered.

Laughs Loud's face was void of expression, her small lips drawn into a tight line. Frank and Winema took Laughs's and Green Basket's hands, then followed the crowd to the gallows. Two wagons clattered around the corner. Kentapoos, Black Wound, Whusum, and Boston rode in the back of the first wagon, sitting atop pine coffins. Slolux and Barncho rode likewise on the second. Frank's grip tightened around Winema's hand. Murmurs rippled through the crowd.

A breeze brought the smells of freshly cut pine and damp hemp. The wagons halted in front of the gallows. A soldier helped Kentapoos and the three others down from the first wagon, then pointed to the steps. Chains clanking, and with a strange loping movement, they shuffled to the gallows stairs. Then Kentapoos looked questioningly at the second wagon. Barncho and Slolux were left sitting on their coffins.

Why? Winema wondered. What is happening?

A soldier gave Kentapoos a shove. *Kash! No need to be rough.*

Kentapoos climbed the stairs, followed by Black Wound, Whusum, and Boston. A gangly Sunday doctor, his face suitably somber, awaited the prisoners on the platform with Colonel Wheaton, but Kentapoos gave them no notice. Instead, his eyes searched the crowd. Green Basket's lip trembled as she watched him. She murmured something Winema could not hear. Winema moved Laughs Loud between her and Frank, caressed the side of the child's face, gently pressed it against her hip.

The minister stepped over to Kentapoos. "Do not be afraid, son. You go to a better place. You will never want for anything. God will furnish you everything without asking."

Kentapoos appraised the man. "Is that so? Do you like this place you call heaven?"

The preacher smiled. "It is a beautiful place."

Kentapoos nodded, then, "I tell you what I will do. I will give you twenty-five ponies if you will take my place today, because I do not wish to go right now."

The preacher's smile melted into a sickly grin. He glanced at the platform door below him, muttered it was not yet his time, then retreated to the back of the platform.

Wheaton asked Kentapoos if he had any last words. Kentapoos shook his head. Two soldiers slipped gray woolen hoods over the condemned men's heads. Then the nooses.

Winema could hear her heartbeats pounding in her ears. Something hard, something vile, began to form in her belly. She felt light-headed. Everything slowed, became hazy, like a dream. Wheaton was looking at a man hidden beside the platform. Winema's mouth felt as dry as dust. She thought of Tule Lake, of Lost River, of cool, clear water. *They will stop soon—it won't happen. They will change their minds.*

Wheaton nodded.

Winema shoved Laugh's face into her skirts, then heard a noise, a banging door. Then sickening thumps. The earth lurched beneath her feet. *Oh, God, Kemush!*

There were gurgling sounds.

Laughs Loud jerked, pressed her face harder into Winema's dress.

Green Basket's fingers dug into Winema's arm. Moans and wails erupted from the crowd of Modocs. Winema's legs felt suddenly made of tule reeds. Frank squeezed her arm—too hard, she thought, but prevented her from collapsing. She felt Laughs's fingers biting into her side.

There was the sudden odor of urine from the gallows. She found herself gasping for breath. Something was squeezing her throat, choking the air from her.

Sixty-one

FRANK, WINEMA, AND Jeff stood with Green Basket, Shade, and Laughs Loud on the long wooden platform at the train station, surrounded by Kentapoos's people. The women's hair was clipped short in mourning. Black patches of mourning pitch darkened everyone's cheeks.

Keeping a comfortable distance from the frightening steel machine before them, three hundred Modocs milled about, saying their goodbyes to friends and loved ones. Winema saw fear and broken spirits in every eye. She realized her own eyes must reflect the same.

His voice husky with emotion, Frank held Green Basket's hand. "We'll see you again. We'll come visit. I promise."

Shade stood as mute as a tree. She had not spoken since the hanging.

Despite Frank's reassurances, Winema knew she would never see these people again—yet another type of execution. "Indian Territory" had no meaning. They would disappear into a White void never to be heard from again. At least, she reflected sadly, Kweelush and Wild Girl would not have to face this last rending experience.

A sergeant stood on a crate, holding a pocket watch. "Five minutes! Five minutes!"

Tears rushed down Winema's cheeks as Lodge Woman joined them. She held Sleeps-a-lot's and Moonlight's hands. "I know you cannot forgive my husband, but can you forgive me?"

Winema grasped her old friend's arms. "Do you remember the time we turned that angry bear cub loose in Chases Squirrel's lodge?"

Lodge Woman nodded and smiled through tears. "*Ih*. She never liked you since."

Winema wiped her eyes and took her friend's hands. "We have been friends too long to let a man divide us."

Lodge Woman loosed a sob of relief. Green Basket stepped forward and touched Winema's arm. "I know we were never close. It was not your fault. It—it was mine." She kneaded her hands and stared at the ground, struggling for the words as she probed an old wound. "I was . . . jealous."

Winema was confused. "Jealous? Why?"

Basket looked Winema in the eye. "You and Kentapoos were so close. He confided in you, told you things he would not tell me, his *own* wife."

Suddenly there was a tremendous roar and a geyser of steam hissed from under the train, shot through people's legs, misted over their bodies.

"Aiieee!" Lodge Woman, Laughs, Basket, and others screamed. They huddled closer to Frank.

The engineer and fireman looked down from the engine cab and chuckled. While some of the Modocs cowered, others eyed the hulking train with dread and hatred. It breathed and clanked and hissed like some devil conjured by the Whites to ingest them, to carry them away to the "warm place." Or so the Whites had said.

Shade cried, "The iron pack train will take us so far east that we will never be able to join our ancestor's spirits in the west." She started to moan a plaintive death song. Several women near her joined in.

Other nearby Modocs nodded and murmured their agreement. A long, shrill blast of the whistle ripped the air. Children started wailing again. Men cursed the evil thing that signaled their exile to the death land.

Soldiers, carrying rifles with fixed bayonets, started yelling and pushing people into the cars. A low moan emanated from the Modocs, building into wails as families were separated. Arms reached out in a last, desperate effort to maintain contact.

A soldier pried his way roughly in between the Riddles and the Modoc women. "Move! Onto the train!"

He jostled Frank and Winema, shoved them aside.

"Hey!" Frank yelled at the soldier. The two scuffled on the platform. The soldier jabbed his rifle butt into Frank's stomach, knocking him to the platform.

Wheee-whee-wheeee The whistle screamed in their ears. Winema helped Frank up. When they looked around, Basket, Laughs, Lodge Woman and Shade had been hustled into a car. Women were crying, babies bawling. The sounds swirled and mixed with the shrieking steam whistle, the cacophony harkening the images of the day they departed Kalelk for the last time.

Another suffocating cloud of steam hissed out over the platform. The engine clanked, then huffed choking plumes of black smoke. It chugged and belched, showering the platform with its burning spittle. The cars squeaked and protested against the pull, then jerked into motion.

Winema started to sob—dry, convulsive gasps of grief. She looked desperately for Lodge Woman and Basket, but all she saw was the blur of agonized faces pressed against soot-stained windows.

The iron pack train groaned a final protest, and slid away.

SIXTY-TWO

Fort Klamath, August 1874

MORNING DAWNED BRIGHT and clear after the night's storm. Rain had sweetened the air and a warm breeze scoured the sky of clouds and painted a magic palette of soft hues across the sky.

Jeff squatted beside his cousin's grave, digging his fingers into the moist soil, turning it over absently. Closing his eyes, he recalled treasured memories. His fingers touched something solid. He felt around, grasped the object, and pulled from the soil a small buckskin pouch with a thin rawhide tie. After brushing away the clinging dirt, he recognized it—Kentapoos's medicine pouch.

He did not open it. A man's medicine was his own. The items inside were sacred and personal. He looked up at his mother and held out the pouch. She smiled, clutched the pouch a moment, then passed it back to Jeff.

"You were meant to find it, my son. He must want you to have it. When you are alone, you may look inside. His medicine will become your medicine."

They heard a shrill cry above and looked skyward. *Witkat'kis* circled lazily.

Jeff heard a tremble in his mother's voice as she watched the hawk. "His spirit is with us today. He knows we go to fulfill a promise." She straightened proudly. "Come. It is time."

Frank waited in the buckboard loaded with luggage, gifts, and small pouches filled with soil from Lost River Valley.

"Ready for the big train ride?" Frank asked as they approached.

Winema smiled. "Yes, Tchmu'tcham. Let's go and bring Laughs Loud home."

EPILOGUE

  FRANK AND TOBY Riddle lived out their lives near the Klamath Indian reservation, until Frank's death in 1906. Mrs. Riddle lived until 1932 and was frequently called upon to translate and to provide her diplomatic skills between the government and other tribes.

Jeff Riddle married Manda Schonchin, daughter of Chief Skonches. Chief Skonches remained the respected head of his people until his death in 1892, at age 95.

Tule Lake was drained to make way for farm land. Lost River was redirected and suffers from pollution.

Many Modoc descendants—the Riddles, the Schonchins, and those of the approximately 150 Modocs who stayed in Oregon—live today, close to home, in southwest Oregon.

Of the 150 Modocs sent to Oklahoma:

Hakar (Hooker Jim) died in Oklahoma in 1879.

Bostin'ahgar (Bogus Charley) died at Walla Walla, Washington in 1881.

Slatuslocks (Steamboat Frank) became a minister and died in Oakland, Maine in 1885 while doing advanced study for the ministry under the auspices of the Society of Friends.

Wieum (William Faithful) died at the Klamath Reservation in 1911.

Krelatko (Scarfaced Charley) died in Oklahoma in 1896.

Cho-ocks (Curly Headed Doctor) died in Oklahoma in 1890.

Slolux spent five years at Alcatraz, then was sent to Oklahoma where he died in 1899.

Barncho died at Alcatraz—the year was unavailable.

As irony would have it, Krelatko was appointed chief of the Oklahoma Modocs by the federal government. After one year in Oklahoma, the Quapaw Indian agent demanded Krelatko force his people to give up gambling and to cease wearing blankets and traditional clothing. He refused and was replaced by Bogus Charley, who remained chief for several years.

The Oklahoma Modocs suffered heavy mortality during their exile, especially the elders and the children. By 1880 almost one third of them had died. While disease and pneumonia no doubt took its toll, Lynn Schonchin, descendent of Chief Skonches, was no doubt accurate when he said many died from broken hearts.

In Jeff Riddle's book, there is a wonderful but sad photo of Slatuslocks ("Rev. Steamboat Frank") and his family taken in Joplin, Missouri, in 1883. There's Frank with his eight-year-old son, his sisters, and their children—five healthy young adults, three healthy children, and a baby—dressed up in fine dresses and suits. They were all dead, save one, by 1911.

The Oklahoma Modocs were given a 4,000-acre reserve purchased from the Shawnees, under the auspices of the Quapaw Indian Agency in the far northeast corner of Oklahoma, just across the border from Seneca, Missouri. Apparently they were not considered important enough to have their own Indian agent and were squeezed in between the small reserves of the Quapaws, Peorias, Senecas, Wyandots, and Miamis.

Many of the Modocs took, or were given, Anglicized names almost immediately. The twisted humor of the agents resulted in names like U. S. Grant and Robin Hood. To the frustration of their descendants, many of the Modocs' true names were never passed on and are now lost to the ages.

In 1874–75 Albert Meacham took the Riddles, Skiet-teteko,

Slatuslocks, and Krelatko "on the lecture circuit." They traveled across the country with Meacham, spinning the tale of the Modoc War to rapt audiences. Meacham may have felt he was helping them make a living when he trussed up Slatuslocks, Skiet-teteko, and Krelatko in fringed buckskin outfits and had them whoop down the aisles, perform war dances and put on archery demonstrations. Eventually the show fizzled out and Meacham had to borrow five hundred dollars to get everyone home. He then published two purple-prose books about the war.

Kentapoos's daughter and only child passed away in childhood, leaving him without descendants. The day after the hanging, Kentapoos's body mysteriously appeared in Yreka. Propped up in a coffin, the body was displayed in front of a general store. Soon after, his remains once again returned to the possession of the army, who decapitated the body and sent his head east to Army surgeons, who "studied" the brain.

His remains were purportedly reinterred in his grave at Fort Klamath. The re-internment remains in doubt, and the burial site is now in private hands. Modoc requests for proof the body still lies there have been denied by both current and previous owners.

As Kentapoos had feared, the government did indeed get "that one last measure" of him.

THE MODOCS

Akroh—Father

*Big Arm—Winema's first husband, who died of smallpox

Black Wound—Tetetekus (Stoney Boy as a youth)

Bogus Charley

Boston—Boston Charley

Charka—Handsome Boy, Jeff Riddle—Winema's son

Cho-ocks—Curly Headed Doctor, Kentapoos's medicine man

*Green Basket—Kentapoos's senior wife (actual name lost to history)

Hakar—Hooker Jim, Leader of the Hot Creek Band

Jakalunus—Head medicine man for the Modocs, loyal to Skonches

Kankush—Little Ike

Kentapoos—Captain Jack, nickname, Waterbrash. Winema's cousin

Krelatko—Scarface Charley

Kweelush—Winema's aunt

Laughs Loud—Kentapoos's daughter

Laulauwush—A child Winema often watched over in her youth

*Fictional characters

*Lodge Woman—One of Winema's friends, wife of Krelatko

Mehenulush—A child Winema often watched over in her youth, captured by the Pit River tribe

*Moluks—Winema's uncle

*Moonlight—Lodge Woman's daughter

Secot—Principal Modoc chief, Winema's father

*Shade, Likes the—Kentapoos's junior wife

Skiet-teteko—Shacknasty Jim

Skonches—John Schonchin, Secot's war chief, later Principal Chief after Secot's death

Slatuslocks—Steamboat Frank

*Smoke—White Loon's husband

*Squinter—White Hair's husband

*Tall Woman—Mehenulush's mother. Also captured by Pit Rivers.

*White Hair—White captive Amanda Slocum, later adopted by Modocs

*White Loon—Friend of Lodge Woman's

Whusum—John Schonchin, Chief Skonches's brother

Wieum—William Faithful

Wild Girl—One of Winema's friends, wife of Wieum

Winema—Toby Riddle (nickname: Little Swallow)

*Woman Watching—Black Wound's wife

KEY MODOC
AND CHINOOK WORDS

Ah-ha—(Chinook) Yes

Alamimakt—Pit River Indians

Atui—Now!

Boshtin—White(s)

Catkum—Blood

Chowotkan—Farewell

Dasi—A deerhide ball stuffed with duck feathers

Dekes—Wife

Ditchee Skoks—The good spirits

Doly Kana?—Where are you going?

Domli ditchki—And you?

Domilus Wopuku—What do you think?

Ena—Mother

Gailawa—Mouse (mice)

Geo' sut'walinai—My friend(s)

Gaw oonok—My son

Gaw pinkuk-fumti—My aunt

Getak—Enough! Quiet!

Haggi—Lo! Look there!

Hunamasht—Is that so?

Ih—Yes

*Ih*ash—A poison root

Itl'willie—Venison (in Chinook)

Juljulius—Crickets

Kai—No

Kaela Ena—Mother Earth

Kailash stani—Two colorful invectives

Kakla—Gambling

Kapka—Come

Kapkablandaks—Be silent!

Kash—Colorful invective

Kau'py—(Chinook) Coffee

Kekina—A small lizard

Kemush—God; The Creator

Ketchkani tchili-lika—Little Sparrow

Kiuks—Respectful title for medicine/holy man

Kloshe'—(Chinook) Good

Klow howya—(Chinook) Hello/Goodbye

Kola—(Sioux) (my) friend

Laki—Chief

Lam'etsin—Medicine

Latinkini—Warm Springs Indians

Lockaa gewo—Call a council

Lok—Bear

Luelótan—Dead

Mak'laks—Indian person/people

Moan ditch hosoyuk—Very good friend

Moi—Squirrel

Mowatoc—Modoc country

Nat keka-istsna—We go

Nawit'ka—Yes, indeed

Nent—Right!; Indeed!; So it is!

Ni'ka mem—My name is (in Chinook)

Oka ilagen—Of course

Otwekatuxe—Depending on inflection and the situation, may mean either "I am done talking" or "All ready."

Paksh—Pipe

Pil chik'amin—Gold

Pusuep—Uncle

Shuldshash—Soldiers

Siastai—Shasta Indians

Skwis'kwis—(Chinook) Squirrel

Sloa—Wildcat

Sot—Paiute Indians

Stois—Mink

Squaw—(French/Indian slang) Vagina

Taghum—(Chinook) Six

Tchwai—Well then

Tchwai na—Let's do it!

Tika—A Bluejay

Tyee—A chief or headman

Wakakatekeh—Brother

Wak'e—(Chinook) No

Waquset—Good

Watchaga auk lum weyus!—You son of a dog!

Wekkis—Large woven reed baskets

Wiga—Penis

Wochaga—Dog

Wochagalam weash—Son of a female dog (you son of a bitch)

Wuk lucee?—How are you?

The Seasons
Jkwo'—Spring
Kchil'wifam—Summer
Sha'lum—Fall
Fol'dum—Winter

FOR FURTHER READING

Andrist, R. K, *The California Gold Rush*, American Heritage Publishing Co., 1961.

Brown, Dee, *Bury My Heart at Wounded Knee*, Henry Holt & Co., New York, 1970. (For a good encapsulated history of the Modocs.)

Bureau of Ethnology, *Chinook Jargon*, Classification No. SI 2.3, #15, 1875.

Curtain, Jeremiah, *Myths of the Modocs*, Benjamin Bloom, Inc., 1912, 1971.

Gatschet, Albert S., *The Klamath Indians of Southwest Oregon*, Bureau of Ethnology, 1895.

Hulbert, A. B., *The Forty-Niners*, Little Brown & Co., 1931.

Landrum, F. S., *Guardhouse, Gallows & Graves* [compiled by] Klamath County Museum, Klamath Falls, OR, 1988.

Meacham, Albert B., *Wigwam & Warpath*, John P. Dale & Co., Boston, MA, 1875.

Meacham, Albert B., *Winema and Her People*, American Publishing Co., Hartford, CT, 1876.

Miller, Joaquin, *Life amongst the Modocs: Unwritten History*, London, Bentley, 1873. Reprinted by Urion Press, 1982.

Mooney, James, *The Ghost Dance Religion: Smohalla and His Doctrine*, Bureau of Ethnology, 1896 (extract facsimile by Shorey Pubs., Washington, 1972).

Murray, Keith A., *The Modocs and Their War*, University of Oklahoma Press, Norman, Oklahoma, 1959.

Ray, Verne F., *Primitive Pragmatists: The Modoc Indians of Northern California*, University of Washington Press, 1963.

Riddle, Jeff C., *The Indian History of the Modoc War*, Urion Press (first published in 1914), San Jose, California, 1974. Available through the Klamath County Museum, Klamath Falls, OR.

Time-Life Books (ed.), *The Indians of California*, Alexandria, VA, 1994.

Yreka Journal, 1869–1873.

Records of the United States Military Academy.

No one knows the American West better.

JACK
BALLAS

__THE HARD LAND   0-425-15519-6/$4.99

__GUN BOSS   0-515-11611-4/$4.50

__BANDIDO CABALLERO

              0-425-15956-6/$5.99

__GRANGER'S CLAIM

              0-425-16453-5/$5.99

The Old West in all its raw glory.